Sleep Softly Baby

carol magill

POOLBEG
Crimson

Published 2008
by Poolbeg Press Ltd
123 Grange Hill, Baldoyle
Dublin 13, Ireland
E-mail: poolbeg@poolbeg.com
www.poolbeg.com

13 5 7 9 10 8 6 4 2

A catalogue record for this book is available from the British Library.

ISBN 978-1-84223 -359-7

Typeset by Type Design in Sabon 10.5/14

Printed by
Litographia Roses, Spain

Note on the author

Carol Magill lives in north County Dublin with her family plus three dogs and three cats. Her hobbies include reading, music and television soap operas. She divides her time between Ireland and Spain.

Acknowledgements

I would like to thank the following:
my family for their loyal support;
the staff of Poolbeg Press, particularly Paula Campbell whose idea it was in the first place and the ever-cheerful Niamh Fitzgerald;
my eagle-eyed editor, the wonderful Gaye Shortland.
and you, dear reader, for being smart enough to buy this book.
Hope you enjoy!

For Anne Green and Eilish Jones,
lifelong friends, with love

Prologue

The graveyard was cold and damp and a swirling mist seemed to rise up off the earth. Above, the sky was dark and overcast and heavy clouds blotted the sun. Erin shivered in her overcoat and pulled her thick woollen scarf tighter around her throat. It was a dismal scene. Even the trees seemed to weep in sympathy, large, heavy beads of dew dripping slowly from their overhanging branches.

Beside her, Erin felt a hand reach out to enclose her own. She turned to look at her mother who stood by her side. Her face was pale and drawn beneath the brim of her black hat.

"Be strong," she whispered. "You must be strong."

Erin's eyes were drawn back to the gaping hole in the earth. The damp clay was piled to one side and now the sombre workmen leaned on their spades while they waited for the coffin to arrive. Soon her child would be lowered into this grave and the earth

1

piled on top of her. She would never see her again. She felt an awful sadness overwhelm her. Her mother's arm wemt around her shoulders drew her close, soothing her, whispering encouragement.

"Don't break," her mother said. "Be strong."

Now she could see the small procession make its way amongst the headstones. As it drew closer, she could see the priest in billowing vestments intoning prayers, the altar boy carrying a tall crucifix and then a small knot of men.

In front, his face grim and worn, was her husband. He seemed to be weeping. In his hands he cradled the tiny white coffin.

The procession stopped when it came to the grave. The group of mourners formed a circle. Across from her, she could see her mother-in-law and the rest of her husband's family. Their faces were grim and downcast as they stared blankly into the dark hole prepared for the dead baby.

The priest had started to read from the black Bible in his hands. His solemn words floated out over the damp morning air. Ashes to ashes, dust to dust. Erin felt a shudder pass through her. Now the priest was splashing holy water on the coffin from a little silver bowl.

One of the workmen stepped forward. He took the coffin from her husband's hands and gently lowered it into the grave. Then another man scooped up a shovel of earth and held it out. Her husband took a handful of brown clay and slowly released it. Erin could hear the sound as it rattled on the coffin lid. Then it was her turn. She let the earth fall from her fingers and tumble into the grave. She fought back the tears. She felt the grief overwhelm her till she thought her heart would burst. She looked up and saw the clouds assembling, dark and brooding and filled with menace.

The workmen were busy again, their spades setting to work. The earth began to fall faster and faster into the grave, quickly smothering the tiny white box. There was a roll of thunder and the first drops of rain began to fall, splashing off the branches and splattering the clothes of the mourners.

Erin turned away. People were unfurling their umbrellas and moving to shelter. Across the grave, her mother-in-law was staring at her. Her eyes were grim and accusing. Erin saw her lips begin to move. She put her hands to her ears to blank the awful words.

"You killed her," she was saying. "How could you murder your own daughter?"

Chapter 1

When Erin O'Neill took up with Harry Kavanagh, she had no idea of the consequences that would follow. She was simply caught up in the glamorous world he inhabited – a world of fast cars and fine food and good living. It could truly be said that he swept her completely off her feet. Harry was tall and dark and had the type of rugged good looks you might see in a movie magazine. And he oozed charm and charisma.

Some cynical observers said she was after his family's money. But nothing could have been further from the truth. When Erin first met him money didn't enter her head. Her big concern was how to disentangle herself from a disastrous engagement to Luke Bradford. That, at the time, had seemed like a huge problem to her – but no one could have foreseen the terrible events that were about to unfold.

Erin was twenty-six years old, tall, with a slim figure and a mane of chestnut hair that caused men to turn in the street and stare. And she had dark flashing eyes to match. She worked as a junior reporter with a big Dublin newspaper called *The Clarion* and was sharing a flat with her cousin, Lora, while she looked for a place of her own. She was finding Dublin a big change from the small rural town of Mountclare, her home-town, where she had spent the previous three years working as a reporter for *The Midlands Champion*. She liked Mountclare. She liked the country lifestyle and got on well with her colleagues. But it wasn't where she wanted to be. She was ambitious and she wanted to be in Dublin working on one of the big national dailies. So when the opportunity came she grabbed it with both hands.

The contract which *The Clarion* gave her was nothing to shout about. It was for twelve months and the salary was barely enough to survive on. But, for Erin, it was the break she had been waiting for. She was absolutely delighted to work for a paper that sold 200,000 copies a day and allowed her to write *real* stories. She knew it would only be a matter of time before she impressed them with her energy and her nose for scoops. She was on her way. At the end of the year, the contract would be renewed and before long, she would be scrambling up the career ladder. She might even be editor some day.

But not everyone was pleased. Her fiancé, Luke Bradford, was livid when he heard the news. Luke was a lawyer working in his father's practice and he hoped to inherit the business when the old man retired. It had been his idea to get engaged. He had been totally smitten by Erin from the first time he met her at the local district court where he was representing a client on a driving charge. He had asked her to join him for a drink and before long they were going out together. Within three months, they were engaged and Erin was wearing a fine solitaire engagement ring. So when she told him she was taking a job in Dublin, Luke was furious.

"You can't be serious," he spluttered after she told him in Cassidy's pub one evening after work.

"Would I joke about a thing like this?"

"Sometimes I can't tell with you," he retorted angrily.

She tried to calm him down. "It's not so bad, Luke. Dublin's only a couple of hours away. I'll come back to see you at weekends."

"And what am I supposed to do in the meantime? You know I can't join you up there. I've got to stay here with my father."

"I'll ring you every day. I'll text. I'll send you emails. It's not as if I'm moving to Beijing."

"You might as well be," he muttered darkly.

He was right to be worried. Dublin was a much faster place than sleepy little Mountclare and for a good-looking woman like Erin the temptations would be greater. Luke was very possessive and didn't like the idea of her being up there on her own. Besides, he had started saving for their wedding and had recently bought a nice plot of land about a mile outside the town where they could build a house. He had assumed she was going to stay with him in Mountclare and never leave. He had never expected her to drop a bombshell like this.

But she was determined. A chance to work for *The Clarion* was too great an opportunity to miss. So she gave her notice to George Slattery, her editor. George was sorry to lose her but he was a kind man and could sympathise with her decision.

"You're doing the right thing," he said. "You'll get more experience up there. If you stay here you'll still be reporting the Agricultural Show when you're an old lady. Call in and see me anytime you come back."

A couple of weeks later, Erin left for Dublin after a farewell party that went on till three o'clock in the morning. Her cousin Lora worked in a bank and had agreed to put her up in her flat in the Docklands till she found her feet.

Luke drove her to Dublin with two suitcases packed in the boot of the car. He had a raging headache from the party and to make matters worse, it was a miserable January day and the rain never stopped from the moment they left Mountclare. As a result, they were both in foul humour and argued the whole way.

"If you loved me, you'd never do something like this," he complained.

"What do you expect? My career was never going to get off the ground if I stayed with *The Champion*. Even George Slattery said I was right to go."

"What about our wedding? What about the house I was going to build?"

Privately, Erin already had serious doubts about the wedding and the house but this wasn't the time to go into them.

"We'll work something out," she said.

"I know what's behind this. You think Mountclare isn't good enough for you," he snapped.

"That's not true. I'm very fond of Mountclare but Dublin is where the opportunities are."

"Well, I just hope you're happy. You'll soon find out that Dublin is not the bed of roses you think it is."

Eventually the outskirts of the city appeared and they encountered serious traffic. By now, the car had got hot and steamy and the sweat was trickling down Luke's face. Erin decided to say no more in case he lost his temper and ran into the back of a truck, so they both sat with gritted teeth till they arrived at the flat.

Lora opened the door after several minutes and took one look at her cousin.

"You'll have to sleep on the couch," she announced. "The radiator in the spare bedroom is flooding."

Erin's first impression of *The Clarion* was not encouraging. She was given a desk in a poky little corner of the newsroom and put on the morning shift because it was the worst job in the office and nobody else wanted to do it. She quickly discovered why. She spent the entire time between 9 a.m. and 6 p.m.

ringing the fire brigade and the gardaí and asking if there was anything happening. In between making phone calls, she monitored the radio news.

The news editor was a tall, thin man in his thirties called Ger Armstrong. He wore corduroy slacks and open-necked shirts and had the harassed look of someone who was constantly under pressure. After the first day, he told her she had done such a good job on the morning shift that he was keeping her on it for the entire weekend. As a result, she had to ring Luke and tell him she wouldn't be able to join him back in Mountclare. He hit the roof and said this was what he knew would happen. So they had another row.

Matters didn't improve. On Monday she was given a pile of press releases and told to sift through them and see if they contained any news. On Tuesday she was sent to a meeting of the city council where she almost fell asleep from boredom while the councillors argued over the site for a municipal waste dump. By the end of the third week, she had written a grand total of four short paragraphs which were buried in the back pages of the paper. She began to wonder if Luke was right and she should have stayed in Mountclare.

By now, her dreams of writing big stories and getting her name on the front page were rapidly disintegrating. She was on the edge of despair. The idea that she could just come to Dublin and take the city by storm had been sadly mistaken. As far as the reading public was concerned, she didn't even exist.

She began to wonder if George Slattery would take her back again if she asked him politely.

Meanwhile, Luke was ringing her every day wanting to know when he was going to see her again. She dreaded his phone calls. The tension came to a head in a particularly stormy session one Friday afternoon.

"Well? Are you coming down to Mountclare this weekend?" he demanded.

Erin swallowed hard before replying. "I can't. I'm working."

Luke exploded. "I don't believe it!" he thundered. "That's the third weekend in a row."

"I'm sorry, Luke, but I've got to do what I'm told."

"That's where you're wrong, Erin!"

She could hear the fury rising in his voice.

"There are laws against this kind of thing! You can't let them kick you around like this. I think I'll ring your editor and give him a piece of my mind."

"Oh God, no," she stammered, mortified at the very idea. "Please don't do that. You'll get me into trouble. I'll come down as soon as I get a break."

"And when is that going to be?"

"I don't know. Right now, we're short-staffed."

"I'm running out of patience," he said menacingly. "We're supposed to be engaged."

"I know. I'll make it up to you. Honest."

But Luke was far from satisfied.

"You've got to stand up for yourself, Erin. They're exploiting you. The next thing you know they'll have you selling the damned paper on the street corners. This is no way to conduct a romance."

She knew he was right. It *was* no way to conduct a romance. But by now Erin was seriously wondering if there was any romance left to conduct. Ever since the engagement, she had felt trapped and every day that passed, the feeling grew.

She was an attractive young woman but it wasn't till she'd started working at *The Midlands Champion* and met Luke Bradford that she'd had her first serious relationship. Luke was no Brad Pitt. He was twenty-eight, broad and swarthy with mousey-brown hair that was already thinning at the temples. People said he would go bald by forty. He was prone to put on weight and already had a paunch straining against his waistband. But he was kind and generous and clearly doted on her to the point of obsession. When he asked her to marry him one evening after a boozy dinner, she was flattered. Afterwards she wondered what had possessed her but by then it was too late. She was wearing his ring.

Immediately, she noticed a change in his attitude. Now, he became much more assertive. He began to make decisions without consulting her, like buying the plot of land to build a house. He spent his time drawing up plans for the wedding which he insisted should be held in nine months' time. He even decided on the number of bridesmaids (four) and the size of the cake (three tiers). One morning, Erin woke up to the fact that she was now riding a rollercoaster that would inevitably deposit her at the altar of her local parish church if she didn't do something fast.

But unknown to her, events were already moving in a direction that would shape her career and bring her troubled romance to a head.

Chapter 2

One afternoon, as she was sitting at her desk, reading press releases and silently feeling sorry for herself, Erin saw the financial editor come striding in her direction. James Chapman was tall and distinguished-looking and always dressed immaculately in fine shirts and pin-striped suits as if he had just stepped out of a boardroom. He had his own office and personal secretary on the second floor and rarely appeared in the newsroom at all.

He stopped when he came to her desk.

"Hello," he said in his confident, south-Dublin accent. "You're the new reporter, aren't you?"

"Yes," Erin replied, surprised that he even knew who she was.

He held out his hand and introduced himself. "James Chapman, financial editor. And I've got a job for you."

"Oh?" Erin felt her stomach turn a somersault. She

hoped he wasn't going to ask her to write something complicated like an analysis of the Dow Jones Index. She knew absolutely nothing about financial matters. They made as much sense to her as Mandarin Chinese.

But it was something else entirely.

"I'm looking for someone to interview Charlie Kavanagh tomorrow. He's just bought the Conway Hotel in Ballsbridge."

Charlie Kavanagh was the chairman of Kavanagh Construction, a major property-development company and one of the richest men in the country. He was reputed to live in a fabulous mansion in Malahide.

"It's all fixed up," Chapman went on. "The interview is arranged for ten o'clock in the morning. I'm sending a photographer out this afternoon to get some pictures. Old Charlie will be expecting you."

"Me?"

"Sure. You've done interviews before, haven't you?"

"Oh yes, of course, many times."

"Well then, there shouldn't be any problem. I need a thousand words by four o'clock."

"Sssure," Erin managed to reply.

James Chapman smiled. "So it's all sorted. I'll talk to the news editor and get him to release you."

He made it sound like she was being let out of a cage.

"Where am I supposed to interview him?" she asked.

"At his home – Belvedere. You can take a taxi out there. Just get a receipt and I'll reimburse you."

With a sinking feeling, Erin watched him stroll back to his office. Charlie Kavanagh was a very powerful figure and he rarely gave interviews. Besides, he was supposed to be very bad-tempered. She had heard a story one time about him throwing a glass of wine over some politician who had upset him. What would he do to a reporter who got on his wrong side?

Her apprehension was fuelled by a remark from a colleague when she mentioned the job she'd been asked to do.

"Charlie Kavanagh?" he said. "Rather you than me. I was sent to interview him one time and it was like talking to a bear with a hangover. All I got out of him were grunts."

Nevertheless, Erin was beginning to see that this could be the chance she'd been waiting for. She knew that the editor read everything that went into the paper so that meant he would read her interview. But she would have to produce the best article she had ever written in her entire career. She would have to write such a fantastic piece that the whole newsroom would be talking about it.

She spent the rest of the afternoon in the newspaper library going through the clippings file on Charlie Kavanagh and taking copious notes. She hardly knew where to start. There were acres of material about him. By the time she left, she had filled twelve foolscap pages.

She went home to Lora's flat. Thankfully, her cousin was out with her boyfriend, Jack, who worked as a graphic designer for a magazine company, so she had the place to herself. She made an omelette for supper, poured a glass of wine and sat at the dining-table where she slowly condensed her notes and drew up a list of questions to ask. When she had finished, she felt she had known Charlie Kavanagh all her life. Then she booked a taxi for the morning, had a shower and went to bed. She was fast asleep by the time her cousin got home.

The sound of a car backfiring outside her bedroom window woke her up. It was half past seven but it was still dark. Erin was tempted to lie on in bed but by now she could hear her cousin moving about, so she got up too.

Lora looked like a ghost in her faded dressing-gown with her pale complexion.

"Good night?" Erin inquired.

Her cousin was gulping down a mug of hot coffee.

"Too damned good. Now I'm paying the price."

"No gain without pain," Erin said cheerfully but Lora only scowled.

Mornings were never her cousin's best time and this morning seemed worse than most. By the time she left for work it was eight o'clock. Erin decided to have a shower and get dressed.

The taxi was booked for nine. She wondered what she should wear. On her meagre salary, she didn't have a very extensive wardrobe. It mainly consisted of useful everyday items she had bought in the sales. In the end, she settled for the grey business suit she had worn for her job interview and a sparkling white blouse. A few pieces of simple silver jewellery and a touch of make-up and she was ready.

On the way through north Dublin in the taxi, she went over her notes and rehearsed the questions she had prepared. This could be her big opportunity. Despite Charlie Kavanagh's tough reputation, she was determined not to let him intimidate her. Nevertheless, she found herself practising deep-breathing exercises until the taxi finally deposited her at the gates of Belvedere.

The sight of the place did little to dispel her growing feeling of unease. The estate was surrounded by a high wall and heavy wrought-iron gates that gave it a dark, sombre appearance. Just beyond the wall, she could see rolling green parkland and a copse of trees, their tall branches blocking out the sun. I don't like this place one bit, she thought. There's something creepy about it.

But just then her thoughts were interrupted by a deep, masculine voice.

"Are you the reporter?"

She turned quickly to see a young man, perhaps in his late twenties, coming towards her.

"Yes," Erin replied.

"I've been asked to escort you to the house," he said. "So, if you would just follow me."

Her new companion started up the driveway and

Erin fell in beside him. It gave her an opportunity to study him. He was tall and wore a heavy weatherproof jacket over a thick woollen pullover. His trousers were tucked into a pair of Wellington boots and strands of black curling hair escaped from underneath his check cap. She assumed he was one of the gardening staff.

"You're a bit young, aren't you?" he said casually and Erin felt her skin bristle.

"I beg your pardon?"

He smiled, playfully. "Don't take offence. I always assumed reporters were older. You know, with a trilby hat and a pencil stuck behind their ears? Maybe I watch too many films," he laughed.

"I think you do," she said tartly.

But he didn't appear to be put off. He continued chatting as they made their way up the long winding drive. By now, the house was coming into view. It was three storeys high with tall chimneys pointing towards the sky. The walls were crusted with ivy. On the top floor a row of windows seemed to look out blankly over the lawns. There was something vaguely unsettling about the house that made her feel uncomfortable. As they approached, her companion turned to her.

"What are you going to interview him about?" he asked.

Erin was beginning to get annoyed with his familiarity. Besides, the closer she came to Charlie Kavanagh, the more nervous she was becoming.

"I don't see how that is any of your business," she snapped.

"Oh dear," he said. "You're not in very good form this morning. What happened to you?"

"I met *you*," Erin growled.

But the young man only laughed once more. "He doesn't usually give interviews, you know. He doesn't really like the media very much. You're lucky he agreed to see you."

Erin decided that silence was her best resort. Her chattering companion appeared to be one of those people who just couldn't take a hint.

"He's meeting you in his office at the back," he said, leading her to the rear of the house and stopping before a door. "Here it is."

"Thanks."

As he was about to depart, he leaned closer and whispered, "Be sure to ask him about the early days. How he started in business with nothing and had to fight his way up. He always enjoys talking about that."

He gave her a playful wink and departed.

She stared after him. What an impertinent young man, she thought. You'd think he owned the place the way he carried on. But she had no time to think about it. The moment had arrived when she had to face the awesome figure of Charlie Kavanagh. She took a deep breath and knocked on the door.

"Come in," a brisk voice answered.

She opened the door and found herself in a large office with a comfortable settee and a wall lined with filing cabinets. The man she had come to interview was sitting behind a desk in front of the window, his head bent over a large map spread out before him. She recognised him at once. He was a big, heavy-set man in his early sixties with a florid weather-beaten face, silver hair and large plump hands like a farmer.

"Yes?" he asked, glancing up and staring at her.

"I'm Erin O'Neill. From *The Clarion*. I have an appointment for ten o'clock."

"Yes, yes," Kavanagh grumbled, rolling up the map and setting it aside. He looked at her again, as if he had been expecting someone else.

"Where's Chapman?" he demanded. "I thought he was coming himself?"

"He asked me to do it."

"Hmmhhh," Charlie Kavanagh growled.

Erin felt her spirits sink. This interview was not getting off to a very good start.

But before she could proceed, another door opened and a small bird-like woman with blue-rinsed hair entered the room. On seeing Erin, the woman's countenance darkened. Her inquisitive eyes bored deeply into Erin's till she was forced to look away. The woman walked briskly to Charlie's desk and whispered something in his ear. Then she turned and left. At the door, she turned once more and stared at Erin so intensely that she felt the flesh crawl up her back.

Who on earth was that, she thought? And why did she give me such a withering look? But Charlie Kavanagh snapped her from her reverie.

"Right," he said, pointing to a chair. "Take a seat and start shooting. I've got somebody coming to see me at eleven."

The episode with the older woman had unsettled her further. Erin fumbled for her bag and took out a small portable voice-recorder.

But immediately Charlie Kavanagh waved it away.

"I'm not talking into that thing," he said. "It puts me off. Haven't you got a notebook and pen?"

"Sssure," Erin replied and dug into her bag again. She glanced at the list of questions she had prepared and began the interview.

"What is your business philosophy?" she asked in an unsteady voice.

Kavanagh stared at her. "Business philosophy? What do you mean?"

"What are the values that inspire you? What drives you on?"

He screwed up his weather-beaten face and thought for a moment. "Making money, I suppose. And hard work."

"Anything else?"

"No."

It wasn't the response she had been expecting but Erin scribbled down his answer and looked at her next question. Maybe it would take a few minutes for him to warm up.

"Do you believe the property market can continue to expand?"

"Yes."

"Yes ... what?"

"What you just said. The market will expand. People have to live somewhere. That's why I build houses for them."

Within ten minutes she had arrived at her final question. The interview had turned into a nightmare. So far she had managed to fill a mere half page with Charlie Kavanagh's replies. He had answered her with one-line responses and tired old clichés that everyone had heard a hundred times before. There was absolutely nothing new or exciting. And now he was giving her the distinct impression that he wanted the interview finished as soon as possible.

"What is your favourite method of relaxation?" she asked at last, hoping desperately for something that might rescue the situation.

"Going to the races."

"Is that all?"

"Yes," he grunted. "I'm a busy man. I don't have time for silly pastimes."

"I see," Erin muttered.

She stared at the notebook in her lap. James Chapman had asked for 1000 words. She'd be hard pressed to get 200 from the material she had managed to extract from the gruff developer. The interview had been a catastrophe. Far from establishing her reputation, it was more likely to finish her career.

She was preparing to leave with a heavy heart when she suddenly remembered the advice of the young man who had met her at the gates.

"Mr Kavanagh, can I ask you one final question? What was it like when you started out in the early days?"

It was if someone had waved a magic wand. Charlie Kavanagh's attitude immediately changed. He sat back in his chair and a dreamy look came into his eyes. He stretched his arms behind his neck and began to talk.

"Those were the days," he said. "I began with a van, a couple of shovels and a hundred pounds I borrowed from my uncle. And I never looked back."

For the next forty minutes, the developer talked like he was totally invigorated. He was a young man again working eighteen-hour days, hammering together deals, making money and reinvesting it as he built up his property empire. Erin's pen flew across the pages as she struggled to keep up with the torrent of anecdotes and stories that poured from his mouth. It was as if Charlie Kavanagh was lost in that bygone world of his youth when he was setting out to make his fortune and take the industry by storm.

She was still taking notes when the phone on his desk gave a loud ring. Kavanagh suddenly straightened up and pressed it to his ear.

He spoke for a moment, then replaced it and turned back to Erin.

"I'm sorry," he said. "My next appointment has arrived."

He came out from behind his desk and warmly

shook her by the hand. His face was still glowing with enthusiasm.

"You're a very sharp reporter," he said. "You ask the right questions."

Erin managed a nervous smile.

As he walked her to the door, he drew a business card from his pocket and pressed it into her hand.

"That's my personal number. In a few days' time I'll contact you again and I'll have a big story for you." He nodded gravely. "A *very* big story."

She left the room with a tremendous feeling of relief. She had come close to disaster but now she had enough material for three articles and the promise of a good story as a bonus.

She was still feeling light-headed when she ran into the young man again outside on the drive. He was standing beside a gleaming black BMW car.

"How are you getting back to Dublin?" he asked.

"I'm taking the DART," she replied.

He opened the door of the car. "Hop in. I'll drive you to the station."

As she settled into the passenger seat, she inquired: "You never introduced yourself. Do you mind if I ask who exactly you are?"

"I'm sorry," he said, with a playful smile. "I'm Harry Kavanagh. You've just been talking to my father."

Chapter 3

THE MAN WHO BUILT A PROPERTY EMPIRE WITH £100 AND A SHOVEL ran the headline above the story that appeared on the front page of the finance supplement two days later. Not only did it have her name on it but it carried her picture as well. *By Erin O'Neill,* it said. She was so happy that she gazed at it till the type began to swim before her eyes. It was her first by-line for *The Clarion.* She cut it out and inserted it into a plastic cover to keep with the other important mementoes of her life like the menu from her Debs ball and her first payslip from *The Midlands Champion.*

She wasn't the only one who was pleased. James Chapman was delighted.

"I don't know how you managed it," he said, "but you're the first person who ever got two words of sense out of that old devil."

"Maybe they didn't ask the right questions," Erin replied with a knowing grin.

More praise quickly followed. Ger Armstrong came over to her desk and congratulated her. The features editor stopped by to say she had read the piece and liked it – Erin had a nice, quirky interview style and she would make sure to put some work her way.

Erin had confronted her first test and it appeared she had passed with flying colours.

But she didn't have long to bask in her new-found glory. A few days later, she was sitting in the newsroom when the phone rang.

It was Harry Kavanagh.

"My father wants to see you," he said.

Erin had been wondering how the interview had gone down at Belvedere.

"Did he like the article?" she asked cautiously.

"He loved it. He bought two dozen copies of the paper to send to his friends. Now he wants you out here again tomorrow at midday. He's got something important to tell you. Can you make it?"

"Sure, I can."

"Okay, same as last time. I'll be waiting for you at the gates."

She put the phone down with a trembling feeling of excitement. This would be the big story that Charlie Kavanagh had mentioned. Gamblers talked about a winning streak and the same thing happened in journalism. You got a good story and it spawned more stories. She wondered what Charlie Kavanagh was going to tell her.

* * *

The following morning she got up as soon as Lora had left for work. She had a breakfast of cereal and fruit and washed it down with strong black coffee. Then she had a shower and began to get ready. For this occasion, she decided to dispense with the sober business suit in favour of something less formal. She chose a blue wrap-around dress in the softest wool and her new knee-length aubergine swing coat. Thankfully, she had recently smartened up her wardrobe for her new life in Dublin. She spent fifteen minutes brushing her long chestnut hair and applying her make-up. When she was finished, she studied herself in the full-length mirror.

"Yes," she said to herself. "That looks an awful lot better."

Harry was waiting at the entrance to the estate when she arrived. He was wearing a warm ski jacket and casual slacks and his thick, dark hair had been brushed carefully. Erin thought he looked quite handsome. His blue eyes smiled in welcome.

"I'll carry that," he said, reaching for her briefcase as they started up the drive.

"Thank you," she replied and handed over the case which contained her notebook and laptop computer.

"Am I allowed to tell you that you're looking great?"

"Certainly. Every woman likes to be complimented. It's not a crime."

"Well, you are. In fact you're looking fabulous."

Erin smiled with satisfaction. "Do you work with your father?" she asked.

"Yes. I'm his assistant. I organise his schedules, sit in with him at meetings, carry out research. My father likes to keep the business within the family."

"You must be busy?"

He nodded. "I'm going to be even busier in the days ahead, as you're about to find out. But I'll let him tell you about that himself."

They were approaching the house. Erin studied it once more as they drew near, wondering what it was about the place that continued to make her feel uncomfortable. She thought of the woman she had met in Charlie Kavanagh's office on her first visit here and felt a shiver run along her spine. She could still remember that cold penetrating stare that seemed to pierce right into her soul. Who was she? And why had she shown such hostility?

"Do you live here?" she asked.

"Most of the time but I also keep an apartment in town."

"Do you never feel isolated? It's so big and …" she was about to say eerie but thought better of it, "solitary."

"But that's what I like about it," he laughed. "It's so peaceful. Listen." He held up a finger.

In the distance she could hear the whirr of a tractor. But the overwhelming sound was the noisy chattering of the birds coming from the copse of trees near the gates.

"There are twenty acres here," he said. "There's an old wood over there which is nice for walks. And every season brings new pleasures. We're moving into the spring now and soon the fields will be alive with colour. Look," he pointed to a verge, "can you see the daffodils beginning to come up?"

She followed his finger and, sure enough, she could see the tender green shoots pushing through the earth towards the sun. She looked again at Harry Kavanagh. What an interesting guy, she thought. I've never met a man before who could spot daffodils growing.

"I never thanked you for the tip," she said.

"What tip?"

"You told me what to ask him, remember? You said I should get him to talk about the early days when he was starting out."

Harry gave her a playful grin. "You were appealing to his vanity. Deep down, everybody is vain. My father is no exception."

"Well, it certainly worked. That's why I got such a good interview."

"Ah but *you* must take the credit. You *are* the one who wrote it, after all."

Charlie Kavanagh was waiting for them in his office and this time he had a pot of coffee ready and a tray with cake on a table beside his desk. He took hold of Erin's hand and clasped it warmly.

"That was a brilliant interview, absolutely bloody

brilliant. The phone hasn't stopped ringing with people telling me how much they enjoyed it. You made me look human for a change. I didn't recognise myself." He chortled and let go of her hand.

"I'm glad you liked it," she said, pleased.

"I loved it. Now why don't you sit down and have a cup of coffee to warm you up? It's nippy out there today."

Coffee was exactly what Erin needed right then. Charlie poured the steaming brew into a mug for her and pointed to containers of milk and sugar.

"Help yourself. And have a piece of cake. You'll like it. It's walnut. It's made from a special recipe."

He went and sat behind his desk. Harry had taken a seat and was gathering together some papers and drawings.

"I said I'd have a good story for you," Charlie went on, "and I have. You know I've bought the Conway Hotel?"

"Yes," she replied. It was the reason she had interviewed him in the first place.

"Well, everyone is dying to know what I'm going to do with it. There's been a lot of speculation that I'm going to refurbish it and open a luxury hotel in its place. But I'm not."

"No?" Erin asked.

"I'm going to build apartments."

For a second, she thought she had misheard. "Did you say apartments?"

"That's right."

"In the middle of Ballsbridge?"

"Correct."

"How many?"

"Five hundred."

She put down her coffee mug for fear of spilling it. This was amazing. Ballsbridge was the most exclusive neighbourhood in the entire country. When word of this got out there was bound to be huge controversy.

"Do you think you'll be allowed?"

Charlie Kavanagh's chest heaved and he chuckled. "Well, that's what we're about to find out."

She felt her excitement begin to mount. So he hadn't been joking when he said he had a very good story for her. This was a major scoop. She could barely contain herself.

Meanwhile, Harry had unrolled a sheet of drawings and spread it out on his father's desk.

"Let me show you exactly what we have in mind," he said.

Erin got up and bent over the table to take a look. A red line had been drawn round the site of the Conway Hotel and in its place six apartment blocks had been sketched in.

"It won't be just apartments," Harry continued. "We're planning shops, gardens, a leisure centre and a restaurant. It will be a community. We're calling it Conway Village. What do you think?"

"It certainly has a pleasant ring," Erin said. "But I suppose the big question is: will you get planning permission?"

The two men glanced at each other. She had got to the nub of the situation. This was what made the story such big news.

"We expect there'll be some opposition," Harry said at last. "But we're confident."

"The local residents will go ballistic," Erin said. "You know how defensive they are about their area."

Charlie had now assumed an aggressive tone. "Why should those Ballsbridge snobs dictate where people can live? The city is growing so fast that people are commuting for miles. We can't keep pushing them further out into the suburbs. What's wrong with building apartments?"

Erin had now taken out her notebook and was busy writing this down.

"We're not talking some grim tower blocks here. These will be luxury units designed to the highest standards and constructed with the very best materials. They will have all modern conveniences. But most important, they will be reasonably priced so that ordinary people can afford them, particularly young families." He looked directly at Erin while he spoke. "Now I'd like to see those snooty residents object to that."

When Erin finally left Belvedere, she went straight back to the office. She had a notebook bulging with quotes and under her arm she carried a copy of the plans that Harry Kavanagh had given her. She knew she had a mega story on her hands.

As soon as she got in, she made a beeline for Ger Armstrong.

"I need to talk to you," she said, drawing him aside. "You're not going to believe this."

"Try me."

"Charlie Kavanagh is planning to build five hundred apartments in the middle of Ballsbridge."

The news editor's face dropped. "I hope this isn't a wind-up, because I'm not in the mood for jokes."

"It's not a joke, Ger. He's deadly serious. I've just come from his house. And I've got the plans right here."

She held out the documents for his inspection.

"Five hundred? Did you say *five* hundred?"

"Yes."

"He'll never get away with it."

"He thinks he will."

She leafed through her notebook. "*Why should those Ballsbridge snobs dictate where people can live?*"

"He said that?"

She nodded. "Exact quote."

"And he said you could use it?"

"Yes. Everything was on the record."

"My God," the news editor said, "we've got a cracker on our hands."

For the next couple of hours Erin hammered furiously at her word processor. Every so often, she stopped to consult her notebook to check comments and quotes. By now, the adrenalin was pulsing through her system like a building on fire. She was on a high. All her senses were on alert. As she worked, the story began to take shape. The pictures editor had been brought in and several reporters had been set to work preparing background pieces on Kavanagh Construction and the Conway Hotel. Ger Armstrong had decided not to seek reaction in case it alerted the rival media to the big story they were running. That would come tomorrow and give the paper another lead.

At eight thirty Erin leaned back from her desk. The report was finished and would now go to the sub-editors and the layout people for processing. It was going to be tomorrow's lead story. She felt exhausted. But she wasn't finished yet.

The editor emerged from his office, rubbing his hands together in satisfaction.

"Great work," he said. "We're putting on an extra 30,000 copies. When we hit the news-stands in the morning, everybody will want to read this stuff. Now, I think it's time to buy you a celebratory drink."

Chapter 4

Erin was dragged from her sleep the following morning at seven o'clock by the loud ringing of her phone. It was RTÉ radio wanting her to go on the breakfast news programme.

"Let me check," she said, still drowsy with sleep. "I'll call you back."

She rang Ger Armstrong and asked what she should do.

"Go on," he said, enthusiastically. "This is great publicity for us."

"Okay, I'll tell them."

She called RTÉ and then dived into the shower and quickly got dressed in her smart grey suit. Fifteen minutes later, she was sitting in the back of an RTÉ car speeding out to Donnybrook. She had never done a broadcast interview before. Normally, she would have been nervous but this morning she felt relaxed and in control. She had all the facts at her fingertips and felt supremely confident.

The interview went off without a hitch. Erin repeated all she had learned the previous day from the Kavanaghs including Charlie's comments about the need for more housing in the city centre, particularly for young families. By nine o'clock, she was in the RTÉ canteen drinking coffee and eating a chocolate muffin with the programme producer as she tried to come to terms with the whirlwind that had suddenly engulfed her. Yesterday, only a handful of people in the entire country knew who she was and this morning she had been broadcasting to the nation.

She wasn't due back in the office till two o'clock. She thought briefly of going home and catching up on her sleep. Last night had been bruising. The editor had insisted on buying drinks for everyone and she hadn't left the pub till one thirty, what with colleagues coming up to shake her hand and congratulate her on the scoop.

But she knew she wouldn't sleep. She was wide awake now and the adrenalin was pumping again. In any case, the decision was taken out of her hands when her mobile suddenly started to ring.

"Hello," she said, quickly pressing the phone to her ear.

"Hi, Erin," a deep, male voice responded.

"Harry!"

"I'm ringing to congratulate you on your report and your excellent radio interview. I've just been listening to it."

"So you think I've got a future in this business?"

"Are you looking for an agent?"

She laughed. "How about your father?"

"He's over the moon. This is exactly what he wants. He knows we'll have a battle to get that development built. But he wants all the facts laid out so that people can make up their own minds."

"Well, I'm glad to hear it."

"That's not the only reason I called."

"No?"

"I wanted to invite you to lunch."

Erin was growing to like Harry Kavanagh. He did wonders for her morale and lunch with him would be a welcome diversion. And, besides, she had some time to kill before going into work.

"Sure," she said. "Tell me where."

The place he suggested was a little Italian restaurant called Nessun Dorma which was situated in a lane off Grafton Street. She agreed to meet him there at half twelve. She barely had time to get back to her apartment and change out of her business suit before she was rushing back into the city again. But it was worth it – she felt much better meeting Harry Kavanagh in her little green cashmere V-neck sweater which clung to her figure in a most flattering way, black jacket and black bootleg slacks.

She found Harry dressed in a smart navy suit, sparkling white shirt and red tie, waiting for her at a discreet table near the back. He stood up and smiled as she came in.

"There she is!" he said, taking her hands and kissing her gently on the cheek. "Erin O'Neill, star of stage, screen and radio!"

"Steady on," she laughed. "That's the first broadcast I've ever done."

"But it won't be the last. You have a glittering career ahead of you. I can confidently predict it."

He waited while she settled into her chair, then handed her a menu.

"Were you nervous about doing the broadcast?"

"Not a bit. I've been on an adrenalin jag since your father gave me that story."

"Then tell me something. How do you always look so well with the hectic lifestyle you lead?"

Erin thought of all those boring days she had spent in the office rewriting press statements and listening to the radio. If only he knew that until recently her lifestyle had been about as hectic as watching paint dry. But she wasn't about to tell him that.

"Clean living," she said and watched his face break into a grin.

The menu had a large selection of Italian dishes and by now she was ravenous. Apart from the chocolate muffin in the RTÉ canteen, she'd had nothing to eat all day. She chose scallop of veal with fettuccine and a side salad. Harry had chicken al forno and insisted on ordering wine. Erin normally drank moderately but she was quickly discovering that life in the fast lane presented plenty of opportunities for boozing.

"I'll just have a glass," she insisted. "I've got to keep a clear head. I have a busy evening in front of me. We're expecting the reaction to your apartment proposals."

"I can tell you what it will be," Harry predicted. "You'll get the usual suspects jumping up and down about the environment. They'll complain that a development like Conway Village is out of character for a place like Ballsbridge. What they won't tell you is that they just don't want anybody else living beside them in case it lowers the value of their fancy houses."

Erin knew there was some truth in what he said. But she also knew that many of the objectors would have valid reasons for opposing the scheme. As a journalist, it was her duty to give both sides of the argument.

"But we welcome a debate," Harry went on. "That's what we want. We've got nothing to hide. And that's why your report was so important. Now the matter is out in the open and people can decide for themselves."

"So you admit that the media can get things right?"

Harry pretended to consider. "Occasionally," he said and she playfully flicked her napkin at him.

It was a pleasant lunch. Harry turned out to be a very entertaining companion. He reminded her of his father when she got him talking about his early days.

"Enough about me," he said eventually. "Tell me about your family."

"There's just four of us: mother, father and little sister, Anne. My dad says he's the only man on the island. I'm the eldest. They're all living happily in a little town called Mountclare in County Offaly but Anne is hoping to come to Dublin soon."

"They must be very proud of you."

Erin shook her head. "I'm not so sure about that. I think they'd prefer to stay out of the limelight. They're just ordinary country people who want to live a quiet life."

"So why did you choose a career in journalism?"

"You'd only laugh if I told you."

"No, I won't."

"Because I was top of the class in English."

His face broke into a smile. "I could think of worse reasons. Stick with what you're good at."

"But I've learned that journalism is more than just being able to string sentences together. It requires a good nose for news."

"Well, I don't think you've anything to learn in that department. You certainly made the most out of the Ballsbridge story."

She waved the compliment away. "What about *your* family?" she asked.

He swirled the wine in his glass. "You've met my father. He's exactly what you see. He's a self-made man who can't stop working despite my mother's constant complaints. In every other respect, Mum's the power behind the throne. She keeps a tight rein on everything. I've an older sister, Susan, who's a vet and lives with her husband, Toby, in Kinsealy. Toby is my father's solicitor. That's how he and Susan met. And finally, there's Tim. He's the baby. Tim's twenty-four."

"Does Susan have any children?"

"No. Susan is only interested in her career and her horses. She keeps a stable on the Belvedere lands. She's a very keen horsewoman. It's a big disappointment to my mother. She would love a grandchild. I think she's worried that the Kavanagh dynasty will die out. Not that it's likely to happen."

"Tim's not married?"

"No. He doesn't even have a girlfriend."

"What does he do?"

"Nothing. He's a perpetual student. He's a very bright guy. But he doesn't know what to do with himself. My father is forever at him to settle down and take a job in the company."

"So why won't he?"

Harry shrugged. "You'd need to ask him. I think it has something to do with his pride. Tim doesn't want to be beholden to the family. He thinks he can make his own way in the world. But my father says he's just plain lazy."

Eventually, the meal came to an end and Harry signalled for the waiter to bring the bill.

"I've really enjoyed talking to you, Erin. But now I have to get back to the house. Dad's called a meeting for this afternoon to decide how to proceed with our planning application. It could turn into a heavy session."

"Will you promise me something?" Erin pleaded. "Will you call me if there are any developments?"

"Of course. You'd never speak to me again if I didn't."

After he had paid they walked outside.

"I've got the car nearby. Can I give you a lift back to your office?"

But the sun was shining and there was a nice bright feel to the afternoon.

"I think I'll walk," Erin replied. "The exercise will do me good."

The newsroom was buzzing when she got to the office just before two o'clock. Since she was the person who had broken the story, she was put on it again to handle the reaction. It was already starting to pour in and a pile of press statements was waiting on her desk.

She took off her coat and sat down once more at her word processor. She began by sifting out the most important reactions and put the remainder aside for use on an inside page. By five o'clock, she was ready to start writing. But she still had to wait for news from the Kavanagh camp. It came at six o'clock. The phone gave a ring and Harry was on the line again.

"We're going to lodge our application at the planning office tomorrow."

"What time?"

"Why does it matter?"

"We'll get some pictures."

She heard him chuckle.

"This is turning into a bit of a circus, isn't it?"

"Isn't that exactly what you wanted?"

"*Touché*. We'll be there for ten o'clock."

"Thanks."

"You're welcome."

She put the phone down. She had the final piece of the jigsaw. She started to write and two hours later, she finished her story and sent it to Ger Armstrong to read. By now, she was feeling bushed. The Kavanagh development had consumed most of the past twenty-four hours. She stood up, stretched her arms and walked across to the news desk.

"Do you mind if I go home? I need to catch up on my sleep."

"Go right ahead," the news editor said. "You've certainly earned it."

The story ran for the rest of the week, not always the lead but always front page. By now, it had become Erin's story. She had the inside track with Kavanagh Construction and used it to maximum advantage to keep ahead of their competitors. It meant she was in constant demand for radio and television interviews. She had got the big break she wanted and now she was learning valuable lessons in news management.

But there was a downside for her social life. Since coming to Dublin, she had managed to get back to Mountclare on only two occasions. And now that she was making the headlines, Luke Bradford had started ringing every day to complain. It reached a crisis one afternoon a few weeks later with an angry phone call.

"I'm fed up with this business," he began. "Everybody is talking about you."

"What do you expect?" Erin snapped back. "I'm a reporter. I'm in the news."

"Well, I don't like it. It makes me look bad."

"How do you mean, Luke? I don't understand."

"People are saying I've no control over you. They think I should rein you in."

Erin couldn't believe what she was hearing. "You should *rein* me in? Like I was a horse?"

"Yes. We're supposed to be getting married in six months' time. People are saying you should be down here with me instead of gadding around all over Dublin. You seem to be never off the radio."

She could feel her blood begin to boil. This was like an episode of *The Simpsons*.

She took a deep breath. "Luke, I don't think you realise just how hard I've been working. I'm in the big league now. I'm not reporting horse shows and garden parties any more."

"That's the problem," he retorted. "You've no time left for *us*."

Erin decided she had heard enough. "I'm going to pretend we didn't have this conversation."

"The thing is, those people are right. You *should* be down here. We've got to find somewhere to live till the house is built. I never wanted you to go to Dublin in the first place and now this has happened. You're making a show of me, Erin."

She switched off the phone and uttered a silent scream.

But the conversation presented her with an unpalatable truth. It was becoming clear that she couldn't continue to ignore Luke Bradford and the dilemma he represented. He hovered over her life like a ghost from the past. How long could she continue to dodge the fact that she didn't love him and never wanted to get married? It was time for some hard talking.

She made up her mind. She would go down to Mountclare on the following weekend and present him with the brutal reality. When she broke off the engagement there was bound to be a dreadful scene. She could just imagine the recriminations. But it would have to be done and the sooner she did it the better. In preparation she took off her engagement ring and slipped it into a drawer.

By now, Kavanagh Construction had lodged their planning application and all the interested parties had given their reaction. The story began to fade from the front pages. It wouldn't become news again until the decision was made and Harry had promised she would get first bite at it once it was announced.

But Erin didn't return to the obscurity of the morning shifts. She had earned her spurs and now was given a higher profile. One afternoon, she was asked to accompany the political correspondent to an important press briefing and write a colour piece.

The meeting was being held in Government Buildings. She sat through the lengthy question-and-answer session, taking notes and watching for little snippets of information that might come in useful. At last, the meeting came to an end and she left with the rest of the reporters. But she was no sooner outside in the corridor when she felt a gentle tug at her sleeve. She turned to find a tall man in sunglasses smiling at her. He whipped off the glasses and she saw that it was Harry.

"My God," she said. "It's James Bond! What are you doing here?"

"Ssssh," he said and drew her aside. "I've been meeting some politicians but I don't want everyone to know." He glanced at his watch. "Have you time for a quick cup of coffee?"

"Sure."

They went to a quiet bar a few streets away.

"Our paths seem destined to cross," he said with a grin, after he had ordered two caffé lattes. "Fate must be drawing us together."

Erin smiled. "Dublin's a small place. It's difficult to stay hidden. Were you lobbying about your planning application?"

"Good Lord, no," he replied. "That would be much too dangerous."

"So what was it?"

He looked around before responding. "It's just general stuff. I do it all the time. It's part of my job. We like to be well informed about what's going on – government contracts, stuff like that."

"So, is there any news about the application?"

He shook his head. "I don't expect to hear anything for a while. But don't worry, Erin. You'll be the first to know. What were you doing there?"

She told him about the political briefing and the colour piece she was writing.

"Sometimes I wish I had been a reporter," he said, wistfully. "It must be very exciting. There's always something happening. You'd never get bored."

"Don't be fooled, Harry. It can get pretty boring at times."

A thoughtful look had appeared on his face. "Something has just occurred to me," he said. "The last time we met you asked about my family. How would you like to meet them?"

She stared at him. "What do you mean?"

"We're having a party at the house on Saturday night. Would you like to be my guest?"

"I . . . don't know," she stammered.

"I'm sorry. Perhaps you're seeing your fiancé?"

Immediately, she felt a blush creep into her cheeks. "How do you know about my fiancé?"

He pointed to her finger. "You used to wear an engagement ring. But I notice you're not wearing it any more."

"You're pretty observant. Maybe you would make a good reporter, after all."

Harry smiled. "So if I'm ever down on my luck, you'll have a word with your editor?"

"Depends how well you behave."

He laughed. "Look if you're already tied up, it's okay. It was just an idea that popped into my head."

"No," Erin said. "I'm not tied up. I'd like to come."

"Well then, I'll send a car for you. The party is at eight o'clock. Shall we say seven thirty?"

"In that case, you'd better take my address," she said, tearing a leaf from her notebook and writing it down for him.

He glanced at it and stuck it away in the pocket of his jacket. "I'm looking forward to this, Erin. I think you're going to enjoy it."

He stood up and kissed her boldly on the cheek before marching out of the bar.

She watched him go as she languidly stirred the remains of her coffee. It would be no harm to attend the Kavanaghs' party. She would get to see how the other half lived. She might even pick up some interesting gossip. At the very least, she was bound to make some useful contacts.

And then a terrible thought struck her with all the force of an express train. This weekend she was supposed to be going down to Mountclare to tell Luke Bradford their relationship was over.

Immediately, she felt a pang of conscience. The sooner she confronted Luke the better. The farce of their engagement had gone on long enough. But she also wanted to go to this party. And anyway, she hadn't told him she was definitely coming down to Mountclare this weekend. She could ring him and say she was working the Sunday shift and couldn't get away. He'd complain like hell, of course, but she could live with that. It was only for one more week and then she would definitely go down and deliver the bad news.

Once she had made the decision, she felt good again. She left the bar and sauntered along Nassau Street towards her office in the bright afternoon sun, admiring the window boxes and tubs of flowers that adorned the shop fronts.

With each contact, she found herself coming more under Harry Kavanagh's spell. He was tall and handsome with a strong, athletic build and a head of thick, dark hair. And he was entertaining company, always witty and courteous. What was more, his family was extremely wealthy. During her research for the interview with his father, she had come across an article that put the Kavanagh family fortune at €50 million.

A strange thought occurred to her. Why had he noticed her engagement ring? Had he been looking for evidence that she was involved in a relationship? And if so, why would he do that? Erin was aware that there was a frisson that passed between two people when they were attracted and she had certainly felt it with Harry. And now he had invited her to this party. What did it all mean?

Immediately she dismissed the thought from her mind. This was just her wild imagination playing games. Harry could have his pick of women. They would be fighting over him. Why should he be interested in her? She had to be realistic. He moved in rich money circles. If he was looking for a partner that was the class he would choose from. His mate would be the daughter of some millionaire like himself, not a poor, struggling reporter who didn't even earn enough money to afford her own apartment.

As for the engagement ring, Harry had noticed it for the very same reason that he had noticed the daffodils coming up – because he was a smart, intelligent man who spotted these things.

Still it was pleasant to daydream and as Erin turned into Westmoreland Street and *The Clarion*'s offices came into view, these thoughts continued to play on her mind.

Chapter 5

On Friday Erin worked till lunch-time, then told Ger Armstrong she had to go home to type up some notes. She had been working hard recently so no one raised any objection. But instead of going home, she went straight to the hairdresser's where she had already booked an appointment. If she was going to the Kavanaghs' party, she was determined to look her best. She owed it to Harry who had invited her. And she owed it to herself. She had her dignity to maintain. She didn't want a crowd of society madams looking down their noses and feeling sorry for her.

She sat in the hairdresser's chair for over an hour while she had her hair washed and trimmed and blow-dried. When it was finished and she examined herself in the mirror, she was delighted with what she saw. If nothing else, her hair would be sure to draw attention. She was so pleased that she gave the hairdresser a €5 tip which she could ill afford.

Then on her way home, she passed a boutique that had a sale and, on impulse, she went in and bought a stunning little black evening dress with a silver trim and some beautiful silk blouses. When she left, her credit card had been wildly overdrawn. But it was all in a good cause. Something told her she would get plenty of use out of that dress in the months to come.

On Saturday morning, she felt so tired that she slept till lunch-time. When she got up she found her cousin vacuuming the flat.

Erin went into the kitchen and put on the kettle to make some tea and Lora immediately came to join her.

"You've had your hair done," she remarked.

"Yes. I've been invited to a party."

"Oh," her cousin replied. "Is it a newspaper party?"

"Not really. But it's sort of work-related. Harry Kavanagh invited me."

"The building family?"

"Yes. I've been writing about them a lot."

Lora looked suitably impressed. "Well, that should be very grand. Where is it?"

"At Belvedere, his father's house in Malahide."

Her cousin could barely conceal her envy. "Will Luke be going with you?"

At the mention of his name, Erin felt her back stiffen. "He hasn't been invited. I've really only been asked because of the interview I wrote."

A cautious look had now entered Lora's eyes. "You

need to be careful, Erin. If Luke finds out he'll be furious."

But Erin merely smiled and waved her hand dismissively. "It's all very innocent, I can assure you."

"I know. But sometimes these things can get twisted out of context. Anyway, you go off and enjoy yourself. And don't forget to bring home some roast pheasant in a doggy bag. We'll have it for Sunday lunch."

Erin was glad when her cousin left for the afternoon to meet her boyfriend. He was taking her for a meal and later to a rock concert. Harry had promised to send a car to pick her up at seven thirty, so at six she began to get ready. She filled the bath and soaked herself for half an hour in the nice warm water, feeling the tiredness and tension easing out of her bones. Then she dried herself, pulled on a towelling robe and sat down at her dressing-table to begin her make-up.

By seven fifteen she was ready. The black dress she had bought looked great. She slipped on a pair of silver earrings and did a little pirouette in front of the mirror. She looked good and the sight bolstered her confidence. Tonight, no one would be able to look down on her. She would be more than a match for any of the society ladies at Belvedere. She applied some finishing touches, dabbed a little perfume behind each ear and slipped on a pair of black and silver heels just as the bell announced the arrival of her cab.

It deposited her at the front door of Belvedere at

five past eight. The place was ablaze with lights and cars were parked all along the driveway. Harry was waiting. He came down the steps to greet her. He looked magnificent in a black velvet jacket and white dress shirt and tie. His dark hair tumbled across his forehead and his eyes glowed with obvious delight.

He took her hand and kissed her gently on the cheek.

"There you are," he said. "Come inside. We can't have you catching your death of cold."

But as Erin approached the front door, she felt a strange apprehension take hold of her. There it was again – that uneasy feeling that the house inspired. She had felt it from the first day she had set eyes on it. And now she could feel it again, an overpowering sense of malice that made her baulk and want to turn back.

But Harry was gently leading her forward and suddenly the door opened and she entered a brightly lit hall where a crowd of people were milling about. They clutched glasses of champagne and chattered like magpies in little groups of four and five.

"Let me introduce you to some people," he said.

He led her through the crowd, pausing to pick up two glasses of champagne as he went.

"You look wonderful," he whispered.

"Thank you."

"Already you're turning their heads. Look."

She glanced about her. He was right. Behind them, people had stopped chattering long enough to stare in her direction. No doubt they were wondering who she was. But their reaction only served to increase her unease. She didn't belong here. She shouldn't have come. Harry led her by the hand and then stopped abruptly next to a small group who were chatting together at the foot of the stairs.

"Let me introduce my mother," said Harry, placing his hand gently on the shoulder of an elderly lady in a white silk dress.

She turned and Erin's heart jumped into her mouth. It was the same woman she had seen in Charlie Kavanagh's office on her very first visit to Belvedere. Once again, the sharp, inquisitive eyes travelled over Erin and looked her up and down.

"Mother, this is my friend, Erin O'Neill."

The frosty look remained on Mrs Kavanagh's face as she slowly extended her hand.

"I'm pleased to meet you, Ms O'Neill. Have you travelled far?"

"Just from Dublin."

"But that's not a Dublin accent I hear."

"No, I'm from Offaly."

Mrs Kavanagh did not react. Her cold, unwelcoming eyes continued to bore into Erin's face.

"I see. Well, I trust you will enjoy yourself."

Harry now turned to the other members of the group.

"Erin, this is my sister Susan and her husband Toby."

A thin woman of about thirty extended her hand. She had a pointed chin, sharp angular features and grey eyes that didn't smile.

"You're welcome," she said.

Toby also put forward his chubby hand. He was a small, plump man of about forty with a shiny, pink complexion.

"How do you do, Ms O'Neill?" he said and inclined his head politely.

"And finally, this is my little brother, Tim," Harry announced.

A younger, thinner version of Harry was grinning at her with bright, boyish eyes.

"I know who you are," he said, eagerly grasping her hand. "You're the woman who wrote that flattering interview about Dad."

"Yes," Erin said, pleased that one member of the Kavanagh family at least was showing her some warmth.

"It certainly put him in good form. He said it was the best interview ever. He said you really captured him down to a tee."

"You can always write a good interview if you have an interesting subject," Erin remarked, "and your father is certainly that."

"Now you're being modest," Harry said, then turned to the others. "Where is he anyway? I want him to meet Erin."

"He's shut up in his office with the architect and that man from the bank," Tim replied.

"Well, he'd better get out of there soon," Mrs Kavanagh complained. "He's got guests to attend to. It's very rude to disappear like that." She shook her head and spoke to the general company. "He works all the time. Never relaxes. That can't be good for anyone."

"How are you enjoying the party, Ms O'Neill?"

It was Susan. She was still studying Erin intently.

"I've just arrived."

"You must get to lots of wonderful parties. You newspaper people spend your whole time gadding around town to fancy receptions, don't you?"

"Not really," Erin replied. "This is the first party I've been to in months. I've been working extremely hard."

She felt Harry's hand on her shoulder.

"We're going to circulate," he said to the group. "We'll catch up with you later."

She was relieved to get away. Apart from Tim, Harry's family had given her a very cool reception. She was certain that they didn't approve of her and it made her upset. She had been invited here by Harry and the least she might have expected was some civility. But it just reinforced her initial feeling of discomfort and unease. It had been a mistake to come here. These were not her sort of people and she didn't like them.

She spent the next hour being whisked from one group to another while Harry proudly introduced her to friends and associates and soon her head was swimming as she struggled to remember all the names and faces, till in the end she gave up. And everywhere she went, she noticed the inquisitive glances. At nine o'clock, a magnificent buffet supper was served in the dining-room and people gathered to sample the lobster and smoked salmon and other fine food that was laid out on long trestle tables.

She was glad of the opportunity to sit down. Harry left to fetch his father who was still closeted with his advisors in his office and Erin found a comfortable settee and balanced a plate on her knees. But she had no sooner started to eat when she saw Tim approach through the crowd, carrying a plate of food.

"Mind if I join you?" he asked.

"Not at all," she replied and moved over to let him sit down.

"Buffets are fine," Tim commented. "They are much less formal than sitting around a big dining-table. But they have one major disadvantage. You can't eat comfortably."

"True," Erin replied, "but we seem to be managing all right."

"So, are you having a good time?"

"Well, I've met a lot of people."

"But now you just want to escape and unwind?"

"Exactly," Erin said with a gentle smile.

"Well, you've certainly caused a stir," Tim went on. "They're all wondering why Harry invited you here."

She looked more closely at him. "Really?"

"Oh, yes. It's always the same whenever he brings a new female friend to a party. It sets all the tongues wagging." He lowered his voice. "You see, there are a lot of women here tonight who have their sights set on

Harry. And they see you as a possible rival."

He turned his head in the direction of a beautiful blonde woman in a stunning magenta evening dress who was sitting across the room and staring openly at Erin. She hadn't noticed her till now.

"That woman is Samantha O'Malley. She was Harry's girlfriend till quite recently. I don't think she likes you. She believes you've stolen him away."

"Oh."

Erin looked again at the woman, then turned back to Tim. He nodded and grinned.

"But I wouldn't worry about it if I were you. I don't think Harry is in any rush to get married. And one other thing, don't mind Susan or my mother. They are very protective of my brother. At heart, my mother doesn't really believe that *any* woman is worthy of him."

He winked and returned to the buffet, leaving Erin to ponder the meaning of his words.

But just then, Harry came back.

"I can't find Dad," he said. "I don't know where he's disappeared to."

"I want to go home," Erin said.

Harry's face dropped. "But you've only just got here. There's dancing later."

"I don't feel well. I really need to get home to bed. Could you organise a taxi for me?"

"I'll do no such thing. I'll drive you myself."

"Oh, no," she protested. "I couldn't drag you away from the party."

But he dismissed her protests and went off the collect her coat. A few minutes later, he returned.

"The car's outside," he said.

"Are you sure you want to do this? You have your guests to think about."

"I've seen them all before," he said. "Many times. You're the only guest I'm interested in."

Thankfully, the roads were clear of traffic and half an hour later, Harry was pulling in beside her apartment.

"You didn't really enjoy the evening, did you?"

"No," Erin said.

"May I ask why not?"

"It's not your fault, Harry. I just felt uncomfortable. I shouldn't have come. Those were not really my sort of people. They didn't like me."

"Well, I'm sorry for them but they'll just have to get used to you."

His strong arm encircled her shoulders and drew her close.

"I know this sounds crazy," he said, "but I think I'm falling in love with you."

Next moment, his warm lips were pressed on hers and they were locked in a passionate embrace, Erin's body shuddering with pleasure as her arms went around his neck.

Chapter 6

The following morning she was dragged awake by a loud banging on the front door. She rubbed the sleep from her eyes and looked at her bedside clock. It was five past ten. Outside her window she could see that the sun was out and the city was enjoying a quiet Sunday morning.

The banging started again, more urgent this time. Who on earth can this be, she thought as she slipped out of bed and hurriedly pulled on her dressing-gown. She opened the door and gasped. Luke Bradford was standing in the hall with a thunderous look on his face.

"Luke? What are you doing here?"

"We have to talk."

She quickly gathered her thoughts. Lora's bedroom door was ajar which meant she was spending the night at Jack's place, so she was on her own in the flat. And she didn't like the look on Luke Bradford's face. He appeared ready to pull someone's head off.

But before she could do anything, he brushed past her and entered the apartment.

"Where is he?" he growled, glancing round furiously.

"Who are you talking about?"

"You know who," he said with a sneer. "The man you've been seeing, this Kavanagh guy. Have you got him in the bedroom?"

"I've got no one in the bedroom. I'm alone here."

"I don't believe you."

"Then go ahead and search the place."

"Are you hiding him?"

"I'm not hiding anybody! Now tell me what you're going on about?"

He suddenly took hold of her hand. "Where's my engagement ring? Why aren't you wearing it?"

"I took it off," she said. "Now why don't you just calm down and tell me what the hell this is all about?"

"You know damned well what it's about," he continued, following her into the living-room. "You've been carrying on with Harry Kavanagh behind my back. And don't try to lie about it. I've got all the details. I know you were with him last night."

"*What?*"

"I got a phone call at seven o'clock this morning. I drove up straight away."

"A phone call? Who from?"

"Joe Spears."

"Who's he?"

"A friend of mine. I asked him to keep an eye on you."

She gasped in astonishment. "You asked someone to spy on me?"

"Damned right I did. I knew something like this would happen. I never wanted you to come to Dublin in the first place."

Luke seemed to be getting worse. By now he was practically foaming at the mouth.

"I'm going to make a cup of tea," Erin said. "And then we're going to sit down and discuss this in a rational fashion."

She went off to the kitchen and left Luke fuming on the settee. Inside she was boiling with rage. The thought of him spying on her, asking this Joe Spears person to follow her around and now barging into the flat, made her seethe with anger. She wondered how long it had been going on. But there was one good aspect to this. It had brought matters to a head.

She returned with two cups of tea and gave one to Luke. By now, he had a piece of paper in his hand and was waving it about.

"I have all the evidence right here," he said. "All the times you saw him, the lunches, the cups of coffee, the cosy little conversations. And this party out at his house last night."

"Just for the record, Luke, I had one lunch with Harry Kavanagh and one cup of coffee. And they were both connected with work."

"I don't believe you. And I've had enough. You're coming back to Mountclare with me right this minute."

He stood up and took hold of her arm.

"Let go of me!" she protested.

"I'll let go of you when you're safely in my car. C'mon!"

But Erin resisted. "I'm not going anywhere. And I'd advise you to let go of my arm. You know the law. If you don't release me I'll have you charged with assault."

The mention of charges forced a change of mind. Luke let her go and sat down again.

"Don't you dare manhandle me," she said. "Who do you think you are?"

"Your fiancé," he said bitterly. "Although you wouldn't think it the way you've been carrying on."

"I'll carry on exactly as I please. You have no rights over me."

"Well, that much is obvious," he snorted.

"I've been meaning to have this talk with you for some time," she said. "The truth is, I want to break off the engagement."

His face went pale. "You can't do that. We'll be a laughing-stock."

"I can put up with that."

"Yes, but that's easy when you're in Dublin. I'm the one who has to live in Mountclare."

"Listen, Luke, I don't know why I got engaged in the first place. I don't love you. I've never loved you. And there is no way I'm letting you railroad me into a disastrous marriage that would mean misery for both of us."

His mouth dropped open. "You don't know what you're saying. You're off your head."

"I am not off my head and I know exactly what I'm saying. This charade has gone on too long and it's stopping right now."

"This is all Kavanagh's fault, isn't it? He poisoned you against me!"

"It's nobody's fault. It's just reality."

"You'll change your mind. You'll settle down once you're back in Mountclare. Coming to Dublin was a big mistake. All these bright lights have turned your head."

Erin heaved a deep sigh. How was she going to make him understand?

"I'm never going to change my mind, Luke. You and I are totally incompatible. We'd be awful for each other. If we got married it would be a catastrophe."

She went into the bedroom and returned with the ring.

"Take it," she said. "I should never have allowed matters to get this far. I'm sorry if I hurt you."

By now he had sunk his head in his hands and was sobbing loudly. "I love you, Erin! And now my life is ruined. What am I going to do?"

"You'll get over it," she said. "You'll find another nice woman and you'll both be very happy."

After he was gone, she sat staring out of the window. A couple of swallows were building a nest nearby and she watched the birds ferrying pieces of straw and leaves in their tiny beaks. She was sorry the way events had turned out. She wished she had been able to sit down with Luke and discuss their situation like two reasonable people. But at least it was over and that was a big relief.

Perhaps she had been a bit hard on him. She had never intended to reduce him to tears but he had given her little choice. And the thought of asking Joe Spears to spy on her still rankled.

Luke was the second man to mention love in the past twelve hours. She knew it was a much abused word. People tossed it around without thinking what it meant. She was certain that Luke didn't love her. And she definitely didn't love him. He saw her as a possession, a trophy to parade around Mountclare so that people would admire him. If he truly loved her, he would never have behaved the way he did. But was Harry Kavanagh any different?

She thought of last night, after they had left the party and that wonderful moment when he had taken her in his arms and she had felt her heart melt with pleasure. He'd told her that he was falling in love with her.

But something warned her to be careful. A relationship with Harry would be fraught with danger. They inhabited different worlds and, after last night, she knew his family were firmly set against her. They would do everything in their power to keep them apart.

Still her thoughts kept returning to that wonderful moment in the car and the other occasions she had been with him in the last few weeks. He excited her and flattered her. He made her feel important. He was a joy to be with. Yet everything had happened so fast that Erin barely had a chance to catch her breath.

Was it possible for two people to fall in love with such breakneck speed? Was it love or mere infatuation? Was Harry just dallying with her as he had with other women like Samantha O'Malley, that beautiful creature she had seen last night? And what was she to make of Tim's remark that his brother was in no hurry to get married?

She was still turning these thoughts over in her mind when she heard the key in the lock, the door opened and her cousin returned home. She came into the living room with a lively spring in her step, then stopped when she saw Erin.

"You look upset," she said.

Erin raised her eyes to look at her cousin. "I had a visitor."

"Oh, anyone interesting?"

"Luke Bradford was here."

Lora clasped her hand across her mouth. "Don't tell me. He found out about the party! Oh, my God!"

"He knew about the party, all right. He knew about Harry Kavanagh. You won't believe this but he asked this friend of his to spy on me."

Lora looked shocked and excited at the same time. "So what happened?"

"We had a big argument and the upshot is I broke off the engagement."

Lora's eyes were almost popping out of her head with excitement.

"Did you give him back the ring?"

"Yes."

"The wedding's off?"

"Yes, Lora, did you not hear me? Everything is off – the wedding, the relationship, the whole *enchilada*. There's no going back."

"Oh my God!" Lora said again. "There're going to be ructions in Mountclare when this gets out."

Mention of Mountclare reminded Erin that she had better ring her mother and warn her. Her cousin was right. When word of the broken engagement got around, the town would be abuzz with rumours.

But if she was expecting her mother to be disappointed, this was not the case.

"I'm not surprised," Mrs O'Neill said matter-of-factly. "You two were never meant for each other."

"Those are my sentiments exactly."

"So, you're not upset or anything? I wouldn't like you to be hurt."

"Mum, I'm absolutely delighted. I feel like I just got out of jail. I'm sorry for Luke but I'm sure he'll get over it."

"He's going to have an awful lot of explaining to do."

"He'll manage. He'll probably blame it all on me. And in a way he'd be right. I should never have allowed it to go so far."

"You know, I'm actually quite happy it's off," Mrs

O'Neill said. "I never told you this but I didn't really like Luke very much. I thought he was a bit full of himself, if you know what I mean."

"I know exactly what you mean."

She put down the phone feeling greatly relieved. She was proud of her mum. Imagine if she had sided with Luke and tried to persuade her to go back to him! But her mother was much too sensible for that. She was glad of her support. It had been a momentous couple of days and she was still struggling to come to terms with all that had happened.

For their dinner she made a pasta dish with salad and opened a bottle of wine she found in the back of the cupboard. After they had eaten, she watched a DVD with Lora for the remainder of the evening. Shortly after eleven o'clock she went wearily to bed and within a few minutes she had faded off to sleep.

Chapter 7

Next morning, she rose early. She felt relaxed and energised. It was another bright day with a definite hint of spring in the air and the weather seemed to chime with her mood. It was time to move on and make a new beginning. Luke Bradford was a chapter in her life which she had now firmly closed. But she would draw the lessons from it. From now on, she would think very carefully before she got involved in another serious relationship.

She was in high spirits as she set off for the office through the bustling city streets. It was just before nine o'clock when she arrived into the newsroom. As usual, she checked her pigeonhole to see if any mail had arrived. Inside, she found a letter. She took it out and gave it a casual glance. Her name was written in block capitals which was odd.

Since joining *The Clarion*, Erin had got used to people writing to her. Many of the letters were from cranks but occasionally they were from people tipping her off about some story that might be worth pursuing. She took the letter to her desk and opened it. Immediately, she felt herself freeze as her eyes scanned the message inside

STAY AWAY FROM BELVEDERE. YOU ARE NOT WANTED. AND STAY AWAY FROM HARRY KAVANAGH IF YOU KNOW WHAT IS GOOD FOR YOU. YOU HAVE BEEN WARNED!

She stared at the letter till it began to swim before her eyes. Its message had instantly shattered the light airy feeling that had been with her since she woke. Now she experienced again the unease she had encountered at Belvedere.

She looked at her hands and saw they were damp with perspiration. Her first instinct was to roll the letter in a ball and dump it in the waste bin. But before she could do anything, she was startled by a loud voice. She looked up to see Ger Armstrong towering over her.

"Are you okay, Erin? You look a bit shocked."

She quickly covered the letter with a newspaper and forced a smile onto her lips.

"I'm fine, Ger."

"Let me get you a cup of coffee."

"No, it's okay."

"Are you sure?"

"Yes."

"Well, in that case, can I ask you to get your butt

over to the Department of Health? The Minister has just called a press conference for ten o'clock."

"What about?"

"I'll give you three guesses."

"Another crisis in the health system?"

"What amazing perception!" Ger Armstrong said with a world-weary grin.

Erin gathered her things together and set off. She had plenty of time so on her way out, she ducked into the bathroom, found an empty stall and locked the door. She took out the letter and studied it once more. By now, the worst of the shock had worn off and she was able to think rationally.

The person who had written the note had deliberately used capital letters to disguise the handwriting. That much was clear. But the intention was obvious. It was meant as a warning. But who could it be? Was it possible that Luke Bradford had sent it in an effort to win her back? But that sounded so far-fetched as to be ridiculous. It had to be someone who had seen her at the party on Saturday night, someone who bore her a deep dislike.

For some reason, Mrs Kavanagh came into her mind. Erin remembered the sharp, penetrating eyes that had bored right through her. She recalled the cold, dismissive way she had treated her at the party. And she remembered Tim's remark that his mother didn't believe any woman was worthy of her son. Was it Mrs Kavanagh who had sent the letter to warn her off from any further involvement with Harry?

Now she felt a new emotion rise up in her breast Her pride was hurt and it made her indignant. Who did the Kavanaghs think they were that they could look down their noses at her? And why did they believe she would be interested in their precious son? Harry Kavanagh had invited *her* to the party. He was the one who had made all the running. *He* was the one who had pursued *her*.

These thoughts restored her confidence. She felt her old self-esteem return. There was no way she was going to join the queue of wannabe brides fighting to become the new Mrs Kavanagh. She had more self-respect. She emerged from the bathroom and went down the stairs to the busy street. Ten minutes later, she was taking her seat at a packed press conference and listening to a beleaguered Minister for Health as she attempted to explain yet another failure in the hospital system.

It was after one o'clock when she got back to the office, after stopping off for a quick bar lunch at a pub on the way. She sat down at her desk and wrote up her report. She was just sending it to Ger Armstrong when she heard her mobile go off. She dug it out of her handbag and pressed it her ear.

"Hi," she said.

"Erin, it's Harry."

At once, she felt the colour rush to her face. She braced herself. If he was ringing for another date she would tell him politely to take a running jump.

But it was something else entirely.

"I promised to ring you. We've just received the planning decision."

She felt her heart give a leap. This was the big story she had been waiting for, the chance of another scoop.

"What does it say?" she asked, breathlessly flicking open a notebook.

"It's a classic compromise." He sounded as excited as she was. "They're allowing us to build three hundred apartments."

"Three hundred?"

"That's right."

"What about the restaurant and shops?"

"We get that too."

By any yardstick, this was a victory for Kavanagh Construction.

"Are you happy with it?"

"We certainly are. Of course, we would have preferred the full five hundred. But it appears Ballsbridge isn't ready for that degree of development just yet."

"Who else has got the decision?"

"Just us."

"Is it possible to get my hands on a copy?"

"Sure. But I'm not trusting it to a courier. Can you meet me at Sammy's Bar? It's at the back of Dame Street."

"I know it."

"I'll be there in half an hour," he said.

She immediately informed Ger Armstrong and

grabbed her bag. Immediately, the news editor swung into action, clearing pages and allocating angles to other reporters. Erin could feel the buzz begin to rise. She had got another exclusive and the razzmatazz was about to start all over again.

He was waiting for her in a secluded corner of the bar with a gin and tonic in front of him.

"What can I get you?" he asked.

"Nothing for me, thanks. I'm under pressure, got to get back to the office."

He opened his coat and slid a large buff envelope across the desk. Erin quickly tore it open and leafed through the bulky contents. She could tell at once that there was enough material to fill half a dozen pages of *The Clarion*. Her biggest challenge would be to condense it all. He reached into his pocket and took out another envelope.

"That's our response," he said.

It was a prepared press statement. It expressed regret that the development hadn't been granted in full but accepted that local concerns had to be taken into account. It reiterated the company's belief that ordinary people had the right to decent housing and that no one should be allowed to block the democratic decision of the planning authorities. On the whole, the company welcomed the decision as a fair compromise. Erin detected the hand of some highly-skilled PR advisor.

She stood up.

"Thanks, Harry. You kept your word."

"I always do."

She started to leave but he reached out and caught her hand.

"Is that all I get, a brief thank-you? When can I see you again?"

"Not tonight. I've got a busy shift ahead."

"I could buy you dinner when you're finished?"

She shook her head. "I'll be too tired."

But it hurt her to see the downcast look that came over his face.

"Tell, you what," she said. "Give me a ring some time. Maybe we can grab a coffee together."

The newsroom was in uproar when she returned. Reporters were scurrying around like worker ants as they prepared for the busy night ahead. In the midst of all the excitement, Ger Armstrong stood in shirtsleeves like a general directing his troops.

Erin took off her coat and gave him the planning report. Immediately he got a couple of reporters to run off copies.

"The editor has decided to go big on this," Ger Armstrong said. "He's giving it three pages inside plus the front-page lead. Do you need any help?"

"No. I should be okay. I've got the company's response and I know who else to ring."

"Okay, if you need assistance just holler."

She got herself a coffee, sat down at her desk and started to work. She leafed through her contacts book and made her first call. It was to the chairperson of the local residents' association, a feisty woman called Maeve Brennan. Erin had already dealt with her on the original story and was on first-name terms.

"Hi, Maeve," she began. "Are you sitting down? I've got the decision on the Conway Hotel development."

"I don't like the sound of this," Maeve said.

"They've been given permission to build three hundred apartments."

She heard a sharp intake of breath.

"Erin, if you're pulling my leg, I'll never forgive you."

"No, Maeve. I'm deadly serious."

"Is this official?"

"I have the planning report right here on my desk."

Maeve Brennan exploded. "They must be crazy! Three hundred apartments? What are they trying to do, turn Ballsbridge into Hong Kong?"

Erin was busily taking notes. "What are you going to do about it?"

"We'll fight it, of course. We'll take it to every court in the land. We'll take it to Strasbourg if necessary. We'll lie down in front of the diggers."

Maeve Brennan was working herself into a frenzy.

"If Charlie Kavanagh thinks he's getting away with this, he's got another think coming! By the time we're finished with him, he'll be lucky to build a dog-kennel never mind three hundred apartments!"

When Erin put down the phone she glanced at her

notes. Maeve Brennan had just provided her with some brilliant quotes. Already the story was building. She moved on to the next contact on her list, the environment spokesman for one of the opposition parties.

She worked steadily, fielding phone calls and typing frantically as she battled to fashion the lead story. It had to distil all the main elements of the decision so that a casual reader could grasp the essential news points. The inside pages would amplify the story and carry the less important angles.

Beside her desk, her waste bin began to fill up with discarded coffee cups. But she wouldn't swap this task for anything. It was like a drug. She felt high on the energy and the excitement of knowing she was at the centre of a very important development that was going to have the country talking. By nine o'clock, she had finished. She sent her report to the news desk and went over to watch the evening news on television.

And here she met a disappointment.

They led with the planning decision. At once she felt her spirits sink. She had been hoping that she could keep the story for herself and have another scoop. But somehow it had leaked out and tomorrow all the papers would all have it. She couldn't disguise her frustration.

She felt Ger Armstrong's comforting hand on her shoulder.

"Don't feel bad about it. A story this big was bound to break. But we've had a head start on the others, thanks to you. Tomorrow morning we'll wipe the decks with the opposition, you'll see."

"Thanks, Ger," Erin said.

"And if it's any solace, the editor has asked me to pass on his congratulations."

She took a cab back home and found her cousin watching television.

"You look whacked," Lora said.

"That's exactly how I feel."

"Busy day?"

"You could say that," Erin replied, with a tired grin. "Do you mind if I don't sit up with you? I think I'll get my head down."

"Be my guest," Lora said.

Erin went into the bathroom and stood under the hot shower. Five minutes later she was snuggling into her cosy duvet. She felt exhausted. She was just drifting off when she remembered her conversation with Harry Kavanagh and his request to see her again. I'll deal with that tomorrow, she thought. Two minutes later she was fast asleep.

Chapter 8

He rang just after nine o'clock as she was eating a breakfast of toast and cereal at the breakfast bar in the kitchen. Lora had already left for work.

"Congratulations," he began. "I've just been reading the paper. You've pulled off another triumph."

"It's all down to you, Harry. You provided me with the material."

"Oh, for God's sake! Can't you take a compliment? You know what your problem is? You're too damned modest."

"Okay, thank you for your kind words."

"You know why I'm ringing?"

"To congratulate me?"

"Yes and to invite you to lunch."

Erin took a deep breath. There was no easy way to do this. She was about to turn him down when he interrupted her.

"I'm determined, Erin. I won't take no for an answer. I've booked a table at the Café de Paris for half twelve and I expect you to be there."

There was a click and the phone went dead.

She reached for her coffee cup and stared off into space. She would have to face him and tell him that she didn't want to see him again. And she would tell him why. She still had that threatening letter in her bag. She was glad now that she hadn't destroyed it.

He was waiting for her when she arrived at the restaurant at twelve thirty. He was dressed immaculately in dark jacket and blue shirt and a little corner of handkerchief peeped jauntily from his breast pocket.

He pulled out a chair for her to sit down.

"I've taken the liberty of ordering champagne," he smiled, pointing to the ice bucket that stood beside the table. "This is a celebration. Will I pour?"

Erin quickly covered her glass with her hand. "I won't be staying, Harry."

His face fell. "Why not?"

"Because I've decided I don't want to continue seeing you."

He looked aghast. "What are you talking about? What has upset you?"

"Let's not beat about the bush. You and I come from different social backgrounds. I would have been blind not to have noticed the hostility your family showed me on Saturday night. Your mother gave me a look that could have killed me stone dead. And then I got this."

She opened her bag and handed over the letter. Harry quickly read it and gave it back.

"When did it arrive?"

"Yesterday morning. I think I can guess who sent it – your mother. She doesn't like me although I have never done anything to harm her. I suppose she thinks I'm going to steal away her darling son. You and I will never work, Harry. I'm not prepared to be treated like some cheap gold-digger. I'm sorry."

"Hold on a minute," he said. "You have no proof that my mother wrote that letter."

"So who did?"

"I think I know. There is a woman I was seeing until recently, Samantha O'Malley. I broke off our relationship and she took it very badly."

"How can you be sure?"

"Because she's done it before. She made a threatening phone call to another woman I was seeing. Samantha's neurotic, Erin. I'll bet my next month's salary this is her work."

She stared at him across the table. This revelation put a completely new slant on the situation. What if she was wrong? What if Mrs Kavanagh hadn't written the letter after all and she was blaming the wrong person?

"I'll admit my mother can be very possessive. I could be seeing a royal princess and she wouldn't approve. But she's not a psychopath."

"She doesn't like me, Harry. She doesn't even try to hide it. She makes me feel very uncomfortable."

"Give her time. She'll come around." He reached out and took her hand. "Erin, you're the most gorgeous woman I've ever met. You're the most lively and the most entertaining. I've fallen head over heels for you. Why walk away from what could be a beautiful relationship?"

She looked into his bright eyes, pleading openly with her. She looked at that handsome face, at the lock of dark hair falling carelessly across his forehead. And suddenly, she felt her resolution dissolve.

"All right," she said. "But there are conditions. I don't want to have anything to do with your family. And I will never set foot in Belvedere again."

With the hurdle overcome, their relationship began to blossom. On their next date, he took her to the theatre and afterwards for supper to a cosy little restaurant at the back of the Central Bank where there were candles on the tables and a pianist played romantic melodies. Soon, they were seeing each other almost every day.

Suddenly, Erin was happy, far happier than she had ever been in her entire life. Her career was on an upwards curve and now she had met this exciting man. Her initial caution gave way to trust and she discovered that Harry was unlike any man she had ever known.

He believed in himself and, unlike Luke Bradford, he regarded her as an equal and allowed her space to breathe. Here was a man who was secure, who didn't treat her as a prize possession that had to be jealously guarded. Here was a man with energy and tenderness who made love to her in a way she had never experienced before. Here, at last, was a man she could relate to as a partner.

"How do you manage sex like that?" she asked, after one particularly beautiful session when they had both exhausted themselves with passion.

He smiled languidly from beneath his dark lashes. "Because I love you, Erin and you inspire me like no woman ever has. Making love to a woman as beautiful as you takes no great effort. It's a joy."

She smiled, snuggling closer to him and nibbling his ear.

"By the way," he asked, "whatever happened to your fiancé? I was concerned about that. I hope I wasn't the cause of you breaking up?"

"Oh no," she said, quickly shaking her head. "That affair was never going anywhere. It was doomed to failure."

"So he survived?"

"Oh yes, he survived. The last I heard he was seeing someone else."

"That's good," Harry said, pulling her closer. "I like happy endings."

Most of their lovemaking occurred in Harry's apartment beside the river. It was a spectacular place – a three-bedroomed penthouse in an exclusive development that the company had built several years before. Harry had kept this one for himself.

No expense had been spared. The bathroom was

tiled with Italian marble. The kitchen was stocked with top-of-the-range equipment. The walls and floors were covered with expensive prints and carpets and it was filled with the very best furniture. To cap it all, it had a large wrap-around terrace with views over the whole city. It was exactly the sort of place that a wealthy businessman like Harry might own.

"You know, I've been thinking," he said one morning after they had spent the night together and were lying in bed. "This place is empty most of the time. You should move in."

She leaned on her elbow and stared into his face. "Are you serious?"

"Of course. You're still sharing with your cousin, aren't you? I'm sure it must be a bit cramped for you both."

Harry obviously didn't know just how cramped. One small bathroom for two people and sometimes three, if Jack stayed over, underwear drying on the radiators, dishes piling in the sink. The miracle was that they hadn't had a screaming match by now.

To move from her apartment to Harry's penthouse would be like moving to another world. This place was so spacious and quiet. She could use one of the bedrooms as an office where she could set up a desk and keep her laptop and books. And in the summer she could have coffee on that fabulous terrace while she and the city woke up together.

"If you're concerned about upkeep, don't be," he continued. "There's a housekeeper who comes in once a week. She looks after laundry and cleaning. She keeps the fridge stocked. She even waters the plants."

"I don't know what to say."

"Just say yes. The place is lying idle. I only use it occasionally. I'd feel much happier if you were here. And, of course, if you were, I'd see a lot more of my fabulous penthouse too!"

She flung her arms around him and covered him in kisses.

"Oh, Harry, you wonderful man! Now you're inviting me to be your concubine."

"It's your decision," he laughed, as his hands found her rump and he pulled her closer.

She moved in the following weekend. Her total belongings fitted comfortably in two large boxes and a suitcase and took a single trip in Jack's car. Her cousin was bowled over when she saw where Erin was moving to. She ran around the penthouse like a child in a sweetshop, opening doors and peering into wardrobes and uttering gasps of astonishment.

"This is like something you might find in Beverly Hills," she said as she stood on the terrace and gazed out over the rooftops and spires. "You are one lucky wagon, Erin O'Neill. I hope you know that?"

Erin did know. She still hadn't completely come to terms with her good fortune in finding such a generous lover. The thoughts of going to sleep in that massive king-size bed or eating breakfast on that beautiful sunlit terrace filled her with joy and anticipation.

But one dark cloud still hung over their relationship. Since they had got together, Harry had observed her conditions. He hadn't once mentioned his mother or invited her back to Belvedere. But now that they were living together almost full-time, it would surely only be a matter of time till Mrs Kavanagh found out. Erin wasn't entirely convinced that she hadn't written that letter. And now she dreaded the consequences.

However, she didn't have long to brood about it. A few weeks later, Harry surprised her one morning as he was coming out of the shower.

He stood in the bedroom, vigorously towelling himself as water dripped onto the carpet.

"How would you like to come to Los Angeles with me?" he asked.

Erin sat bolt upright in bed.

"Do you mean Los Angeles, California?"

He smiled and drew her close. "Is there another one that I don't know about? I have to go there on business and I'm asking you to come with me."

She threw her arms around him and held him tight.

"I'd love to come. When do I start packing?"

It turned out that there was a company in LA that had developed a new technique for pre-cast concrete and Kavanagh Construction wanted to investigate it. Now that the Conway Village development had secured approval, the time seemed right to go. Harry would be able to combine some business and pleasure.

"How long are we going for?" Erin asked.

"Ten days."

"And will you be stuck in meetings all the time?"

"I sincerely hope not," he grinned. "I figure I'll be tied up in business for a couple of days at most. I want to talk with these guys and then I'll have to visit the factory and see this process for myself."

"And then what?"

"We're on our own. We could spend a few days in LA and travel back via Las Vegas if you like."

It sounded like a dream. Los Angeles, Hollywood, Santa Monica, Venice Beach – it was too good to be true! And then the prospect of visiting Las Vegas as a bonus!

Erin fell back on the pillows and kicked her heels for joy.

The trip was arranged for the following week. She organised her leave, and Harry's efficient secretary booked the flights and hotels and made all the arrangements. Then there was the usual flurry to organise passports and visas and holiday insurance. Finally there was the question of what to pack.

"Don't take too much," he advised. "You can use this break to do some shopping. The dollar is weak right now so you might pick up some bargains."

The thought of some serious shopping only increased Erin's excitement. This was her first trip to the U.S. and she couldn't wait to go. She rang her mother to tell her.

"Is the newspaper sending you?" Mrs O'Neill wanted to know.

"No, it's a holiday."

"Who are you going with?"

"This man I've been seeing."

"Well, that's your business but I hope you know what you're doing. He's not another version of Luke Bradford, is he?"

"Oh God, no, there can't be too many men like *him*!"

"Don't bet on it," her mother said. "Now you go off and enjoy yourself. I'm sure you're going to have a wonderful time."

Chapter 9

Los Angeles came at them out of the blue, a small shimmering image on the edge of the ocean that grew and expanded as they approached till at last they were gazing with wonder on a vast, sprawling city with ribbons of highways and buildings that almost touched the sky.

They were relieved to arrive. The flight had been long and tiring with a two-hour stop off at Newark. Even though they were travelling first class and were able to doze, they both felt jaded. But when they disembarked and found their way outside, it was still only lunch-time and the sun was boiling in the sky. Harry's secretary had made reservations at the Sheraton Hotel in Santa Monica so they climbed into the back of a cab and sped away.

They had been allocated a spacious room with a massive bed and en-suite bathroom. From the terrace, there were views of the ocean. Erin was thrilled to

discover that the hotel had a spa and several outdoor
pools. This was where she planned to spend some of
her time, working on her tan.

"Why don't we take a nap for a couple of hours to
get over the jet-lag?" Harry said. "And when it's
cooler we can explore the place. What do you say?"

Erin, who could barely keep her eyes open, nodded
her agreement. Fifteen minutes later they were sound
asleep in each other's arms.

That evening, after they had showered and dressed,
they ventured out of the hotel. Erin was immediately
seized with the magic of the place. The sun was going
down over the ocean and a soothing breeze blew in
from the sea. They strolled along the pier, hand in
hand, till they found a seafood restaurant where they
had a relaxing dinner. Afterwards, they wandered
back to their hotel in the moonlight.

The following morning early, Harry set off for his
business appointment. Erin was left to her own
devices. After breakfast, she took off to explore the
locality some more. She spent several enjoyable hours
wandering round a vast shopping mall and ate lunch
at a deli bar. Back at the hotel, she changed into her
bikini, took her sunblock, towel and a paperback
novel she had bought at the airport and headed down
to the pool.

The days passed very pleasantly. Once Harry's
business had been concluded, they were free to relax.
They took a few days to visit Disneyland and

Hollywood and Universal Studios. But the last few days were passed relaxing by the pool. Lunch was a snack at the poolside bar and the evenings were spent dining at some of the fabulous restaurants nearby. Before they knew, their time was up and they were headed for Las Vegas.

This was a fabled destination in Erin's mind. It conjured up images of luxurious casinos and fabulous hotels, Elvis Presley and Frank Sinatra and the stunning spectacle of the Grand Canyon. She had seen countless films and television programmes about this city. It spelt glitter and high living. It would be the ideal place to spend the remaining part of their trip. And there were excellent stores and retail malls where she could shop to her heart's content.

But Erin didn't know that Las Vegas was about to change her life.

Her first impression was the flatness of the terrain. As far as the eye could see, the landscape stretched in a clear unbroken line. The second thing was the heat. By this stage of their trip, they had grown used to the increased temperature. But they weren't prepared for the searing heat that greeted them when they stepped off the plane at Las Vegas. It was like opening the door of a furnace. Within minutes, Erin could feel her blouse sticking to her back with sweat. They were grateful when they reached the cool interior of the arrivals lounge.

Harry's secretary had booked them into the

Ambassador Hotel on the famous Las Vegas strip. It was air-conditioned and provided every convenience. And, of course, it had its own casino. There was no need to endure the brutal outdoor heat if they didn't want to.

"So what do you make of it?" Harry asked after they had finally settled into their suite and he had asked room service to send up some cold beers.

"It's a bit overpowering," Erin confessed. "I'm still struggling to take it all in."

"That reminds me. Celine Dion is playing at Caesar's Palace. Why don't we book dinner and take in the show?"

"I think that's a great idea."

"Okay, I'll do it this afternoon. Then I'm going to spend a session in the gym." He patted his midriff. "I'm afraid all this high living is beginning to take its toll. I need some exercise."

While Harry was at the gym, Erin set off to explore the hotel. It was a vast expanse of shops, restaurants and bars. The casino was on the ground floor and, as she went past, something urged her to go in. The sight that met her was amazing. She was in a large, carpeted room with no windows and no natural light but it was crowded with people. And they were interested in only one thing: gambling.

Everywhere she turned she could see roulette wheels, poker tables and the constant clamour of slot machines. Around the tables, intense groups of men and women concentrated on the throw of a dice or the turn of a card. It was an electrifying atmosphere.

As she strolled past, she heard a roar from one table and turned to see a smartly dressed woman collect a pile of winning chips. She didn't smile or show any emotion as she gathered her winnings. Without even pausing to count, she continued to play.

Erin watched in fascination. Within fifteen minutes, the chips had dwindled away till they were all gone. Erin calculated that $10,000 had been lost. But the woman didn't seem the least bit concerned. She calmly summoned a cashier and paid for more chips so she could carry on gambling.

Erin returned to her room, changed into her bikini and bathrobe and went out to the pool. After what she witnessed in the casino, she'd concluded that sunbathing was much more relaxing and an awful lot cheaper.

Dinner at Caesar's Palace had been booked for eight, with the show scheduled to follow at ten o'clock. By now, they were both hungry and looking forward to the performance. The hotel was only a few blocks away and Harry suggested that they walk, now that the evening was cool. Celine Dion was a major attraction and when they arrived, they found the restaurant packed. They ate a lovely dinner and then settled back to enjoy a superb evening's entertainment from a star performer.

It was after midnight when they got back to their hotel. But before going to bed, they stopped at a little cocktail bar to have a nightcap.

"So, have you enjoyed your first day in Vegas?" Harry asked.

"I've enjoyed the entire trip, thank you. I don't think I've had a single dull moment since we arrived."

"That's the whole idea," he said, gazing lovingly into her face. "I'm glad you came. I would have missed you terribly if I'd been here alone."

She smiled and stroked his arm. "I would have missed you too."

He put down his drink and held her hands.

"You know, I can't imagine living without you, Erin. You mean everything to me, my reason for being. I want to spend the rest of my life with you."

She closed her eyes and felt her heart swell in her breast. "Me too."

"So why don't we get married?"

She was stunned. She sat up and stared at him. For a brief moment, she thought he was joking but the intense look on his face told her he was deadly serious.

"Are you proposing to me, Harry?"

"I hope so."

"And when would we do it?"

"As soon as possible."

"There'd have to be an awful lot of preparation."

"Not necessarily. We can do it right here in Vegas. All we need is proof of identity."

By now, she was totally confused. This was not how she had imagined a proposal of marriage. It had come right out of the blue and taken her completely by surprise.

"Is it valid?"

"Oh yes, it's valid all right. There were over 100,000 marriage licences issued in Las Vegas last year. It's a minor industry. What do you say?"

"I'm not sure, Harry."

She thought of his family. They would be outraged if they went ahead with this. And they would blame *her*. They would be convinced she had trapped him. Mrs Kavanagh would be furious.

"What about our parents? They might be offended if they're not told."

"We can ring them in advance and let them know. The bottom line, Erin, is this is none of their business. It's between you and me."

He was right, of course. She loved this man and he loved her. And she wanted to spend the rest of her life with him. Why worry what others thought?

She took a deep breath.

"Okay," she said. "Let's do it."

A huge smile engulfed Harry's face. He pulled her close and covered her face in kisses.

"You don't know what this means," he whispered "Those are the most beautiful words I will ever hear."

The following morning after breakfast they set off to make the arrangements. The place they chose was called The Little Chapel of the Silver Bells. It was a small red-bricked building with a steeple on the roof. It was just like dozens of similar little wedding chapels in Las Vegas.

Here, they talked to a pleasant man in glasses who introduced himself as the Rev Herbert Johnson. He explained that he was licensed by the state of Nevada to marry them. Once they had produced their passports and filled out some forms, the Rev Johnson's assistant took them to look at wedding attire. The Little Chapel possessed a complete wardrobe of wedding dresses and suits.

"Of course you don't have to hire wedding costumes if you don't want," the assistant explained. "Some people prefer to get married in their everyday clothes."

But Erin had long harboured dreams of a white wedding and there in the wardrobe was a beautiful satin dress that was exactly her size. She tried it on and it fitted her perfectly.

"I'll wear this," she said.

"The man smiled and turned to Harry.

"And you, sir?"

Harry chose a dark dress suit, white shirt and bow tie.

"What about music?" the man continued. "Where are you from?"

"We're Irish," Harry replied.

"We have 'Danny Boy'!" the man said, enthusiastically. "It's a beautiful orchestral recording. It's very popular. Lots of couples choose it. Or you could have 'Galway Bay'?"

Seeing Erin's little grimace, Harry hastily said, "I think we'd prefer something . . . classical."

The details were concluded without further fuss. For a fee of $500, Rev Johnson would marry them, supply the witnesses, provide a marriage licence, hire out a wedding dress and suit, supply the music and also arrange for wedding photographs and a video. Harry paid the money and everyone shook hands and agreed to return the following day at noon.

The wedding ceremony went as smooth as clockwork and was concluded in twenty-five minutes. Despite the surroundings, it was strangely touching. They stood before the Rev Johnson in their hired clothes and took their marriage vows while a sound system softly played Verdi's 'Chorus of the 'Hebrew Slaves'. The Rev Johnson's assistant and a plump, jovial woman in an elasticised trouser suit acted as witnesses. Then Erin and Harry exchanged matching wedding rings bought at the hotel jewellery shop. Finally, they all signed the register and Rev Johnson declared them man and wife.

On their way out of the chapel, they met another couple anxiously waiting their turn. Harry stood blinking in the blinding sunlight. He turned to Erin and kissed her.

"Hello, wife," he said.

She looked at him. This was the most important day in her life. It had been entirely different to anything she could have imagined. Yet she felt an immense joy as she looked at the handsome man who stood beside her in his hired suit and bow tie. She knew in her heart she had made the right decision.

"Hello, husband," she replied

Chapter 10

But their joy was short-lived. At last, the trip came to an end and they had to return to Dublin. Erin feared the reception that awaited them. As she had predicted, Harry's mother had been furious when he rang to tell her of their plans, threatening him with all sorts of dire consequences if he went ahead with the wedding. Now they had to face the music.

It wasn't long in coming. He returned from work one evening with his face looking sombre. Now that they were officially married, he had moved into the penthouse to live with her full-time and travelled out to his father's office at Belvedere each morning.

"My mother is going ballistic," he announced as he sat down wearily in front of the television in the sitting-room. "She's spitting blood."

"I did warn you," Erin said, gently stroking his neck to soothe him. "How is your father taking it?"

"He's fine. I never expected any trouble from him.

In fact he's very fond of you. But my mother is going bananas."

"This only confirms the wisdom of our decision, Harry. Now that we're married, there's not a thing she can do about it."

"I wouldn't be too sure about that," he said, ominously. "She's barely speaking to me. She's accusing us of making a fool of her. She says our wedding is the talk of all her friends."

"You *did* tell her we're also planning a proper church wedding in due course?"

"Yes. But she says the damage is done. She says she can't look people in the eye any more."

"Well, I'm sorry if she takes that view," Erin said gloomily.

In contrast, her family had taken the announcement very well. In fact, her mother had been entirely sympathetic when Erin explained why they wanted a quiet wedding and would go for a full ceremony when they were ready. The only question Mrs O'Neill asked was if Erin was happy.

But Erin was concerned for Harry. He looked miserable.

"Don't allow it to upset you."

"You don't know my mother, Erin. She's a very domineering woman. She wants everything her own way."

"She'll just have to learn there are some things she can't control."

He held his head in his hands and stared at the floor.

"That's not as easy as it sounds. Nobody has ever thwarted her like this before."

"I wasn't aware that we were thwarting her," Erin replied, coolly. "I thought we were simply getting married."

"That's not how she sees it. She regards it as a snub. But what's really bothering her is that she wasn't consulted. By doing this, we robbed her of her big opportunity to organise everything."

"Including your choice of a bride?"

The remark stung him. He turned to look at her.

"Why do you say that?"

"Because it's true, isn't it?"

He lowered his eyes again. "Yes, if I was being honest."

A memory of the last time she had seen Mrs Kavanagh flashed into Erin's mind. She thought of those cold, unfeeling eyes penetrating right into her heart. What sort of cruelty would she be capable of if she set her mind to it? She felt a little tremor of fear as she took her husband's hands.

"Harry, I want to make something absolutely clear. I hope you understand that money had nothing to do with me marrying you?"

He looked aghast. "What put that idea in your head?"

"I would have married you even if you didn't have a brass farthing."

"I know that."

"And while my family may not be as wealthy as

yours, they are decent people and they have decent values and they raised me properly. I have nothing to be ashamed of."

"Oh, Erin," he said, angrily, "stop talking like this."

"You brought it up," she said, tartly.

"It will all blow over. After we've had the church wedding, they'll all calm down. It's just going to take a bit of time, that's all."

But it didn't blow over. Time passed and Harry seemed to grow more depressed. It was clear that he was suffering. He was now torn between his wife and his family. For Erin's part, she would have been happy never to see the Kavanaghs again or set foot in their gloomy house but she hated to see him hurting like this.

In an effort to lift his spirits, she took him down to Mountclare to meet her parents. He was warmly received and treated as a welcome addition to the O'Neill family. It made a stark contrast with the Kavanaghs' stony silence. But she was adamant that she would not allow them to drive a wedge between her husband and herself. So, despite her difficulties, she determined to put the matter aside and get on with her life.

At work, her colleagues were anxious to hear about her American trip and in particular her impressions of Las Vegas. None of them had ever been there and they had dozens of questions. Was it true that there were no windows in the casinos so that the gamblers wouldn't know whether it was night or day? And no clocks so they wouldn't know what time it was? And that the casinos provided free food and drink so that the gamblers never had to leave?

She told them what she had seen and the travel editor commissioned her to write an article about shopping in Vegas for which she would be specially paid. But Erin withheld one important piece of information. She didn't tell anyone she had married Harry on the trip. They had both removed their wedding rings and agreed to keep the information to themselves. News of the wedding had caused enough reaction among the small circle of people who *were* aware of it. They could only imagine what the newspapers would make of it when they got hold of the information. For the time being, the fewer people who knew, the better.

Apart from the tension with his family, their marriage didn't make much difference to their established routine. They continued to see their friends and go to parties and eat out in nice restaurants. But there was one development. Now that they were married, Harry decided he wanted to dine at home more often. What was more, he wanted to do the cooking. And Erin soon discovered he was quite an accomplished chef.

"Where did you learn to cook like this?" she asked one Sunday evening after he had prepared a succulent meal of roast Wicklow lamb.

"You like it?"

"I certainly do. It's delicious. And the vegetables are exactly how I like them too, *al dente*. Not boiled away to mush."

Harry smiled proudly as he poured the wine. "I took a course," he confessed.

"You did? I'm surprised. What made you do that?"

"It was a birthday present from a friend. It was a course of ten lessons. I thought if I was ever marooned on a desert island some time, being able to cook might come in handy." He laughed. "But I really enjoyed it. The man who was giving the lessons was a very good teacher and he knew his stuff. He did away with all the mystique and made cooking simple and easy."

"Well, it certainly rubbed off on you," she said. "This food is wonderful. By the way, this friend who gave you the present, she didn't happen to be a woman, did she?"

He glanced up, shyly. "Yes, she was. Does it bother you?"

"Not at all," she replied. "We all have past histories, including me. Why shouldn't you have previous girlfriends? It would be very odd if you didn't."

"Well, I'm glad you take that attitude, Erin. Because I've discovered that some women can be very jealous."

"Like Samantha O'Malley, for instance?"

He paused before looking at her. "Yes. Samantha gave me a lot of trouble. She was intensely possessive."

Erin thought briefly of the willowy blonde she had seen at the party. Did she really write the threatening note or was it Mrs Kavanagh as she suspected?

"Well, *I'm* not," she said. "I can't stand possessive people. You're an adult. If you ever want to leave, I won't try to stop you."

"How on earth did we get onto the subject?" Harry said, pouring more wine. "For God's sake, we're hardly married a wet week."

He tipped his glass against Erin's and proposed a toast.

"Long life and happiness."

They laughed and drank their wine.

Soon afterwards, Erin followed Harry's example and enrolled in a class in Basic Cuisine for Beginners. She was determined to improve her culinary skills. Within weeks, she was enjoying the classes and eagerly hurrying off after work to attend them. Soon, she was producing adventurous dishes like Beef Wellington and Duck á l'Orange which she would never have dreamed of attempting in the past.

Now they took turns cooking at home. Harry drew up a roster and stuck it to the fridge door with a magic magnet so they knew whose turn it was and could shop for the ingredients in advance. They both had adventurous tastes in food and as the time passed, they tried out many new recipes from around the world. Erin even picked up the courage to organise a dinner party one Saturday night for a couple of

Harry's friends and some colleagues from the paper.

She made a simple salad of tomatoes and mozzarella cheese sprinkled with fresh basil leaves and followed with a hearty Coq au Vin. Dessert was a tiramisu she bought at a nearby patisserie. It was a boozy affair but very enjoyable. Everybody admired the apartment and went out onto the terrace to view the dazzling aspect over the city. When they had all gone home and the dishes had been piled in the sink to be washed the following day, Erin sank into Harry's arms.

"I love you," she said.

"And I love you."

"I'm glad I married you and I don't give a damn what anybody thinks."

"Hear, hear."

"Have you ever been as happy as this?"

"Never," Harry said.

She snuggled closer into his breast.

"Make a wish," Harry said.

Erin closed her eyes.

"I wish this happiness can go on forever. I wish it may never end."

But issues remained that had not been resolved. There were still tensions that both of them skirted around. Chief among them was the question of the church wedding.

"We should do it soon," he urged one evening when they were having a drink after work. The longer we put it off, the harder it will become. Once we have the church wedding over, my mother will have no more excuse to ignore you."

By now, Erin had grown to hate any mention of Harry's mother. She had become like a ghost at the banquet, a malign presence constantly hovering over their marriage. And a new thought had been gaining ground in her mind. What would happen if they organised the church wedding and his family decided to boycott it? It would be an absolute catastrophe. It would be a terrible insult to her. And it was exactly the sort of thing his mother might be capable of. Even worse, it would cause an impossible strain between Harry and her.

"Let's wait a bit longer," she said. "Why the hurry?"

"Don't you see?" he insisted. "It will give my mother something to do. She would be in her element organising everything."

But Erin's patience with Mrs Kavanagh had finally worn out.

"Why does it always have to be your mother who calls the shots?" she said. "Why do we have to keep her happy? What about *my* mother? She's got feelings too. And if there's going to be a wedding *she* is the person who should be organising it. She *is* the bride's mother after all."

"There's a very simple reason," Harry replied. "Your mother is totally sensible and mine is not."

"And because she's sensible she ends up getting

sidelined. I don't think that's very fair. Do you?"

"Oh please, Erin. No one's being sidelined. Can't you see how difficult this is for me? I'm caught between a rock and a hard place. All I want is to keep everybody happy so we can get on with our lives."

She *did* see how difficult it was and it made her sad. It fuelled the resentment that was steadily building against Mrs Kavanagh and her selfish behaviour. She was the source of the conflict that was beginning to seep into the marriage. And it occurred to Erin that this was exactly what she wanted.

The situation caused her deep unhappiness. She went around for days feeling dull and depressed. Christmas came and that caused further problems. Harry was expected out at Belvedere but Erin wasn't invited. It was another snub and he refused to go without her. So they spent Christmas Day together in the penthouse and Harry cooked a beautiful dinner of poached hake and prawns with tagliatelle and mixed vegetables .

As a concession to the season, they finished up with plum pudding. And the following day, she took him down to Mountclare to spend the remainder of the holiday with her family where he was made to feel very much at home.

By now, the gulf that had opened up with the Kavanaghs was causing an increasing strain. She hated the way it was hurting Harry. Sometimes she even wondered if it might have been better if they had not got married in Las Vegas, at all. But most of the time she was defiant. She had married the man she loved. It was Mrs Kavanagh who was causing all the problems. And the longer it went on, the harder it became for Erin to forgive her.

And then, towards the end of March, something happened to change the situation dramatically.

Chapter 11

"I'm pregnant," she announced one evening after Harry had returned from work.

His eyes popped. He opened his mouth. Then he closed it. Then he opened it again. Eventually he managed to speak.

"Did you say *pregnant?*"

"Yes. Like, I'm going to have a baby."

"Oh, Erin, that's wonderful!" He gathered her in his arms. "I'm thrilled to bits. I'm absolutely over the moon. When did you find out?"

"This afternoon," she grinned. "I've suspected it for some weeks but sometimes it can be a false alarm so I wanted to be sure before I told you. But Amanda Foley confirmed it today."

"How pregnant are you?"

"Six weeks."

"That's it!" he said, all excited. "You must stop working right away. I want you to rest up and take it easy. And you must start eating properly. Did the doctor give you a diet sheet?"

"For God's sake," Erin said between the laughter. "I'm only having a baby. I'm not having a heart transplant. And I'm already eating perfectly well. You don't have to wrap me up in cotton wool."

"You're my wife," he replied, gravely, "and I love you. And that's our baby you're carrying. So from now on, you get special treatment."

"I might come to enjoy that," she said with a smile. "But there's no way I'm stopping work at six weeks pregnant. People would think I was crazy. Besides, what would I do with myself all day long?"

"Then promise to take it easy. And there's to be no heavy housework. If anything like that needs done, ask me. Okay?"

"Sure. I'll be delighted."

"Now what would you like for dinner? I'll cook something special. And I'll stick a bottle of champers in the fridge right now. This calls for a celebration."

He stopped and turned to her.

"Something has just occurred to me. This is the last glass you'll be having for some time. You know you can't drink when you're pregnant?"

"Yes," she laughed. "I have read the books too."

Erin was every bit as excited as Harry about her news. She loved children and the thought of having one of her own filled her with enormous joy. And the pregnancy wouldn't interfere with her career. Half the staff at *The Clarion* were women and the paper was very flexible when it came to taking maternity leave.

But the effect on Harry was dramatic. Suddenly he started taking an intense interest in babies and all matters relating to childbirth, devouring books on maternal health and childcare. For a man whose favourite relaxation was curling up on the settee with a couple of beers while he watched the sports on television, it was a marked change.

"Folic acid is very important," he announced one evening. "I've just been reading about it. Are you sure you're getting enough?"

"If I get any more folic acid, I'll start sprouting leaves."

"This isn't funny, Erin. You get folic acid in food like spinach and beans. Liver is a particularly good source. Maybe you should put it on your grocery list."

"Harry!" she shouted. "I'm paying a doctor to take care of these things. I'm perfectly healthy. Now why don't you just relax and let nature take its course?"

"I can't relax. This is the biggest thing on my mind right now. Do you think I should get a copy of *Dr Spock*? I'm told he's coming back into fashion."

"Don't you think it might be a good idea to wait till the baby is born before we start buying books on child rearing?"

"You can never start too soon," Harry replied. "I think I'll nip down to the bookshop tomorrow lunchtime and buy a copy."

But while she might smile at his enthusiasm,

privately she was delighted. She could see that he was going to be an excellent father. Harry wouldn't need to be reminded to spend time with his child and help with the baby chores. On the evidence of his initial reaction, he couldn't wait to get started.

But they weren't the only people interested in this baby as she was about to discover. A few days later, she was sitting at her desk in the newsroom when the phone rang. She answered it and heard a voice she didn't recognise.

"Am I speaking to Erin O'Neill?"

"Yes."

"Good afternoon, my dear. I thought I'd ring to congratulate you on your good news."

"Who am I speaking to?" Erin asked cautiously.

"It's Caroline Kavanagh, Harry's mother."

She felt herself freeze. Mrs Kavanagh was the last person in the world she expected to call. What should she do? She was tempted to slam down the phone immediately but good sense prevailed.

"Yes?" she asked.

"Harry told me you were pregnant and I thought I'd ring to offer my good wishes. I'm absolutely delighted for you, my dear."

"Thank you very much, Mrs Kavanagh."

"Oh come now, Erin. I think we can address each other by our first names, don't you?"

The woman's audacity took Erin's breath away. She was on the verge of terminating the call but she thought of Harry and restrained herself.

"How are you keeping?" Mrs Kavanagh continued. "Any sign of morning sickness?"

"No," Erin replied, coolly. "Not so far. In fact, I'm perfectly healthy."

"Well, that's very good news. You might be one of the lucky ones. Some poor creatures have a terrible time. I remember when I was having Tim I suffered dreadfully for the entire pregnancy. But, please God, you'll be spared that sort of thing."

"I hope so."

"You know, I've been thinking. You and I should sit down and have a good chat. We have a lot to discuss. I know what we'll do. Some day next week you must come out to Belvedere."

"I'm very busy right now," Erin interrupted.

"But not too busy to have afternoon tea with your mother-in-law, I hope? Which day would suit?"

"I can't decide," Erin said abruptly. "Give me some time to think about it."

She put the phone down as if it was on fire. The sound of the woman's voice had set her nerves on edge. She couldn't get over the brazen cheek of Mrs Kavanagh. Suddenly she was being sweet as pie to her but Erin couldn't forget her attitude that night at Belvedere or the sullen silence that had followed her marriage.

That evening over dinner, she told Harry about the call. But he showed no surprise.

"I know. She told me she was going to do it."

"Really? You mean you discussed it between you?"

"She called me at work. She's really excited about the baby. This is going to be her first grandchild and she's like a kid on Christmas Eve waiting for Santa to arrive."

"I don't understand," Erin said. "Why did she need to consult you?"

"She wanted to know how you would react."

"*What?*"

"She wasn't sure if you were going to accept her call. I think she half expected you might put down the phone."

"She's very lucky I didn't."

"Well, I'm delighted you talked."

"But there's no way I'm going to meet her. I told you at the beginning that I was never setting foot in Belvedere again. She doesn't fool me, Harry. Your mother hates my guts."

He turned his pleading eyes to her. "Please, Erin, do it for me?"

"Can't you see this is just a charade she's putting on? Nothing has changed. I don't trust her."

"No, something *has* changed. My mother is no fool. She knows when she's no longer in the driving seat. You've got something she desperately wants. You're going to have her grandchild."

Erin suddenly remembered Harry telling her that his mother was desperate for a grandchild. Susan had been a disappointment. She was more concerned with her career and her horses. And Tim had shown no interest in even finding a job let alone getting married.

She realised that Harry was right. Something had indeed changed and now Erin held the whip hand.

"Please go and talk to her," he pleaded. "It will make everything so much easier."

"I can't, Harry. We'll end up fighting. She hates me and I don't like her."

"Please," he begged.

Reluctantly, she agreed. Despite her best instincts, she allowed Harry to ring and make an appointment. But it was a trip that she was not looking forward to.

The visit was arranged for the following Thursday morning, which was the first day that Erin was free. She put on a smart linen dress, olive green with a white flower print, brushed out her long hair and wrapped up the box of expensive Belgian chocolates that Harry had bought. At last she set out for Belvedere in the car that Caroline Kavanagh had sent to pick her up.

The moment they passed through the high iron gates, Erin felt the chill return. She remembered her first visit here and the gloomy feeling that had come over her. And now it was back. There was something about Belvedere, some eerie atmosphere that made her skin crawl.

Her mother-in-law was waiting in a small sitting room with a fire burning cheerily in the grate. She got up and kissed Erin warmly, then graciously accepted the present she had brought.

"My favourite chocolates," she declared. "That's

very thoughtful of you. Now come and sit down by the fire. It's cold today." She rang a bell for tea. "You've no idea how delighted I am," she went on. "When Harry told me your good news I was absolutely thrilled. Do you mind if I ask? Were you planning on getting pregnant?"

"No," Erin replied. "I was just as surprised as you."

A smile broke on Mrs Kavanagh's lips. "I think that is always the best way. How many weeks are you now, my dear?"

"Seven."

"And your gynaecologist is happy with your progress?"

"I don't have a gynaecologist," Erin replied. "My local GP, Amanda Foley, is taking care of me and she seems to think everything is coming along just fine."

A concerned look had now appeared on Mrs Kavanagh's face. "Oh but you must have a gynaecologist! Your GP may be an excellent doctor but she's not a specialist. And I happen to know the very man. Professor O'Leary. He's the most eminent gynaecologist in the field. He's a personal friend."

"Do I really need him? I thought my GP was properly qualified."

"Oh yes, you need him. I'll ring first thing in the morning and make an appointment for you. You can never be too careful, my dear. I don't want to sound alarmist but you hear the most awful horror stories."

At that moment the tea arrived, served in a bone china service by a maid in uniform. Caroline

Kavanagh poured and offered some fruit cake on a dish.

"Have you decided where to have the delivery?" she asked.

"Not yet."

"Well, that's the second thing you must do. I can strongly recommend St Angela's nursing home. That's where all my children were born. They have the most up-to-date facilities and the care is superb."

"Better than one of the big maternity hospitals?"

"There is no comparison, my dear. It's like the difference between a bed and breakfast and the Shelbourne Hotel. In St Angela's you will have your own private room and individual attention. And if, God forbid, there are complications, you will have the very best medical expertise on hand."

The thought crossed Erin's mind that all these facilities would also be available in the maternity hospitals but she didn't want to spoil this visit by having an argument. Besides, Mrs Kavanagh was now a completely different person to the cold tyrant she had met before.

Soon, it was time for lunch. They dined alone on smoked salmon and lamb chops while Mrs Kavanagh kept up a steady stream of conversation. It was obvious that she was making a big effort to be conciliatory while at the same time maintaining a firm grip on the discussion. Erin found herself swept along by her mother-in-law's enthusiasm. But the topic of conversation was about to change.

"I've been thinking we should discuss your wedding," Mrs Kavanagh eventually said when the coffee was served. "We don't want malicious tongues to start wagging, do we?"

Erin had been expecting this. But whereas a few weeks ago she might have flared up and told her mother-in-law to mind her own damned business, now she took the announcement completely in her stride. Besides, what harm was there in listening to what she had to say? She didn't have to agree to it.

"I've given the matter some thought," Mrs Kavanagh directed an ingratiating smile at Erin, "and I've come to the conclusion that we should have a big event. It's what people would expect. What are your views, my dear?"

Erin thought briefly of the wedding in Las Vegas before Rev Johnson and the two hired witnesses. Nothing could be smaller than that.

"I haven't made up my mind," she said.

"You see, if we have a small, private wedding, people might think we've got something to hide. We must avoid that at all costs."

"Hide what?" Erin asked.

Mrs Kavanagh gave her a look. "You don't realise how malicious people can be. Some of them like nothing better than gossip and scandal. If we had a small wedding there would definitely be questions, believe me."

Erin wasn't exactly sure what she was hinting at but she let it go. "How big did you have in mind?"

"Susan had three hundred guests."

Erin caught her breath. Off the top of her head, she couldn't think of thirty people she would invite to her wedding. But doubtless Mrs Kavanagh was thinking of all their friends and business associates.

"I know this might sound old-fashioned but we have certain standards to keep up." She smiled sweetly. "I was thinking we could have the reception here in the grounds of Belvedere. We can put up a marquee. And it's much easier to maintain security."

"It all sounds very expensive," said Erin, her heart sinking.

Mrs Kavanagh gently patted Erin's hand. "Don't let that concern you. Harry's father will pay for everything."

"But shouldn't we discuss it with Harry?"

Caroline waved the suggestion away. "There's no need. Men know absolutely nothing about these things. Harry will agree to whatever we decide."

"I'd still like an opportunity to think about it."

"Of course, but don't take too long, my dear. We don't have much time. And there's an awful lot to organise."

Chapter 12

Erin left Belvedere with her head in a spin. She had sworn never to set foot in the place again or to have any more contact with the Kavanaghs but she had just spent several hours discussing wedding plans with her mother-in-law. And Caroline could not have been sweeter. She had been warm and welcoming. There had been no recriminations. The subject of the wedding in Las Vegas had not even been raised. Nor had the chilly silence that had greeted her since her return. To all intents, Erin could have been having a cosy little chat with one of her best friends to talk about her pregnancy.

But she couldn't escape the feeling that Caroline Kavanagh had simply been acting a part and had manipulated her. Her mother-in-law had done most of the talking and made all the decisions. It was as if she had come to the meeting with an agenda and had stuck rigidly to it. While she was careful to defer to Erin and

127

ask her opinions, she was the one who had been in control of the conversation from start to finish. And she had done it so skilfully that Erin had found herself being carried along. The meeting left her with an uneasy feeling. She still didn't fully trust Mrs Kavanagh.

"How did the chat with my mother go?" Harry asked after she got home.

"It went very smoothly. She couldn't have been nicer."

He beamed with pleasure. "Well, that's exactly what I wanted to hear. I want you two to get along together. You know, my mother is actually a very kind woman, Erin. She has many very generous qualities. And she is really delighted about this baby."

"We talked about our wedding. She suggested we do it in style. She said Susan had three hundred guests at her wedding."

He laughed. "That was because Susan's best friend, Deirdre Mulcahy, had two hundred and fifty at hers. Susan didn't want to be outshone."

"Do *you* want a big wedding?"

"It's all the same to me," he shrugged. "But I can understand why my mother wants one."

"Why?"

"Because it sends out a statement that you've been accepted. Don't you see, if we had a small wedding, it might appear that the family didn't approve of you and I was marrying against their wishes. It would give rise to all sorts of gossip. My mother wants to avoid that at all costs."

So this was what Mrs Kavanagh had been hinting

at when she suggested a small wedding would not be a good idea.

"So do you think we should go along with her?"

He nodded. "I do. I know you don't like a lot of fuss. But it would probably be for the best."

That evening, Erin sat down and made a list of all the people she would invite. There was her family, of course, and various aunts and uncles and cousins. Then there were friends from school and other people she had got to know in Mountclare. And finally there were colleagues from *The Clarion*. But even though she went over the list several times, she couldn't make it grow beyond fifty people. If they invited three hundred guests, her friends were going to be outnumbered by six to one.

She decided to ring her mother and seek her advice.

"You'll be relieved to know that we're getting married again, properly this time – a real church wedding."

"Is this what you want?" Mrs O'Neill asked.

"Yes. It was always our intention from the beginning. But it's being brought forward because of the baby."

"I suppose that makes sense," her mother said. "Although I don't always pay attention to what people think."

"The Kavanaghs want a big reception, anything up to three hundred guests. I should add that they will be paying for it so cost isn't a factor. Have you any thoughts about it?"

"Not really. I think it's entirely up to you and Harry."

"Harry thinks we should go along with it."

"Well then, why are you asking me? I made a decision not to interfere in my children's lives once they became adults. I think you're well able to make up your own mind, Erin."

"It's just that our side is going to be swamped. You don't think that will be a problem?"

"Why should it be? If the Kavanaghs are footing the bill, they can invite the Dublin football team if they want. Where is the reception being held?"

"In the grounds of their house."

"So we can look forward to a good day out. Your father will be pleased."

The following week, Mrs Kavanagh rang and arranged to see her again. Erin was beginning to enjoy the power she suddenly had over her mother-in-law. It gave her a quiet satisfaction that their roles had been reversed and Mrs Kavanagh now had to defer to her and seek her approval.

This time, they sat in a beautiful conservatory looking out across the lawns and over tea and scones agreed that two hundred and fifty guests should be invited to the wedding. Caroline Kavanagh was delighted.

"There's another point that needs to be decided," she said. "I know it's traditional to have the service in the bride's parish church but that could be awkward if we're going to have the reception here."

Erin had already thought of this. "What do you propose?" she asked.

"I've spoken to some people and I think it's possible to have the service in Malahide."

She smiled winningly at Erin. "I think it would be more suitable. Can you imagine the nightmare of trying to ferry all those people from Offaly to Dublin? All it would take is a traffic hold-up and the reception could be delayed for hours."

"I can see that."

"So shall we go ahead with Malahide?"

"Yes," Erin said. "It's for the best."

With these major items successfully agreed, it was now a question of deciding on the wedding dress and the number of attendants. On these matters, Mrs Kavanagh tactfully left the decision in Erin's hands. She was happy to have got her way on the big areas that mattered. Erin settled for three bridesmaids – her sister, Anne, an old school friend called Tara McCoy and, as a conciliatory gesture to the Kavanaghs, she included Harry's sister, Susan.

However, the choice of a wedding dress caused an unforeseen problem. Erin wanted something stylish and chic but a search of Dublin bridal shops left her disappointed. Despite spending two weeks traipsing all over the city, she could find nothing she liked. But once more, Mrs Kavanagh came to the rescue.

"I have a very good dressmaker, Erin. Why don't we talk to her? Just tell her what you have in mind and

let her produce some sketches. I'm sure she'll be able
to sort it out for you."

An appointment with the dressmaker was duly
arranged and if Erin was expecting someone staid and
old-fashioned, she was pleasantly surprised. Julia
Emerson was in her mid-thirties and thoroughly
modern. It took her half an hour to rustle up
something that suited Erin perfectly and, after taking
measurements, she drove away in her black Audi with
a promise to arrange for a fitting within ten days.

Now that the major decisions had been made, Erin
was happy to leave the rest of the arrangements in the
hands of her mother-in-law who seemed only too
willing to take on the task. There was a mountain of
detail to be looked after including the despatch of the
invitations which were issued in her parents' names
but with Belvedere as the address for reply. Then there
were the bridal flowers and the hiring of the organist
and singer for the service and the dozens of other
important items that had to be taken care of. Mrs
Kavanagh eagerly immersed herself in this tedious
work.

She seemed genuinely happy to take it over and
was careful to consult with Erin about even the
smallest matter, including the printing of the menu.
And she did it all with skill and efficiency. Erin's view
of her mother-in-law began to undergo a subtle
change. She decided that her initial impression of her
might have been mistaken. Perhaps there was some
truth in what Harry had said. Perhaps Caroline

Kavanagh did have a generous side to her nature.

The wedding was scheduled for June. As the date approached, the pressure on Erin began to grow. She still had to report for work every day and undertake whatever duties the news editor had assigned for her. But she also had to attend for fittings and rehearsals and deal with the constant phone calls from Mrs Kavanagh as well as visiting Professor O'Leary for regular check-ups on her medical condition. She decided that the pressure was getting too much. She approached Ger Armstrong and arranged for a couple of weeks' leave.

There was also the question of the honeymoon. After some discussion, they decided to go off to Paris for ten days. June was supposed to be a good month to visit the city. The weather would be dry and not too hot.

And finally there was the question of accommodation for her parents during the wedding celebrations. Her sister Anne had recently moved to Dublin to take up a job with an interior design company and was in the process of buying an apartment but it wouldn't be ready in time. And Erin wasn't entirely happy with the idea of putting them up in a hotel.

Once again, Mrs Kavanagh came up with a solution.

"Why don't you and Harry move into Belvedere till after the wedding?" she said. "We have a beautiful flat that my husband uses when he has business guests staying with us. It would simplify matters enormously. It's only a short drive to the church and then your family can have the use of the penthouse in town."

Erin baulked at the prospect of moving into the big old house. She still had not overcome her initial dislike of Belvedere and its grim, forbidding atmosphere. But she could see that her mother-in-law's suggestion made a lot of sense. Besides, she would only be staying there for a few days till the wedding was over.

And after seeing the flat, she was won over. It was actually a spacious self-contained apartment on the top floor of the main residence. It was almost as big as Harry's penthouse. It had three large bedrooms, kitchen, bathroom and a large living-room with big windows looking over the rolling parklands. And it had its own separate entrance so their privacy was ensured.

She packed a couple of suitcases and they moved in straight away.

At last, the wedding day arrived. She was up early and ate a light breakfast of coffee and toast. The service was scheduled for midday and at nine o'clock the hairdresser arrived, quickly followed at ten by Julia Emerson and the three bridesmaids for a final fitting of the dresses. The night before, Harry had been bundled out of the flat and closeted in another couple of rooms of the house with the groomsmen in deference to the superstition that it was unlucky for the groom to see the bride until they met at the church.

The dress that Julia had designed was a beautiful strapless creation of champagne taffeta. At one of the early fittings, Erin had looked at herself in the mirror and felt the breath escape her.

"It's stunning," she gasped. "It fits me like a glove. Oh Julia, you're a wonder!"

"Well, I have excellent material to work on," the dressmaker replied with a smile. "Not every bride is as elegant as you, Erin."

"Thank you," Erin replied, delighted at the lovely compliment.

Now, as she slipped into Julia's beautiful creation, Mrs Kavanagh arrived with a tray of champagne and added her appreciation.

"You're going to look magnificent when you walk down that aisle, my dear. People will gasp in admiration. This is a day they will remember for a very long time."

Soon the time was approaching to leave for the church. Harry and his party had already departed along with the rest of the family. The bridal limousine was parked outside the front door, decked in ribbons and sprays of flowers. Erin's father had turned up to travel with her. There was a final check to make sure all was in order and they set off.

It was a beautiful summer morning and the warm sun glittered off the bonnet of the car as they drove down the avenue past the broad expanse of parkland and the trees bursting with bloom.

"Are you nervous?" her father asked.

"Not really."

Despite all the excitement around her, Erin felt strangely calm. There had been no last-minute hitches, thanks to her mother-in-law's meticulous preparations. The whole operation appeared to be going like a dream.

"You were always very confident," her father replied. "Even when you were a little girl. I wish you many happy days, Erin. You've been a good daughter."

Suddenly, her eyes filled up with tears. This was a momentous day for her. She was glad that she had opted for a proper church wedding where she could have her family and friends around her.

"Thank you, Dad," she whispered as he gently squeezed her hand.

As soon as they entered the church, the organ swelled out with the strains of 'The Trumpet Voluntary' and the guests rose to greet her. Erin slowly made her way down the aisle, nodding and smiling to those she recognised. In the front row, her mother and family were seated; on the other side, the Kavanaghs and their entourage. Waiting at the foot of the altar was a grinning Harry and the bridal attendants. A glow of pleasure swept over her.

The service lasted forty-five minutes but it seemed to be over in a flash. Then it was outside to the waiting photographers and the crowds of onlookers who had gathered. This was a big society wedding and it was attracting great interest. Erin posed for photographs and accepted the congratulations of the well-wishers who surrounded the couple. Eventually, they got back into the bridal car and made the short journey back to Belvedere.

A splendid reception awaited them. The Kavanaghs had spared no expense. A jazz band played on the lawn in front of the house while inside the marquee, champagne was being served and a fabulous buffet lunch was prepared. There were further photographs and more handshakes and introductions to people Erin had never met. But at last, they were able to extricate themselves. Harry found a couple of chairs under the shade of a tree and Erin took off her shoes.

"You look beautiful," he said.

"Thank you."

"How does it feel to be the centre of all this attention?"

"Bewildering," Erin confessed. "I've shaken so many hands that my arm is sore."

Her eyes drifted along the lawn to Belvedere where it sat in all its gloomy splendour. Suddenly she was seized again with the sense of unease that she had always associated with the house. It seemed to be looking down on the proceedings, mocking them in its splendid isolation. What grim secrets did it hold? What terrible deeds had it witnessed within its cold, grey walls?

She drew her eyes away and, at that moment, Mrs Kavanagh made her way towards them. She took hold of Erin's hands and kissed her.

"You did us proud, my dear. You look absolutely magnificent. I want to welcome you into the family. I couldn't wish for a more beautiful daughter-in-law. I think you and I are going to get on splendidly."

She was glad to escape to Paris. After all the excitement of the last few months, Paris seemed like an oasis of tranquillity. They were alone at last and could do as they pleased. She had never been to the city before so everything was new to her. And to cap it all, the weather was bright and sunny and perfect for walking.

They stayed at a little hotel near the Luxembourg Gardens and spent the days wandering the avenues and boulevards, visiting attractions that Erin had read about but never seen. In the evenings, they dined at quaint little restaurants in cobbled streets and tiny squares. There was a magic about the city, something that Erin could feel yet couldn't explain. She began to understand why Paris had always held such fascination for artists and poets.

One evening, as they dined on the terrace of a little bistro on the Rue Monge, Harry took her hand.

"I don't think I have ever thanked you properly for coming into my life."

"What a beautiful thing to say!"

"You have transformed it, Erin. You have given me a meaning and purpose that I didn't have before. And soon you will have our baby."

She thought of the little ball of life that was taking

shape inside her womb. Already it was beginning to kick. Before long it would emerge into the great big world. Then her joy would be complete.

Harry gently kissed her lips.

"You have transformed my life too," she said.

She lifted her head and gazed at the sky, blanketed with stars. I am so fortunate, she thought. I have this lovely man. I have a wonderful career. My life is perfect. What more could I possibly wish for?

Chapter 13

After the honeymoon they returned to Belvedere to spend a few more weeks there on Caroline Kavanagh's insistence. Erin wasn't entirely happy about this situation but decided to grin and bear it for another little while as a courtesy to her mother-in-law – after all, she had been wonderfully generous about the wedding.

But one morning, as they were eating breakfast, Harry happened to say casually: "I understand you're booked into St Angela's for the delivery."

Erin glanced up sharply from the morning paper she was reading. This was news to her. So far, she hadn't made any arrangements for the birth of her baby.

"Am I indeed?"

"Yes, my mother told me."

"Well, it's a pity she didn't tell me."

"I'm sorry," Harry said, putting down his coffee cup. "I thought you had agreed it between you."

"No," Erin said. "This is the first I've heard of it."

"Oh, dear," he said. "I've put my foot in it, haven't I?"

Erin felt peeved. At the very least, Mrs Kavanagh should have consulted her. But she didn't want to risk a row with her husband.

"It's not your fault," she said, gently kissing his cheek. "I just wish your mother would talk to me before doing something like this, that's all. It makes me feel like I don't count."

"You're right," Harry said. "I'll have a word with her."

"No, please don't. I don't want any ill feeling. It's all the same, I suppose. I've got to go somewhere."

"It's just that she's got a thing about St Angela's. That's where we were all born. My mother swears by it. She was acting for the best, Erin. She didn't mean any harm."

"I know," she sighed.

"And it *is* a wonderful place. The treatment and care is absolutely top-notch."

"I've no doubt it is. But it would be nice if I could be allowed to make some decisions for myself from time to time."

The decision over St Angela's wasn't the first such incident. Since coming back from Paris, Erin had watched as her mother-in-law's encroachment on her life had grown slowly but surely. There were a number of small things like the arrival one day of a large box of baby clothes from one of the leading children's boutiques in Dublin. It turned out they had been ordered and paid for by Mrs Kavanagh.

"You don't have to thank me," she said when Erin asked about them. "I happened to be in town one day and I saw them in the window and they looked so cute that I had to have them. You can regard them as an early christening present."

"But they're in pink," Erin pointed out. "What happens if the baby is a boy?"

"They'll exchange them. It's not a problem. I've already discussed it with the shop."

Erin examined the clothes. They were beautiful and they must have cost a small fortune. It was difficult to argue with her mother-in-law when she was going out of her way to be so generous.

"Thank you," she said. "You're very kind and I'm truly grateful."

But the biggest change of all was yet to come.

One evening, Mrs Kavanagh suggested that they should remain at Belvedere instead of going back to live at Harry's penthouse. Work was due to commence soon on a new house in Kinsealy which Harry's parents were giving them as a wedding present. However, there were planning issues still to be resolved and it could be a year before the house was completed. In the meantime, Mrs Kavanagh suggested they might like to stay with her at Belvedere.

"I like to think of you being near me till the baby is born," she said. "And the flat is lying empty so you might as well have it. I must confess that I don't care for you being isolated in that penthouse in town. God knows how you would cope if anything went wrong."

Erin knew she would cope pretty well. There were three major maternity hospitals within half a mile of Harry's penthouse. And the chances of anything going wrong seemed pretty remote. On her regular visits to see him, Professor O'Leary had told her she was perfectly healthy.

"But the penthouse is closer to where I work," Erin pointed out.

"Don't worry your head about that," Mrs Kavanagh replied. "We'll get you a car. Or if you don't want to drive we can have someone take you in and pick you up again. I want you here. You're part of the family now and I want you near me."

Erin was far from happy with the plan. She didn't want to find herself living so close to her in-laws. She enjoyed city life and the fact that she was at the centre of everything. But most of all she disliked Belvedere and the gloomy atmosphere it projected.

She decided to speak to Harry about it.

"She does have a point," he said. "It has a lot of advantages. You won't be on your own like you would be in town. And I'll be at hand whenever my father needs me. Besides, we won't be staying here forever. Once the new house is built we can move out again."

"I'm nervous," she said.

"Whatever for?"

"Don't be offended, Harry, but there's something about Belvedere that gives me the creeps. I've felt that way about it from the very first day I saw it."

He began to laugh. "Gives you the creeps? It's not a haunted house, Erin! I've lived here for most of my life and I can assure you there are no headless ghosts wandering the corridors at night."

"Don't ask me to explain it. It just makes me feel uneasy."

He smiled indulgently. "It's your imagination, Erin. Once you've settled down at Belvedere, you'll grow to love the old place."

Many young married women would have envied Erin. She was living in a fabulous house with acres of land. She had every comfort. She didn't even have any household chores to carry out. A maid arrived every morning to clean the flat and do her laundry. She was being treated like gentry.

But no matter how much she tried, she couldn't warm to Belvedere. She couldn't escape her initial feeling that there was something eerie about the place, something she couldn't quite put her finger on. She felt like a prisoner there. Her mother-in-law was careful never to intrude on her privacy but she was always hovering in the background. And to make matters worse, Harry had taken to travelling regularly on the firm's business now that the issue of the Conway Hotel development had been settled in their favour. As a result, she was often alone.

But she felt she had no option but to knuckle down. She took solace in the thought that once the new house was built, she would be able to escape from the claustrophobic atmosphere of Belvedere and breathe freely again. But she often wished that her mother-in-law would be less manipulative and would allow her to make some choices for herself.

Not that she disagreed with everything Mrs Kavanagh proposed . . .

One morning she got a phone call to say her mother-in-law wanted to see her. Erin went down to the living room and found her seated beside the window where she could gaze out across the lawns.

"There you are, Erin. You look radiant this morning. How do you feel?"

"I'm fine, thanks."

"You're the picture of good health, my dear. When is your next appointment with Professor O'Leary?"

"I'm seeing him in two weeks' time."

"He's a wonderful man. I would trust him with my life. Listen carefully to everything he tells you. Now, is there anything I can do for you?"

"You're very kind," Erin replied, "but I have everything I need."

"Good. I'm very glad to hear that." She rang the little bell for tea. "I wanted to consult with you, Erin. I've been thinking. What you need up there in that flat is a nursery."

Erin had been thinking the very same thing. "Those are my thoughts exactly. It occurred to me that we might use one of the bedrooms. But I wanted to get your permission."

Mrs Kavanagh beamed. "Isn't it amazing that we should be thinking alike? You need somewhere for the baby when it arrives, its own little space. They sleep better when they're alone. There are fewer distractions. And it's important that you get the baby into a routine as quickly as possible." She smiled. "Otherwise, you'll never get a proper night's rest."

"I was thinking of the room beside ours."

Her mother-in-law clapped her hands with excitement. "So was I. You will need to keep the baby close and that room would be ideal. It's bright and gets the sunlight. Have you had any thoughts about how you might furnish it?"

"All we really need is a playpen and a cot and a few mobiles and toys."

"Why stop at that?" Mrs Kavanagh said. "Why not decorate the whole room?"

"You mean a proper nursery?"

"Yes."

Erin was delighted. A proper nursery would be wonderful. "Are you sure?" she asked. "I don't want to cause too much inconvenience."

But Mrs Kavanagh made a tutting sound. "There would be no inconvenience, my dear. We'll decorate the whole room. I'll get some of the staff to move out the furniture and put it into storage. When this little mite comes home to Belvedere, it must have its very own nursery!"

At that moment, the tea arrived, accompanied by a freshly baked raisin cake. The two women fell into animated conversation about how they would transform the bedroom. Erin had definite ideas about how to decorate the nursery and she outlined them now to her companion.

"That sounds fantastic," Mrs Kavanagh said when Erin had finished. "You have a very creative mind, my dear. That's exactly how we'll do it."

"So you agree?"

"Of course, I agree. It's your baby and your nursery. And you can't improve on perfection."

By now, Erin was caught up in the excitement of the plan.

"I saw a catalogue," she said. "They have this lovely wallpaper, bright, warm colours, little animals, flowers. It's all designed to stimulate the baby's imagination."

"I know what we'll do," her mother-in-law announced, finally. "The first day you're free, we'll go into town together and select the materials. We'll get started on this project right away. There's no point in wasting time."

The following Saturday they drove into Dublin in Mrs Kavanagh's car and spent a delightful few hours visiting children's stores and choosing the items they would need. Caroline was in high spirits as she examined toys and baby strollers and brightly coloured mobiles to hang above the cot. But for once she didn't interfere and allowed Erin to make the final choices, although she did insist on paying.

On Monday, two of the staff arrived at the flat and

removed all the furniture and the following day they began painting the ceiling and putting up the wallpaper. On Wednesday, the cot and playpen and the toys arrived. When everything was in order, Erin gazed lovingly at the transformation that had taken place. Now the room had been turned into a proper nursery that any parent would be proud of. As well as the cot and playpen, there was a chest of drawers to store the baby's clothes with a changing mat on top and a comfortable armchair where Erin could relax while feeding the baby.

She turned to her mother-in-law.

"I think it looks wonderful," she said.

"And so do I."

"How can I thank you?"

"You don't need to thank me," Mrs Kavanagh replied with a wave of her bony hand. "It's been a joy. I want my grandchild to have the very best. And you too, my dear."

By now, Erin's condition was beginning to show and she decided it was time to tell Ger Armstrong.

"Congratulations," the news editor said. "I'm delighted for you. Although I can't deny that I'm going to miss you, Erin. When is the baby due?"

"Early November."

"And when do you plan to take your maternity leave?"

She had made up her mind to work as long as possible. All the mothers she had spoken to agreed that the leave would be more valuable after the baby was born.

"I thought I might go towards the end of October."

"Okay. I'll make arrangements to hire a freelance to cover for you. Just let me know if you need to go sooner. And if it's possible for you to work from home, I'll try to arrange that too."

So far, her pregnancy had been trouble-free. She had her regular consultations with Professor O'Leary who checked her blood pressure and arranged for her to have several scans taken to monitor the foetus's development. All the reports were positive and indicated a normal birth.

But as the summer progressed and the weather grew hotter, she began to feel tired. She mentioned this to the gynaecologist at her next visit.

"That's normal," he said. "There's nothing to be concerned about. Remember the extra weight you're carrying around. Anybody would be tired," he smiled.

But it didn't make Erin feel any more comfortable. She took to wearing the lightest dresses and loose clothes and Ger Armstrong tried to ensure that she was given work that didn't require her to be rushing madly about the city. Nevertheless, she was grateful when October came to an end and she was able to begin her maternity leave.

She went down to Mountclare to visit her family. They were delighted to see her and made a big fuss.

"Is there anything you need?" her mother inquired.

"Nothing," Erin replied. "The Kavanaghs have

been really brilliant. A racehorse wouldn't get any better care and attention."

"Do you want me to come up to Dublin for the birth? Would you like me to be with you?"

"Yes," she replied. "I would love that. But only if you can easily manage it."

"I can manage. Your father can fend for himself for a few days. I'll stick a few ready-made meals in the freezer."

"You can stay with me at Belvedere, if you like," Erin said. "We have a guest room at the flat."

"Oh God no," Mrs O'Neill said with a shudder. "I wouldn't dream of it. We'd all be getting in each other's hair. I'll find a nice little bed and breakfast somewhere nearby and that will do me fine."

But the waiting seemed to drag and Erin began to get bored. With Harry at work or travelling, she now had lots of time on her hands. It was the first period in years when she had nothing to do but wait. She took to going for walks around the grounds of Belvedere. Professor O'Leary had told her it was important to get exercise and she was glad to escape the confinement of the house. And before long, she had found a companion.

One day as she was walking in the woods of the estate, she came across Tim engaged in the same pursuit.

"Hi," he said. "Fancy meeting you here."

"I could say the same thing about you."

"Oh, I go for a stroll most afternoons," he replied.

"It gives me an opportunity to think."

"And what do you think about, might I inquire?" she said with a grin.

"My studies, the meaning of life . . . the book I'm writing."

"Oh! I didn't know you were writing a book. I often wondered what you did besides study all the time."

"But you were too polite to ask?"

"Yes."

"I've got two university degrees, Erin," he smiled. "A primary degree in English Literature and a masters in Modern European Literature, so it shouldn't surprise you that I have decided to write a book! It's something I've wanted to do for a long time."

"What's it about?" she asked, falling in beside him.

"It's a sort of philosophical novel. It's a parable of our times."

"That sounds interesting."

"Yes," Tim said. "I think so too. I'm very excited about it. You see, I've been pondering something. We've never been so well off in our entire history. You'd think people would be happy but they're not. We have all this drug and alcohol abuse. We have rising suicide rates. We have marriage breakdown. Why do you think that is?"

"You tell me," Erin said.

He stopped and held up a finger. "It's because people have lost their moral compass. They have no spirituality in their lives. They've been too busy pursuing money and fame and glamour and they've been disappointed. They feel cheated and empty. And now they don't know where to turn."

"That sounds fascinating," Erin agreed.

"You think so?"

"Yes. I think it would make a wonderful novel."

He looked pleased. "Well, like I said, I've only just started. I'll let you know how it comes along. But what about you? You look like your baby is due any day."

"It is," Erin said.

"My mother will be pleased. You've no idea how much she wants this child. You'd think it was her own baby the way she goes on. She has become obsessive about it."

"I kind of got that impression," Erin said with a smile.

"Yes. But do you really know how much?" Tim had stopped and was staring at her again. "I think she'd go completely off her head if anything happened to it."

Erin thought the remark a bit insensitive but excused Tim on grounds of his youth. Then before she could comment, they came to a fork in the path.

"This is where I leave you," Tim said. "I'm heading off towards Kinsealy. It's been lovely talking to you, Erin."

He waved goodbye and started across the fields.

But she didn't have long to contemplate Tim's remarks on his mother. A few nights later, as she was lying in bed beside Harry, a sharp pain in her abdomen woke her. She sat up and felt the pain come darting back again in spasms. And then she became aware of a warm, damp feeling slowly spreading along the bed.

She began to shake Harry awake.

"Wake up, wake up!" she cried. "The baby's coming."

Chapter 14

"It's a little girl," the doctor announced holding up a little bloodstained bundle and giving it to the nurse to bathe.

Erin was only vaguely aware of his words. Her overwhelming feeling was that the terrible pain had finally stopped and now in its place there was a dull, throbbing ache and a feeling of utter exhaustion. She sank her head back onto the pillows. She would like nothing better than to drift off and sleep, sleep, sleep. She had just come through the most gruelling experience of her life.

But she wasn't allowed to sleep just yet.

"Three point seven five kilos," the nurse declared. "That's a fine, big, healthy baby! And already she wants her mother. Would you like to hold her, Mrs Kavanagh?"

Erin nodded and reached out her hands. She looked at the trembling infant in her arms, the mass of thick, black hair, the tiny hands, the upturned nose, the dark, shining eyes that she had inherited from her. Immediately, she felt an enormous love sweep over her. She cuddled her baby to her breast and she began to suck.

"Hungry too," the nurse said as she wiped the sweat from Erin's brow.

Now she became aware of Harry's handsome face smiling down at her. He kissed her damp forehead and held her hand.

"How do you feel?" he asked.

"Knackered."

"I'm not surprised. I'm so proud of you, my wonderful, wonderful wife."

St Angela's nursing home was everything that Mrs Kavanagh had promised. The following morning, Erin was gently wakened at eight by a cheerful woman bearing a tray with tea in a china teapot.

"Did you sleep well?" she inquired, putting the tray down on the bedside locker and smiling broadly at Erin.

Erin sat up and blinked. She recognised the woman. She remembered that she had been on duty last night when she arrived in labour.

"I slept like a log."

"Well, I'm not surprised. That was some ordeal you went through. Now we've got to get you back on your feet again. How do you feel?"

She had taken hold of Erin's wrist and was measuring her pulse.

"A little bit groggy but I'm sure that will pass."

"Professor O'Leary will be in to see you later. He'll give you a thorough examination. But I must say, you look pretty healthy to me."

"Where's my baby?" Erin asked, quickly glancing around. She wanted to see her again, to hold her and cradle her, to look once more at that angelic little face.

"She's in the nursery being well looked after, I can assure you. Now we have to take care of the mother."

She put a thermometer in Erin's mouth and gave her a printed folder which on closer inspection turned out to be a menu.

"Just tick off the items you require, Mrs Kavanagh. I'll pick it up on my way back. Breakfast will be served shortly." She withdrew the thermometer and wrote something on a file. "Temperature's normal. You're doing just fine."

She made for the door but Erin quickly called after her.

"I'll get her back again, won't I?"

The woman gave a gentle laugh. "Oh, you certainly will. Any time you want. But now I'd advise you to concentrate on breakfast."

Erin edged herself up against the pillows and took in her surroundings. Now that she was wide awake, she could see that she was in a beautiful room painted in soft, yellow pastel shades. Beside her, there was a window looking out on a garden with flower-beds and closely-pruned rose bushes.

On a table in a corner, several large bouquets of

flowers already stood in vases beside a couple of congratulations cards. They must have been delivered earlier this morning while she was asleep. There was another door which led to a bathroom. The bed was large and comfortable with crisp white sheets and a nice patterned duvet. A large television gazed down at her from a little stand on the wall.

She lifted the remote control and turned it on. Immediately, *Sky News* flashed onto the screen. She pressed the buttons and ran down the channels then switched it off and poured a cup of tea from the pot the nurse had left. She raised it to her lips and took a sip. It was the most delicious tea she had ever tasted. She lay back against the pillows and gave a contented sigh.

After breakfast, the baby was brought back to her. As she was feeding her, she heard a knock on the door and a young nurse put her head into the room.

"Are you decent? You've got a visitor."

"Oh! Send them in," Erin said.

The nurse stood aside and Mrs Kavanagh came bustling in. She immediately hurried to the bedside and stared at the little pink bundle curled up at Erin's breast. For a full two minutes she gazed lovingly at the infant as her eyes brimmed with pleasure.

"Oh, Erin, you don't know how happy I am. A little girl! It was what I have been praying for. I am so, so pleased."

Erin smiled proudly.

"May I hold her?"

"Of course – just be careful she doesn't mess up your dress."

"Oh, who cares about the dress? This is the moment I've dreamed about for so long. Just look at her! Did you ever see anything so beautiful? She's a perfect little angel. Aren't you, my love?" She looked transfixed as she gently rocked the baby in her arms. "There, there, there," she whispered, making cooing sounds into the tiny face. But the baby was unhappy at being parted from her mother and began to cry.

"I think you'd better give her back to me before she screams the place down," Erin said. "You've interrupted her feed."

Reluctantly, Mrs Kavanagh returned the baby and watched as Erin began to suckle her again.

"You're so fortunate. You don't know how much I envy you."

"You had babies of your own. You know what it's like."

A wistful look had now come over Caroline Kavanagh's face. "But it was all so long ago. I'd give anything to be in your place, to hold her in my arms and nurse her as you are doing now."

Erin was struck by the sadness in her voice. "You can hold her again once I've fed her," she said. "You're her grandmother. You can hold her any time you want."

Eventually, Mrs Kavanagh left, promising to return again in the afternoon. After lunch, the visitors began to arrive in earnest – her parents, her sister Anne, Tim,

Susan, Ger Armstrong and some of her colleagues from work, friends old and new. They all left presents for the baby which Erin had them stack in the bottom of her wardrobe until such time as Harry could take them home. They also brought magazines, flowers, fruit and chocolates for the new mother till her locker could hold no more.

At last, Harry returned. He beamed with joy as he cradled the baby.

"I'm very proud of you," he said.

Erin reached out and ran her fingers gently along his arm.

"I'm so happy," she said. "Don't you think we're the luckiest couple on earth?"

Every afternoon Erin's mother and sister came to see her. Charlie Kavanagh was a frequent visitor too – he would lift the baby in his big rough hands and look embarrassed as he tickled her chin, but Erin could see he was delighted to be holding his first grandchild.

But Mrs Kavanagh was the most frequent visitor. She turned up faithfully every day, sometimes several times, always solicitous, always bearing gifts of flowers and books. She was entranced with the baby. She loved to hold her in her arms and gaze longingly into her tiny face as she sighed and cooed.

One afternoon, she said to Erin: "Have you decided on a name for her yet?"

Erin and Harry had devoted much thought to this topic. She wanted to please her mother by including her name – Rosemary – and, to be diplomatic, they agreed that they would also add Caroline for Mrs Kavanagh. But they hadn't finally settled on the baby's first name.

"Not yet," Erin said. "At least, we haven't arrived at a firm decision."

Her mother-in-law came and sat on the bed beside her.

"There is something I would like to ask you. I would regard it as an enormous favour."

"What?" Erin asked.

"Would you call her Emily?"

"Emily?"

"Yes. It was my mother's name. If I had been able to have another little girl, that's what I would have called her."

Erin was somewhat taken aback. It was an unusual request. She thought the name itself was somewhat bland and maybe even a little old-fashioned but she had no great aversion to it.

Mrs Kavanagh was staring at her intently and there was a pleading look in her eyes.

"You've no idea how much it would mean to me," she said.

"You understand it's not entirely my decision," said Erin. "I would have to discuss it with Harry."

"Yes, of course. By all means do that."

"Let me talk to him and come back to you."

That evening when Harry visited, Erin raised the matter.

161

"I had a strange request today from your mother. She asked if we would call the baby Emily. After her mother."

He looked up quickly from admiring his little daughter's sleeping face. "Really?"

"Yes. What do you think?"

"I've no great objection. What do *you* think?"

"She said she would regard it as an enormous favour. I suppose if it keeps her happy, we could do it."

"Okay," Harry said, turning back once more to his scrutiny of the baby. "Tell her we'll call her Emily."

Mrs Kavanagh was overjoyed when Erin told her. There were tears welling in her eyes as she took hold of her hands and held them tight.

"Oh. I'm so grateful, so very, very grateful. I don't know how to thank you. You are such a wonderful daughter-in-law!"

"And you are very good to me too," Erin said. "It hasn't all been one-way traffic. So let's call it quits, shall we?"

As the days passed, Erin began to grow restless. She wasn't used to lying in bed all day and having people fuss over her. The nurses moved a cot beside her bed so the baby could be with her, only moving it out again at night so that Erin could sleep. They showed her the basic things like how to wash the baby and change her nappy – things that Erin already knew by instinct. But for long stretches of the day, there was nothing to do but gaze out the window at the garden or watch television and read.

There was a recreation room with magazines and books and occasionally she would walk down there and talk with the other mothers. But by now she was anxious to be up. She longed to get back to the real world where things were happening. She was aware of the fact that, had she not been in a private nursing home, she would be home already.

On the fifth morning, after Professor O'Leary had been to see her yet again and declared her fit and healthy, Erin asked: "Is there any reason why I should stay here any longer?"

"The short answer is no."

"So when can I leave?"

"Today if you want, but you'll still have to take it easy for a while."

Immediately, Erin rang Harry and told him she was being discharged. He unfortunately was tied up with work for the morning but promised to come just after lunch. Erin could hardly wait.

By lunch-time she was dressed and packed. She had cleared out her locker, giving the remaining presents of fruit and sweets to the staff, together with some lavish boxes of expensive chocolates Mrs Kavanagh had brought in specially for them.

After lunch, which she hurriedly gulped down, came the exciting task of dressing little Emily for her first trip outdoors. Then, baby swaddled in a warm pink blanket, she sat down to wait for Harry.

* * *

It was a bright, crisp afternoon with a hint of frost still lingering on the lawns at Belvedere as they drove up to the house. Mrs Kavanagh was waiting on the front steps. She took the baby in her arms and led Erin into the warm house.

"Welcome home, my dear," she said.

Chapter 15

Erin was glad to return to the comparative freedom of Belvedere. Despite her misgivings, it had now become her home, at least for the foreseeable future. It was good to be once more in familiar surroundings and to sleep in her own bed with her husband's strong body pressed close against her. It was good to be independent again and do things for herself. No matter how pleasant life in St Angela's had been, she had still felt restrained there.

The baby settled into her new nursery quite happily and Erin developed a routine for feeding and bathing her and putting her down for regular naps. Before long, Baby Emily was sleeping most of the night which was a big relief, particularly for Harry who greatly valued his sleep. In these tasks, Erin was eagerly assisted by her mother-in-law who enjoyed the work and keenly looked forward to it.

Caroline Kavanagh seemed determined to avoid

friction. She was at pains to adopt the role of assistant and not to interfere. Erin was the mother and this baby was *her* child. Her mother-in-law claimed no rights or privileges over her although it was obvious to everyone that she doted on the little girl.

This was an arrangement that suited Erin well. With her mother-in-law on hand and only too eager to help, she was able to find some time to attend to a few things not strictly baby-related. Chief among them was her mission to get back into good physical shape.

After the birth, she was shocked to weigh herself one morning and discover she had put on almost three and a half kilos during the pregnancy. She was determined to get it off as soon as possible and regain her figure. She made an appointment to see her GP. Dr Foley was in her mid-thirties and very progressive. Erin liked and trusted her.

"Get undressed and let me weigh you," Amanda Foley said when Erin explained her concern.

Erin did as instructed and stepped onto the scales.

"Hmmmh," the doctor said, writing the weight down on a chart. "You could certainly lose a few kilos, all right. But with a little bit of effort we can get you back to your proper size. Are you breast-feeding the baby?"

"Yes."

"Well, that should help to get some of the weight off little by little. It also means your priority should be to eat well – this is no time to go on a drastic diet which might interfere with the all-important milk supply! But you should concentrate on highly nutritious food and cut down on empty starches and sugar." She gave Erin a diet sheet. "How much exercise do you get?"

Erin told her about the daily walks she used to take during pregnancy on Professor O'Leary's advice.

"Well, I recommend that you start again immediately. Begin with half an hour at a good brisk pace. You can build up as you get more comfortable with it. Exercise is good for you anyway and not just for weight loss. And, as you're breastfeeding, you've probably been told to avoid alcohol. That should help get the weight down too."

The following morning Erin left Emily with Mrs Kavanagh, put on an old pair of tracksuit bottoms and set off for a brisk walk around the grounds of Belvedere. It was quiet and peaceful and far removed from the sound of distant traffic. She found herself thinking about the new house that was being built for them at Kinsealy. The planning difficulties had been overcome and construction was well under way. They had decided to name it Larchfield because of a copse of trees that had once stood on the site.

Now that the baby was born, Erin was anxious to move in as soon as possible. She was eagerly looking forward to leaving Belvedere and becoming mistress of her own home.

But as she approached the woods, her reverie was interrupted. She saw a figure emerge from a path and recognised Tim.

carol magill

"Hi!" she called.

He looked surprised to see her. "Shouldn't you be at home looking after the baby?"

"What a thoroughly sexist remark," she responded with a smile.

"That's not what I meant. I was simply wondering."

"Your mother is taking care of her. I needed to get some fresh air and some exercise. I've got to lose some weight."

"Well, she's in good hands then. My mother will spoil her rotten if you're not careful. She loves that child, Erin. But you don't need me to tell you that."

"I know. You told me once you thought she was becoming obsessive about her. I'm inclined to agree with you."

A thoughtful look came into Tim's face. "It's a natural grandparent's love, I suppose," he mused, "plus the fact that she's probably bored and lonely. You know how my father is totally immersed in his work. It's one of the reasons why I don't want to join the company despite all their attempts at persuasion."

"So what are you going to do with your life? You can't study forever."

He turned to stare at her. "Why not? Lots of people did it in the Middle Ages. Nobody thought it was odd for a young man to devote his time to learning. In fact it was something to be admired. It's only in this modern age that people insist everybody should have a job. Besides, I do have a job. I'm writing my book – and that reminds me . . ."

"Yes?"

"I've got some good news to report. I sent the first chapters to a publishing house in London and guess what?"

"Tell me?"

"They rang this morning. They've read them and they're very excited. They want me to send them more."

Erin threw her arms around her brother-in-law and hugged him. "Oh, Tim! I'm delighted for you. That really is good news."

He blushed and tried to hide his embarrassment. "Yes. I'm quite pleased, really. Maybe I'll surprise everyone one of these days."

The weather grew cold and damp as Christmas approached but Erin steadfastly maintained her exercise regime. And she began to see results. Combined with the diet which Amanda Foley had set her, she watched the excess weight slowly drop away. Gradually, she saw her slim figure return and she was able to get into clothes that had previously been too tight. And she discovered another positive effect of the exercise regime – she got her old energy levels back.

However, now she had another issue on her mind. It was six weeks since the baby was born and it was time to get her christened.

After discussing the matter with Harry, it was decided to bring her to the church on the second Sunday in December. It was a date that suited everyone including Erin's family in Mountclare who would travel up for the occasion. Mrs Kavanagh suggested that they should have the christening party at Belvedere and invite some of their friends and she threw herself into the organisation with her usual zeal and efficiency.

The run-up to the christening proved to be quite hectic, particularly since it coincided with the onset of Christmas. But it seemed to bring out the best in Mrs Kavanagh. She immersed herself in all the little organisational details just as she had with the preparations for the wedding and Erin was quite happy to leave everything in her capable hands.

But two days before the event, something happened to shatter her contentment.

The post usually arrived around 10a.m. and any personal mail for Harry and her was delivered to their apartment by one of the household staff. Erin had just finished bathing the baby when she heard a soft knock at the door.

"Come in!" she called out.

Mrs Martin came in, a bunch of letters in her hand. She was a middle-aged woman who helped out in the kitchen.

"Some letters for you," she said with a smile.

"Thank you, Mrs Martin. Just leave them on the table."

She did so and then came to bill and coo over the baby.

After she had left, Erin dried and dressed Emily,

then put her down to sleep in the nursery. On her return, she picked up the letters and glanced at them. They were mainly for Harry but there was one for her. She sliced open the envelope and a page torn from a notebook fell out.

Immediately she felt a chill run through her.

She picked the page up and read.

YOU DON'T LEARN, DO YOU? YOU WERE WARNED BEFORE AND IGNORED IT. NOW YOU HAVE BROUGHT YOUR BASTARD TO LIVE IN BELVEDERE. YOU ARE GOING TO REGRET IT. MARK THESE WORDS!

She stared at the letter. It was written in block capitals just like the previous one and clearly had come from the same person. She felt a tremor pass through her. Who was doing this to her and why? A list of possible suspects flashed through her mind – Harry's old girlfriend, Samantha O'Malley? Mrs Kavanagh? She had suspected her mother-in-law for the first letter but she couldn't have written this vile threat – not in a million years.

She examined the envelope. The postmark showed it had been posted in central Dublin the previous day. She put it away in a drawer and, sitting by the window, struggled with the torrent of emotions that were raging through her mind. What was happening? Who was doing this? What had she done to incur such hatred?

She waited till dinner was over before showing the

letter to Harry. As he read it, his face grew dark.

"This is some crank," he said. "Some sick person who is bent on upsetting you."

"Samantha O'Malley?"

He looked at her sharply. "No. I don't think Samantha is responsible for this. She may be neurotic and she was very upset when we broke up but I don't think she is capable of anything as vicious as this."

"So who is it? It must be someone who knows us, Harry."

"I've no idea," he sighed.

"This one has a postmark. Maybe we could attempt to trace the sender?"

"It would be a waste of time, Erin. There's only one thing to do."

He rolled the letter in a ball and threw it into the fire. He put an arm around her and pulled her close as they watched it burn.

"Whoever sent that letter wanted to upset you. If you let yourself worry about it, they will have succeeded. The only way to deal with this is to put it entirely out of your mind."

But it wasn't so easy to follow Harry's advice. The episode had brought back all the old doubts and concerns about Belvedere. Whoever had written that letter knew her. And the fact that it had mentioned the baby made her fearful that some harm might come to her child. Now she took care never to leave Emily alone even with Mrs Kavanagh. And her desire to get away from Belvedere and into their new home took on a greater urgency.

A few days later, she asked Harry when Larchfield would be ready.

"Early in the new year," he said. "The building work is coming along very well."

"Can you be more specific?" she asked with a hint of irritation.

"I can't give you an actual completion date, Erin. You appreciate that the weather is a big factor. If it's raining, the men can't work."

"I want to know," she said firmly.

He stared at her. "I thought you had settled down here? I thought you and my mother were getting along fine? You even agreed to name the child for her."

"We are getting on and she's a great help to me but I want to live in my own home, Harry. It's not unreasonable. Surely you can understand that?"

"Of course, I can."

"So when will we be moving to Larchfield?"

"Early in the spring," he said.

Chapter 16

The christening party was much larger than Erin would have liked. There were about fifty people gathered in the drawing-room at Belvedere for the celebration when they returned from the church around three o'clock. The core of the group was the two families and she was pleased to see her parents mixing well with the Kavanaghs. Her father spent most of the afternoon discussing property with Charlie Kavanagh in front of the fire and Tim made sure to keep the drinks flowing while simultaneously conversing with her mother and sister Anne on a sofa in the corner.

But there was no doubt about the centre of attraction. Baby Emily, in a beautiful embroidered silk christening gown, which was an O'Neill family heirloom, lay comfortably in her mother's lap on a big settee in the middle of the room as people crowded round to take photographs. Harry sat beside them, looking extremely handsome in a neat blazer and slacks while Mrs Kavanagh proudly brought guests to admire the new arrival like a curator in an art gallery showing off some treasure.

Eventually people began to drift away. The O'Neills were among the first to leave. Mr O'Neill was driving and wanted to get on the motorway ahead of the traffic. By seven the last of the guests had departed into the night.

Caroline Kavanagh came and sat on the settee beside Erin.

"I want to thank you," she said.

"But you did all the work."

"I mean about the baby. I want to thank you for calling her Emily. It means an awful lot to me. I'll never forget your kindness."

Erin looked at her and wondered how she could ever have suspected her of anything malicious.

"You don't have to thank me," she said with a smile. "I was only too happy to do it."

Before Erin knew, Christmas was upon them. She had been so busy that she hadn't even had an opportunity to buy any gifts. So with four days to go, she persuaded Harry to brave the crowds and take her into Dublin. It was like a madhouse. Grafton Street was a solid mass of heaving bodies and within minutes Harry was complaining about how much he hated shopping. Erin realised she would get far more accomplished if her husband wasn't with her.

"I'll tell you what we'll do. Why don't you go off with Emily to Bewleys and have a coffee and I'll soldier on alone?"

"Are you sure?" he asked.

"I'm absolutely certain. The truth is I can get around much better on my own."

"Well, if you'd be happier."

"I would," Erin replied. "Go off, amuse Emily and read the paper and I'll see you in an hour."

She set off into the crowds of shoppers and buskers and charity collectors rattling tins at her from every doorway. But she was on a mission and she needed to accomplish it in double-quick time before Emily became fractious. She had already made a list of what she wanted and she persevered till she had got it all.

When she returned, she found Harry peacefully reading *The Clarion* in a corner of the café while Emily slept soundly in her buggy.

"Care to join me?" he asked.

She nodded and he went off for two more lattes.

When he returned she took a grateful gulp of her coffee, then snuggled in close to her husband.

"You know, we rarely get a chance to spend time together like this," she said.

"All that will change when Larchfield is finished," he replied.

At the mention of their new house, her spirits rose.

"Is it nearing completion?"

"It should be ready for Easter."

"That long?" she protested. "I thought you said it

would be finished for the spring."

"So I did but the builders ran into some snags." He patted her arm. "Don't worry. The time will go faster than you think. And I've got the perfect house-warming present for you."

"Oh?" she said, excitedly.

"I'm taking you away on a break. You and Emily. It will be our first family holiday together."

Christmas at Belvedere was a quiet family affair. On Christmas Eve, they all attended Midnight Mass in Malahide and came back to the house to have drinks. It was late when Erin finally got to bed but Emily had settled well into a sleeping routine by now and didn't wake.

On Christmas morning Mrs Kavanagh was up early to supervise the lunch and soon the appetising smell of roasting turkey was wafting through the house. Harry and Erin and Tim went for a walk with Emily in her baby buggy while Susan remained behind to help her mother. And then at one o'clock they all sat down to eat.

It was like something out of a Dickens novel. Charlie Kavanagh sat at the head of the table and carved. There was a cheery fire blazing in the grate and a Christmas tree twinkling in a corner beside the window, while outside they could hear the wind rattling the panes.

After lunch, it was time to exchange presents. Erin had tried to find something appropriate for each member of the family. Harry got a tie, his father got cuff links, Tim got a novel, Susan got a book on horse breeding and her husband Toby was given a boxed set of classical music CDs. For Mrs Kavanagh she had bought a knitted shawl which she found in a craft shop off Dawson Street.

One by one, she opened her own gifts till finally she came to her mother-in-law's present. She tore off the wrapping paper to discover a small box. When she opened it she let out a gasp of surprise. A beautiful necklace and pendant nestled on a bed of white silk.

She drew it slowly from the box and held it up to watch it sparkle in the light. She was sure it was solid gold.

"It's beautiful," she said, turning to Mrs Kavanagh. "But it looks much too expensive. You really shouldn't have done this."

Caroline Kennedy placed her thin hand on top of Erin's.

"I want you to have it, my dear. You have brought so much pleasure into my life."

Erin held the necklace against her throat. All the heads around the table were turned to look at her.

"Thank you so much," she said.

There was only one discordant note.

Out of the corner of her eye, Erin caught Susan scowling at her.

One evening a few weeks later, as she was watching late-night television with Harry, he turned to her: "I've been meaning to say this, Erin. You've made a big impression on my family and that makes me very happy."

"Thank you."

"I know there was a lot of tension at first. But you've totally won them over. You have my mother eating out of your hand. Look at the lovely Christmas gift she gave you. My father is always talking about you. He thinks you're the best thing that ever happened to me. And Tim is one of your biggest fans."

"Well, that's nice to know," Erin replied, feeling a warm glow of satisfaction.

"There's only one person left to convince and that's Susan."

At the mention of her sister-in-law's name, Erin felt herself stiffen. Harry was perfectly correct. Since coming to live at Belvedere, Susan's attitude had remained lofty and aloof.

"Well, I've certainly done nothing to offend her. In fact, I chose her as one of my bridesmaids."

"You've had Emily," Harry said.

She turned to face him. "I don't understand."

"I hope I'm wrong about this," he continued, "but I think she might be jealous of you."

"That's ridiculous."

"Is it? My father and mother are both doting on the child, particularly my mother. Susan used to be the only daughter. And then you and Emily turn up and you edge her off the stage. I'm beginning to think she resents it."

Erin recalled the scowl at the Christmas lunch when she received the gold necklace from Mrs Kavanagh. What if Harry was right?

"If Emily is bothering her why doesn't she have children of her own?" she said.

Harry sat closer. "I've often thought about that. I always believed that Susan didn't want children. But I'm beginning to change my mind. What if she *can't* have them? That would put a completely different perspective on things."

"There are treatments she can have."

"Maybe there are other problems we don't know about?"

Erin let this thought run through her mind. If it was true then it really did put Susan's situation in a new light.

"What if she's been desperately trying all this time to have a child to please my mother and meeting no success? And then you turn up out of the blue and in a matter of months, you have Emily and everyone is falling over themselves with delight. Don't you think she might feel a little envious?"

"Yes," Erin said. "Now that you put it that way, I do. But there's nothing I can do about it."

"There is," Harry said. "You can make an effort to be nice to her."

"But she just snubs me."

"Try harder. I want you two to become friends. She spends most mornings at the stables. Why don't you visit her some time? Why don't you tell her you'd like to take up horse-riding?"

"But I've absolutely no interest in horse riding."

He took her hand. "Please, Erin. Give it a try. Do it for me."

Chapter 17

The following Saturday morning, Erin asked Harry to take care of Emily while she put on some old jeans and a sweater and set off across the fields to the stables. They were situated about a quarter of a mile from the house in a group of outbuildings. It was a crisp, winter morning with a coating of frost powdering the grass and her breath hung in little clouds as she walked.

When she arrived, she found Susan deep in conversation with a man she hadn't seen before. They looked up when they saw her approach and lowered their voices.

"Good morning," Erin said cheerily as she drew near.

Her sister-in-law glanced suspiciously at her. "Good morning," she replied.

The man she had been talking to stood awkwardly by her side. He was small and thin and dressed in an old check jacket and scarf. On his feet was a pair of black Wellington boots. Erin saw him watching her carefully.

"This is Cornish," Susan said. "He helps me with the horses."

Cornish took off his cap and nodded. "Good morning, ma'am."

"Good morning, Cornish," Erin smiled. Then she turned her attention back to Susan.

"I've come to ask you about riding. Harry thinks I should get more exercise."

"Oh!" Susan looked taken aback. "Have you ever ridden before?"

"Never."

"You'll need a helmet and proper boots." She glanced at the walking shoes that Erin was wearing. "I could lend you some, I suppose."

"Would you?"

Cornish took his leave, lifted a pitchfork and began shifting some straw into a stall.

"Come with me," Susan said and led Erin to a little storeroom at the back of the stables. "Here," she said, taking out a pair of riding boots and a black helmet. "Try them on."

The boots were a bit tight but the helmet fitted perfectly.

"And you'd better put on a jacket."

She took a padded jacket from a peg and Erin put it on.

"Let me look at you," Susan said, running her eye over Erin. "Yes," she nodded, "you'll do."

Next, she took Erin to the stalls where the horses were stabled. The animals raised their beautiful heads and snorted as the women approached. Susan expertly ran her hand along their flanks and whispered to calm them down.

"I think we'll start you with Gypsy," she said. "She should be easy. She's a placid little thing."

Erin watched, fascinated, as she led a little grey mare out into the yard and began to saddle her up while the horse waited patiently.

"You're very good with them," she commented.

"It's important to let them know who is boss," Susan replied. "You'll quickly get the hang of it. Now put your toe in the stirrup and mount."

But it was easier said than done. After a couple of attempts, Susan put a hand under Erin's rump and pushed her up and into the saddle. She spent another few minutes giving instructions about posture, how to hold the reins, grip the horse's sides and steer.

"Keep your toes in the stirrup," she said. "Do you feel comfortable?"

"Yes," Erin replied, though in fact it felt very precarious.

"Now, I'm going to lead you round for a few minutes while she gets used to you."

She gripped the halter and slowly took the horse and rider round in a circle.

"How is that?"

"Fine."

"Try to relax. They're very intelligent animals. If

185

you get nervous, they will know."

"Okay."

"Do you want to try a trot?" Susan asked, at last.

"Okay."

"Please wait a moment."

Susan went back into the stables and returned with a magnificent black stallion.

"This is Thunder," she said, adjusting her helmet. "He's my favourite mount. Aren't you, Thunder?"

She took some sugar lumps from her pocket, cupped them in her hand and gave them to the horse.

"Now," she said. "If you're ready, Erin, let's go."

She dug her heels into the horse's flanks and they sat off at a gentle trot, with Susan calling out instructions all the way. It felt very awkward at first and Erin was quite nervous but then soon she got the hang of it and overcame her initial fear. Soon she was enjoying the experience enormously. She had always wondered about the pleasures of horse-riding and now she knew. It was fantastic. When they returned to the stables twenty minutes later, she was red-faced and out of breath.

"You did very well," Susan said as they dismounted. "How do you feel?"

"Wonderful."

Susan nodded and took off her helmet. "Good," she said. "I'll see you here again at the same time tomorrow."

That evening when they were eating supper, Harry asked her how she had got on.

"I thoroughly enjoyed it. My first time on a horse and Susan said I did very well."

"Well, I'm pleased to hear that. Susan's not a bad sort, really. A bit stiff and reserved, perhaps. But she'll loosen up. I think you'll get to like her."

But Susan didn't loosen up. Despite visiting the stables and going riding most mornings, Erin's sister-in-law continued to maintain her distance. There was none of the warmth or the little shared jokes and confidences she would expect from a friend.

She rarely asked about baby Emily or Erin's job. She never talked about her own work or her husband, Toby, despite several inquiries from Erin. It was as if she was merely putting up with Erin for the sake of politeness because she was now part of the family. Indeed, she seemed to have more in common with the groom, Cornish. Erin often came across the two of them huddled together in conversation.

It was becoming obvious that Susan simply didn't like her. Perhaps she really was jealous as Harry had hinted. Erin enjoyed the morning rides but Susan's attitude meant they were fast becoming a trial. After a fortnight, the relationship between the two women had barely progressed at all – unlike her relationship with Tim. He had become a regular companion.

Because Tim had no regular job, he seemed to have plenty of time on his hands. He would often drop up to the nursery to have a chat with Erin while she took care of the baby. And in the afternoons, he liked to go for walks in the woods. He invited Erin to join him. This suited her because she was still keeping up Amanda Foley's exercise regime.

On their walks, she got to know Tim better. She began to grow quite fond of him.

"How is the novel coming along?" she would ask.

And Tim would relate the latest developments with the publishers in London.

"They're very excited. They think the novel could be a big hit."

"Have you found a title for it yet?"

"No," Tim admitted, "but it will come. My main concern right now is getting it finished. I've kind of reached a sticky patch. I can't seem to move it forward."

"It's not easy writing a novel, is it?"

"You can say that again. It's bloody hard work. But at least my publishers are enthusiastic and that's very encouraging."

"Think of the satisfaction when you get it finished," she said. "Think of the applause and the praise."

"I'm dreading it," he confessed. "I think that's going to be the worst bit. What if nobody likes it? What if the critics pan it?"

"They won't," Erin said to reassure him. "I'm sure the book will be a great success. I know I'll certainly buy a copy."

"But will anyone else?"

"Oh, Tim! You must have more confidence in

yourself. Why don't you just forget about the critics and concentrate on getting the book finished."

"You're right," he said. "That's exactly what I'll do."

On another occasion, she asked: "Have you got a girlfriend, Tim?"

He looked startled. "Why do you ask?"

"No reason. It's just that you've never mentioned it so I wondered."

"I used to have a girl. Her name was Sarah Ferris. I met her at college and we got on very well together. But she wanted to get married and, well, I don't have a job or anything and I didn't think it was the right thing to do."

"I'm sure you'll easily find another girl," Erin said. "You're a handsome man and you're excellent company. Lots of women would find you very attractive."

Tim seemed to brighten up.

"Thank you for saying that, Erin. But I'm sure you're only trying to please me."

"No, I'm not. I'm telling you the truth."

He stopped and looked at her. "If I could find a girl like you, it might be different. You are so kind and understanding. You are sympathetic. I can talk to you. I'd have no problem marrying *you*, Erin, but unfortunately Harry has beaten me to it."

He laughed loudly and they moved on.

But a few days later she had her most interesting conversation with Tim and one that disturbed her.

It was a bright, sunny afternoon with the air cold and dry and perfect for walking. Erin wrapped Emily up well in her buggy and set off with Tim, following a path across the fields till they entered the woods.

"Your new house will soon be ready," he said as his boots crackled on the undergrowth at the side of the path. "You'll be leaving us."

"At Easter," Erin replied. "That's provided we don't have any more hold-ups."

"We're all going to miss you. You've brought a joy and a life into the house that was missing before."

"But we won't be far away. And we'll come and visit often."

"It's not the same thing as having you living with us. You've become part of the family. Mum dotes on you. I don't know how she is going to cope. She's going to miss you terribly, particularly little Emily."

Erin knew this was true. She was secretly dreading the moment when she had to leave Mrs Kavanagh even though she was keen to get away and start her own home.

Tim paused, as if he was turning something over in his mind. At last he said: "Has Harry spoken to you about it?"

"About what?"

"My mother and Emily?"

"No," Erin said.

"There's something you should know. But promise you won't mention that I told you. You must never tell another single person."

By now, Erin was intrigued. "I promise."

He lowered his voice and spoke softly.

"My mother had one more child after me. It was her last baby. It was a little girl and she called her Emily."

"*Emily?*" Erin said, feeling a little nervous shiver pass over her.

"Yes," Tim said.

"And what happened?"

"She died in her sleep. It was a cot death."

Erin was shocked. But what Tim had told her made everything fall into place. It explained Mrs Kavanagh's odd behaviour. It explained her obsession with having a grandchild and her strange request to call the child Emily.

"That's very sad," she said. "It must have been awful."

"It was," Tim agreed. "I was only a little boy at the time but I can still remember it. I noticed a change in my mother after the baby died. I think she went into a depression. And even when she eventually came out of it, she wasn't the same. She seemed to grow into herself, bottle up all her grief inside her. Until you and the baby arrived."

"And why won't people talk about it?"

"It's a family secret. My mother won't allow the subject to be raised. I think she's ashamed. And that's why you must never mention it, Erin. If you did, it would cause all sorts of trouble."

"Don't worry," she said. "The secret is safe with me."

"Ever since the baby arrived and you've come to live with us, she has been a changed person. I've never seen her look so happy. It's almost as if little Emily has given her a new lease of life. That's why I'm not looking forward to you leaving."

Tim's prediction proved accurate. As Larchfield neared completion and their departure drew near, Mrs Kavanagh began to grow increasingly anxious. She would ask Harry about the progress of the new house as if it was some terrible calamity that was threatening to overtake them. And with each piece of good news, her face grew dark and unhappy. When the weather turned wet and windy in February, she greeted it as if it was a cause for celebration.

"The builders won't be able to work in that weather," she remarked one evening.

But Harry brushed the remark aside.

"It won't make any difference. The roof is on and now they're concentrating on the inside work."

"Oh," she said, her face looking downcast.

Erin couldn't help feeling sorry for her. What Tim had told her somehow made Caroline seem more vulnerable and human. She had suffered a terrible loss which had been devastating for her. Erin could only imagine the pain and grief she must have endured. But at the same time, she was determined to move ahead. She wanted to get away from Belvedere as soon as possible. She had already stayed longer than she planned.

Meanwhile, her attempts at developing a friendship with Susan were not meeting much success. She had continued her morning riding sessions and had grown more confident and skilled with each day that passed. She was proving to be a natural rider. This should have brought the two women together but it didn't. Susan continued to remain cool and aloof. She was never rude or disrespectful but it was clear to Erin that they would not be good friends. But now, with the impending move to her new home, Erin had a very good reason to discontinue the lessons.

The construction of Larchfield was almost completed but much indoor work still remained to be done. The colour schemes and interior decoration had to be agreed. Curtains and fabrics had to be selected not to mention bathroom and kitchen appliances. Furniture had to be ordered. Harry had said he wanted the very best for his new house but he was busy at work and was often travelling, so the burden fell onto Erin's shoulders. She decided to call on her sister, Anne, to help.

Anne was working for an interior design company and had a good eye for colour and decoration. She would be the ideal person to assist her. When Erin rang to seek her advice, she volunteered at once.

"I'd love to help," she said. "I'd really enjoy it."

"So why don't we start on Saturday? I'll take you out to the house and you can get an idea of what's required. The electricians have just finished the wiring so it's empty right now."

"That's perfect," Anne said. "I like a fresh sheet to work on."

On Saturday morning, Erin left the baby with Harry and the two women drove the short distance to the new house. It still looked like a building site with rubble and scaffolding lying around the front lawn. But as they approached, a magnificent five-bedroomed structure came into view. Larchfield was a spectacular house sitting on a quarter-acre site.

As soon as Anne saw it, she let out a cry of admiration.

"It's massive," she said. "How are you going to heat it?"

"Solar panels," Erin said.

She pointed to the large sheets of glass that covered sections of the roof.

"Don't ask me how it works, but I'm told that it does. Besides we'll also have conventional sources like gas and electricity as back-up if required. But Harry is very big into renewable energy. I expect that will be the main source."

Inside the rooms were bare. The walls had been plastered and the windows painted and someone had gone over the floors with a powerful commercial vacuum cleaner so that the place was spotlessly clean of dust and grime.

"At least it's tidy," Anne remarked as she took a large notepad from her bag and looked around the spacious living-room. "Why don't we start in here? Did you have any thoughts about the decor?"

They spent almost three hours going from room to room while Anne made suggestions about colours and fabrics and took copious notes.

Harry had plans to turn one of the upstairs bedrooms into an office where he could conduct business and Erin was toying with the idea of doing something similar with a smaller bedroom. Another room was already earmarked as Baby Emily's nursery.

As they progressed, Erin began to envision the house as it would look when they were finished – a comfortable, modern, smartly furnished home where there would be plenty of room for them to live and work and for Emily to grow up.

When they finally ended their tour, they sat in the car and Anne went over her notes again.

"Are you on a budget?" she asked.

"No. Harry wants the best so I don't think cost will be an issue."

"In that case, there is some marvellous furniture I'd like you to see. And it's not too expensive. I'm available on Monday if you're free to come to the warehouse with me."

By now, Erin was entirely caught up in the excitement. "That sounds ideal. But I'd like Harry to come with us. He's got to live here too."

"Okay. Why don't you talk to him and you can ring me later?"

When Monday arrived, Harry and Erin drove into town and picked up Anne and the three of them had a very productive time visiting warehouses and show, rooms. Meanwhile, Anne had arranged with one of her colleagues to co-ordinate the fabrics and curtains.

When it was over they went for coffee.

"Everything seems to be falling into place," Harry said. "If you give me a colour plan for each room, I'll have the painters start work next week."

"How long will they take?" Anne asked.

"It shouldn't be more than a week or ten days."

"Okay. Then we can start work on the curtains and fabrics."

"So," Erin said, with a growing sense of satisfaction, "we should be ready to move in about three weeks' time?"

"April 13th," Harry said. "A little bit later than we planned."

Erin spent the available time preparing for the move. It was surprising the amount of possessions they had accumulated in the short time since they had been married. There were her clothes and CDs and books plus all of Harry's belongings including a set of golf clubs that he rarely used. And there was all the baby equipment. Since Emily's arrival, she had been deluged with presents and gifts from their friends and families, mainly of useful items like clothes and toys. Erin ordered a number of large boxes and began the laborious task of packing and marking them.

One evening, Harry said to her, "Susan tells me you've stopped the riding sessions."

"Yes," Erin replied. "With all the preparations for

the move, I decided I just didn't have time."

He looked at her. "That's not the real reason, is it?"

"No, it's not," she confessed.

"It wasn't working out?"

"The sessions were enjoyable. But the reason you asked me to go along was so Susan and me would become friends and I'm afraid that hasn't happened. I did my best."

"I'm sorry," Harry said. "She likes you, you know. She told me. And she thinks you've got real riding potential."

Erin let out a sigh. "Well, she didn't communicate it to me. Every session was a trial, Harry. She gave the impression that she was only putting up with me and didn't really want me there. She was more friendly with that groom, Cornish, than she was with me. And there's only so much cold shoulder anyone can take."

"Have you cancelled?"

"Not formally. I told her I was going to be busy with Larchfield and wouldn't be coming back for a while."

"So you might resume?"

"It's doubtful. What's the point?"

"Never close a door permanently," he said. "You never know when you might need to open it again."

Meanwhile the decoration for the house was proceeding smoothly. Anne prepared a colour plan with detailed instructions for every room and a team of four painters was set to work. The highlight was the living-room which was going to be painted in bright, airy yellows and whites. To complement the colour scheme, they had ordered several large leather settees and chairs, a couple of low coffee tables and a plasma-screen television and sound system. The drapes were also in bright yellow. And Anne had even helped her choose some large prints for the walls. The room was going to look stunning when it was finished.

The large open-plan kitchen/diner had been fitted with top-of-the-range appliances. A magnificent Neff cooker and oven dominated the room while a huge walk-in fridge stood beside the door. In the centre of the kitchen was a large marble-topped island with stylish stools. Upstairs, the bathrooms gleamed with shining suites and jacuzzi baths.

By now, Erin was in a state of high excitement. She was finally making the break from Belvedere. She had been looking forward to this event for a very long time. Two days before they were due to leave, she sat down to have a heart-to-heart talk with her mother-in-law. In the last few weeks she had watched Mrs Kavanagh grow ever more depressed at the prospect of their departure.

"I won't pretend that I'm happy," Caroline said. "I don't know what I'm going to do when you've gone."

"You'll find plenty of things to do. You've got your husband and Tim and this big house to look after. You won't be bored."

"Oh, that's not what I mean. Of course, I've got

plenty of *chores*. But what am I going to do for my own personal satisfaction? You and little Emily have become the centre of my life."

"We won't be far away," Erin said, reassuringly. "We'll keep in touch. I'll come and visit and bring Emily. And you can drive over to see us any time you want."

"But it won't be the same. You won't be living here. I'm going to miss you dreadfully. You know, Erin, I would do anything to keep you here."

"It's not possible. The house is almost ready. We have to go."

Mrs Kavanagh looked as if she was on the verge of tears.

"Why is it always like this? Whenever I find something to love, it is taken away from me."

"Don't talk like that. We'll still be available for you. Things will be just the same."

"No," Mrs Kavanagh said. "They won't. I know what life is like. Once you leave, things will never be the same again."

That afternoon, Erin had to drive over to Larchfield to take delivery of some bedroom furniture. She was glad of the opportunity to escape from Belvedere. With their imminent departure, the atmosphere had grown sad and depressing. It was beginning to get her down.

The delivery van was turning into the drive as she arrived. She parked the car and waited while the furniture was unloaded and taken upstairs to the bedrooms. Then she signed the receipt and watched the van drive off again.

On the way back to Belvedere, she saw the sky grow dark and overcast and a wind began to shake the branches of the trees. The weather was changing and it looked as if a storm was on the way. As she drove up the long drive, the big house rose up out of the gloom like some ghostly spectre. She had just parked the car when there was a low rumble and the skies opened. Next moment, the rain was pouring down.

She pulled her jacket over her head and ran up the steps to the front door. As she entered the hall, she immediately sensed that something was wrong. The staff were standing in hushed little groups, looking shocked and distressed.

At that moment, Harry came out of the drawing-room. His face was ashen grey.

"Thank God you're back," he said.

"What's happening?" she asked with panic rising in her breast.

"It's Dad," he replied. "He's had a heart attack."

Chapter 18

She felt the blood drain from her face.

"How bad is he?" she asked, clasping a hand to her mouth.

"He's still breathing, thank God. We've called an emergency ambulance and it's on its way."

"Where is he?"

"In the drawing-room. My mother is with him."

"And where is Emily?"

"She's in the nursery. I asked one of the maids to stay with her."

"Can I see him?" she asked, as she struggled to come to terms with the enormity of what was happening.

"Better not," Harry said. "There's nothing you can do. It would only distress you."

"Then I'd best go and see to Emily. If you need me, call."

She kissed Harry and quickly made her way

upstairs to the nursery where she found the baby sleeping peacefully. She went into the living-room and stared out the window at the rain lashing the lawns around the house.

She had grown fond of her gruff old father-in-law and the thought of something bad happening to him filled her with dread. But she was helpless in the face of this awful thing that had occurred. Please God the ambulance would come on time. They had special equipment to deal with situations like this. Once Charlie Kavanagh was in the ambulance his chances of survival would be much improved.

She felt a terrible sadness come over her. Charlie had always been a lively presence around the house. The thought of that big, healthy man with his life hanging by a thread was difficult to take in. Yet she realised he was an ideal candidate for a heart attack – overweight, rarely exercising, drinking too much, always working, pushing himself to extremes to conclude deals and complete contracts. And according to Harry, he had been smoking heavily until recently – Cuban cigars.

Charlie had always been kind to her, had taken a special shine to her. He had given her the big break she needed to advance her career with the scoop about the Conway Hotel. And he doted on his granddaughter, just like his wife. Erin felt the sadness overwhelm her. It was awful. They would all be devastated if he should die like this, so suddenly and without warning.

She heard the sound of a siren drawing near and

saw a light flashing at the bottom of the drive. She watched as the ambulance slowly made its way closer till it reached the front door. Harry and Tim emerged into the driving rain and spoke hurriedly to the driver. Two attendants quickly opened the back of the ambulance and returned with a stretcher and a third man followed with what looked like an oxygen mask and cylinder. They disappeared from view into the house.

She wondered if she should go back downstairs. But she would only get in the way. After several minutes, she saw the attendants come back out again carrying the stretcher while the third man walked alongside holding the oxygen equipment. Harry and his mother got into the ambulance and the doors were closed and it set off again down the drive, moving faster now till at last, it was gone from view.

She remained at the window, battling with the thoughts that were swirling round in her head. The pall that had always hung over the house seemed to have intensified with what had occurred. She thought of the bright new home that awaited her at Larchfield. It was her opportunity to break free, to make a new start and leave all the old doubts and fears behind. She couldn't wait to get away.

She was startled by a loud knock at the door.

"Come in," she said and looked up to see Tim enter the room. He looked pale and shaken.

"How is he?" she asked, turning from the window and going to him.

He gave a helpless shrug. "Not good, I'm afraid. They were able to revive him but there is nothing more they can do till they get him to hospital. Harry has promised to ring as soon as he has news."

"Would you like a drink?" she asked.

Tim nodded and lowered himself into a chair. He covered his head with his hands and Erin could see he was on the brink of tears.

"This has been a terrible shock. I still haven't taken it in." He took the glass that Erin poured and drank about half of it before wiping his chin. "It happened so quickly. It took us all by surprise."

"Were you with him when it happened?"

"No. Harry was. They were in the drawing-room discussing some new scheme that Dad is planning when he suddenly complained about chest pains and collapsed onto the sofa. By the time I got there, he looked as if he was dead. He looked awful, Erin. His face was pale as chalk and he was barely able to breathe. It was terrible. I thought he was gone."

She bit her lip. "There was no warning?"

"None. Only yesterday he was making plans to go to the races with some of his pals."

"I don't know what to say. Your poor mother must be devastated."

"She's keeping up a brave front but she's as shocked as the rest of us. Thank God, Harry was here. He was the one who took charge and rang for the ambulance. If I had been on my own I would have been useless."

"You would have been fine," Erin said reassuringly. "At times like this we always find the strength to cope."

"Well, we're going to need it now," Tim said, finishing his drink. "Are you all right up here?"

"Yes. I've got Emily to keep me occupied."

"Then I'll leave you. Harry has asked me to ring a few people and cancel meetings that Dad had lined up. I'll be downstairs if you need me."

At the door, he turned back into the room.

"You know, this proves that you can take nothing for granted. But one thing is certain. If he survives, he will have to slow down. He can't continue to work the way he has. This is a turning point, Erin. However this pans out, things will have to change."

He left, promising to contact her as soon as he heard news from the hospital.

She checked on Emily and found her still sleeping soundly. She thought of what Tim had just said. He was right. If Charlie Kavanagh survived this heart attack, he could not resume his gruelling work schedule. And that meant only one thing. Harry would have to take his place!

This thought only served to make her even more gloomy. The impact would be far-reaching. She would see even less of her husband. And he would be the one putting his health at risk for the sake of the company. It was not something that Erin could bring herself to think about.

* * *

After what seemed like hours, she heard her mobile ring. It was Harry.

"Well?" she said, urgently. "Any news?"

"Dad's undergone emergency surgery and he's now in intensive care. The main artery to his heart was blocked. They had to perform a by-pass."

"Is he going to survive?"

"They won't say. The only information I could get from the surgeon is that they'll monitor him during the night and check again in the morning. The next twelve hours will be crucial. But Erin, the good news is, he's still alive."

"Thank God. What are you going to do?"

"Mum wants to remain at the hospital. I'm going to stay with her."

"What do you want me to do?"

"Just wait and pray. I'll ring you again if there are any developments."

"All right," she said. "I'm sorry, Harry."

"I know."

"And I love you."

"I know that too."

Emily woke and Erin fed her and changed her nappy and played with her for a while till she grew tired and finally dozed off once more. She turned on the television and watched some film but she couldn't concentrate and switched it off again. It was now eleven o'clock. It seemed like an eternity had passed in the last six hours.

She thought of Harry and Mrs Kavanagh in that hospital waiting room, counting the minutes as they slowly passed and Charlie's life was weighed in the scales. There was nothing she could do. She checked once more on Emily and decided to go to bed. But her mind was still in turmoil and it was a long time before she began to feel drowsy and the waves of sleep at last overpowered her.

When she woke, the rain had stopped and the fields around Belvedere looked fresh and green in the bright spring sunshine. The sight filled her with hope. Surely nothing bad could happen on a morning such as this. She looked in on Emily and found her sleeping still. She went into the bathroom and had a quick shower. When she emerged, her mobile was ringing. She hurried to the dressing-table and picked it up.

"Hi," Harry said. His voice sounded tired.

"Anything to report?"

"Dad had a good night. I've just been speaking to the cardiologist and he seemed upbeat."

"Oh, thank heavens! Is he conscious?"

"No, he's still sedated. He'll come around later in the morning."

"How is your mother?"

"Exhausted, as you can imagine. Same as me."

"So what are you going to do?"

"We're coming home. Mum has to get some sleep.

207

Susan and Tim are going to relieve us. They're on their way in now and they'll stay till this evening. I'll see you in about forty minutes."

She switched off the phone and felt her courage rise. Charlie Kavanagh was a tough old bird and now that he had survived the crucial first hours, he would surely pull through. She finished dressing and made a cup of tea and some toast and soon she saw Harry's BMW coming up the drive. She gathered up the sleeping Emily, wrapped her in a shawl and went down to the hall to meet them.

She watched Harry help his mother out of the car. She looked utterly worn out. It was obvious that she hadn't slept. Harry didn't look much better. When Mrs Kavanagh saw her, her face broke into a tired smile.

"What a wonderful sight to greet me," she said, peering at the baby in Erin's arms. "Can I hold her?"

"Certainly."

She took the child and gently bent to kiss her forehead. At that moment, Emily woke and laughed into her face.

"Look at that," she said. "Wouldn't that warm the coldest heart?" She turned to Erin and smiled. "Thank you, my dear. And now I'd best try and get some rest. It has been a tiring night and I'm going to need all my energy for what lies ahead."

One of the maids took her hand and slowly helped her climb the stairs.

Once they were back in the apartment, Harry

turned to Erin and took her in his arms.

"I feel drained," he said. "What kept me going was talking to you and knowing you were here supporting me."

"Ssshh," she said. "Everything is going to be okay. Now why don't you follow your mother's example and get some sleep? Do you want me to make breakfast?"

He shook his head. "I think I'll just have a shower and get between the sheets for a few hours."

"Do that," Erin said. "I'll take Emily for a walk so the place will be quiet."

"You've been a tower of strength," he said.

She managed a smile. "Get some sleep. Your father is going to be fine."

Harry slept till lunch-time and when he woke he immediately got on the phone to Tim. Erin bit her lip as she watched. Slowly, she saw the contours of his face begin to change. As he continued to talk, his mood shifted from fear into hope. He was laughing when he finally switched off the phone. He swept Erin into his arms and kissed her.

"Dad is conscious and his breathing has returned to normal. They've been monitoring his heartbeat and it appears to have stabilised. They think the operation has been a success." He closed his eyes tight to hold back the tears. "Oh, Erin, I feel so happy I could shout for joy."

"That's great. Does your mother know?"

"Yes. Tim has been speaking to her. They're going to let us in to see him for a short time at four o'clock." He glanced at his watch. "I'd better get ready."

"Slow down," she said. "You've got plenty of time and you're going nowhere without some food. When was the last time you had something to eat?"

"I can't remember."

"I'll fix something. Go and have a shower. And shave that stubble off your chin. You look like you've been sleeping on a park bench."

Harry was far hungrier than he realised and now that he had some good news, his appetite returned with gusto. Erin heated some soup and a chicken casserole she dug out of the freezer. She watched as he greedily demolished it. By three o'clock he was ready to set off again with his mother for the hospital. But this time he was in a far better mood.

"Do you want to come with us?" he asked as he straightened his tie in the bathroom mirror. "I'm sure he would be glad to see you and Emily."

"Not this time. I don't want to tire him. Anyway, it's doubtful if the doctors would even let us in. But tell him that I'm thinking about him and I'll visit in the next few days."

She waved goodbye as the car set off once more down the drive. The news of Charlie Kavanagh's recovery had spread throughout the household and now there was a brighter, cheerier atmosphere around Belvedere. She went back upstairs and made a cup of tea then rang her mother to tell her what had happened.

Shortly after five o'clock, she heard Harry's car coming back up the drive.

He came into the apartment with a huge grin on his face.

"Well?"

"You're not going to believe this. He was sitting up in bed and complaining that they wouldn't allow him boiled eggs for supper."

She found herself smiling too. "Sounds like your father all right."

"He's in excellent form and the doctors are very pleased with his progress. But he's not getting out of there for another few weeks. And when he does come home he's got a long period of convalescence ahead of him."

"How did he react to that news?"

"Not very well, as you might have guessed."

"Well, I'm glad someone has finally laid it on the line for him. Your father has to rest, Harry. That was his problem. He was working too hard."

"I think he knows that. The bad news is I will have to take over the running of the company, at least till he's back on his feet."

"I was expecting that."

"There's something else."

The smile had left his face and was replaced by a frown.

"We'll have to postpone the move to Larchfield. We can't leave my mother now, Erin. Not with all this on her plate."

Chapter 19

This was a bitter blow but she couldn't resist the logic of Harry's statement. Mrs Kavanagh needed all the assistance she could get to nurse her husband back to health. To leave now in the middle of this calamity would be unthinkable. With a heavy heart, Erin put all thoughts of Larchfield out of her mind and concentrated on helping her mother-in-law and looking after her child.

Three weeks later, Charlie came home. When Erin saw him get out of the car she was shocked. He looked so frail. The clothes seemed to hang in folds from his ravaged frame. His face looked tired and worn and there was a grey pallor to his cheeks. She remembered the big, heavy-set man with the ruddy face she had first encountered in this very house only two years before and couldn't help comparing the two. It struck her that Charlie Kavanagh had some way to go before he was fully restored to health.

But she kept these thoughts to herself for now the mood of the house was positive.

Everyone welcomed Charlie back and fussed over him. He had been put on a strict recovery programme and told that he would have to take some exercise each day. He had been given a range of medication and a diet sheet which Mrs Kavanagh had copied and circulated to the kitchen staff. Finally, he was told to regulate his drinking and quit smoking.

It sounded like a recipe for trouble and sure enough, it wasn't long before she began to hear stories about Charlie arguing with the cook about his food and demanding that he be allowed a glass of wine with his dinner. He was anxious to return to work and Harry and his mother had to take a firm hand with him and insist that he adhere to the doctor's instructions. But on one matter, Charlie offered no resistance. He agreed to go for a walk each morning with Erin and Emily round the grounds of Belvedere.

By now the weather had turned fine. Spring was well advanced and summer was clearly on the way. It was a perfect time to be out of doors. The flowers were in bloom and the birds were nesting and everywhere Erin looked she could see nature stirring from its winter sleep. So each morning after breakfast, she dressed the baby, strapped her into her buggy and came down to meet Charlie in the hall. He would be waiting for her, wrapped up in a thick woollen parka and scarf and together they would set off.

At first, his progress was slow and after fifteen

minutes, he would get tired. But gradually, as his strength began to return, the walks were extended and soon they were walking for an hour. On his way around the grounds, he would point out things of interest to Erin and relate the history of the place.

"I bought Belvedere in 1968. I had just made my first million pounds which was a lot of money in those days. Now millionaires are ten a penny but back then they were pretty thin on the ground." He chuckled at the memory. "This property belonged to a family called Dunwoody. They had lived in it for generations but gradually they had been dying off and they found themselves in financial difficulties. I bought it for £200,000. I was thinking of knocking down the house and building houses on the site. Malahide was still a village at that time but I could see the potential. And then I thought: Why not live in it myself? Of course there was a lot of opposition from the old families around here. They regarded me as an upstart. I wasn't seen as the proper sort of person to own a place like this. But I didn't give a damn. I brought people in to renovate the house and cultivate the lands. And when I started to give parties, my neighbours quickly changed their tune. They were soon falling over themselves to get invited." He laughed. "Money is money at the end of the day, Erin, and it has a language of its own."

"You sound like a man who has had a very happy life," she said.

He shrugged. "I've enjoyed myself but I do have

some regrets. I won't say there haven't been disappointments along the way. I'm sorry we don't have more grandchildren." He smiled wryly from the corner of his mouth. "I don't want to end up like the Dunwoodys with no heirs to keep the family line alive. But thankfully, you came along and changed all that."

He bent down to tickle Emily's chin. "This little mite had brought great pleasure into our home. I can't remember when Caroline was so happy, or me, for that matter. Don't be fooled by my exterior, Erin. I have a tender heart."

"I know," she said.

"You don't miss much, do you?" he went on. "I could see that the first day we met. I knew you were a smart cookie."

Over the next few weeks as she got to know her father-in-law better, Erin found a strong bond of affection springing up between them. He was a tough man who didn't suffer fools gladly and he could be determined and stubborn when he wanted his own way. But there was a gentle side to Charlie Kavanagh and she saw it often on their morning walks. Gradually, Erin found her love for him growing.

Meanwhile, Harry had taken over the day-to-day running of the company. It involved lengthy meetings with architects and accountants and bankers, visits to building sites, correspondence with planners and officials, trips to factories to inspect new processes and purchase materials. With the onset of dry weather, work had started on the Conway Hotel development and the bulldozers were already knocking down the old hotel and clearing the land. But there was still opposition to the plan and regular pickets at the gates of the site.

Harry seemed to revel in the work. He rose every morning at seven, had a shower and breakfast and by eight o'clock he was at his desk in Charlie's office, taking phone calls and directing the business of Kavanagh Construction. And he also had his father's lengthy experience to call on. Every morning when he returned from his walk with Erin, Charlie spent an hour closeted with his son while together they confronted problems and hammered out solutions.

But there was one area where Erin drew the line. She was determined that Harry should learn from his father's mistakes. She insisted that he get proper sleep, eat a healthy diet, have a medical check and take regular exercise. For his birthday, she presented him with a five-year membership of a leisure complex in Swords that had a gym and a swimming pool.

"I want you to use it," she said. "And I won't hear any excuses. You can go in the evenings when you finish work. We've had one heart attack in this family and that's one too many."

By now, Erin's maternity leave was coming to an end and she was beginning to think of returning to work at *The Clarion*. But since receiving the threatening letter, she had become very protective of Emily and was wary of leaving her in the care of anyone else. The ideal solution would be to work from home and she was already preparing some suggestions to put to Ger Armstrong. These thoughts of work were brought sharply into focus one morning when she received a phone call from a young reporter at the office.

"I'm sorry to bother you, Erin, but I've been asked to give you a call."

The reporter sounded nervous.

"Yes?"

"We've heard that Charlie Kavanagh has had a heart attack. I was wondering if you could tell us anything about it."

She was immediately taken aback. It had never occurred to her that her father-in-law's condition would be the subject of media attention. The family had been careful to ensure that only a handful of friends and colleagues knew about Charlie's illness but obviously word had leaked out.

"I don't think so," she said. "His health is a private matter."

"So he did have a heart attack?"

"I didn't say that. I said that his state of health was private."

"But he's a public figure. People are interested in him."

Suddenly, she was back again as a cub reporter in the newsroom. She could understand exactly what had happened. Someone had heard about Charlie and suggested a news story and this unfortunate reporter had been detailed to write it. It wasn't his fault. There was no point getting into an argument with him.

"Let me speak to the news editor," she said.

A minute later she was talking to her boss.

"Hi, Ger," she said. "I've just had a reporter call me about my father-in-law's health."

"I know, I asked him to do it. We heard he had a heart attack."

"But don't you think this is intrusive?"

"Erin, what's happened to your news judgment? Just because you're involved, suddenly it's intrusion. If it was anyone else, it would be a scoop."

"A scoop? Somebody has a health problem and suddenly it's a scoop?"

"Not just somebody. Charlie Kavanagh is a powerful man. He's in the public eye. You can't have it both ways, Erin. You should know that."

"Well, I don't think the family will be pleased."

"The story is already out there. Someone recognised him in the hospital. It's only a matter of time before the tabloids have it. I'm giving the family an opportunity to put their side of it first."

"Let me talk to them," she said. "I'll call you back."

She rang Harry and told him what had happened. As she expected, he exploded when he heard.

"I don't believe this. They want to write a story about my father's heart attack? Is there nothing sacred?"

"They *will* write it. I know the way they work."

"Can't you use your influence to keep the lid on it?"

Erin felt like laughing at the naivety of her husband's question. "You might as well try to stop water running downhill. If *The Clarion* doesn't write it, the tabloids will. And believe me, they will be much worse."

"Can't we just tell them to go to hell?"

"I don't advise it. That will only get their backs up."

"We could threaten to injunct."

"And then what happens? If it ends up in court we'd be a laughing-stock."

Harry let out a weary sigh. "So what do you think we should do?"

"Issue a statement. I'll draft it if you like. Just tell me exactly what your father wants to say."

"Okay," Harry said. "I'll talk to him. But I know he's not going to like it."

Charlie was just as incredulous as Harry when he heard what was going on.

"Who do they think I am? The Pope? I never thought I'd see the day when my heart attack became front page news."

"It won't be front-page if we handle it properly."

"Is there's no way out of this?"

Erin shook her head. "Afraid not."

"Well, they must have very little to write about. Tell me what I should say."

An hour later, Erin had the statement prepared. It said that Mr Charles Kavanagh, managing director of the building firm, Kavanagh Construction, was resting at home following surgery to correct a heart complaint and was making a good recovery. It went on to thank the many well-wishers who had contacted the family and particularly the media for their delicate consideration of the family's privacy at this difficult time.

"You think that will keep them quiet?" Charlie asked.

"We're about to find out."

She rang the statement through to Ger Armstrong.

"Anyone else got this?" he asked as he read it.

"Only *The Clarion*."

She heard him chuckle.

"*Delicate consideration of the family's privacy*? I like it, Erin. You're a fast learner. You should be in PR. Thanks a bundle."

The report appeared the following day on an inside page half hidden near the bottom. There were a couple of enquiries from the evening papers and then the story disappeared. Everyone at Belvedere breathed a sigh of relief. But the episode had a salutary effect on Erin. It made her look at the other side of her job and how reporting appeared differently to those on the receiving end.

Her morning walks with Charlie meant that she didn't see so much of Tim. He seemed to have faded into the background although occasionally she would run into him around the grounds, always with his brow furrowed and deep in thought. But that didn't stop

Harry complaining bitterly about him.

"Wouldn't you think he'd lend a hand now that my father is ill? But he hasn't raised a finger. Too busy wasting his time with his bloody studying."

Erin knew he had a case. Nevertheless, she felt compelled to put in a word for her brother-in-law. "What help would he be?"

"That's not the point, Erin. He hasn't even made an offer. And he benefits from the success of Kavanagh Construction just like the rest of us. I can tell you my father isn't very pleased. He takes a dim view of Tim's behaviour."

"But he knows nothing about the business."

"That's because he hasn't bothered to find out," Harry said with some force. "He doesn't want to get his hands dirty with real work. He prefers the role of the permanent bloody student."

"Look, Harry, you have to be reasonable. If Tim started working with you, he'd quickly get in your hair. You'd probably end up firing him."

Harry started to laugh. "You're right. I probably would. But it would be nice if he showed a little interest now and again."

A few days later when she came back from a shopping trip to Malahide, she met her brother-in-law as she was getting out of the car.

"Let me help you with that stuff," he said, taking hold of her bags.

"Thank you, Tim. That's very kind."

He came up the stairs with her to the apartment

and put the bags down in the kitchen.

"Would you like a cup of tea?" she asked. "I'm just about to boil the kettle."

"Yes. I'd appreciate that."

"Then go and sit in the living-room. It'll be ready in a minute."

When she came into the room, she found him leafing through a couple of magazines.

"So how have you been?" she asked, pouring the tea and pushing a plate of biscuits across the table.

"Okay."

"Book coming along all right? You got over that sticky patch you mentioned?"

"Oh yes. The publishers are very happy."

"So when can we expect a signed copy from the author?"

"I don't know, Erin. I'm not in the mood for writing just now."

She scrutinised his face. She thought he was looking downcast. "Why? What has happened?"

He shrugged and allowed his gaze to drift down to the floor. "I feel guilty," he said. "Here's Dad has had a heart attack and Harry immediately steps in and assumes the reins of the company. And what do I do? Nothing."

It was uncanny. This was exactly the conversation she had with her husband a few days earlier.

"Why don't you talk to Harry and ask if you can help?"

But this suggestion only made Tim more depressed.

"I'd be no good at it. I'd be useless."

"At least you could offer."

"I'd only make a fool of myself. And if things went wrong, I'd get blamed. They're blaming me already. I can tell. I know this family much better than you, Erin, and believe me they harbour grudges. They're going to say I stood by and did nothing to help when the company was in trouble."

"Then prove them wrong. Go and talk to Harry."

He looked at her helplessly. "I can't."

She reached out and stroked his arm. "Your father is getting better every day. He'll soon be able to get involved again. This will all be forgotten."

"No, it won't," Tim said, staring into her face. "This family never forgets anything."

Later, when she was alone, Erin mulled over Tim's strange comment. What had he meant when he said the family never forgets? Was he trying to tell her something? It wasn't the first time he had made some remark that alarmed her. It made her wonder if there were more secrets buried in the Kavanagh family history that she knew nothing about.

She was sorry to see Tim depressed. He was a sensitive soul and it upset her to see him so unhappy. But she could understand the family's vexation if he refused to help in their time of trouble. She had offered him a way out and he had refused to take it. There was little else she could do.

The conversation stoked her determination to get

away to Larchfield as soon as was decently possible. The house was furnished and decorated and ready for occupation. If it hadn't been for Charlie's heart attack, they would be living there now, away from Belvedere and its gloomy secrets. But the good news was that her father-in-law was recovering fast and spending more time with Harry on company affairs while Mrs Kavanagh seemed to be coping quite well. One day soon they would be able to take their leave without having to feel guilty. Erin could only look forward to it with anticipation.

But a phone call from Ger Armstrong a few days later soon distracted her.

"Hi, Erin," he began. "I've been checking the rosters and I see you are due back to work next week."

"That's right. I was going to call you."

"How is the baby?"

"She's growing fast."

"Playing with her word processor yet?"

"I expect that any day soon," Erin laughed.

"Well, I've been thinking. We'll be glad to have you back again but perhaps I should ease you in."

"How do you mean?"

"I've got an idea for a series of profiles I want to run. It will be called *Movers and Shakers*. You get the idea? People who are making things happen on the local scene. It can be businessmen, politicians, musicians, writers. I'll leave the choice up to you. You could write them from home, no need to come into the office."

This was exactly what she had been hoping for. It would mean she could continue to look after Emily.

"That sounds like a great idea," she said.

"Aim for a gender balance. You could probably get a lot of information on your subjects from the internet before you interview them."

"How many do you want?"

"I thought we might start with six. We'll kick off with the Saturday review and run them all the following week in the features pages."

"Okay, I'll start working on a list right away and email it to you."

"Incidentally, how is your father-in-law?"

"Are you asking out of personal or professional interest?"

She heard her boss laugh.

"Personal, of course."

"He's fine. He's making a very good recovery. I never thanked you for burying that story, did I?"

"You don't have to. You were right. It wasn't much of a story. And when you're sick, the last thing you want is to find the fact splashed all over the papers."

"Well, thanks anyway. I'll tell him you were asking."

"Talk to you," the news editor said and was gone.

Erin put the phone down and felt the old familiar excitement return. It was good to be working again and to feel valued. This was what she was meant for. She made a cup of coffee, checked on the baby and sat down at the dining table and started to draw up a list of possible subjects.

Two hours later, she had a dozen names. They ranged from a young dress designer who was shaking up the fashion world to a singer/songwriter whose compositions were beginning to attract rave reviews. She had just finished emailing the list to Ger Armstrong for his approval when she heard Emily wake up and start to cry for her feed.

Now she had something to work on and it felt great. The following day, the news editor came back to her. He had whittled her list down to six candidates and suggested she keep the others in reserve in case they decided to extend the series later. But right now she had more than enough to keep her occupied. She decided to start with the songwriter. He was an eighteen-year-old piano player called Jamie Stone who had no formal musical training. But he had a magical touch with melodies and lyrics. She downloaded as much information as she could from the internet and then phoned to ask him for an interview.

He was delighted. An interview with *The Clarion* was a great opportunity to raise his profile. They arranged to meet at a café in Malahide the following afternoon. Erin bundled Emily into her carrycot and borrowed Harry's car for the short journey. When she got there, it took ten minutes to find a parking space so she was late when she arrived at her destination.

Jamie Stone was waiting for her with an empty cup of coffee on the table before him. Erin took one look at the gangly youth with his mop of untidy hair and a couple of days' stubble on his hollow cheeks and knew that he was exactly what she was looking for. To complete the picture, he was dressed completely in black crew-neck sweater, jacket and tight-fitting jeans.

"Is Jamie Stone your real name?" she asked after she had ordered a couple of fresh coffees and settled Emily on a seat beside her.

"Yes. Why do you ask?"

"Because it seems just right for you. Aloysius McGillicuddy wouldn't have the same ring to it, don't you think?"

"I suppose not," he laughed.

"So tell me how you got started."

"Playing the piano or writing songs?"

"Writing songs, Jamie, that's why I'm interested in you. There are loads of people who can play the piano but not everyone can write."

"I used to play in a band when I was at school."

"What do you do now?"

"I'm unemployed."

It was getting better. She turned on her portable voice recorder.

"Sorry to interrupt you," she said. "Keep talking."

Thankfully, Jamie Stone was a voluble young man with plenty to say for himself. In no time, Erin had got reams of material.

"So where do you get your ideas?" she asked.

He scratched his untidy head. "I'm not sure. They just sort of come to me. I might be walking along the street and the first few bars of a melody will pop into my head or maybe a phrase that I can work into a song. I can't explain it really."

As they continued to talk, Erin found herself warming to Jamie. He was totally unselfconscious. He didn't pretend that his songs had subtle depths of meaning or were touched by some great creative genius. She found this very refreshing. Many of the writers and musicians she had met were so full of their own importance that they were almost unbearable. She would try to capture that in the piece she wrote.

Eventually, the interview came to an end. When she looked at her watch, she discovered that two and a half hours had passed. Amazingly, Emily had slept through the whole thing. But Erin had found Jamie Stone so interesting that she could have talked to him all evening.

"Would you mind coming into *The Clarion* office some day to get your photograph taken?" she asked.

"My photograph?"

"Yes. People will want to know what you look like."

"Do I have to get dressed up?"

"Oh God, no, that would spoil everything. Just come exactly as you are. Don't even wash your hair."

He fingered his greasy locks. "You're sure?"

"Absolutely."

"So what do I do?"

"Just ring and ask for the pictures editor. I'll tell him to expect you. And then you can arrange a suitable time between you."

"Thanks very much," Jamie said as they got up to leave. And then he remembered something. He opened a bag which was slung across his shoulder and took out a CD.

"This is for you," he said, taking out a pen and scribbling something on the cover. "How do you spell Erin?"

"E – R – I – N. Like the old name for Ireland."

"Right, Erin, that's my demo CD. Thanks for the interview."

"Thank you, Jamie, and good luck with your career."

She was still in a light-hearted mood as she drove back to Belvedere. Jamie Stone had been a dream to interview and had given her some magnificent quotes. She knew she was going to write a superb profile. She might even suggest to the news editor that they kick off the series with it.

As she was parking the car, the front door suddenly opened and a small, burly figure came bustling out. She recognised Susan's husband, Toby.

"Hi, Toby," she said. "How are you? I haven't seen you for a while."

"Busy as usual," he said. "But I'm not complaining. I enjoy my work. Now I must scoot. Susan serves dinner on the dot of seven." He waved and was gone.

Later after supper, when Emily had been fed and washed and bedded down, Erin put on Jamie Stone's CD while she went back over her notes.

"That's a catchy tune," Harry said, raising his head from the sports pages of the evening paper. "Who is it?"

"Just a young musician I interviewed this afternoon," she replied.

"He sounds very good."

"Incidentally, I ran into Toby as I was coming home. He nearly knocked me down he was in such a hurry to get away for his dinner."

"I think Susan has him very well house-trained," Harry said with a grin.

"I haven't seen him for ages. What was he doing here?"

"Going over my father's will."

"Ah."

"After that health fright he got, Dad decided to bring his will up to date. I suppose it's a sensible precaution."

"Your father is looking marvellous now, Harry. I wouldn't be surprised if he outlived us all."

It took Erin a couple of days to write up the profile and email it to Ger Armstrong. He came back to say he loved it.

"This kid is amazing," he said. "Most of these musicians have their heads so far up their backsides I'm surprised they can hear themselves play. But Jamie Stone seems like a nice, unpretentious guy. In fact he's just the sort of young man I wouldn't mind my daughter going out with."

"Don't you think you should ask your daughter's opinion first?"

"She's only eight, Erin."

"So you like it?"

"I just told you. I *loved* it. I'm going to run with it as the opening profile of the series. Now when do you think you can get the next one to me?"

"I'm working on it already," she said.

Over the next few weeks, she spent a very enjoyable time carrying out her interviews and writing up her profiles. But not all her subjects were as easy or as pleasant as Jamie Stone. However, Erin was sufficiently experienced to know that she held the whip-hand. She was providing the publicity so she was in charge. Her interviewees needed her more than she needed them and if anyone proved awkward she wasn't slow to let them know.

She found the routine very convivial. She worked at her own pace and to her own deadlines. There were no barking phones or radios blaring in her ear. It made a change from the hectic atmosphere of the newsroom. Erin was in her element, delighted to be working again and gaining real, creative satisfaction from writing her articles.

And then, to complete her joy, Harry said the words she had been waiting so long to hear.

Chapter 20

"I think we can move to Larchfield."

They were having dinner one evening while Emily was sleeping comfortably in the nursery.

Erin immediately put down her knife and fork. "You mean it?"

"Yes. I've been talking to my father and he thinks he's well enough to resume the reins of the company. I'll continue to work closely with him but I don't think we need to hang around Belvedere any more."

"Oh, Harry, that's great news."

He smiled, playfully. "I thought you'd be pleased."

"What do your father's doctors say?"

"They agree. In fact, they think some regular work will be good for him. I don't know if you noticed but he's been getting very bored lately."

"It would be difficult not to notice," Erin said. "He's been pacing around the house like a panther in a cage."

"He won't be working in the manic way he used to," Harry continued. "Mum will keep a close eye on him and I'll be sharing the burden. We might also promote one or two people and delegate some of the workload."

"So when is this all going to happen?"

"Next week. It also means we can finally move into our new house, Erin. We can go this weekend, if you like. I know you can't wait to get away."

"I'll stay here as long as necessary," she said, quickly.

He reached out and took her hand. "I know. You've been solid as a rock throughout this crisis. But I think the time has come for us to make the break. The house is sitting empty, we might as well be living there."

"Does your mother know?"

"Yes. I've already spoken to her."

"How is she taking it?"

He shrugged. "She's resigned to it by now. There's no longer any reason for us to stay."

That night, Erin could scarcely sleep for excitement. She was delighted finally to be going to their new home. She had been waiting so long that there had been occasions when she had wondered if they would ever make the move. For the first time since they had married, she would be mistress of her own house. They would have their own space, invite their friends and have dinner parties where she could put her recently acquired culinary skills into practice.

Emily would have her own little nursery and Erin would have her study. It was all set up with bookshelves and desk and a broadband connection for her laptop. She would talk to Ger Armstrong and persuade him to let her work from home on a regular basis. It would be perfect.

And she would be free at last of Belvedere.

The following morning after breakfast, she drove over to Larchfield. It had been almost three months since she had last seen it. As she approached, she could see the house sparkling in the sun like a bright, shining jewel and a gush of pleasure filled her heart. At long last this beautiful house was going to be hers. She quickly opened the front door and was met by the smell of fresh paint so she set about opening windows to let in air.

The house was ready for occupation. The furniture was all in place, the bathroom and kitchen fittings, the carpets and curtains that Anne had helped her choose, the pictures and ornaments. As she wandered from room to room, she was immediately struck by the way the sunlight came flooding in to bathe the house in a bright, airy light. The contrast with Belvedere and its gloomy, oppressive atmosphere could not have been more obvious.

There were still some small things that needed to be done, some little personal touches that she had in mind when she got time. The garden required attention. She could see how the lawn was now growing fast and would need to be trimmed. And the winter rains had encouraged the weeds that were sprouting wildly along the borders. But this was something for Harry to do at weekends.

She went upstairs to the master bedroom with its large en-suite bath and shower. Next door was the room that would be Emily's new nursery. It was painted a nice bright pink with matching curtains. A colourful mobile hung above the cot and a little chest of drawers stood in a corner of the room with cartoon characters stencilled on the sides.

She stood for a moment and pictured her daughter growing up here. Perhaps in time she would be joined by a little brother or sister. She thought of the happy years they would spend here in their own home as the children grew up. It was as if a new chapter was opening in her life but this would be the main chapter where everyone lived happy ever after.

She smiled to herself as she went back round the rooms, closing the windows and pausing occasionally to allow her imagination to take flight. Eventually, she dragged herself away, locked up and drove the short distance back to Belvedere.

As she entered, she met Mrs Kavanagh coming down the stairs. She looked downcast and there was a strange look in her eyes.

"So you're finally moving?" she said. "Harry told me."

"Yes, we're going this weekend."

She solemnly nodded her head. "You know my

236

feelings. We've been through it all before. I don't want you to go."

"We're not moving very far . . ."

"I know. And you'll visit and ring and keep in touch. But it won't be the same. We both understand that." She looked at Erin with her piercing eyes. "I'll talk to you before you go," she said as she turned and walked away.

Erin watched her go. Her mother-in-law was a complex woman and her moods could change quite dramatically. She had known that the departure from Belvedere was never going to be easy. She just hoped Caroline Kavanagh didn't turn cold on her again.

But she had no time to brood. The next few days were extremely busy. She had an article to finish for Ger Armstrong and he wanted it for the weekend. She concentrated on getting it written and on Thursday evening she emailed it to him. The following morning she decided to take another trip to Larchfield and start moving some of their personal belongings across.

Much of their stuff had already been packed in boxes which were stored in the spare bedroom of the flat. But there were still a lot of baby clothes and books to be transported. If she took them now it would leave more room in the car tomorrow when they made the final journey. She quickly loaded the stuff into bags and asked one of the gardeners, a young man called Tommy Murphy, to help her carry them down to the car.

She wondered if she should take little Emily along

but when she checked she found the child sleeping soundly. It would be a pity to disturb her. She decided to ask her mother-in-law to keep an eye on her. But when she rang Mrs Kavanagh, there was no response.

Now she faced a dilemma. It would take forty-five minutes to complete her business at Larchfield. She would be there and back in no time. But she had never left Emily alone for so long. She wondered what she should do. In the end, she decided to turn on the baby monitor. Downstairs, she sought out Mrs Martin who was working in the kitchen and asked her to listen for Emily on the monitor and also to go upstairs and check on her a couple of times.

Tommy Murphy put the last of the bags into the car and Erin set off.

The road was free of traffic and she soon reached Larchfield. She opened the door and carried the bags up the stairs to the master bedroom. She looked around once more at the spanking new house and felt the sense of anticipation return. But she had no time to delay. She locked up and hurried back again to Belvedere.

As she turned the car into the driveway, she checked her watch. She had been gone for less than an hour but already she was feeling guilty for leaving the baby alone.

She quickly climbed the stairs to the apartment and found it in silence. Good. So Emily was still sleeping. She tiptoed into the nursery and approached the cot.

The baby was lying on her face with her head

buried in the pillow. Immediately, an uneasy feeling came over Erin. She had left the baby sleeping on her back. She quickly lifted Emily to turn her over. But the body felt limp and lifeless. Suddenly, she felt an icy panic seize her.

"Oh, no!" she screamed and clutched the child to her breast.

Little Emily was not breathing.

Chapter 21

Within minutes, the house was in pandemonium. It was Tim who got to her first and found her screaming hysterically and clutching the baby to her breast. Immediately, he alerted Harry and within minutes, the room was filled with excited people, family members and staff aghast at the terrible tragedy that had occurred under their roof.

Harry rushed to the distraught Erin and took her in his arms. His face was a mask of horror. Gently, he prised the baby from her grasp and gave her to Tim.

"There, there," he kept saying as he cradled his wife's head and softly stroked her face.

Meanwhile Tim was frantically pressing on the baby's tiny chest in an effort to revive her. But it was in vain.

"Has anyone called an ambulance?" Charlie Kavanagh demanded as he stood supporting his trembling wife.

"I did," Tim said, "and I also called Dr Bellows. He's on his way right now."

"Get her a glass of brandy," his father instructed. "She's in shock. We have to calm her down."

Tim went into the living-room, returned with a tumbler and gave it to Harry.

"Drink this," Harry said, forcing the glass against her teeth. "Please swallow, Erin. It will be good for you."

Charlie quickly assumed control. "Harry, get her onto the settee and lay her down," he ordered. "Tim, you give him a hand."

Together the two men lifted Erin and carried her to the settee in the living-room.

"Is there anything we can do, sir," one of the kitchen staff asked.

"Go down to the hall and wait for Dr Bellows. Then bring him up here straight away. And close the door like a good man. We need to be alone for a few minutes."

Erin's screams had now dissolved into wracking sobs that threatened to convulse her. Harry sat beside her and desperately tried to calm her down. Charlie bent and looked into her face. She stared back at him with glassy eyes, then shook her head frantically back and forth like a madwoman.

"Can you tell us what happened?"

She gulped and the words came spilling out in short disjointed phrases.

"I went out – in the car – when I came back – she was dead."

242

She started to weep but Charlie persisted with the questions.

"How long were you gone?"

"An hour."

"Where was the baby when you left her?"

"Sleeping in her cot."

"Did you leave her alone?"

"Yes."

Across the room, Mrs Kavanagh sat ashen-faced. At the mention of what had happened, her head shot up and she stared at Erin in disbelief.

Meanwhile, Erin had started wailing again. She tried to get up but Harry restrained her.

"Tell me she's not dead! Tell me she's not dead!" she screamed.

Charlie shook his head and turned to his son. "One short hour," he said, "and she'll remember it for the rest of her life."

It seemed like forever before they heard a knock on the door and Dr Bellows came hurrying in. He was the Kavanagh's family doctor, a small, precise man with white hair and a neat, three-piece suit. But he had an air of professional competence.

"What's happening?" he asked and Charlie quickly told him.

"Where's the child?"

Dr Bellows went to where the baby now lay on her parents' bed and began feeling for a pulse. He put his ear to the baby's chest and began to massage it. After a few minutes he gave up.

"Dead," he said heavily. He checked his watch, then took out a notebook and wrote down the time.

He went back to Erin. She was still sobbing and struggling to get up. Dr Bellows took one look at her, opened a black leather bag and took out a syringe.

"I'm going to give you a sedative," he said. "And then you're going to sleep. It won't hurt."

He pulled up her sleeve and slid the needle in just below the skin. Erin's body went limp. Thirty seconds later she was out.

"The gardaí will have to be informed," the doctor said, standing up and putting the syringe away.

At the mention of the police, Charlie's face became grim. "Is that necessary?"

"Afraid so," the doctor replied. "In a situation like this, they will want to take statements. It's routine."

"That's all we need," Charlie said with a sigh.

"This is an awful business," the doctor said. "You have my profound sympathy."

"What killed her?" Charlie asked.

Dr Bellows shrugged. "Looks like SIDS," he said. "Sudden Infant Death Syndrome. What used to be known as cot death."

A few minutes later, the ambulance arrived and Emily was taken to hospital for an autopsy to be carried out. Erin was put to bed and Mrs Martin was detailed to sit with her. The family decided to hold a conference in the downstairs drawing-room, together with Dr Bellows. Susan and Toby were summoned to join them. They all sat around the room looking pale and shocked. Once more, Charlie took charge.

"We'll have to try and piece this together. Tim, you got to her first."

"I was going up the stairs when I heard screaming coming from the flat," Tim said. "When I got there she was hysterical. She had Emily in her arms and was shouting that she wouldn't breathe. I looked at the baby and she seemed to be already dead. I tried to calm her but she was in a state of shock, just like you saw. That's when I rang Harry, the ambulance and the doctor."

Harry sat with his head buried in his hands. He looked dazed by all that had occurred.

"I've spoken to Tommy Murphy," he sighed. "He tells me Erin asked him to help her load some bags into the car to take across to Larchfield. He confirms that she was gone for about an hour."

"Did Murphy see the baby?"

"No. Erin told him she was sleeping in the nursery. Mrs Martin says that Erin asked her to listen out for the baby waking on the monitor and to check on her. She says she looked in twice and there was so sound so she assumed the child was still sleeping."

"So Erin was alone when she found the child?"

"Yes."

Charlie turned to Toby who was sitting quietly beside his wife. "What do we do now?"

"Wait for the gardaí to arrive," he said, glancing nervously around the room till his eyes came to rest on Mrs Kavanagh.

Caroline sat grim-faced and stern, her hands folded before her in her lap. "She should never have left the baby alone," she said, coldly. "Then it would never have happened."

Charlie gave her a dark look. People exchanged glances. No one said anything for a moment.

"What about funeral arrangements?" Tim asked at last.

"We can't do anything till the hospital has finished the autopsy," Dr Bellows replied.

"We should keep the service private," Charlie said. "I don't think Erin's in a fit state to be meeting people. What do you say, Harry?"

Harry nodded.

"I'll take care of it," Charlie continued. "You have enough to do looking after your wife. And I'd better ring Erin's family and let them know." He turned to Toby. "I want this kept quiet. The fewer people who know about it, the better. If we get any enquiries, I want them referred straight to you."

Toby nodded his agreement.

"Anything else?" Charlie asked, glancing round the room.

No one spoke.

"What a bloody awful day," he said.

Soon afterwards, the gardaí arrived, a sergeant and a young woman constable. They interviewed each person separately about what they had seen and heard. But the key witness, Erin, was sedated and unable to give a statement. They said they would call again in the morning and interview her then.

When they had gone and everyone but Harry had departed, Charlie went to the sideboard and poured two large glasses of whiskey. He gave one to his son.

"What are you going to do about Erin?" he asked.

Harry shook his head. "I don't know."

"She's in a terrible state. And God knows what she'll be like in the morning when that sedative wears off. She'll go through hell. She'll blame herself, mark my words."

"Why should she blame herself?" Harry said, quickly. "You heard Dr Bellows. It was Sudden Infant Death Syndrome."

"Because she will. After the funeral, you should take her away."

"I was thinking of taking a break when we moved to Larchfield," Harry said.

"Then do it. We can spare you. Just take her away. She needs a complete rest from all this." He cast a sad eye on his son. "She's been cooped up too long in this damned house. You have too. You should have moved long ago."

Chapter 22

The agony began soon after dawn, as the first rays of daylight began to filter into the bedroom. Erin's initial realisation was that she was alone in the bed. Where was Harry? Why was his warm body not here beside her?

She turned and saw a strange face staring at her. It looked like Mrs Martin. What was she doing here? Why was she watching? And where was her husband? She felt drowsy, her eyelids still thick with sleep and her mind heavy and slow to respond. It was as if she was climbing out of a deep, black hole. It took her drugged brain a couple of moments to adjust to the familiar contours of the room.

Mrs Martin was getting up and leaving. As Erin heard the door click shut behind her, her mind immediately turned to Emily. She would want her feed. She must get up and go to her. She pushed herself up in bed and suddenly the terrible events of the previous day came crashing in on her. Emily was dead!

Now she recognised the awful thing that had been lying submerged on the edge of her consciousness. Emily had stopped breathing. She was lying in her cot and she wouldn't breathe. She put her hands to her head and began to scream.

The bedroom door opened and Mrs Martin came rushing back in, Harry on her heels. He came quickly to the bedside and took her in his arms.

"Sssssh," he said, in a soft, caressing voice, just above a whisper. "Don't fret. Everything is going to be all right."

Erin stared at him with wild eyes. "Emily is dead!" she screamed. "Our child is dead. How can everything be all right?"

"You must trust me," Harry said. "Please, Erin!"

He glanced at Mrs Martin who turned quickly and left the room once more.

Erin clung to her husband as the tears poured down her face. He stroked her hair till at last the sobbing eased and the well of grief was exhausted. Slowly, she wiped her eyes.

"What are we going to do?" she asked.

"It's all taken care of."

"Where is she?"

"At the hospital."

"I want to see her."

"You can't, Erin. No one can see her till they've carried out the autopsy. They have to find out what happened."

"I *want* to see her."

"Later, Erin. Not now. The police will be coming to talk to you"

"What for?"

"It's just routine. They want you to tell them what happened."

She sank back on the pillows and closed her eyes. The blackness was returning. She could feel it coming at her like a wave and, with it, the terrible feeling of emptiness and loss.

Mrs Martin came back with a tray containing tea and toast. Erin took a piece of toast and began to eat. It was strange that she was able to eat like this when her child was dead. She saw Harry watching and put down the cup and took his hand. It felt soft and warm. She gently squeezed his fingers.

"You have a terrible ordeal ahead of you," he said. "I want you to do something for me."

"Yes?"

He was taking a silver strip of tablets from his pocket. "These are tranquillisers. Dr Bellows gave them to me. He said they would help you to relax. Will you take them?"

She nodded.

Harry broke off two tablets and placed them in her palm. He watched as she washed them down with tea.

"Everything is going to be all right?" she asked. "You said that?"

"Yes," Harry said. "Everything is going to be all right."

When she had finished eating, Mrs Martin cleared away the tea things and assisted her into the bathroom. At first, her steps were shaky but then she gained confidence and walked with a more steady tread. Mrs Martin filled the tub and Erin lowered herself in and began to soap her body. The bath was warm and comforting. She lay back and let the water caress her. She could lie here forever, insulate herself against the world. But she knew she had to press on. There were things that must be done. She stood up and rinsed away the suds. Mrs Martin wrapped her in a towel and began to rub her dry. Then she sat down at her dressing-table and began to brush her hair.

It was amazing but she found these simple tasks consoling. As she brushed out her long chestnut hair, she began to consider what she should wear. It would have to be something dark. She was in mourning now. She had a pair of dark tights in a drawer somewhere and a navy business suit in the wardrobe and black shoes. That was the outfit she should wear.

She congratulated herself that she was able to figure these things out. She had never felt this way before. It was as if her mind was working on two separate levels. She was able to rationalise yet the terrible pain and emptiness lurked just below the surface ready to pounce.

As she finished dressing, Harry came in and sat down beside her. He too had got changed and shaved and now he wore a dark suit and tie.

"The gardaí have arrived," he said. "They're downstairs."

The tranquillisers were working. Erin could feel the

wall of fear and depression being pushed back and in its place there was calmness like a balm being applied to a wound.

She gave her statement in the drawing-room. Harry went with her. The police were apologetic and kept their questions to a minimum. When they were finished, the young woman constable placed her hand on Erin's wrist and told her how sorry she was.

Erin nodded. It was just routine. They would go away and type up her statement and that would be their day's work done.

Soon after, her family arrived. Harry had arranged for them to stay at Belvedere so she would have them close.

As soon as she appeared, her mother came quickly forward to embrace her.

"Oh, Erin!" she said, holding her close. "I don't know what to say. My heart is breaking. That poor little mite!"

But Erin felt strangely calm. It was as if she was standing apart from everything and observing.

"She's in heaven," she said. "That's where babies go when they die."

Mrs O'Neill looked at her. "Yes, that's exactly where she is. And right now she's asking God to give us the strength to survive. Try to see it like that and it will be easier."

Her father took her in his arms and then her sister. Anne held Erin for a long time and stared into her face.

"I'm so sorry," she said. "I know it's hard but you must try to accept it. Try to think of the future."

"I will," Erin said.

"You know we will always be here for you. You have lots of friends who will support you. You have your husband who loves you. You'll get over this, Erin, and things will get better. You must believe that."

Erin blinked and nodded her head. She kissed her sister.

"Thank you for coming," she said.

Around lunch-time, the hospital rang to say their examination was finished and they were ready to release the body for burial. Their analysis concurred with Dr Bellows'. Emily had died of Sudden Infant Death Syndrome.

Charlie and Tim had taken care of the arrangements. The local priest, Fr McCarthy, agreed to conduct the service at the hospital chapel with the funeral immediately afterwards. He was the priest who had married them.

"Will I be allowed to see her?" Erin asked when they were alone again in the upstairs flat.

"Yes."

Her eyes slowly filled with tears. "It will be like burying part of myself," she said. "I don't think I will ever be the same again."

"We must be strong," Harry said. "We must bury her with dignity. Do you think you will be able for it?"

"Yes," she said.

"Will I give you another tranquilliser?"

She held out her hand and Harry placed a tablet in it, then poured a glass of water.

"There's one thing I want to do," Erin said.

She began to walk across the room towards the nursery.

"Don't!" Harry said.

But it was too late. Before he could stop her, she had pushed open the door.

The room was empty. The cot and playpen had been removed along with all the baby clothes and toys. Nothing remained to remind her of the child who had once slept in this room.

She turned to stare at him with a questioning look in her eyes.

"Why?" she asked.

Harry lowered his face. "We thought it was best."

In the afternoon, the weather changed. The bright sunshine that had marked the morning gave way to dull, cloudy overcast skies and the threat of rain. It compounded the feeling of gloom for everyone in the house. Erin dressed in a dark skirt and coat and thick woollen scarf. Harry had sent one of the staff into Malahide to buy black mantillas for the women. He gave one to Erin and she put it on.

When everyone was ready, he took her hand and led the party outside where the funeral cars were waiting. The O'Neills got into the back with Erin, and

Harry sat beside the driver. The Kavanaghs followed behind in separate cars.

The hospital was twenty minutes away. Erin's mind was dulled but still the waves of pain kept trying to break through. She steeled herself for the ordeal that lay ahead. One of the worst parts was coming now when she would have to look at the body of their dead child for the last time. The burial would be another when little Emily would be laid in the ground and the earth piled on top of her.

At last, the grey hospital building came into view through the swirling mist. They got out of the cars and made their way into the chapel. Fr McCarthy was waiting. He was a young priest, not much older than Harry. He welcomed them and offered kind words of sympathy. Then he walked with them to where the baby lay. He stood beside Erin and held her hand.

The undertakers had done a fine job. A little white coffin rested on a silver trestle, surrounded by a bank of lilies and a row of tiny candles. It reminded Erin of the decorations on a birthday cake. She bent her head to look at the dead body of her child.

Emily had been dressed in a little white gown. Her eyes were closed and her tiny hands crossed on her chest. To a casual observer, she might have been asleep. Erin gazed at the tiny body resting in the satin folds of the coffin like a doll in a crib. She looked at the soft contours of her little face, the gentle down of hair brushed carefully back from her broad forehead. This was her child. She had brought her into the world and now she was about to watch as she was confined to the dark earth.

She felt her resolve begin to crack. A sob choked in her throat and she forced it back. This was not a time to show emotion. If she broke down now, God knew what would happen at the graveside. She willed herself to be strong and see it through. And miraculously, the strength came. She bent down and kissed the cold forehead of her child then turned to her mother. Mrs O'Neill, who could restrain herself no longer, broke down in tears. Anne put an arm around her shoulder and led her sobbing to a pew.

Harry remained. He stood looking at the little body, then he too kissed the child and walked back to where Erin was sitting in the front row. One by one, the other mourners filed past the open casket. When it came to her turn, Mrs Kavanagh stared into the coffin with a strange intensity in her eyes. She stood motionless for a while. Then she carefully reached out her hand and gently touched the baby's face. She turned away and walked to her seat without glancing at anyone.

Fr McCarthy rose to conduct the service. He spoke about the love that Jesus had for children and quoted several passages from the scriptures. He said it was a terrible thing for a parent to bury a child. It went against the natural order. But sometimes things happened that were difficult to understand. God's ways were not our ways. It was through accepting these difficulties as part of a larger plan that we could achieve true peace of mind. The death of little Emily was such an event. It was a hard blow for Erin and Harry and their families and he prayed that in time they would be reconciled to it.

As the priest continued to speak, Erin could hear people begin to sob. She clutched Harry's hand and felt the warm pressure of his fingers as he held it tight. Then Fr McCarthy concluded the service and came and spoke to them again.

Now the undertaker's men were extinguishing the candles and preparing to leave. They gathered the flowers and took them outside to the hearse. One of the worst moments was approaching. Erin couldn't watch. She buried her face in her hands as the men quickly stepped forward and began to screw the wooden lid of the coffin into place.

Outside, the sky looked heavy and overcast. Erin's head reeled from the barrage of emotions that fought for possession of her brain. She knew she should feel distraught but all she could experience was this leaden dullness. The tranquillisers were doing their job, isolating her from her feelings. She turned and saw Mrs Kavanagh walking towards them. She stopped and Erin thought she was going to speak but she ignored her and spoke to Harry instead.

The two families seemed to have gathered in separate camps, the O'Neills in a huddle at one side of the driveway and the Kavanaghs on the other. Dr Bellows, who had also turned up, looked out of place as if unsure who he should be with. At last he approached Harry and Erin.

"How are you?" he asked, coming close to Erin and looking hard into her face.

She saw his lips move but her brain was fogged and she had difficulty understanding what he was saying.

"How are you coping?" He studied her closely as if he was examining her.

She looked at him with dazed eyes. So much was happening, so many people, and the terrible grief that was waiting to overwhelm her if she let her guard slip.

"I'm sorry I was so upset yesterday."

"That was only to be expected," Dr Bellows said. "I would have been more concerned if you had not shown some emotion. You were in shock. Anyone would be. But you feel a little better now?" He looked at her closely again.

"Yes."

"Those tranquillisers I gave you? You're taking them?"

She opened her mouth. She was having difficulty framing her words. For some reason her tongue would not co-operate with her thoughts. She felt Harry's strong hand on her arm.

"Yes," she said.

Dr Bellows nodded. "Come and see me again if you feel the need. Later when all this is over, you might become depressed. That often happens. If you do, I can give you something for it."

"Thank you."

He turned to Harry and said something that she couldn't hear. Then his voice seemed to grow louder.

"Dreadful tragedy," he said. "I offer my sincere condolences."

He shook hands with them both and walked off towards the Kavanaghs. Erin watched him go. Across the driveway, she saw her mother-in-law still watching her. She blames me, she thought. She thinks I'm responsible for Emily's death. They all do. In fact, I even blame myself.

Now the coffin was being carried from the church and loaded into the hearse. People began to disperse to the funeral cars. Fr McCarthy and an altar boy sat in the hearse with the driver as it began its slow progress away from the chapel. The other cars fell in behind.

The graveyard was about half an hour away. The whole way there, Erin had an image of Mrs Kavanagh's face with its cold, accusing stare. Only a few short days ago that face had been warm and friendly. Now it was filled with malice. But she had little time to ponder these thoughts. They had arrived at the gates of the graveyard and the hearse was stopping. They pulled into a parking space and they got out. Harry turned to embrace her.

"Are you ready for this?" he asked.

She nodded. Since that moment back in the chapel, she knew she could find the strength to see it through. This was for her dead baby. There must be no scenes. The funeral must be conducted with decorum.

"Okay, go down to the grave with the other women. We'll be there in a moment."

One of the undertaker's men led the way. The

graveyard was cold and damp and a swirling mist seemed to rise up off the earth. Above, the sky was dark and overcast and heavy clouds blotted the sun. Erin shivered in her overcoat and pulled her thick woollen scarf tighter around her throat. It was a dismal scene. Even the trees seemed to weep in sympathy, large, heavy beads of dew dripped slowly from their overhanging branches.

Beside her, Erin felt a hand reach out to enclose her own. She turned to look at her mother who stood by her side. Her face was pale and drawn beneath the brim of her black hat.

"Be strong," she whispered. "You must be strong."

Erin's eyes were drawn back to the gaping hole in the earth. The damp clay was piled to one side and now the sombre workmen leaned on their spades while they waited for the coffin to arrive. Soon her child would be lowered into this grave and the earth piled on top of her. She would never see her again. She felt an awful sadness overwhelm her. Her mother's arm went to her shoulder and drew her close, soothing her, whispering encouragement.

"Don't break," her mother said. "Be strong."

Now she could see the small procession make its way amongst the headstones. As it drew closer, she could see the priest in billowing vestments intoning prayers, the altar boy carrying a tall crucifix and then a small knot of men. In front, his face grim and worn, she saw her husband. He seemed to be weeping. In his hands he cradled the tiny white coffin.

The procession stopped when it came to the grave. The group of mourners formed a circle. Across from her, she could see her mother-in-law and the rest of her husband's family. Their faces were grim and downcast as they stared blankly into the dark hole prepared for the dead baby.

The priest had started to read from the black Bible in his hands. His solemn words floated out over the damp morning air. Ashes to ashes, dust to dust. Erin felt a shudder pass through her. Now the priest was splashing holy water on the coffin from a little silver bowl.

One of the workmen stepped forward. He took the coffin from her husband's hands and gently lowered it into the grave. Then another man scooped up a shovel of earth and held it out. Her husband took a handful of brown clay and slowly released it. Erin could hear the sound as it rattled on the coffin lid. Then it was her turn. She let the earth fall from her fingers and tumble into the grave. She fought back the tears. She felt the grief overwhelm her till she thought her heart would burst. She looked up and saw the clouds assembling, dark and brooding and filled with menace.

The workmen were busy again, their spades setting to work. The earth began to fall faster and faster into the grave, quickly smothering the tiny white box. There was a roll of thunder and the first drops of rain began to fall, splashing off the branches and splattering the clothes of the mourners.

Erin turned away. People were unfurling their umbrellas and moving to shelter. Across the grave, her mother-in-law was staring at her. Her eyes were grim and accusing. Erin saw her lips begin to move. She put her hands to her ears to blank the awful words.

"You killed her," she was saying. "How could you murder your own daughter?"

Chapter 23

It was several weeks before Erin was able to face the world. As the numbing tranquillisers were gradually withdrawn, the grief that had been patiently waiting seized its opportunity and she was enfolded in its warm, passionate embrace. For days she was so wracked by guilt and loss that she unable to leave her bed. She lay gazing at the ceiling or watching the sun's shadow as it slowly moved across the curtains and day melted into night.

She couldn't sleep. She could barely eat. She could do nothing but endlessly retrace the events of that terrible day and blame herself for what had happened. If only she hadn't left Emily alone, if only she had taken her with her, if she hadn't visited Larchfield at all but waited until later to bring the bags across to the new house. Back and forth she went in her tormented mind while she picked at every little thread of solace and it unravelled in her hands.

She was responsible and she deserved the awful remorse that now gnawed at her relentlessly day after day. She had left her defenceless child alone and unattended for death to claim her when she should have been there, guarding her, shielding her from harm as any mother would. No wonder everyone hated her, especially her mother-in-law. She had seen it in her eyes and heard it in her voice. What Erin had done was unforgivable. How could she ever face people again?

Meanwhile, Harry could do nothing but watch and grow increasingly distracted. He tried to reason with her. He told her the verdict of the autopsy, that Emily had died from Sudden Infant Death Syndrome as the hospital report stated. No one was to blame. It could have happened even if Erin had been in the house with the baby. She had to stop blaming herself for something that was not her fault.

He wanted to bring Dr Bellows to see her but Erin resisted. Bellows would only drug her again and she knew by now that drugs and sedatives were not the answer. They brought short-term relief. They simply blotted out her emotions but left the wound untreated. The only way to get over this grief was to face it head on and work her way through.

By the end of the second week, she was exhausted. She looked pale and haggard and twice her age.

"I'm worried sick about you," Harry confessed one evening as he sat by her bedside. "We all are. You've got to snap out of this, Erin. You're going to make yourself seriously ill."

She looked at her husband. She loved him. He had always been kind and considerate. He had his own grief to bear and now she was adding to his pain.

"I can't," she said. "Everywhere I look, there is a grey wall surrounding me."

"Break through it."

"How?"

"By getting up and living your life again. By engaging with the world instead of withdrawing like this. I've got a suggestion."

"Yes?"

"Come away with me. We'll go on a cruise. The change of scenery will do you good. It will give us a chance to be alone together."

She didn't want to go. But she had to do something. Maybe it would work. Besides, it would give her the opportunity to escape from this dreadful house with all its terrible memories. She turned her face to her husband. He was pleading with her.

"Please," he asked.

She sighed. A cruise could not be any worse than lying here in this bed all day, staring at the ceiling.

"Okay," she said.

As soon as they left Southampton, the weather suddenly improved and the sun came out. The passengers on the cruise ship *SS Montpelier* took to sitting in the deckchairs after breakfast and enjoying the air while they relaxed and watched the sea roll by. This was what they had paid hard cash for and they were determined to get their money's worth.

Harry persuaded Erin to join them. They found a couple of chairs in a quiet part of the deck and read their books till lunch-time. He had picked up a biography of a rugby star in the ship's library and Erin had found a novel – *Blackberry Wine* by Joanne Harris. She had seen the reviews and had wanted to read it but had never found the time until now.

She very quickly came to realise that the cruise had one big advantage she hadn't considered. No one knew them. She could face people without constantly being reminded of what had happened. She didn't have to endure the judgement of others that she had witnessed at the graveside or listen to embarrassed expressions of sympathy. She could be a different person. She could escape. And just possibly, the trip might provide the chance to leave her grief behind and pick up the rhythm of her life once more. But first there were some hurdles to cross.

From the first moment they set foot on the ship, they had been wrapped in a warm, cosseting blanket. A young man in smart naval uniform stepped forward and introduced himself as Carshaw and announced that he was to be their steward for the trip. He carried their luggage to their suite – a large, bright cabin with a double bed, bathroom, wardrobes, writing desk and views of the sea from a large porthole window.

Carshaw, who didn't supply any first name, offered to unpack for them and when they declined, asked if he could get them anything to drink before dinner.

They ordered gin and tonics and five minutes later he was back with two glasses on a silver tray.

Before he left them, he explained the drill. He would be on hand to serve them at any time, day or night. He would wake them in the morning at eight o'clock with coffee or tea unless they preferred to sleep on and order breakfast in their suite. If they required tickets for any of the on-shore tours, he would arrange them. If they needed clothes laundered, he would do that too. If there was any comfort they required, it was Carshaw's role to supply it. The steward gave them his mobile phone number and departed.

Harry turned to Erin and took her in his arms.

"Do you like it?"

"It's beautiful. You've been so good to me, Harry. I'll never be able to thank you."

"You don't have to thank me. I want you to be happy, Erin. Now promise me you'll try to enjoy this trip."

"I promise."

He smiled. "I've never had a personal manservant before, have you?"

"No," she replied, "but I think I could get used to it."

"Carshaw," he mused. "Odd name, sounds like something out of *The Forsyte Saga*."

On the first evening, they had dinner together in a quiet part of the dining-room and afterwards went out on deck and watched the lights of the ships passing on the vast sea. The cruise was to take them right around the Mediterranean to Gibraltar, Valencia, Barcelona, Nice, Naples and finally Palma, Majorca before returning to Southampton. They had two weeks to unwind and find their bearings again.

On the second evening they were invited to dinner at the captain's table. There were to be seven of them and it was a black-tie affair which meant dressing up. This was the first major test for Erin and she was nervous.

"I'm not sure I can face it," she said.

"Nonsense."

"I won't know anybody. What am I going to say?"

"What you would say at any dinner party. You just make small talk."

"Couldn't we pretend that I'm not feeling well?"

"We have to go, Erin. It's an honour to be asked."

He sat down beside her on the bed.

"Look, darling, we've talked about this. You agreed that you can't hide away forever. At some stage you've got to get involved with the world again."

"What if these people turn out to be bores?"

"That could happen anywhere."

"But you don't have to put up with them for two whole weeks."

But she needn't have worried. Besides the captain, a tall distinguished-looking man called Brown, the other guests were a young couple named McKenzie who were on their honeymoon and a retired stockbroker and his wife from Kingston-on-Thames whose name was Benson.

The meal was superb and even Erin's poor appetite was tempted by the succession of splendid dishes that were placed before them. And the guests turned out to be interesting company and not the bores she had feared. As the meal progressed, she felt herself relax as Captain Brown regaled them with stories about his twenty years' experience at sea.

When it was over, they were invited to join the other couples at a little cocktail bar where a pianist played soothing melodies and they continued the earlier conversation. The Bensons had been on several cruises and were able to pass on useful information and Harry picked up some market tips from the former broker. It was after one o'clock when they finally retired to bed.

Back in their suite, they found that the bedcovers had been turned down, some expensive chocolates had been placed on their pillows and a vase of fresh flowers left on the writing-table.

Harry turned to her. "That wasn't so bad now, was it?"

"No," she admitted.

"Do you think you could try it again tomorrow evening?"

"Yes."

In the morning, they woke on the high seas, the sun streaming into the room and the Bay of Biscay rolling past their window. Carshaw had left a pot of coffee and some biscuits on the table along with a

271

programme of events for the day. These included classes in ballroom dancing, aerobics, flower arranging, still-life painting, clay-pigeon shooting, and bridge. They studied the programme in bed while they drank their coffee.

Every hour of the day seemed to have been catered for. Besides these activities, there was the gym, four swimming pools, a cinema, theatre, casino and the ship's ten bars. The staff of the SS Montpelier were clearly determined that none of their passengers should ever feel time on their hands.

They fell into a comfortable routine. They spent their days reading on the deck and their evenings dining and chatting in the bar. Every couple of days the ship docked in a new port and they went ashore with the other passengers to visit the tourist sights. But even though Erin was slowly coming out of her shell, she still had moments when the blackness came back.

One night, she woke in a distressed state with her nightdress sticking to her skin with sweat. She sat up in bed and stared at the unfamiliar room as the vision that had frightened her slowly receded from her mind. She had been back again in the rain-swept graveyard as Emily's coffin was lowered into the ground and her mother-in-law stared at her with those cold, accusing eyes.

Roused from sleep, Harry sat up and put his arms around her.

"What's the matter, Erin?"

"Nothing, It was just a dream. Go back to sleep."

"Can I do anything for you?"

"Just hold me," she said. "Cuddle close to me."
She took his hand and placed it on her breast. "I love
you," she said.

"I love you too."

"Don't ever leave me, no matter what happens."

She drifted back to sleep and when she woke the
next morning, the sun was shining and they were in
Barcelona. Yet the nightmare wasn't forgotten nor the
heavy weight of guilt that hung over her like a yoke.
But these moments gradually receded and she began to
have more good days than bad. Slowly, she felt herself
getting better. The depression began to lift with each
passing day and the distractions that it brought. One
night as they prepared for bed, she confessed to Harry
that she was glad she had come. She could feel the
holiday doing her good.

He coaxed her to the swimming pool and the
sundeck where she stretched out each morning with
the other sunworshippers and developed her tan. One
evening at dinner, a remark from Mrs McKenzie
brought back a forgotten feeling. She had decided to
wear a little pale yellow satin cocktail dress. As she sat
down, the other woman turned to her.

"You look fabulous. I hadn't noticed your tan
before. And that beautiful dress sets it off perfectly."

Erin found herself smiling. She hadn't smiled in a
long time.

"I've been working on it," she confessed. "I
sunbathe on deck most days."

"I must follow your example," Mrs McKenzie said, holding out her pale white arm. "Look at me. I'm as white as a sheet."

But time was passing and the cruise was coming to an end. In quick succession, the ship put in at Nice, Naples and Palma and then it was time to steam back again to Southampton where they would fly back to Dublin. As the ship neared its final destination, Erin thought of what awaited them when they got back to Belvedere.

She hated the idea of returning to the old house. And now there was the added strain of facing Mrs Kavanagh once more in the knowledge that she held her responsible for little Emily's death. She knew she couldn't face it. If she was to recover fully from the tragedy, she would have to make a fresh start. She made up her mind to move immediately to Larchfield.

One evening as they were passing through the straits of Gibraltar, Harry remarked on how well she looked.

"You've got your complexion back and your appetite has returned. You know, there were times when I began to wonder if you would ever pull through."

She squeezed his hand. "I've got something to ask you."

"Go ahead."

"When we get home, can we move into Larchfield straight away?"

His response surprised her.

"Straight away? Do you mean the day we return?"

"Please, Harry."

"Is that a good idea?"

"Why not?"

"Are you ready to be on your own all day? At Belvedere, you'll have people to look after you."

"Of course, I'm ready. It's what I want, Harry. It's what I need."

"We'll be tired when we get back and the new house will need to be aired. Could you not wait for a few days?"

"No. I don't want to spend another night in Belvedere."

"Why?"

"Because our new house is waiting and I'm dying to get into it."

"There's another reason, Erin, that you're not telling me about, isn't there?"

She lowered her head. "You mustn't breathe a word of this. Promise me."

"I promise."

"I know this sounds crazy but your mother blames me for what happened and I dread the thought of meeting her again."

He put his arm around her and held her close. "Oh, Erin, don't be foolish. My mother was upset like we all were. Of course, she doesn't blame you."

"She does, Harry. I know. I can tell by the way she looks at me."

He stared at her, a reflective look on his face.

"All right," he said. "If it makes you happy, we'll move into the new house straight away."

Chapter 24

But Erin had reckoned without the vagaries of the weather. When they finally arrived back at Southampton, they found the flight to Dublin had been cancelled because of fog. Harry was fuming. He was counting on getting back home as soon as possible and starting work again. His father would be waiting for him to return, struggling alone without his assistance.

After some negotiation, he managed to secure seats on a flight to Manchester and onwards to Dublin. But there was a four-hour delay. By the time they arrived at Dublin airport, it was after midnight and it was half past one when Harry's car eventually made its way up the drive to Belvedere.

He had phoned ahead and some members of staff were waiting to greet them. But Erin was relieved to find that the family had gone to bed.

He switched off the engine and turned to her.

"I'm sorry, Erin. But there's no way I'm going to start moving to Larchfield at this late hour. We'll have to sleep here tonight."

He saw the look of disappointment in her eyes.

"You promised me," she said.

"I know I did. But I wasn't counting on all these hold-ups. I'm utterly exhausted and I'm sure you are too. You can't really expect us to move tonight."

"I don't see why not. I'm prepared to put up with the disruption if you are."

He shook his head. "Erin, you don't get it, do you? If we insist on moving house at two o'clock in the morning, everyone will be convinced we've gone crazy. And my parents will be insulted."

He opened the car door and began to take their suitcases out of the boot.

"C'mon," he said. "It's only for one night. We'll sleep in Larchfield tomorrow night."

Reluctantly, she got out. One of the staff came hurrying down the steps and took hold of their cases. Erin followed him sullenly into the silent house.

Despite her dislike of the place, she slept soundly under Belvedere's roof. She wakened at 8.30 a.m. as Harry was coming out of the shower.

"You must have been very tired," he said, bending down to kiss her. "You fell asleep the moment your head hit the pillow. I'm glad. Now you look really refreshed."

"Yes," she agreed.

"I've got a meeting with Dad at nine o'clock. We'll move our stuff to Larchfield as soon as I'm free. Can you wait that long?"

She smiled. "I've waited so long I suppose a few more hours won't hurt."

"This afternoon," he said. "We'll be in Larchfield in time for dinner."

His words reassured her. She went into the bathroom and when she emerged, Harry had made coffee and toast.

"Give your dad my regards," she said as he set off to meet his father.

She was excited at the prospect of escaping from Belvedere at last. It was amazing the hold the house had managed to exert on her ever since she first came to live here. It was as if it had taken a grip on her and didn't want to let go. But she had to be aware that this was Harry's home, where his family lived and where he had been reared. She had to be careful not to offend him.

After breakfast, she began to pack. A lot of their belongings had already been moved to Larchfield. She gathered the remaining stuff and put it into boxes and bags for the afternoon's trip. She was just finishing when the phone began to ring.

It was Harry.

"I'm coming to talk to you. Something has come up."

Immediately, she felt herself tense. This did not sound good.

Harry arrived looking sheepish.

"I have to go London," he said with a sigh.

"When?"

"Right away."

She felt her heart sink. "Oh, Harry!"

"I'm sorry," he said. "This is a major deal my father has been working on with some developers. He wants me to go over and make sure everything is in order."

"How long will you be gone?"

A frown clouded his face. "Ten days."

"They can't do this to you! You've just got back and –"

"Erin, this is something I have to do. My father would have undertaken it himself six months ago. It's the reason he got his heart attack. He's too old for this sort of stuff. But it has to be done. I'm a senior director of the company and I can't shirk my responsibility."

She bit her lip. "You're right. I'm sorry. I apologise. But I was so looking forward to moving into the house with you. Now I'll just have to do it on my own."

But he was shaking his head. "No, Erin. You're not going anywhere. I want you to stay here at Belvedere till I return."

She opened her mouth to protest but he silenced her.

"I want you here where there are people around you. I can't have you in the new house all on your own. You're not ready for it yet. I forbid it."

"Forbid it?" she said, her anger flaring. "I can't believe you're saying this. You can't hold me here. You know how desperately I want to move."

He took a firm grip of her arm and stared into her face. "Erin, listen to me. Have you forgotten how bad you were when you found Emily dead? You were hysterical. You were incoherent. I've never seen anyone like that before. I was worried sick about you and so was everyone else. That's why Dr Bellows knocked you out. He said you were suffering from shock. Do you remember the following days? It was a nightmare. I had to give you tranquillisers to get you through. You were like a zombie. I'm not blaming you. What you did was a natural reaction to shock. But it was scary stuff, Erin."

"I'm okay now," she said. "You said yourself that I was looking well. I've stopped taking the pills. Do I look like someone who's about to do something crazy?"

"No," he admitted. "But Dr Bellows had a conversation with you outside the chapel on the day of the funeral. He told you that people often get depressed after something like that. He told you to come and see him. Do you remember?"

"But I'm not depressed, Harry. I'm learning to come to terms with what happened. The cruise was a big help. It got me out of my gloom and now I'm beginning to cope with the loss. You're not seriously suggesting that I can't be left on my own?"

"Of course not, but I've just been discussing this

with Dad. He thinks you should stay here till I get back."

"So they can keep an eye on me?"

"No, Erin. So they can help you if you need it."

She sank down on a chair and buried her head in her hands. "Harry, I don't think you realise how uncomfortable I feel in this house. I don't want to hurt your feelings but the hostility is palpable."

"It's your imagination, Erin."

"No, it's real. Your mother hasn't spoken to me since Emily died. Not one single word. Your sister hasn't spoken to me."

He shook his head. "That's simply not true."

"It is. Can't you see that they blame me for what happened?"

He stood over her. "Erin, I won't continue this argument with you. I want you to stay here. I'll be in constant contact with you. It's only for ten lousy days and then we'll finally be able to move."

She didn't reply.

He walked to the door, then turned once more before he left.

"I could never forgive myself if anything happened to you."

She heard his footsteps retreating down the stairs as she stood gazing out over the lawns. She had never seen her husband in this mood before. He sounded frightened. It was slowly sinking in that he believed she might do something terrible if she was left alone.

She paced the floor. This setback was just one in a

series of bizarre events that had conspired to keep her here. She had never wanted to come to Belvedere in the first place and now the house didn't want to let her go. Well, she would go anyway, without her husband. She would defy him, get into the car and drive across to Larchfield in spite of his instructions.

Just then, she heard the sound of a car engine starting up. She ran to the window in time to see Harry's BMW drive away from the house. He had taken the car. She had no means of transport. She was stuck here whether she liked it or not. She would be alone for ten days until his return. She sank down on the settee.

How was she going to endure it?

She sat for a long time feeling a mood of anger slowly build up inside her. How dare Harry hold her prisoner here! How dare he treat her like a child who had to be constantly watched! And his family was worse. What did they expect her to do at Larchfield – burn it down?

She wasn't unhinged. She wasn't deranged. She had suffered a normal reaction to the shocking death of Baby Emily. Any woman in her situation would have behaved in exactly the same way. Dr Bellows had confirmed that. If there was anyone unhinged in this house it was Mrs Kavanagh with her mean, spiteful attitude and that accusing stare that told the world she held Erin responsible for the death of her own child.

It was outrageous and she wouldn't put up with it. She would ring for a cab and leave this house right away and let them try to stop her. She wasn't a prisoner here. She was an adult. She could do as she pleased.

She reached for the phone and heard a small voice in her head tell her to pause. If she defied Harry and left, it would cause him untold worry. He would probably have to abort the London trip and come back again. It would lead to all sorts of trouble. And he had more than enough to cope with. He was grieving too. And he had the burden of the family business to carry as well. Her desire to leave battled with her sense of duty. It was only for ten more days, a mere week and a half. Maybe she should just knuckle down and see it through.

Gradually, she felt her anger begin to cool. There were plenty of things to keep her busy. She could contact Ger Armstrong and ask for some work. She should ring her mother and tell her she was back. And she had unpacking to do. She swallowed down her disappointment and stirred herself. She picked up the phone again and rang her mum.

"Erin! So you're back. Did you have a nice time?"

"We had a fabulous time."

"Do you think it helped you?"

"Oh yes. I think it did me a power of good."

"Well I'm glad to hear that. How was the weather?"

"It was marvellous. There was rarely a cloud in the sky. I lay out in the sun and got a tan."

"And you weren't seasick?"

"It was a big ship, Mum – they don't rock. And like I said, the weather was fine. There were no storms or anything like that."

"And how is Harry?"

"He's gone to London on some business."

"So you're alone? You could come down here and stay with us if you liked. We'd love to have you."

"Thanks, Mum, but I think I'll be okay."

"Well, you know where we are if you need us. Take care of yourself, love."

She put down the phone feeling pleased. If things really did become unbearable at Belvedere, she had a bolthole to escape to. She could always return to her family in Mountclare. That thought cheered her up.

Next she rang Ger Armstrong. It was several weeks since she had been in touch with the office and he knew nothing about Emily. This wasn't going to be easy.

"Erin! Where the hell have you been? I was looking all over for you. I rang your home and they told me you had gone away."

"I'm sorry, Ger. Something terrible happened."

"What?"

"My baby died."

There was a shocked silence. Next moment her boss was mumbling embarrassed apologies.

"Oh my God, Erin, that's terrible. I'm really sorry. I don't know what to say."

"It was a Sudden Infant Death. That's what the autopsy found."

"I knew absolutely nothing about it. I'm so sorry. I really am."

"We didn't want publicity. You can understand."

"Of course, it must have been awful for you. I can't bear to think about it. How are you coping?"

"I'm getting over it. But it's tough."

"If there's anything I can do," he said.

"There is. You can give me some work."

"Are you sure, Erin? Under the circumstances…"

"No, really. I have to get busy again. It will be good for me. I need to be active."

"Okay, if it's what you want. Give me some time to think about it and I'll get back to you. If you've got any ideas of your own, give me a ring."

When she put down the phone, she was feeling better. Hearing those friendly voices gave her encouragement. She wasn't alone. There were people she could call on who would help her if things got too much for her. And Harry would be ringing her every day. The time would go quickly enough. Erin felt a calmer mood descend on her. She glanced from the window and saw that the sun was out and the fields looked glorious in the morning light. She made up her mind. She wouldn't sit here any longer. She would go for a walk while she thought of what she could write for Ger Armstrong.

She set off from the house at a brisk pace towards the woods. There were wild flowers in bloom along the path and she remembered as a little girl how she used to pick bunches of them at this time of year. She would do the same thing now. They would brighten up the flat. Within ten minutes, she had picked an armful. She was setting off again when suddenly she heard a voice hail her. She looked up and saw Tim.

"Ah, Erin, picking flowers. When did you get back?"

"Late last night. Our flight was cancelled so we were badly delayed."

"You had a pleasant time, I can tell. Look at your lovely suntan."

"We had a very nice time, thank you, and the weather was superb."

"And now you're back to dull reality." He stopped and looked directly into her face. "How are you feeling?"

"You've probably heard that Harry has gone to London?"

"Yes, I did. Looking into fresh business opportunities, I believe."

"And you know how much I was looking forward to moving into our new house now that it's finished."

He was nodding his head in sympathy. "So you have to wait and you don't like it one bit? It's a bummer, Erin."

"Precisely."

"Don't worry, I'm sure you'll find plenty to keep you occupied. And if you ever need someone to talk to, just give me a call."

He gave her a peck on the cheek and set off again.

Erin stared after him. She was glad she had met Tim. He was another cheerful face she could rely on if she felt down in the dumps. And he had one big advantage over the others. He was right here in Belvedere.

Her first day alone in Belvedere passed uneventfully. In the evening, Harry rang as promised. It was comforting to hear his voice. They chatted for half an hour. He seemed to be in good spirits. He had managed to set up a number of business meetings which he regarded as a major achievement since he didn't have his efficient secretary with him to make all the arrangements. But he was missing Erin dreadfully. How was she getting on, he asked?

She told him of the small details of her day, her talk with her mother and Ger Armstrong, the walk in the woods and her meeting with Tim. All this seemed to please him.

"You see, it isn't so bad after all."

"I'm trying to keep busy till you return."

"Well, if my business continues as well as today, I might be home sooner than I thought."

"That would be fantastic, Harry."

"And don't be worrying about my mother. I know she can be awkward sometimes but she has a heart of gold. And she likes you, Erin. She really does."

He rang off, promising to call her again tomorrow.

Soon after, Charlie Kavanagh called to see if she wanted to join the rest of the family for dinner. But Erin had already eaten and wasn't hungry so she declined. And so she passed the remainder of the evening, watching television and working on some ideas for feature work which she planned to present to her news editor the next day.

At eleven o'clock, she went to bed. But she couldn't sleep. Her mind kept drifting back to the evening's conversation with Harry. There was something he had said about his mother liking her and having a heart of gold. Was it possible for the two of them to have such divergent views about the same person? Was it possible she *was* imagining the hostility from Mrs Kavanagh?

She allowed the thought to play around in her head. During the funeral she had been distraught. Her thinking was confused. She was doped and much of what went on was now a blank. Perhaps she *had* misjudged Mrs Kavanagh. Perhaps she had mistaken some sign of the older woman's grief for something more sinister? Was she judging her mother-in-law unfairly?

But then she remembered that the funeral hadn't been the first time Caroline Kavanagh had behaved badly. She had ignored her for months after they came back from Las Vegas. It wasn't till Erin became pregnant that her attitude had changed and she had started cosying up to her. That much was real. She hadn't imagined that.

Her mother-in-law hadn't spoken to her since the baby's death and neither had Susan. Those were facts. Caroline had reverted to her old behaviour. She was ignoring her again, trying to freeze her out. And Erin knew why. Now that the baby was dead, she had no more need for her. Despite what Harry might say, this was *not* some figment of her imagination. Mrs Kavanagh hated her. She could feel it. And she blamed her for the baby's death.

There was one person she could talk to, someone she could rely on to tell her the truth – Tim. He didn't mind sharing family secrets with her. He had shared several already. She made up her mind. She would talk to him tomorrow and ask him what he thought. And with this decision made, Erin finally slipped off to sleep.

Chapter 25

But when the morning came, something occurred to divert her. She was just finishing breakfast when her phone rang and she heard Ger Armstrong on the line.

"I've got a job for you," he said.

"Great!"

"Something right up your street and you won't have far to travel. There's an American writer in town. A guy called Tom McClure. Ever hear of him?"

"Vaguely."

"He's quite big on the other side of the pond, new American realism or something like that. His publicist rang yesterday offering an interview. Are you interested?"

"Sure," Erin said.

"He's staying at the Grand Hotel in Malahide. You could nip down there and talk to him. Say a thousand words of your usual zippy prose. I'll arrange for photographs."

"Okay," Erin said. "Give me the details."

She wrote down the writer's room number and Ger promised to email some background material.

"If you could get the piece in by tomorrow, I'd be delighted."

"I'll start right away," Erin said and switched off the phone.

She rang the hotel, spoke to Tom McClure's publicist and arranged to interview him at midday. It was a fine sunny day so she didn't mind walking the short distance into Malahide. The exercise would do her good.

At a quarter to eleven she set off down the drive with her notebook and voice recorder in a bag slung across her shoulder. She was looking forward to resuming work and getting back into the swing of things again. In preparation, she had digested the material her boss had sent, mainly clippings of articles that had appeared in American magazines.

According to one piece, McClure was 'the vibrant voice of a new generation, challenging the certainties of the age'. She pictured an angry young man in denims and leather motorcycle jacket – a 2008 version of Bob Dylan, perhaps. But the reality was somewhat different.

The man who rose to meet her in the lounge of the hotel was in his mid-40s, slim and somewhat effete and dressed in a well-tailored white linen suit. His feet were clad in a pair of handmade leather brogues while his hair had recently been worked on by an expensive stylist. He took her hand and pressed it gently while his soft blue eyes smiled intently into hers.

"I'm pleased to meet you, Miss O'Neill. Can I get you something to drink?"

"Coffee would be fine," Erin said and a pot of coffee was immediately ordered from the waiter.

Tom McClure's publicist sat beside him on the couch. She was an eager, bustling young woman dressed in a severe skirt and blouse who was clearly intent on protecting her client.

"Before we begin," the publicist said in a rapid New York accent, "Tom's divorce is not a subject for discussion, nor is his current romantic situation. Is that clear?"

She stared at Erin with eyes that brooked no argument.

So it's going to be one of those interviews, Erin thought as she took out her voice recorder and switched it on – tightly controlled and bland to boring.

"Can I start by asking for your impressions of Ireland?" she began.

This was an easy one for Tom. He relaxed into the comfortable settee and placed one long leg over the other.

"Well, Ireland is a must for any aspiring writer. I mean, the Irish take writing seriously. They value it. In Ireland, writers and poets are regarded as important members of society – the conscience of the race, you could almost say. Wasn't it James Joyce who used that very phrase himself and Joyce is rightly admired as a literary giant of the 20th century?"

The publicist was smiling. This was good safe stuff that was sure to please Irish readers and keep her client out of controversy.

McClure continued to talk about his admiration for Irish writers such as Seamus Heaney and Maeve Binchy and his intention to visit the grave of WB Yeats in Sligo. Tom McClure could certainly talk. At this rate she was not going to be short of material.

They moved on to the current state of American literature and politics and, at this stage, the publicist began to get alarmed. She shifted uneasily on the couch.

"Tom doesn't have any political opinions," she intervened. "He tries to remain above politics."

"Oh?" Erin said. If this was true then Tom McClure was the first writer she had ever met who didn't have political views.

"He has general opinions but not specific party affiliations," the publicist clarified with a tight smile.

"What about the state of American publishing?" Erin asked. "Would you say it is healthy? Do many people continue to read books?"

"Not as many as we would like," McClure replied but before he could continue, the publicist interrupted once again.

"We would like to point out that Tom's books have always sold extremely well. He was sixteen weeks in the *New York Times* bestsellers list last year."

The writer smiled and preened himself and Erin was tempted to ask if she should stop talking to Tom McClure altogether and interview the publicist instead. But she pressed on.

"When did you decide to become a writer?" she asked.

This was another easy question which gave McClure the opportunity to talk about his boyhood growing up in a small town in New Jersey. His family was so poor that they couldn't afford a television and his only entertainment was to be found on the shelves of the town library.

"That's where I discovered the American classics, writers like Hawthorne, Melville and Mark Twain. They fired my imagination. I think I was about eight years old when I made the momentous decision to become a writer."

He closed his eyes and a serene smile came over his face. He seemed to be enjoying himself. He looked as if he could talk for hours about this part of his career but the eager publicist was getting uneasy once more. She glanced at her watch and reminded him that he was due for another interview at a local radio station at two.

"Tom has a few minutes left," she said. "Would you care to ask him about his latest novel?"

Erin knew this was the whole point of the exercise. Tom McClure was here to sell his new book and it would be churlish not to allude to it so she listened for another five minutes while he told her that the work, which was called *The Troubled Heart,* was a veiled critique of corporate America and how it impacted on the individual. Then he presented her with a copy and signed it and the interview was at an end. As she was leaving, the photographer arrived to take the pictures.

Erin left the hotel and wandered down along the estuary. It had turned into a glorious day and the sun sparkled off the still water like burnished silver. From the marina, there came the sound of tinkling bells as the yachts rolled and tossed in the gentle swell. It had been an undemanding interview and would be easy to write. Tom McClure had given her plenty of good, if uncontroversial, quotes and she felt a buzz of achievement about her morning's work.

It was good to be working again. She needed this therapy to keep her mind away from Emily. She missed the child desperately and her thoughts kept returning to small memories that filled her heart with regret. Now she would never see her daughter grow up, take her first teetering steps, say her first words, go to school. There was so much that died with Emily and was buried in that cold, windswept grave. Some day she knew she would have to face it and accept it. But right now, she needed distraction and work provided it.

It was also good to get away from the house and out into the world again. She had come to associate Belvedere with sadness and loss. But when Harry returned from London, they would finally make the move to their new home and start afresh. They would settle down and begin their life anew. They would have more children. They would finally put the past behind them and rebuild. And they would be happy she knew this instinctively.

She made her way by the water's edge, watching the swans make their graceful progress along the estuary. The interview was beginning to take shape in her head. She had the opening sentence already framed and she knew which quotes she would use. Eventually, she left the shore and took a road that led inland, till at last she saw the tall trees and the gates of Belvedere come into view. At once, her bright spirits dissolved and a morbid mood settled over her like a cloud.

As she was climbing the steps to the front door, she ran into her brother-in-law.

"Ah, Tim," she said, "I was meaning to call you. Are you free for a moment?"

"Sure."

"Would you care to pop up to the flat? There's something I want to ask you."

He beamed. "That would be a pleasure, Erin."

Tim followed her up the stairs.

Inside the flat, she carefully deposited her bag with its precious notes and recorder on the table and took off her jacket.

"Would you like a cup of tea? I'm just about to put on the kettle."

"Well, in that case I'll join you," he said, seating himself at the window and gazing out over the lawns.

"I forgot to ask you yesterday how the novel is coming on," Erin said.

A frown passed over his face. "They're very keen to publish it but first they want me to make some changes."

"You should listen to them," Erin said. "These people are professionals. I've often found my work has improved enormously after I have taken constructive criticism."

"I hate editors," he growled. "They're always interfering."

"Well, that's their job."

"Just give them a blue pencil and they feel obliged to start cutting and changing. I'm sure if Shakespeare was alive today some of them would want him to rewrite Hamlet and give it a happy ending."

Erin brought in the tray with the tea things and biscuits.

"You should look on the bright side," she said. "You've found someone who wants to publish your work. There are plenty of aspiring writers who would die for that."

She poured the tea and passed him a cup.

"I want to ask your advice," she began. "You're the only one I can trust around here now that Harry has gone to London."

Tim immediately sat forward and gave her his full attention.

"Fire away," he said.

"But first, I want to stress that this is strictly confidential."

This obviously served to whet his appetite.

"Everything that passes between us is confidential, Erin. My lips are sealed."

"Since little Emily died, I've noticed a distinct chill towards me," she went on. "It almost amounts to hostility. Do you know that your sister and mother have not spoken a single word to me since her death? Don't you think that is odd?"

"Of course, it's odd. But we're an odd family."

"At the funeral your mother gave me such a look of hatred that I was convinced she blamed me for the child's death." She didn't mention the fact that she thought she saw Caroline Kavanagh actually mouth the words.

"And you were right," Tim said. "She *does* blame you. I've heard her say so with my own ears. She said if you hadn't left the baby alone it wouldn't have happened."

His words served to confirm her worst fears.

"But that is so irrational!" she protested. "Emily suffered from Sudden Infant Death Syndrome. How could I possibly have prevented it? I couldn't stand over her every minute of the day."

"No, you couldn't. But you aren't dealing with rational people. Now let *me* tell *you* something confidential."

He put down his teacup and took her hand.

"My sister Susan is in a very strange marriage. I don't think there is very much love between herself and Toby. I'm not even sure if they sleep in the same bed."

"Really?"

"Yes. It's none of my business but I've sometimes doubted if he's interested in women at all. But that's by the by. Susan has been desperate for a child ever since she got married but no child came along. Some of it is probably normal maternal instinct. But a big part has to do with wanting to please my mother – to provide a child to replace the one she lost. And she hasn't been able to do it. And then you come along and within months you are pregnant. Now put yourself in her shoes and ask a simple question. How would you feel?"

This was the same line of argument she had heard from Harry and now it was being reinforced by Tim.

"My mother is absolutely devastated by the death of Emily. All her hopes have been dashed for a second time. She has taken this tragedy very hard. And sadly, you are the one she blames."

"So this hostility is not my imagination?"

Tim was vigorously shaking his head. "No, Erin. Unfortunately it's not."

Chapter 26

So she wasn't imagining the hostility. It was real. Tim had confirmed it. In a strange way, the news came as a relief to her. Not because she welcomed the hostility. She wished with all her heart that she and Caroline Kavanagh could get along well together. But until she spoke to Tim, she had begun to doubt the evidence of her own senses. She had begun to wonder if the shock of little Emily's death had unhinged her brain and caused her mind to play tricks on her. Now she knew for certain this was not true.

But the news only increased her feeling of unease. She was alone in this great house with at least one person who was hostile to her. It was going to make her stay here extremely uncomfortable and possibly even dangerous. What if Mrs Kavanagh's resentment drove her to some desperate act of harm? She debated again if she should disobey her husband and move to Larchfield despite him. She might even be able to enlist the help of Tim. He had access to a car and could help her.

As the day wore on, these thoughts continued to grow and with them came an increasing sense of fear. Why wait any longer? She should go now.

By the time six o'clock arrived she had worked herself into a state of agitation. She was about to start packing a bag when the phone rang.

It was Harry.

"Thank God you called," she said, clutching the phone tightly to her ear. "I'm missing you terribly."

"And I'm missing *you*. I've had a hell of a day. I've had six business meetings since breakfast. But the good news is: I'm making substantial progress. But enough about my problems, how are you?"

"I want to move," she blurted out.

"What?"

Her pent-up unhappiness came pouring out in a torrent. "I can't stay here any longer, Harry. I hate this place. I feel afraid. I want to move immediately to Larchfield."

"Afraid, what are you afraid of?" He sounded shocked.

"I don't know. I just feel so isolated and vulnerable. Why can't I move to Larchfield?"

"Erin, please don't start this. We agreed we would move when I got back. Why are you bringing it up all over again?"

"Because I'm more than ever convinced that your mother hates me. So does your sister. I know they blame me for what happened to Emily. I feel like I'm a prisoner here. I can't breathe."

"Has something happened? Has someone said something to you?"

"No," she said quickly.

She heard him give a weary sigh.

"Nobody hates you, Erin. You're imagining this. It's all in your head."

This only made her furious. Why wouldn't he believe her? Why wouldn't he stop defending them and take her side for once?

"You've turned against me," she said, bitterly.

"That's outrageous. I haven't turned against you. I love you, Erin. I love you more than anything in the world."

"If you loved me, you'd allow me to leave. Tim could drive me over. I'd feel much safer in our new house. Please, Harry, don't force me to do something I don't want to do."

"Erin, you're beginning to worry me. Do you want me to ring my father and arrange for Mrs Martin to spend the night with you? Would that make you feel any better?"

"No," she said. "I don't need that."

"Then please let me think this over. I've just told you I've had a difficult day. I'm about to meet some people for dinner. Promise me you'll do nothing until we talk again tomorrow?"

Her hand tightened on the phone so hard that she saw her fingers go white.

"All right." she said, at last. "Just till tomorrow and then I'm going whether you agree or not."

"I'll call in the morning. If anything happens to upset you, ring me at once."

She felt tears of frustration begin to course down her cheeks. "I'm sorry," she said. "I didn't mean to alarm you."

"Forget it," he said. "We're both going through a very stressful time. Just try to relax, Erin. Nothing's going to happen to you."

Later, she suffered a pang of remorse for the way she had behaved. Harry was alone in London carrying out work for the company – work from which they would all ultimately benefit. Why add to his problems? So Caroline Kavanagh didn't like her. But what did she expect was going to happen? That her mother-in-law would break into her room in the middle of the night like a mad axe-woman out of some horror movie?

She was exaggerating the situation out of all proportion. And just now she had behaved like a spoiled drama queen. She should feel ashamed of herself.

But the worry and the fear wouldn't go away. And as the evening settled in, she felt her isolation grow and her anxiety increase. In an effort to relieve her mind, she opened her laptop and began to work on the interview with Tom McClure.

She poured all her energy into the work, losing herself in the article, forgetting her present worries in her determination to finish the interview and send it to Ger Armstrong that night. It was after one when she finally sat back from her desk and read over what she had written. Despite the bland material, the article she had written was good. It was *very* good. It was one of the best things she had ever written. She pressed the SEND key and watched the article disappear from her screen.

She felt exhausted. She made a cup of hot chocolate and sat at the window gazing out at the lawns in front of the house, sparkling ghostly in the moonlight. She tried to empty her mind of all thoughts to prepare herself for sleep. Eventually, she undressed and got into bed but not before making sure that the door was securely locked and bolted and the chain was in place.

The following morning when she woke, the house was silent. She glanced at the bedside clock. It was ten o'clock. She had slept for almost nine hours. She got up and showered and went into the kitchen to make some breakfast. She had just filled the kettle when she heard a gentle knocking on the door. She opened it and found Charlie Kavanagh standing on the landing outside.

"Can I come in?" he asked.

"Of course," Erin said and stood back from the door.

Her father-in-law slowly entered the room and sat down. There was a look of concern etched on his face.

"Have you got a moment to talk?" he asked.

"Sure," she replied. "I'm making some coffee. "Would you like some?"

"Okay."

She went back to the kitchen and returned with two mugs.

"Harry rang me this morning," Charlie began when she was sitting down.

"Yes. I was speaking to him last night."

He stared at her and creased his lips. "He's very worried about you, Erin. He says you don't feel happy here in Belvedere. You want to move to your new house?"

"Yes. The house is ready. We should have been in it long ago. We were preparing to move when Emily died."

"You can't move," her father-in-law said, firmly.

"What?" she said, looking up sharply.

"I said you can't move."

"Why not?"

"Because you're not well."

Erin became indignant. "There's nothing wrong with me. I'm perfectly well."

Her father-in-law laid a gentle hand on her shoulder. "You're not, Erin. Don't be offended. You're suffering from post-traumatic stress. Sometimes the victim is the last person to know. But others can see it. It's not unusual. You've been through a shocking experience. The death of the baby has affected us all. It would be criminal negligence to allow you to go to that house on your own right now. I can't allow it till Harry comes back."

Her face went pale. Her father-in-law had been one of those she had counted on to support her. Now he too had gone over to her enemies.

"There is *nothing* wrong with me," she insisted. "I should know my own mind. You're trying to say I'm deranged."

"Not deranged, Erin. But ill. Sometimes the reaction is delayed. It might take some time to recover. We all feel the best thing is for you to stay here with us."

"I am *not* ill." She noticed that her voice was rising and now she was shouting. Charlie Kavanagh sat calmly watching her. She lowered her tone again.

"I'm sorry," she said. "I shouldn't get angry. I just feel so annoyed with everyone. Why won't you listen to me?"

"You told him you feel like a prisoner here?"

"I do."

"You're not a prisoner. You're free to come and go as you please. You went into Malahide yesterday. Did anyone try to stop you?"

"That was different. That's not what I mean."

"You said my wife hates you, that she blames you for the death of the child?"

"She *does* hate me," Erin said. "I'm not stupid. I know the evidence of my own eyes."

"She cares very much for you, Erin. She's terribly upset about what has happened. She loved the baby, you know that. Emily was her first grandchild. It's been a terrible blow for her too."

"If she cares so much for me, why doesn't she talk to me? Do you realise that she hasn't spoken a single word to me since the baby died?"

Charlie sighed patiently. "Erin, that's not true. She has spoken to you several times. I witnessed it myself. She spoke to you at the funeral. She tells me you have treated her with outright antagonism any time she has approached you."

Erin's mouth fell open. This was like some fantastic charade where the truth was set on its head and everything turned out to be something different. She felt a wave of confusion wash over her and her strength desert her. She no longer had the energy to sit here and argue with her father-in-law. Suddenly she began to weep.

She felt Charlie Kavanagh's strong arms encircle her shoulder.

"Here," he said, pulling a crisp white handkerchief from his pocket. "Wipe your eyes."

She did as he instructed.

"Now listen to me carefully," he said. "You're safe here, Erin. No one wants to harm you. If there is anything you want, you just have to ask. Harry is going to cut short his trip to London. He'll be home in a few days and then you can decide between you about moving house. Is that acceptable?"

She nodded.

"In the meantime, I'm going to ask Dr Bellows to come and see you. He might be able to prescribe something for you."

At the mention of the doctor's name, Erin immediately recoiled.

"No," she said. "I won't see him. I don't need a doctor. There's nothing wrong with me."

"What's the harm? He might be able to help you."

"I said no. I won't see him."

"All right," Charlie said, resignedly. "That's your decision. But will you do one thing for me? Will you join us for dinner tonight? I'd like us all to eat together as a family."

"I'll think about it," she said.

Charlie left and she heard his heavy footsteps descending the stairs. She sat at the coffee table and stared at the walls. She had no intention of joining them for dinner. And the nerve of him insisting that Mrs Kavanagh had wanted to speak to her and she, Erin, had been the one who had shown antagonism. It was the complete opposite of the truth. But now she knew one thing for sure. Her father-in-law was in the conspiracy as well and this dinner invitation was some sort of trap they were preparing for her. Just like the trap he had tried to set with Dr Bellows. But she had seen through that quickly enough. If she allowed him to visit her, it would be tantamount to admitting she was ill. And she wasn't ill. She was perfectly well. But what was she going to do?

It was a long time later when she heard her phone ring. She picked it up. It was Ger Armstrong. She brightened at the sound of his voice.

"Hi, Ger," she said. "Did you get that article I sent you?"

"That's what I'm ringing about," he said in a grave voice.

"What do you think? Do you like it?"

"Is this meant to be a joke?" he asked.

"A joke?"

"Are you trying to get us sued? I thought you understood the laws of libel, Erin?"

"I don't know what you mean," she stammered.

"Then let me read the intro you wrote: *'Tom McClure, the well-known American serial killer is visiting Dublin. I met him recently in the Grand Hotel, Malahide, and he looked perfectly normal. Dressed in a smart suit and with his hair neatly groomed, you would never think the man drinking coffee with me had already murdered sixteen women and is being sought by police in seven countries.'*"

Chapter 27

Erin gasped. Had she written those lines? She had absolutely no memory of it. But evidently she had. Was her mind really beginning to go like everyone said?

She frantically tried to think.

"Just testing you, Ger," she said, with a forced laugh. "You passed with flying colours. Congratulations."

"What do you mean, testing me?" her boss demanded in a disbelieving voice.

"I was checking if you were wide awake and alert like a good news editor should be, that's all."

"So this *is* a joke?" he said, sounding relieved.

"Of course, it is, what did you think? I was just having a bit of fun. I'll send you the proper intro right away."

"Erin, I don't like this sort of stuff," he grumbled. "It's dangerous. It could get us into trouble."

"I'm sorry, Ger. I was in one of my giddy moods."

"Please don't joke like this again. You almost gave me a heart attack. My job is stressful enough as it is."

She put down the phone. Her head was in a whirl. How on earth had she written that stuff? If it had managed to slip into the paper, McClure could have taken them to the cleaners.

She sat down at her laptop and quickly typed out a fresh introductory paragraph and sent it immediately to the news editor.

But the episode had worried her. She had never done anything like that before. She was meticulous about checking her copy thoroughly before submitting it. It was a sign that she hadn't been thinking straight. She had been tired last night when she wrote the article and she must have let her mind wander. Ger Armstrong was perfectly right. It *was* dangerous. She must make sure that it never happened again. She was under too much pressure and this damned house was getting her down. That was the reason.

Her thoughts were interrupted when the phone rang again. She lifted it and heard Harry's voice.

"How are you today?" he began, sounding a little cautious.

"I'm fine. Why is everyone suddenly interested in how I am? I had your father here a while ago. He suggested bringing Dr Bellows to see me."

"I know. I was talking to him earlier."

"Well, I refused. I don't want to see Dr Bellows.

There's absolutely nothing wrong with me."

There was a pause before he replied. "Okay. That's your choice. Did you sleep all right?"

"Yes."

"Good. Did Dad tell you I was cutting short the trip? I'll be home in three or four days."

"Yes. And it's the best piece of news I've heard for a long time. I can't wait to see you."

"Just hang in there for a little while longer and then we'll be together again."

She felt so relieved and grateful. With Harry here beside her, she would be safe. They could move to Larchfield and everything would be all right again.

"When I get back we'll sort everything out. I promise you, Erin. You know I love you."

"Yes," she said. "Your father said you were worried about me. Please don't worry, Harry. I'm okay. Honest. I'm not ill. I'm not deranged." Her voice broke off. She felt her emotions spill over and she was sobbing again. "I just feel so lonely and frightened, that's all. Everyone has turned against me, even your father and he was someone I counted on. I feel so isolated, Harry."

"I know," he said, "but it's going to be just fine. Trust me. A few more days and everything will be sorted out."

"Okay," she sobbed.

"Keep your chin up. Be strong. I'll call you again this evening."

"I'll look forward to that."

"And don't hesitate to ring me if you're concerned. You have my mobile number."

"Okay."

"Just try to keep busy. And don't be frightened. Nothing is going to happen to you."

She put the phone down. By now, the tears were streaming down her face. She felt so miserable that she flung herself on the bed and cried her eyes out. Finally she stood up. She stared into the mirror. Her face was red from weeping and she looked dreadful.

What's the matter with me, she thought? Why am I crying like this at every little thing? She went into the bathroom and washed her face with cold water. I'll have to stop this, she thought. I'll have to take a grip on myself. I'll have to get out of this damned house and have a decent civilised, conversation with someone I can trust.

Anne immediately popped into her mind.

Why hadn't she thought of her before? She would be the perfect person. Anne, with her strong common sense, would surely lift her out of this maudlin depression that seemed to have taken hold of her. She lifted the phone and rang. A minute later she heard her sister's voice on the line.

"It's me," she said. "I was wondering if you could get away for an hour. I need to talk to someone."

"Sure," Anne said. "Where are you now?"

"I'm at Belvedere and I'm going up the walls. I need some intelligent human contact."

"Why? What's the matter?"

"Everything is getting me down. I don't know where to start."

"Okay. Help is on the way. I'll see you at Mirabelle's restaurant in Malahide at a quarter past one. We'll have a bite of lunch and you can get it all off your chest. How does that sound?"

"It sounds marvellous."

"Okay," Anne said. "Just let me tidy up a few things and I'll be on my way. See you there in forty-five minutes."

"See you," Erin said as she switched off the phone and felt a wave of relief wash over her like a restful tide.

She decided to dress up. Dressing up always gave her a lift. She went to the wardrobe and flung it open. Most of her clothes had been packed in preparation for the move to Larchfield but there was a pretty gold and brown floral summer dress and a smart little terracotta linen jacket hanging from the rail. She took them out and put them on. Then she sat down in front of the mirror and began to brush out her hair. I must make an appointment with the hairdresser, she thought. That's always good for a morale boost. And I'll look nice for Harry coming home. In fact I'll do it this afternoon when I get back from meeting Anne. Buoyed up by these thoughts, she applied some lipstick and examined herself in the glass.

She looked good and looking good made her *feel* good. And the thought of meeting her sister reinforced the feeling. A burst of hope swelled once more in

Erin's breast. She had only to wait for a few more days and then Harry would be home and all her troubles would be over. They would move out of this ghastly house and begin afresh. She took her handbag from the dressing-table and locked up the flat. Then she went down the stairs to the main hall.

At the front door she paused and glanced behind her. If she was expecting to see someone, she was disappointed. The hall was empty. There was no one around. She opened the door and stepped out into the bright morning sunlight. It was another glorious day. She felt her heart lift. With a feeling of confidence, she marched boldly down the drive.

It took her twenty-five minutes to reach Malahide village. She took her time, savouring the pleasures of the day. The trees and flowers were in bloom and their fragrant scent filled the morning air. From the gardens and fields she could hear the the sound of birdsong. Eventually, she reached the outskirts of the village and quickened her pace till she reached Mirabelle's restaurant.

Anne had taken the precaution of ringing ahead and booking a table. It was beside the window where they could look out and watch the world pass by. The waiter politely pulled out a chair for her to sit down, gave her a menu and asked if she would like a drink. She ordered a glass of chilled white wine and glanced about. The restaurant was a popular spot for women like her who liked to lunch and it was already beginning to fill up. She sipped her wine while she studied the menu.

The walk had sharpened her appetite and now she felt hungry. Today, she was going to treat herself. She would have a steak with creamed potatoes and broccoli and afterwards a slice of the gorgeous chocolate cake that was one of Mirabelle's specialities. Energised by her decision, she closed the menu and took a sip of wine and felt its cool, smooth bouquet explode on her tongue.

Ten minutes passed before Anne came in looking slightly harassed.

"Sorry I'm late," she said, slipping into the seat beside her. "Parking in this town is a nightmare. I've been driving round in circles for the past fifteen minutes looking for a spot."

"I walked," Erin said, somewhat smugly.

"Good for you but I don't have that option." Anne smiled. "You look very smart. I like your tan. So you enjoyed the cruise?"

"Well, enjoy might be putting it a bit strongly. It took me a while to settle down."

"I know. After all you have been through, I'm not surprised."

"But it was really very good. You know, before Harry suggested it, I had this silly notion that it would be full of elderly people wrapped up in cardigans playing dominoes. How wrong I was. It was a lovely experience. I would recommend it to anyone."

"Bit expensive I would think."

"Not when you consider that it's all-inclusive and the food is out of this world."

She was in the midst of describing their trip when the waiter came to take their order.

"So what has you down in the dumps?" Anne asked, after he had left.

"Frustration, I suppose. Harry's gone to London on company business so I'm stuck on my own in Belvedere. And I'm desperate to get into our new house. It's lying idle and I can't move."

"Why not? It's ready, isn't it? The décor has been completed and the furniture is in place. What's stopping you?"

Erin glanced around and lowered her voice. "My husband and his family."

A look of surprise came over her sister's face. "I don't understand. You'd better explain."

"Since Emily died, they've got this idea that I can't be trusted to be on my own. They want me with them so they can keep an eye on me. They're trying to convince me that I'm suffering from post-traumatic stress."

"And are you?" Anne asked.

"I don't believe so. I must confess I get a bit weepy sometimes."

"I think that's only to be expected after everything that has happened."

"So do I. I miss little Emily terribly. I think about her all the time. But I've got to move on, Anne. I can't spend my time brooding. That isn't going to bring her back."

"You're doing the right thing," her sister said, squeezing her hand.

"I miss Harry. And to make matters worse, his bloody family has turned against me. His mother is convinced I'm responsible for the baby's death. His sister has never liked me and doesn't speak to me. And now his father has joined them."

Anne looked shocked. "But how could anyone suggest you're responsible? It was a SIDS death, wasn't it? There was absolutely nothing you could have done about it."

"I know. But Mrs Kavanagh thinks I should have been minding her. I left her alone for one single bloody hour to bring some bags to the new house. She thinks if I had been with her, it would never have happened."

Anne put down her wineglass and looked sharply at her. "How do you know this, Erin?"

"I heard her – at the funeral – across the grave."

Anne stared. "Across the grave? But she didn't say anything, Erin. I was right there."

"No, I saw her mouth the words."

"Are you sure?" Anne said tentatively. "You were really out of it at the time – you were heavily sedated."

Erin flushed. "Are *you* telling me I'm delusional now?"

"No, no, I just mean maybe –"

"Maybe I was imagining it? No. Tim admitted it's true. She's been saying it to the family."

"Oh! Then why do you stay?"

"Because if I leave it will cause a big fuss and I don't want to upset Harry. He has a lot on his shoulders just now. He's helping his father run the business after his heart attack. And he's grieving as much as I am over the death of the baby. I don't want to do anything to make his life more difficult."

Anne pursed her lips and expelled a jet of air. "I have to confess, I didn't realise things were quite so bad."

Erin shrugged. "So now you can understand my dilemma."

"I think the sooner you get out of there the better. You could come and stay with me, if you like. I've got a spare room."

But Erin shook her head. "I'm going to stick it out. It's only a few more days and then Harry will be home and we can move."

"Are you sure?"

"Yes. I'll survive it. But it's great to talk to you, Anne. It's what I needed, someone who would listen to me and not think I was nuts."

"Well, if you need to talk again, I'm your woman," Anne said, reaching out and taking her hand again. "But promise me something. If things get intolerable at Belvedere, ring me and I'll come at once and get you."

"Okay," Erin said, suddenly feeling overcome with relief and gratitude.

After the meal, Anne drove her back and left her at the gates of Belvedere. Her courage had been bolstered by her sister's sympathetic words and promise of help and she felt more confident as she walked up the drive.

As she reached the front door, it suddenly opened and her father-in-law came out.

"Ah, Erin, have you been for a walk?"

"I was meeting my sister for lunch in Malahide."

"You look well. The outing must have done you good. Why don't you invite your sister to come and visit us some evening?"

"Yes. I might do that."

"And don't forget we're expecting you for dinner this evening." He paused and looked closely into her face. "You *are* coming, aren't you?"

"What time?"

"Seven o'clock. So you'll come?"

"Yes," she said. "I'll come."

Charlie Kavanagh's face beamed with pleasure. He clapped her heartily on the back. "That's my girl, Erin! We'll be looking forward to having you join us."

He went down the steps whistling loudly and Erin entered the house. She went up to the flat and let herself in. The dinner would be a trial. But it would please Harry as much as it had obviously pleased his father. Her best course now was the path of least resistance. If she could avoid further friction with her in-laws for a few more days, Harry would be back and she would be free.

But she would have to remain on her guard. This might appear to be a simple dinner but who knew what they were really up to?

Chapter 28

She spent the afternoon checking emails and making phone calls. There was one mail from Ger Armstrong saying her interview with Tom McClure was going into the paper the following day and asking her to ring him soon about more work. This message cheered her up. Work was the one thing she needed right now. She had to keep busy. It would get her out of this damned house and keep her mind occupied.

Once they moved into Larchfield, she would get her life back in order. She would throw herself into her career. She would do something about the ambition she cherished to become a permanent feature writer. That was a job she would enjoy. She could work from home, dictate her own hours, even choose her own subjects. With a bit of luck, she might convince Ger Armstrong to let her do it.

Once they had their own home, all sorts of wonderful possibilities would open up. She would resume those cookery lessons. She would have fabulous dinner parties, invite her friends who would gasp with envy when they saw the new house and sigh with pleasure over the wonderful dishes she would prepare. She and Harry would finally put the tragedy behind them and perhaps, in the fullness of time, they would have more children. If she could just survive these next few days, everything was possible.

It was in this mood that Erin eventually stirred herself for dinner. The Kavanaghs always dressed up for the meal and tonight would be no exception. But she must be on her best behaviour. She would force herself to enter into the swing of things. She would make a special effort to be pleasant. On no account must she give them any further reason to say she was behaving oddly.

She went into the bathroom, filled the tub and sprinkled in some scented bath foam. The bath was so soothing that she could have lain in it forever but, eventually, she braced herself to face the evening. She towelled herself dry and returned to the bedroom. What would she wear? She hadn't much choice. Most of her stuff was waiting to be unpacked at Larchfield. But she had one suitable dress for an occasion like this, a dress that Harry had bought her, one he was especially fond of. She hadn't worn it since Emily was born but thanks to her weight loss, it would fit her again. It was a shimmering eau de nil evening dress with a low neckline which would look good with a simple silver chain and some earrings.

She put it on and admired herself in the mirror. The dress clung to her, emphasising the fine contours of her body. She sat down at the dressing-table and was about to apply a touch of make-up when suddenly the phone rang. She picked it up and heard Harry on the line.

"Hi," she said, joyfully pressing the phone closer to her ear.

"I said I would ring. How are you?"

"I'm well. How are you?"

"Very tired. I've had another hectic day. But I got a lot of work done. I've concluded several important deals for the company. And tomorrow I'm signing a big contract with a key client."

"That's wonderful, Harry. You know, I never asked you what your hotel is like."

"It's pretty functional, Erin. The room is fine, the service is good, the food's okay but it's not the sort of place you would want to spend the rest of your life in. It's central and that's its main attraction."

"Well, I've got news for you that will make you happy."

"Yes?"

"I'm having dinner with your family this evening."

"Oh, Erin, you don't realise how much that pleases me!"

She heard the tone of relief in his voice.

"You know I desperately want you all to get along together," he continued. "This bickering has been worrying me sick."

"I *do* know. And I feel sorry. Really I do. It's just that everything seems to have got on top of me recently."

"You don't have to explain. You lost your baby, for God's sake. Anybody would feel down. I think it's wonderful the way you have coped."

"I had lunch with Anne today and that cheered me up. And when your father asked me about dinner, I decided to accept. You're right, Harry. I should make more effort to get on with them."

"That is the best thing you could have told me. I love you, Erin."

The joy in his voice was unmistakable.

"And I love you too," she said. "I can't wait to see you again."

"Three more days, four at the most and I'll be home. It won't be long, my love."

They talked for a while longer. It was so restful to hear his voice and when Erin finally switched off the phone, she felt a contented glow steal over her. Tonight she would be on her very best behaviour. She was going to this dinner and no matter what happened she would prove to them that she was sane and normal. If for nothing else, she would do it for Harry's sake.

All the family were waiting when she finally entered the dining room at five to seven. When she came in, Charlie Kavanagh rose, took her by the hand and kissed her warmly on the cheek. Around the table, she was aware of their eyes watching her closely.

"You look wonderful, Erin," her father-in-law said. "That dress seems as if it was specially made for you, it suits you so well."

"Thank you," she replied, glancing nervously at the assembled guests.

Charlie led her to a seat beside him. Caroline sat on his other side, dressed in a lavender satin evening dress. She had a frown on her face and Erin thought she looked worn and tired. Across the table, Susan, Toby and Tim were sitting. Tim winked reassuringly as she sat down.

"I've just been speaking to Harry on the phone," she announced.

"He's been working very hard," Charlie remarked, "and achieving excellent results. Did he tell you he's signing a major contract with an important client tomorrow?"

"Yes. But I can't help feeling sorry for him. He's there all on his own. He doesn't say so but I'm sure he must be lonely. Maybe I should have gone with him?"

At this announcement, Mrs Kavanagh coughed.

"You wouldn't have enjoyed it," Charlie said. "You wouldn't have seen much of him, I can tell you that. He has meetings lined up all day from eight o'clock in the morning."

"He works so hard," Erin said.

"Yes, he does," Charlie Kavanagh continued, "but in our business you can't afford to stand still. You have to keep moving forward."

"You went into Malahide today," Tim said, changing the subject and smiling across the table at her.

"I had lunch with my sister."

"Where did you go?"

"Mirabelle's."

"Any good?"

"I thought so. We had a very nice meal and it wasn't too expensive."

"I haven't been there for ages," Tim said. "Maybe I'll give it another go one of these days. Maybe you might even come with me?"

"Sure," Erin replied. "I'd like that."

"Well, I hope you didn't eat too much," her father-in-law laughed. "I hope you still have some appetite left for dinner."

At that moment, the soup arrived and they all bent to their plates.

Her sister-in-law spoke next.

"You haven't resumed your riding exercises," she said.

Erin looked up. These were the first words Susan had spoken to her for more than a month. She must have decided to be nice to her again. What *were* the Kavanaghs up to?

"I didn't think I was much good at it," Erin replied, not wanting to admit the real reason she had stopped.

"Nonsense, you were very good. You're a natural horsewoman. You have a feel for horses. You should take it up again."

Erin looked into the grey eyes staring at her from across the table. But now there appeared to be a softer tone to them, even a hint of smile playing around the corners of her mouth.

"I'm at the stables every morning. I'd be delighted to see you again. Why don't you come tomorrow morning? We'll get Gypsy saddled up and ready for you."

But before she could reply her mother-in-law broke in.

"Are you sure that's a good idea? Erin has been through a terrible time. Maybe it would be better for her to rest a little before taking on such vigorous exercise." Mrs Kavanagh turned to look directly at Erin. "What do you think, my dear? Do you think you'd be ready for horse-riding?

"I . . . I . . ." Suddenly, Erin felt bewildered. She didn't know what to say. Not only had her mother-in-law addressed her directly but there was a warmth and kindness in her voice that she hadn't heard for a long time.

"I'm not sure," she managed at last.

"If you need something to occupy your mind, why don't you come and talk with me? I'm in my room every day. My husband seems determined to work all the time, despite what his doctors have told him."

She gave Charlie a scolding glance but he simply laughed.

Erin felt her face burn crimson. Come and talk with Mrs Kavanagh who had studiously ignored her since Emily died? And worse still, had blamed her for the baby's death? How was she supposed to respond?

"I've started writing some journalism again so I *am* quite busy," she said. But no sooner were the words out of her mouth than they sounded churlish and ungrateful. The woman was extending an olive branch to her and she was refusing it. How did that appear to everyone around the table?

"I'm sure you could find half an hour," Mrs Kavanagh said. "We'll have afternoon tea and we'll be able to talk. We have a lot of things to discuss. Talking to someone is very good therapy. Shall we say three o'clock?"

"Okay," Erin reluctantly agreed.

After that, the ice was broken. Charlie was soon entertaining the table with a story about a rival builder who had been caught by the authorities employing migrant labour at minimum rates and now was in danger of having his licence revoked.

"Serves him right," Toby said. "If he'd been allowed to get away with that sort of thing, he would have undercut legitimate operators like you."

"He's a greedy sod," Charlie said. "Mean as Scrooge, always looking for ways to scrimp on costs, using poor materials, cutting corners. I'm not one bit sorry for him."

The meal progressed quite smoothly. They had poached salmon for the main course and then baked apple tart. After the good lunch she had eaten at Mirabelle's, Erin had little appetite. But she made an effort to eat the food that was placed in front of her at regular intervals, conscious that everyone would be observing her. Although any time she looked up, their attention seemed to be elsewhere.

The conversation swirled around the table and she was drawn in. People asked her opinion. It was pleasant, relaxed dinner conversation with no hint of hostility or animosity. It was the very opposite of what she had expected. And throughout, Susan smiled benevolently at her and Mrs Kavanagh spoke kindly as if nothing had ever occurred to poison the atmosphere between them.

Eventually the meal ended and Susan and Toby prepared to go home. Out in the hall as they were putting on their coats, Susan took her aside.

"Remember what I said about the horses. We'll be glad to see you. I'll tell Cornish to expect you some morning. I think you'll find it will do you good."

Erin said goodnight and climbed the stairs to the flat. It had been a strange evening. It had turned all her expectations upside down. She had been prepared for coldness and hostility and instead had met warmth and welcome. And now she had an invitation tomorrow for tea with her mother-in-law who had given her that murderous glance at the funeral and accused her of killing her own child.

It was all too much to take in. She had drunk nothing more than a glass of wine at dinner but her head felt fuzzy and strange. She locked the hall door, got undressed and slipped under the sheets. Her mind was all over the place. Once again she began to doubt her own judgment. Was it possible that she was wrong about her in-laws? Was it possible that she had imagined the animosity when all along they had been trying to be kind to her?

Or had tonight been an elaborate charade played out to lull her into a sense of false security? That had been her initial thought when Charlie Kavanagh suggested that she come to dinner. Was it part of some elaborate game they were playing with her, some trap they were setting?

She couldn't think straight. Her head was in a muddle. Maybe in the morning, in the light of day, she would be able to see things more clearly and make sense of what was going on. She pulled the sheets tighter around her and gradually, she fell asleep.

But she wasn't to have a restful night. Her slumber was disturbed by wild dreams. In one of them, she thought she heard someone in her room, someone who was coming to harm her. She sat up suddenly in bed and found her heart beating madly and her forehead drenched in sweat. She turned on the light and saw that it was three o'clock.

She looked around the bedroom. It was empty. There was no indication that anyone had been in there. She was about to go back to sleep when she noticed the door of the nursery was ajar. Now a thin sliver of light was seeping out.

She stared at the door and felt terror creep along her spine. The nursery had been closed since the day of the funeral when all little Emily's baby stuff had been removed and the room had been locked. No one had been in there since.

She got out of bed, drawn towards the door as if in a trance. She put her hand on the handle and carefully edged it open. A shaft of light cut across and she was able to see right into the nursery. And at once, she felt her heart leap into her mouth.

Emily's cot was standing in the middle of the room!

Now the blood was roaring in her head. She felt some powerful magnetism draw her deeper into the room. Slowly, she advanced across the floor till she was standing above the cot. She forced herself to look and immediately recoiled in shock.

A baby was lying in the cot!

She felt the breath leave her body. Her hands reached out and lifted the child. But it felt cold and lifeless. And then a look of horror came over her face as she realised what it was. She wasn't holding a baby. She was holding a doll!

She hurled it on the floor and howled in anguish. Around her, the walls shivered and closed in. The light seemed to fade. She felt her legs go weak. She looked down and saw the ground rushing up to meet her.

Chapter 29

She came round to find a familiar face gazing down at her.

"Wake up!" Mrs Kavanagh said, slapping her cheeks gently and shaking her. "Wake up! What happened to you?"

Erin felt dizzy and there was a pain where she had bumped her forehead as she fell.

"I must have fainted," she said, nursing her bruised head.

"What are you doing in here? Why aren't you in bed?" her mother-in-law demanded.

"There was an intruder," Erin gasped.

"An *intruder*?"

Mrs Kavanagh's voice sounded shocked.

Then Erin heard another voice – a male voice, she thought – outside in the bedroom.

Mrs Kavanagh hurriedly arose and went out.

Erin heard the murmur of voices and then her

mother-in-law saying more loudly: "No, no, it's all right. I can manage. You can go back to bed."

Mrs Kavanagh entered the nursery again, closing the door behind her.

"Now," she said, helping Erin to sit up. "What were you saying about an intruder?"

"Someone was in my bedroom and they wakened me."

The older woman stared at her. "Are you talking about a burglar? Should we get the police?"

"No, not a burglar."

"Well, who then?"

"I don't know," Erin said. "I heard a noise. I got up and saw the nursery door was open. And then I saw the cot."

"What cot? What on earth are you talking about?"

"There," Erin said, pointing.

But when she looked, she saw the room was empty. The cot was gone.

"There's no cot, Erin," her mother-in-law said, firmly. "You can see for yourself."

"There was a cot. Right there," Erin said, getting to her feet and indicating the centre of the floor. Her voice was starting to rise. "It was little Emily's cot. And there was a baby in it. Only it wasn't a baby. It was a plastic doll. One I had never seen before."

Mrs Kavanagh gave a loud sigh. "Erin, there is no cot and no doll. Are you blind? The room is empty."

She felt herself getting angry. "There *was* a cot. I saw it with my own eyes."

"No, dear." Mrs Kavanagh's voice was resolute. "There was no cot. You must have dreamt it. Now I'm going to get you back into bed. Let me look at that bump on your forehead." She brushed a lock of hair from Erin's face. "It's nothing serious, just a scratch. I'll put a plaster on it. And I'm going to give you a sleeping tablet. I want you to sleep. Tomorrow everything will be all right again. And we'll have our little talk."

She helped Erin back into bed. A minute later she returned with a medicine box. She dressed the scratch on Erin's forehead then took a tablet from a bottle and poured a glass of water.

"Swallow that. It will help you to sleep. Do you want me to leave the light on?"

"No," Erin said.

"It must have been something you ate. Now forget all about this. Just close your eyes and relax. You'll be fine now."

She turned to leave but a thought jumped into Erin's mind.

"How did you get in?" she asked.

"The hall door was open."

"And how did you know to come?"

Mrs Kavanagh paused. "Why, dear, I heard you scream. You were screaming fit to wake the dead. Goodnight, Erin."

Erin pulled the sheets close around her and snuggled down in the bed as if trying to escape from the world and all its confusion. She felt totally bewildered. Had she seen the cot or hadn't she? And to make matters worse, a dull, throbbing pain had started in her head where she had fallen. But mercifully, relief was at hand. She had barely closed her eyes when she felt the waves of sleep wash over her and she was dead to the world.

When she woke, it was morning. The sun was already high and the room was flooded with light. She checked the time and saw that it was after eleven. She had slept for eight hours. She sat up in bed and looked around. The room was exactly as she had left it and the nursery door was closed again.

She lay back on the pillows and tried to think. What had happened last night? *Was* it a bad dream? But if it was a dream, it had seemed so real. She could remember everything in precise detail, right up to the moment when she had fainted. Normally, Erin's dreams were like wisps of smoke, disintegrating into fragments the moment she awoke. But this dream was vivid. And there was something else. Mrs Kavanagh said the hall door was open. Yet Erin could distinctly remember locking it when she came in last night.

The pain was still there only now it seemed to have shifted deep inside her head. She got out of bed. She felt dizzy and her footing was unsteady. The sleeping tablet which her mother-in-law had given her must have been very powerful, she could still feel the after-effects. She walked to the dressing-table and studied her face in the mirror. There was a bruise above her right eye which Mrs Kavanagh's sticking plaster had barely managed to conceal.

She turned away and for a moment, she thought she saw the room shift out of focus. Was it a trick of the light or a result of the bang on her head? I'm still drowsy, she decided. Maybe I should return to bed? Nevertheless, something drew her back to the nursery. She tried the door and turned the handle. It opened. She walked in, drew back the curtains and the sunlight came pouring in.

The room stood bare and empty and the air smelt stale. She opened the window and tried to remember once more what had happened here last night. She walked unsteadily to the middle of the floor to the spot where the cot had been. She tried to recall if there had been anything else in the room but all she could remember was the cot and the doll that looked so lifelike she thought she was holding her dead baby. But where was the cot now? And where was the doll?

Suddenly, she felt nauseous. She leaned on the windowsill till the feeling passed. Had she imagined the whole thing? Was it a nightmare? The dizziness in her head was now making it very difficult to concentrate. Her brain felt muzzy as if clogged with cotton wool. She needed to get back into bed and rest some more.

But just as she was turning to leave, she caught the sunlight glinting off something on the floor. She bent down and picked it up. She was holding a tiny piece of pink plastic. Immediately, she felt herself freeze. The plastic must have come from the doll. It must have broken off when she flung it on the floor. So she hadn't been dreaming after all. Here was the proof. There *had* been a cot and a doll in here last night and here was the evidence.

She quickly closed the nursery door and returned to the bedroom. She took a piece of paper from her tissue box and wrapped the plastic in it then put it away in a safe place in the dressing-table drawer. And it was only then that the full implications of what had occurred began to dawn on her.

Someone had definitely been in her bedroom last night. It had to be someone who was familiar with the layout of the place. Belvedere was a big house and a stranger could easily get lost. And it had to be someone who felt confident enough to enter her room in the middle of the night and come back later to remove the cot. That meant they also knew that Harry was away and she would be alone. It had to be someone who either lived in the house or worked here.

She felt herself begin to tremble. Someone she knew, someone who she saw every day had done this. But who? Two people immediately sprang into her mind. Mrs Kavanagh and Susan! Those were the people who disliked her the most and had shown her the most hostility. And wasn't it odd that Mrs Kavanagh should be the first person to find her after she had fainted? Her bedroom was on the other side of the house. What was she doing here?

Erin felt her chest tighten. She found it difficult to

breathe. The thoughts that were now swirling around in her head were frightening. They scared her. She needed to sit down and try to focus her mind. The trembling had begun to intensify. She took her housecoat from the bathroom and wrapped it tightly around her, then went into the kitchen and made a strong cup of tea.

She clutched her teacup and tried to make sense of what was going on. Was it really feasible that Mrs Kavanagh or Susan could have put that cot in the nursery for her to find? The thought was absurd. Why would they do it? What motive could they possibly have? And then the answer came to her like a flash of light. They did it to frighten her, to scare her, to make her feel exactly as she did now – slowly growing terrified out of her wits.

She gulped the hot tea. Did they hate her so much that they would want to hurt her so badly? Yet someone had done it. She hadn't dreamt it. It had really happened. She had the evidence right there in her drawer, wrapped in the tissue. And she was convinced that the person responsible lived here under this roof. Who else fitted the profile so well? Caroline Kavanagh and Susan were the obvious culprits.

She willed the trembling to stop. She must stay calm and try to think rationally. Whatever happened, she must give no indication of her suspicions or she could place herself in even greater danger. If the subject was raised again, she must go along with the suggestion that she had dreamt the whole thing. The last time she had argued with them, they had simply turned it against her and said she was ill.

Besides, the culprit would be watching. She mustn't react. Above all, she must give no hint that she had found the evidence that would prove the incident was real and not a figment of her imagination.

She finished the tea and sat down on the bed. Now her mind was racing. She knew exactly what had happened. The culprit had brought the cot into the nursery when she was asleep and wakened her as they left. When she fainted, they had come back again and removed it.

And the motive was plain as daylight. It caused the trembling to resume and fear to come crawling along her spine like a snake. Whoever had done this didn't simply want to scare her. They wanted to strike terror into her. They wanted to drive her insane. Whoever had left the cot and the doll in the nursery last night, hated her enough to tip her into madness.

Chapter 30

She waited till the trembling stopped then went into the bathroom and stood under the shower. The hot water revived her and now she was thinking clearly. Someone associated with this house was intent on driving her crazy. And she thought she knew who.

Well, she wouldn't allow them to succeed. She was determined to act normally and show no fear. She would begin by taking a walk. It would get her out of this dreadful house and provide her with some much-needed exercise.

She dried herself and applied some make-up to the cut on her forehead. Then she made some scrambled eggs and toast and strong black coffee. She dressed in jeans and sweater and set off towards the woods. She hadn't gone far when she heard the sound of hooves coming fast behind her. She stood quickly aside from the path just in time to see Susan thundering up on her charger. She reined in the horse and stopped.

"I thought I might have seen you at the stables this morning," Susan said, peering down at Erin with her inquisitive grey eyes.

Erin took a deep breath. Here beside her was one of the possible suspects. And she seemed bold as brass. But she forced herself not to react.

"I still don't feel strong enough," she replied.

Susan leaned down and examined her closely. "You do look a little ropey. Did you sleep all right last night?"

The grey eyes were now staring at her and Erin felt the fear return.

"Oh yes. I slept very well, thank you."

"Good. Mum was telling me that you had a nightmare. She heard you screaming in your sleep."

"It was just a bad dream," Erin mumbled. "I get them sometimes. Since little Emily died."

"Why don't you let Dr Bellows examine you? He'll be able to prescribe something."

"I – I don't need a doctor. There's nothing wrong with me. I've been told this is a normal reaction."

Susan nodded. "You're probably right. Losing your baby must have been an awful experience. I can't imagine what it must be like. But if these nightmares persist, I would see old Bellows. He's been our family doctor for years. He really knows his stuff."

"Yes," Erin said. "I'll do that."

"In the meantime, try to keep your mind off it. Dwelling on something like that can't be good. Put it behind you. Move on."

"I will."

"And maybe we'll see you at the stables in a week or so?"

"Yes," Erin said. "I'll look forward to that."

Susan dug her heels into the horse's flanks and went galloping off along the path in a cloud of dust. Erin stood and watched till she had disappeared into the woods. She heaved a sigh of relief. Was it her imagination or had Susan been testing her? Well, if she had, Erin was satisfied with the way she had responded. She thought she had handled the conversation very well.

She returned to the house to face another challenge. Mrs Kavanagh wanted to see her at three o'clock. It was now half past two. She went back to the apartment, changed her clothes and tidied herself up, then descended the stairs to the drawing-room.

This was a meeting she would prefer to avoid but if she did that, it would simply play into her mother-in-law's hands. It would be taken as further proof that Erin was becoming unhinged. Or just as bad, it might alert her to Erin's suspicions. She had no option but to go ahead.

Mrs Kavanagh was sitting beside the window looking out across the lawns. She had a book in her hand. She put it down and removed her reading glasses as Erin approached.

"Sit here beside me," she said. "Have you had any lunch?"

"No. But I'm not hungry. I had a late breakfast."

"Then I'll just order tea and sandwiches."

She rang a little bell and gave instructions to the maid.

"How did you sleep afterwards?" she asked when the girl had left.

"Very well. That tablet you gave me worked. I didn't wake till eleven o'clock."

Mrs Kavanagh nodded. "Normally, I don't hold with sedatives. I only use them in emergencies. But I thought under the circumstances you needed something to help you."

"I didn't thank you," Erin said.

"There's no need. You were in distress. What did you expect me to do?" She looked at Erin with her hard, intense eyes. "Since little Emily died, you and I have not been getting along as well as we should."

Erin took a deep breath. She hoped this meeting was not going to turn into an inquisition. "No," she said.

"Or as well as I would like. I want us to be friends, Erin. We were friends once and I would like it to continue. However, I think the time has come for some blunt speaking between us."

Erin lowered her head and made no reply.

"I've been told you believe I am hostile towards you. I want you to know that none of this is true."

Erin continued to remain silent. If Mrs Kavanagh was trying to provoke an argument, she would not rise to the bait.

"You have imagined this so-called hostility," her

mother-in-law continued. "It's in your mind. It's the delayed reaction to the shock of the baby's death."

Erin bit her lip.

"If you are to get well, you must make an effort to pull yourself together. You have said some very hurtful things about me and said them here under my own roof. Normally I would not stand for it but I am prepared to let it go because I realise you are not a well woman. But you have got to start living in the real world."

The longer she talked, the more intolerable it became. Erin was finding it increasingly difficult to sit here like this and be lectured by Mrs Kavanagh. She couldn't bear to be told once again that she was depressed, that her imagination was running riot, that she was mentally deranged.

Just then the maid entered with the sandwiches and tea things and left them on a table beside the window. Mrs Kavanagh poured and placed a cup on a little table near Erin, together with a plate, cutlery and napkin.

But then she continued: "This incident last night, there was no cot and no doll. You realise that you imagined that too?"

Erin snapped. Despite her resolution, she had to defend herself. "I did *not*," she said, vehemently.

Mrs Kavanagh's face went pale. She stared at Erin with open mouth.

"And I didn't dream it either," Erin said. "It happened. Why don't you stop all this pretence and listen to me for a change?"

Mrs Kavanagh gasped.

"You blamed me for Emily's death," Erin went on. "Did I imagine that too?"

"Who told you that?"

"I'm not at liberty to say. But you *did* blame me, didn't you? You said if I had been with her, it wouldn't have happened. Do you deny it?"

Now it was Mrs Kavanagh's turn to lower her eyes. Her lip quivered as she spoke.

"No, I don't deny it. But it was said in a moment of strain immediately after her death. I was in a state of shock too. It wasn't speaking my true feelings. I loved that child. Maybe I loved her as much as you did."

"I left her for an hour," Erin went on. "One short hour and I will regret it for the rest of my life. But to blame her death on me, her mother, who loved her more than my own life? That was an outrageous thing to say."

"I appreciate that. And I apologise for it."

"You never liked me from the very first time we met. Do you remember? It was at the party here in Belvedere. You barely spoke to me. You made me feel unwelcome. You made me feel that I was unworthy of your son. Because that is exactly how you felt about me. You didn't believe I was good enough for Harry. And when we got married in Las Vegas, you refused to see me or speak to me. You thought Harry had married beneath him, that I had somehow trapped him. Yet the truth was, the marriage was his idea, not mine. Did I imagine all that?"

"No," Mrs Kavanagh said.

"It was only when I got pregnant that you softened your attitude to me. And in an effort to please you, I agreed to all your suggestions, the wedding here at Belvedere, living at the flat, Professor O'Leary, St Angela's nursing home. I agreed to everything to keep you happy. I even agreed to name the baby Emily because that was what you wanted."

Caroline Kavanagh raised her face and now it looked sad and pained. "Please, Erin, do we have to fight like this?"

"I didn't choose this. You forced it on me."

"Well, if I did, I'm sorry."

"Do you realise the pain you caused your son by your selfishness? When we returned from Las Vegas you ignored me for months. Do you remember that Christmas when you refused to invite me out here? It almost broke his heart."

"I regret that. I was angry."

"And now that the baby is dead, I am blamed for it. I am treated like someone insane. People tell me I am imagining things or they didn't happen or it was a bad dream. They suggest I should see Dr Bellows. No one in this damned house is prepared to take me seriously and I am heartily sick of it."

She hurled down her napkin and ran from the room.

Back in the flat, she flung herself down on the settee and willed herself to be calm. She could feel her face flush hot with anger. She cooled it with a damp cloth. She had broken her resolution. She shouldn't have reacted. She shouldn't have lost her temper. But she had finally run out of patience with her mother-in-law and her condescending assumption that she was always right and Erin was *always, always* wrong.

As she sat in the quiet room, where the only sound was the ticking of the clock on the mantelpiece, other thoughts came crowding into her mind. Someone had been in her bedroom last night. Someone had left that cot and doll. She knew it and she had the evidence. It was someone who meant her harm, someone connected with this house. And it could well have been the woman she had just been talking to.

And then, amidst her anger and helplessness, another thought came tumbling into her mind. What about the anonymous notes she had earlier received? They had warned her that something bad was going to happen. She felt a cold sweat break out on her brow as the thought developed to its frightening conclusion.

What if little Emily's death had not been a cot death, after all? What if she had been *murdered?* And what if the person who had done it was the very same person who had been in her room last night?

Chapter 31

This thought was so terrifying that it forced her to sit bolt upright on the settee. It made such perfect sense that she wondered why it hadn't occurred to her before. The first note had arrived before she had even come to live at Belvedere. But it had warned her to stay away.

The last note was much more sinister. It had actually mentioned Baby Emily and warned Erin she would regret bringing her to stay at the house. So this campaign against her was no spur-of-the-moment thing. It had been planned a long time in advance. She felt an icy coldness take hold of her.

She wished now that she had kept the notes to add to the other piece of evidence she had gathered. They had been written by the same person, someone who bore her a terrible grudge for getting involved with the Kavanagh family. She could only guess what lay behind that grudge but she could clearly see the result

– the murder of an innocent child. And it might not end there.

Since she had come to live at Belvedere she had witnessed one strange event after another. It was as if some malign force had been let loose on the house. First there was Charlie Kavanagh's sudden heart attack, then Emily's death. And last night there was the incident with the cot and the doll. There were too many coincidences. Put them all together and they added up to something extremely sinister. Suddenly, the memory of a conversation she had with Tim came surging back into her head. *"You are not dealing with rational people."*

But who? And why? She felt fear grip her like a claw. She had failed little Emily. She had been warned and had chosen to ignore it. And she hadn't picked up on the multiplying signals that told her something bad was going to happen. She felt the old guilt return, the old remorse she had felt after Emily died. She had let her baby down. She was just as guilty as the person who had murdered her.

Tears welled up in her eyes and her chest began to heave. Suddenly she was weeping again – for her dead child, for herself, for the terrible fear that was now holding her in its icy grip. She needed to talk to someone she could trust. Anne came immediately to mind.

She wiped her eyes and with trembling hands, took out her phone. She heard the number ring and ring but no one answered. She tried again and still there was no reply. She left a message asking Anne to call her back and rang Harry. But his phone too, was not picking up. She remembered that he was signing an important contract today. In desperation she thought of Tim.

He was her last hope. She quickly locked up the flat and went off in search of her brother-in-law. His room was in another wing of the house. She had to go along a corridor and down some stairs before she reached it. When she arrived, she found the door slightly ajar. She knocked and heard Tim's cheerful command to enter.

She had never been in his room before. It was bare and sparse. Apart from a single bed pushed against the wall, the only pieces of furniture were a bookcase and a chest of drawers. Tim was seated at a desk before an old-fashioned typewriter. And on the floor beside it was a wastepaper basket, overflowing with balled-up sheets of paper. He turned round as she entered and his face broke into a smile.

"Why, Erin, this is a pleasant surprise. What can I do for you?"

"I needed someone to talk to. I thought of you."

"Well, I'm flattered. I'd offer you something to drink but all I have is whiskey. I don't suppose you'd like a glass?"

She refused. Her head was muddled enough without adding whiskey to the mix.

Tim got up and pulled the chair out from the desk.

"Sit down. Tell me what's bothering you."

He went and sat on the bed, elbows on knees.

"I feel awful," Erin began. "I just had a terrible row with your mother."

"Bully for you. It's time someone gave her a piece of their mind."

"Do you mean that?"

"Yes. My mother has been running people's lives ever since I was a child – me, Harry, Susan, even my father. For years, she has been badgering me to take a job in the company. She accuses me of wasting my time, of not shouldering my family duties. She has even suggested I was responsible for my father's heart attack because I wasn't helping him out."

"Really?"

"Oh yes. Mum is a total control freak. She thinks she has a divine right to order everybody around and make plans for them. And people are so afraid of her, they just let her have her way."

"I'm afraid I lost my temper with her."

"She probably provoked you."

"Yes, she did. But I'm annoyed with myself because I swore I wouldn't react. You see, ever since Emily died, people have been trying to tell me I'm unwell. Just the other day, your father told me I was suffering from post-traumatic stress."

Tim was now listening intently.

"I have to tell you something, Tim. I feel very uneasy here in Belvedere. I am desperate to get away to our new house. It's built and furnished. Everything is in place. It's ready for us to move into."

"So why don't you just go?"

"Because Harry wants me to stay here till he gets back from London. And your father has forbidden me to leave."

"That's a bit rich," Tim said, looking surprised. "I don't think Dad has any right."

"He said I was ill and it would be criminal negligence to allow me to stay in the house on my own."

"You don't look ill to me," Tim said. "You were a bit shocked after the death of the baby. We all were. But you look perfectly fine now."

"But that's the whole point," she went on, quickly. "I do feel well, and yet everyone is treating me as if I was insane. And sometimes I think it might be deliberate."

He looked shocked. "Deliberate? How do you mean?"

"I think someone might be trying to tip me over the edge."

He suddenly sat upright on the bed. "I don't follow you."

"There was an incident last night. About three o'clock, something woke me up. And I discovered the door of Emily's nursery was open and the light on. That room has been closed since she died and Harry removed all her baby things. He thought it was better that we didn't keep reminding ourselves.

"I decided to investigate and when I entered the nursery I saw Emily's cot. That was a big shock. But when I went closer and looked in, I saw a baby wrapped in a blanket. And when I lifted it up, I discovered it was a doll."

Tim's face had gone pale. "My God, that must have been terrifying."

"It was absolutely horrifying. I started screaming and then I passed out. Your mother found me and brought me round."

"So that's what the screaming was about! I heard it too. I came over to investigate but Mum said she you were just having a nightmare so I left."

"So that was you – I heard her speaking to someone, saying she could manage."

"So what did she think when she saw the cot?"

"She didn't. That's the whole point. When I woke up the cot was gone. The room was empty."

"Gone?"

"Please believe me, Tim! Nobody else will, I'm sure!"

"Of course, I believe you," he said.

"There's something else," she went on.

"Yes?"

"I'm certain I locked the door last night. I distinctly remember doing it."

He was staring at her now. "This sounds really sinister. It sounds like someone was definitely playing mind games with you."

"I think so too. But your mother was trying to tell me I imagined the whole thing or that it was a bad dream. That's what infuriated me, the fact that she wouldn't take me seriously. That's what made me lose my temper with her and have the row. I know what I saw, Tim. I know the evidence of my own eyes. And I know that cot and that doll were real. And I have proof."

"Proof?"

"When I found I was holding a doll, I flung it away. And a piece of it must have broken off because this morning, I discovered a little fragment of pink plastic on the nursery floor."

Tim's eyes narrowed. "That certainly sounds pretty convincing," he said.

"There's something else I want to ask you."

"Sure, fire away."

She hesitated. "This may sound crazy but do you think there is any possibility that little Emily's death might not have been SIDS?"

He looked startled. "I'm not sure I understand what you're saying, Erin."

"I'm really asking if you think she could have been murdered."

He stared at her for what seemed like a very long time.

"I don't know," he said at last, "but after what you've just told me, I'm beginning to think that anything is possible. In fact . . ." He stopped and shook his head.

"What?"

"No, forget it."

She reached out and touched his arm. "What, Tim?"

"I don't want to frighten you any further, but if I was in your shoes, I'd begin to worry for my own safety."

Erin left her brother-in-law's room and made her way back to the flat. She was very glad she had spoken to him. At least he had listened to her and hadn't dismissed her as a fantasist. He hadn't told her she was imagining things. He hadn't hinted that she was depressed or tired or ill or used any of the fancy words the people round here employed when they were actually suggesting she was mad. Tim had *believed* her. And that was such a relief in a house where no one took her seriously any more.

Of course, Tim was a little bit like her. He was an outsider. He was the son who wouldn't conform. He was the maverick who wanted to pursue his creative talent despite his parents' insistence that he get involved in the family business. Tim was the black sheep of the family and that meant he was able to stand aside and view them all dispassionately. And what startling conclusions he had drawn – Mrs Kavanagh the control freak who dominated their lives, Susan, the frustrated mother, trapped in a loveless marriage and Charlie Kavanagh, the workaholic who had built up the business from nowhere but was still controlled by his wife.

The only one he hadn't mentioned was Harry and that was probably out of respect for her feelings. Erin wondered what he might have said about her husband if she hadn't been married to him. Harry was the dutiful son who had knuckled down and got involved in the family business and was right this moment working his heart out in London on behalf of the company. But Harry too was under his mother's thumb. She could see that clearly now. She thought of the numerous occasions when they had been forced to change course and alter their plans just to satisfy Mrs Kavanagh's whims.

Talking to Tim had clarified her mind. He had shared her belief that there was something extremely sinister afoot in the house and he hadn't dismissed her suspicion about Emily's death – a suspicion that was rapidly growing into a conviction. And he had said something else that chimed with her thoughts. He had warned her that her own life could be in danger.

The sooner she got out of Belvedere the better. She would have to get hold of Harry and tell him what was happening. She checked the time. It was now almost seven o'clock. The day had flown. By now, Harry should have completed his engagements and be available to talk.

Once she was safely back inside the flat, she double-locked the door and fastened the safety chain. She was taking no more chances. She could feel her heart thumping as she sat down at the dining-table and took out her phone. Harry answered at the first ring.

"It's me," she said, breathless. "I've got to talk to you. Are you free?"

But before she could proceed, he interrupted her.

"You had a row with my mother," he said, coldly.

Erin stiffened. So Mrs Kavanagh hadn't wasted any time getting on to Harry to complain. This wasn't the reception she had anticipated. She had been expecting sympathy and Harry was meeting her with aggression.

"Yes, I did. She provoked me. I'm sorry but I just couldn't take any more of it. I lost my temper."

"Why did you do it, Erin?" She heard the pain in his voice. "For God's sake, could you not live in peace with her for a few more days till I returned?"

She felt herself freeze. She could tell the way this discussion was going to turn out. He was going to take his mother's part and blame her. But this time she was determined not to roll over. This time she was going to fight her corner.

"So you know someone was in my bedroom last night? You know about the cot and the doll?"

"I know what you *think* happened, Erin. My mother says it was a bad dream and she's probably being diplomatic."

"And that's exactly why we had the row, because your mother insists in putting everything down to my vivid imagination. Everybody in this house, Harry, with the exception of your brother Tim, believes I'm insane. Your father told me I was suffering from post-traumatic stress. That's his polite way of saying I'm mad. Do you know what it feels like not to be believed when you have seen things with your own eyes and know them to be true?"

"Mum says there was no cot."

"That's because whoever put it there, removed it again."

"Erin, I'm trying very hard to believe you but from where I am standing all this seems like fantasy. You have no evidence that anyone was in your room. You have no evidence there was a cot and a doll. Any rational person would reach the same conclusion as my mother."

"Ah, but I do have evidence," she said with a small note of triumph. "I found a piece of broken plastic this morning. It came from the doll. I have it in my dressing table drawer."

"Why didn't you tell my mother?"

"You want to know the truth? Because I don't trust her."

She heard a sharp intake of breath.

"Erin, I don't know what you mean by that remark but I don't like the sound of it. You really upset my mother today. She says she went out of her way to make peace with you and you spurned her overture and insulted her. I hate all this constant bickering. You know how much I want you to be friends."

"I don't trust your mother because she doesn't trust me. You know what it's like, Harry; you're a man of the world. You get back what you give out. And your mother has clearly got it into her head that I'm some sort of fantasist. And what's more, she doesn't try to hide it. Why should I trust her?"

She heard him utter a pained groan. But she pressed on.

"Something else, Harry – you don't even trust me yourself."

"What do you mean?" he said, indignantly.

"You've been withholding information from me. You never told me the reason why your mother was so desperate to have a grandchild and why she begged me to call our baby Emily."

"It was because she's wanted a grandchild for years and Susan didn't have any. I've explained all this."

"Ah yes, but there was a more compelling reason, wasn't there?"

"I don't know what you mean."

"Then I'll explain it. It was because your mother lost a child through cot death. And oddly enough, that child was also called Emily."

She heard a loud gasp at the end of the phone.

"Erin, I don't know where you're getting this stuff but it simply isn't true. Who told you that? Was it one of the servants?"

"It was someone who knows the family secrets."

"It isn't true, Erin! My mother never lost a baby. She had three children and Tim was the last. There never was a baby called Emily except our own poor little mite."

"That's the official party line, is it?"

"Erin, I'm beginning to run out of patience. You are really trying me. Why don't you do a couple of simple things?"

"What?"

"I'm not asking you to apologise but –"

"Really? Well, that's good to know."

He ignored her remark. "Please don't mention that story again. It's extremely hurtful and it's totally untrue."

"Harry, you're not listening to me. I have to get out of this house immediately. I don't feel safe here."

She heard him sigh.

"This is your imagination, Erin. I want you to stay exactly where you are. I want you to make a special effort to get along with my mother. It's only for another couple of days and then I'll be home."

"And why should I do that, Harry?"

"Do I have to spell it out? Because I'm asking you and you're my wife and I have a right to expect you to please me with a small thing like this!"

She had heard enough. Even Harry was refusing to believe her. "But that's the cause of all this trouble, isn't it? I have done *everything* to please you. I got married where you wanted. I had the christening where you wanted. I came to live in this goddamned house to please you. And I've stayed in it far longer than I ever intended."

"You know there were very good reasons, Erin."

She could feel her head about to explode. "Were there? Maybe if we had moved to our new house weeks ago, little Emily would still be alive. Has that ever occurred to you? Maybe if we hadn't stayed so long in Belvedere, she wouldn't have been murdered!"

She ended the call and put the phone down, feeling her body shake with nervous exhaustion. She'd just said the unthinkable to her husband but she felt no remorse. Instead she felt a grim satisfaction. She had finally got all the pent-up frustration out of her system and it felt good. She had reached the end of the line. She was fed up being nice to people and playing pretend when all they did was treat her like a fool. And she was not going to spend one more night in this awful house at the mercy of whichever warped individual was playing sick mind games with her and might even kill her. Regardless of what Harry might want, she was leaving now.

Anne had promised to come and pick her up if things became intolerable. Well, they were pretty intolerable now. She had her mind made up. She would ring her sister right away. She would spend the night with her and tomorrow she would move into Larchfield. She would pack her remaining clothes in a bag and go.

Buoyed up by her resolution she lifted the phone again and rang her sister's number. But once again she was passed over to the message minder. Anne must still have her damned phone switched off even though it was long past her finishing time at work. She sat down at her computer and trawled through her emails. There was one from Ger Armstrong asking her to call about work. And there was also one from Anne! She quickly opened it and scanned the contents.

Hi Erin,
I had to go down to Cork at short notice so I'll be out of touch for a few days. Will make sure to contact you as soon as I get back.
Best,
Anne

She felt her spirits sink as she read the mail. She had been counting on Anne. She desperately tried to think what to do next. This was a setback but she wasn't going to give up. There were other avenues she could try. She had the keys to the new house. She could go there directly. And she had her credit card. If necessary, she could simply find a bed and breakfast and stay there for a few days till Anne got back. Whatever it cost, she was getting out of this house tonight.

She dug out a travel bag from the back of the closet and quickly filled it with clothes, her toiletries, make-up bags and a few other essentials. She checked her handbag. She had some spare cash. She considered her next course of action. She could order a taxi to come and get her but that ran the certain risk of being stopped by Charlie Kavanagh or some of the staff. He had already told her he would not allow her to leave till Harry returned.

The other alternative was to try to make her way down the drive unseen and escape on foot. She went to the window and peered out. Tommy Murphy and another man were standing on the front lawn as if on guard duty. Her father-in-law must have posted them there to watch for her. It would be impossible to get past them unseen.

She let the curtains fall back and slumped down on the settee while she considered her options. She could try leaving the house by some other door but even if she was successful, it would be too late. It was now ten to eight. In ten minutes, the gates would be closed. They did it every night for security reasons. Even if by some miracle she managed to make her way from the house and get past Tommy Murphy, she would never get out of the grounds. A sickening feeling was gathering in the pit of her stomach at the realisation that she was trapped.

There was one last possibility. She could ring the police and tell them she was being held against her will. But what would happen? The family would summon Dr Bellows. He would say she was unstable and in need of constant supervision. And who were the police likely to believe? They would surely take the word of a doctor and a respectable businessman before someone like her.

Erin's head began to spin. She felt like weeping with frustration. She was a prisoner. She couldn't leave. She had no choice but to spend another night in this frightening house. The thought left her drained and defeated. Despite her best efforts, they had succeeded in keeping her here. Now she regretted that she hadn't left sooner when she had the chance. If she had gone this morning, she would now be safely away from Belvedere with all its menace and fear. Instead, she was a captive at the mercy of whatever dangers lurked beyond the four walls of her room. And there was no one she could trust, not even her husband.

It occurred to her that it was strange that he had made no attempt to phone her back after she ended the call with that terrible accusation.

She needed a drink. She went to the cabinet and poured a stiff brandy. By now she could feel the shakes start up again. The smooth spirit slid down her throat and warmed her stomach and then she realised she had barely eaten anything all day. She must have food. She must force herself to eat. She needed strength for whatever ordeals might lie ahead. She went into the kitchen and found a spaghetti dish in the fridge. She heated it up and sat by the window slowly eating it while night began to fall.

There was one small ray of hope. If she managed to survive this night, she could make a fresh attempt in the morning. The gates opened again at eight. She had her bag packed. She could leave at dawn and hide in the woods till it was possible to escape. This thought gave her courage. She sat down at her computer once more and wrote a lengthy email to Anne detailing everything that had occurred and telling her sister of her suspicions about Emily and the dangers she felt. Now, if anything happened to her there would be a record with someone she could trust.

Writing the email made her feel better. She showered and checked once more that the door was securely locked and bolted. Then she sat down again at the window. Tonight, she wouldn't sleep. At all costs, she must stay awake. She had to remain on her guard in case harm came to her again. And in the morning, at first light, she would go.

Gradually, an eerie stillness settled over the house. The birds which had been chirping in the eaves fell silent and nothing stirred. Erin sat up and tried to read but she found it difficult to concentrate and her mind kept wandering. Over and over, she rehearsed the events of the last few days till at last her head felt weary. Despite her fear, it was an effort to stay awake. Slowly, her eyelids drooped and her head sank down on her chest and she fell into a sleep.

The dawn light woke her. She sat up with a start, angry with herself that she had slept. She checked her watch. It was ten past seven. It was time to make her move. But first she had to check that the coast was clear. She went to the window and drew back the curtains to see the lie of the land. And as she did so, she felt her chest tighten into a ball.

The early morning mist was beginning to clear and there, plainly visible on the front lawn, was little Emily's buggy.

Chapter 32

For a moment, she was stunned but her initial shock quickly gave way to determination. Here on the lawn was all the evidence she required. Who was going to doubt her now? Suddenly she was seized with fresh energy. She threw on her housecoat over her nightdress and quickly undid the locks of the bedroom door. Next moment, she was frantically racing down the stairs as fast as her legs could carry her.

Her heart was pounding now. She must get to the buggy and seize it. Then she would have her proof. They would have no choice but to believe her. Someone had put the buggy there in another effort to terrorise her. She had absolutely no doubt it was the same person who had left the cot and the doll in the nursery.

The locks on the heavy front door held her back. As she struggled with them, a sweat broke on her brow. Her hands felt wet and clammy. She must get out quickly. She had no time to waste. Every minute counted. At last, she managed to undo the bolts and the doors creaked open. She ran out of the house and into the cold morning air.

The buggy was still there, some distance from the house. She took off across the wet grass, damp and slippery with dew. This was an incredible piece of luck. She would be able to seize it before anyone had a chance to take it away again. But as she drew closer, she got a start. A figure emerged from the back of the house and began to approach the buggy. He was a small, thin man. He walked with his head bowed and seemed unaware of Erin running towards him. When he reached the buggy, he bent down and lifted it on his shoulders and began to walk away.

She shouted after him but he didn't seem to hear. She tried to run as quickly as she could but it was difficult on the wet grass and her bare feet kept slipping. She wished now that she had taken time to put on shoes. The man was getting away from her, making off in the direction of the stables. For a brief moment, he lifted his head and Erin saw who it was. It was Cornish, Susan's groom!

She felt a jolt. So she had been right! This was confirmation of what she suspected. Susan was the culprit and Cornish was her accomplice. This knowledge served to give her renewed energy. She must catch up with the groom and confront him. She redoubled her efforts but suddenly she stumbled and felt her feet slide from under her. Next moment she was sprawled on the wet grass. By the time she got up, Cornish had disappeared.

But she knew where he was going. She set off again, this time at a more sure-footed pace. When she reached the stables, she stopped to catch her breath. She had to be careful now. She approached slowly, keeping her eyes alert for signs of activity. From inside the stables, she could hear the sound of the horses whinnying. Tentatively, she pushed open the door. It was dark inside but a shaft of morning sunlight cut through the gloom. The stables were empty apart from the horses, excited now at her presence. There was no sign of Cornish.

She stepped inside and let the door swing closed behind her. It took a minute for her eyes to grow accustomed to the dim light. There was a strong smell of straw and horse dung. She was able to make out the stalls ranged against the wall, the animals peering out at her with their large expectant eyes, waiting to be fed. Her glance travelled around the small cramped space, the buckets and brushes, the halters and bridles and riding equipment hanging from hooks on the walls.

She began to search each stall in turn. If Cornish was hiding in here she would find him. But they were all empty. And then she came to a door at the end of the wall. Her pulse was racing now. She reached out and pushed it open. It swung wide with a groan. It was a storage room and there propped against the wall was the buggy.

But not just the buggy! The cot was there and all the baby things that Harry had removed from the nursery. This must have been where he had stored them.

And there was the doll. Her hand slowly reached out till she had it in her grasp. In the gathering light, she was able to examine it. What she saw caused her heart to skip. There was a crack on the doll's head and a small hole where a piece had broken off!

She let out a deep breath. She felt vindicated now, justified in what she had done. And with this feeling came a new courage. She left the stables and boldly searched the yard and the outhouses but Cornish had vanished. Reluctantly she set off again across the green lawns which were sparkling in the full glory of the sun.

As she approached, she saw a strange car parked in the drive, a blue Honda that she didn't recognise. By now they would all be awake so her plan of slipping away in the dawn would have to be shelved. But a new strategy was beginning to take shape in her mind. There was no longer any need to slip away. She could walk through the gates of Belvedere a free woman and no one would stop her. For here in her hand she held the doll and in her room was the piece that had broken off it. It was all the evidence she required to prove what she had been saying all along was true.

She looked a sorry sight as she walked up the steps to the front door. She was still dressed in her night clothes and her legs were caked in mud where she had slipped and fallen. Her hair was tossed and disordered after her race across the lawn. But it didn't matter. She knew now who had been tormenting her and she had proof.

As she walked into the front hall, she found the Kavanaghs waiting. But there was someone else, a small, precise figure with shining silver hair and a neatly tailored suit.

He stepped forward and smiled.

"Hello, Erin," he said. "Do you remember me? I'm Dr Bellows. I think it's time we had a little chat."

She felt herself tense. For days now they had been urging her to see Dr Bellows and here he was at last. They led her into the drawing-room and everyone sat down. It was all very civilised. No one shouted or raised their voice. No one laid a finger on her.

"Have you had any breakfast?" Charlie Kavanagh asked. He wore a friendly smile and spoke pleasantly. His wife sat by his side and tried to conceal the concerned look that kept creeping into her face. Dr Bellows oozed calm, professional tact. He looked as relaxed as a man who had been invited for afternoon tea.

"No," she replied to her father-in-law's question. "I'm not hungry."

"Nevertheless," Charlie said, "I think I'll order some coffee and toast. I'm sure Dr Bellows will appreciate it."

He rang the bell. A maid appeared and Charlie gave the order. He stretched his legs and glanced at the doctor.

"Out for an early morning stroll?" Dr Bellows asked her politely. If he was surprised by her disordered appearance, he didn't show it.

"No," Erin said in a firm voice. "As a matter of fact, I was pursuing the person who has been waging a campaign of terror against me."

Mrs Kavanagh's eyelids fluttered. Her husband sat impassive and merely pursed his lips.

"Did you catch him?" Dr Bellows replied. "I'm assuming it was a man?"

"Yes, it was a man. And no, I didn't catch him. But I know who he is. And I also know who has been directing him."

"You mean this person hasn't been acting alone? Is there a conspiracy, do you think?"

"Oh, definitely, a conspiracy would describe it perfectly."

"And would you like to tell us who it is?"

"No," Erin replied. "I would prefer to give that information to the police."

Dr Bellow's eyes drifted slowly across the room till they came to rest on the Kavanaghs. "Why do you think the police would be interested?"

"Because I believe we are dealing with a murder investigation."

"Really?" Dr Bellows said. "That is very interesting."

At the moment the door opened and the maid appeared with a tray containing a pot of coffee and a large plate of buttered toast. Charlie thanked her and she left. He poured coffee for each of them and passed a cup to Erin.

"Drink it," he said. "It will do you good. And why don't you eat some toast? You need food."

Erin sipped the strong black, coffee. It tasted bitter but she knew it would sharpen her reflexes and help her think clearly.

"If we could just get back to this murder investigation," Dr Bellows said, gently, taking a mouthful of coffee and placing the cup and saucer on a table beside him. "Could I ask who the victim is?"

"My daughter."

"Little Emily?"

"Yes."

"But she died from SIDS. That was what the autopsy found."

"The autopsy was wrong."

"Really?"

"Yes. I think she was smothered. I think someone held her face into the mattress and stopped her breathing."

The Kavanaghs sat forward and glanced at the doctor. Charlie replaced a half-eaten slice of toast on his plate.

Dr Bellows cleared his throat. "But there is absolutely no evidence. Why would anyone want to do that?"

"Jealousy," Erin said and took another sip of coffee.

There was a moment of silence.

"You think someone murdered your baby daughter because they were jealous?" Dr Bellows asked.

"Yes."

"Do you have any proof?"

"Yes," Erin said.

"And where is it?"

"Here."

She held up the doll.

In spite of herself, Mrs Kavanagh emitted a loud gasp.

"This is the same doll that appeared in Emily's nursery two nights ago. I don't know if you are aware of the circumstances but I was wakened at 3 a.m. by an intruder in my bedroom. When I went into the nursery I found her cot with this doll in it. I passed out from the shock and Mrs Kavanagh found me."

"But Mrs Kavanagh assures me there was no cot and no doll," the doctor said.

"That's because the person who put them there removed them again."

"And why would they do that?"

"To frighten me, to terrorise me. To make me believe I was going mad. That's what everyone thinks, isn't it? That's why you're questioning me now."

She looked at each of them in turn but they avoided her eyes.

"No one has suggested anything of the kind, Erin," the doctor said. "Do you think you're mad?"

"Of course not."

"But you think your life is in danger? You told

your husband last night you didn't feel safe in Belvedere."

So that explained why Harry hadn't rung her back! Instead, he had got on the phone and reported her conversation to the family.

"No, I don't feel safe. I believe the person who murdered Emily may try to murder me. That's why I'm leaving today."

There was a pained look on Mrs Kavanagh's face while Charlie sank his head in his hands and sighed.

The doctor took a deep breath. "Erin, I have to say that any casual observer would regard your recent behaviour as bizarre at the very least. You have been making wild accusations about people in this house. You have been imagining things that clearly didn't happen. You told your husband that Mrs Kavanagh lost a baby through cot death. I have been the family physician for over thirty years and I can assure you that definitely did not occur."

"Are you going to tell me that the buggy on the lawn didn't happen either?"

The Kavanaghs looked at each other.

"What buggy?" Dr Bellows asked, softly.

"The buggy that was there this morning when I woke up. Emily's buggy. That's why I left the house."

"And where is it now?"

"In the stables, along with all the rest of her stuff. But I also found this." She held up the doll again. "And this is the proof that there was someone in my room that night. Look at its head. Do you see where there is a piece missing? Well, I found that piece on the nursery floor yesterday morning *after* the cot and the doll had been removed. I have it in my room. Come with me now and I'll show you."

She stood up and the others reluctantly followed. Erin wrapped her housecoat tight around her and proceeded up the stairs to the flat. The door was lying open just as she had left it over an hour ago when she ran from the room. They trooped into the bedroom and stood awkwardly around while she bent and opened the dressing-table drawer.

"Here it is," she said, proudly taking out the tissue paper.

She quickly unwrapped it and held it out for their inspection.

The paper was empty.

Dr Bellows was the first to speak.

"Erin, you have been going through a very tough time since the baby's death. I think you need a complete rest. I'm going to refer you to a very pleasant sanatorium where you'll get all the care and attention you require."

She stared at him with horror-filled eyes. "Someone took that piece of plastic. It was there yesterday."

"Please sit down, Erin, while I explain."

"I'm not going to any sanatorium!" she shouted. "I'm getting out of this damned house this morning just as soon as I change my clothes."

Dr Bellows was continuing to speak calmly but

now a harder, firmer note had entered his voice.

"Erin, you are suffering a nervous breakdown brought on by shock at the death of your baby. You are not capable of making rational decisions about your own future. I have interviewed you and in my opinion you require hospitalisation."

"I am not going," she said. "You can't force me against my will."

Dr Bellows was taking a sheet of paper from the breast pocket of his well-tailored suit. "I also have an authorisation to commit you, signed by your husband and faxed to me last night to be used at my discretion. I have the authority, Erin."

She felt a shock run through her. She couldn't believe that Harry would do such a thing. He had betrayed her. Her own husband who she loved and had stood by faithfully all their married life had signed an authorisation to have her committed to an asylum. She felt the betrayal cut through her like a knife.

For the first time, she noticed that Dr Bellows was carrying a little case. He opened it and took out a syringe.

She backed away in terror. "No!" she screamed. "I'm not going. I'm perfectly sane. There's nothing wrong with me."

She tried to run but Charlie Kavanagh quickly stepped forward and took a firm hold of her.

"This is for your own good," Dr Bellows said as the needle slipped in. "In the long run, you're going to thank me."

Chapter 33

Erin's eyes focussed on a cluster of bright red lights. They seemed like the lights of a faraway town but it had to be a small town because there were so few of them and they seemed so close together. And then the lights began to blur and dissolve into a mass of crimson colour and she realised she was looking at a vase of flowers and the sun was shining on them through the window. She pulled herself up and stared at the large bouquet of roses beside her bed.

She felt as if she was emerging from a long, drowsy sleep, the sort of sleep she used to have when she had worked too hard and fallen into bed dog-tired. But now she felt refreshed. She must get up at once and start doing things.

But where was she? She didn't recognise her surroundings. She was in a bright room beside a window. There was another bed next to hers and two more across from her. And where were her clothes?

She was wearing a loose cotton nightdress that she
had never seen before and there was a little plastic
band attached to her wrist with her name written in
large capital letters: ERIN O'NEILL.

She threw back the sheets. There was a pair of
slippers on the floor beside the bed and she didn't
recognise them either. She slipped her feet into the
slippers and walked unsteadily towards a door at the
end of the room.

"It's locked," a voice said.

She turned quickly. A small, pale face was staring
at her from one of the beds across the room.

"Locked?" Erin whispered.

"Yes. You're wasting your time. You can't get out.
If you want something, press the bell above your bed
and a nurse will come."

"A nurse?" Erin said, in disbelief. "Is this a
hospital?"

"That's what they say. I call it the loony bin."

Erin stopped and approached the woman's bed.
She could see that she was about thirty years of age
with short, black hair and pale, white cheeks. She was
sunk deep into the bed so that only her head and face
were visible.

"Where exactly am I?" she asked.

"Avondale Sanatorium."

"I want to go home."

The woman's face broke into a weary smile. "You
can't go home," she said. "That's why the door is
locked."

Erin sat on the edge of her bed and tried to figure things out. What was she doing here? How did she get here? Where was Harry? Her head was muzzy and she seemed to recall having this very same feeling before. It crossed her mind that this was a dream and she was going to wake up and find herself back in her bedroom at Belvedere. And thinking about Belvedere seemed to shift a cog in her brain and the events of the past twenty-four hours began to emerge like familiar objects from a mist.

She remembered the dawn and the buggy on the lawn in front of the house. She remembered running across the wet grass towards the stables. She remembered finding the storeroom with all Emily's baby stuff. She remembered the doll with the hole in its head. And suddenly the pieces of the jigsaw puzzle fell into place in a burst of clarity.

Charlie Kavanagh, Mrs Kavanagh, Dr Bellows. The conference in the drawing-room while they drank coffee and Charlie ate buttered toast. The visit to her bedroom so that she could show them the piece of plastic she had found. She remembered Dr Bellows taking a letter from his pocket, then opening his case and bringing out a syringe while all the time he smiled calmly like a favourite uncle. She remembered screaming in terror and trying to escape. And after that, oblivion.

That's why she had felt like this before. Dr Bellows had given her a sedative to knock her out. She was in an asylum and Harry had put her here. Her own husband had given the doctor authority to have her committed. She closed her eyes and felt the crushing despair descend on her like a black cloud. All the sadness and frustration of the last few weeks overwhelmed her and she felt her chest heave. She began to weep.

Bitter tears streamed down her cheeks. She had come to this: incarcerated in a locked ward in a mental hospital. And she had done nothing wrong. All the wrong had been done to her. She thought of her dead child, the slights and hostility she had been forced to endure, their refusal to believe what she was telling them, things she had witnessed with her own eyes. And instead of sympathy and understanding there was this. Erin flung herself down on the bed and sobbed uncontrollably.

After a while, she felt a hand softly brush her cheek and turned to find the strange woman sitting beside her and looking at her with big, sad eyes.

"Hush," she said. "It's not so bad. Stop crying."

"I don't want to be here!" Erin sobbed. "There's nothing wrong with me!"

"Then the best thing you can do is start acting normal." She took a piece of kitchen roll from her sleeve and gave it to Erin. "Blow your nose. Wipe your eyes."

Erin did as she was told.

"What's your name?" the woman asked.

"Erin."

"I'm Margaret," the woman continued. "Now the

first thing you must do is calm down. They'll be coming to visit you soon. Don't argue with them. Just agree with whatever they say. You'll find that's the best policy."

"My husband signed me in here," Erin said. "Can you believe that?"

"Sure I can. Husbands, fathers, sisters, brothers, they all do it. But there's no point feeling sore about it. They have you here now. What you have to do is be clever."

"How long will I have to stay?"

"Till they say you're ready to go."

"How long have you been here?"

"Two months. But I've been here before."

"Why? What did you do?"

"I set fire to the house."

"I did nothing," Erin said. "Everything was done to me."

She got back into bed and rang the bell. A few minutes later a nurse came bouncing gaily into the room. She was so young and fresh she looked like she should still be in school.

"Hello, Erin," she said. She bent over the bed and smiled into Erin's face. "So you're awake. How do you feel this morning?"

"I feel fine, thank you."

"Good. And look at these lovely roses your husband sent you. Aren't they beautiful?"

She lowered her nose to the flowers and breathed deeply. "They smell wonderful. And there's a card with them. Do you want to see it?"

She held out the card for Erin to read.

*With all my love. Get well soon. We're all behind
you. Harry.*

"I think it's a lovely card," the nurse said, taking it
back and placing it on the table beside the flowers.
"My name is Clara, by the way. What can I do for
you, Erin?"

"I want to use the bathroom."

"Of course, come with me. Can you get out of bed
by yourself or do you need assistance?"

"I think I'll be okay on my own, thank you."

While she waited, the nurse glanced over at the
other bed.

"Hi, Margaret, how are you today?"

"When is lunch?"

"In half an hour. Roast beef today. And apple pie
and custard. You like roast beef, don't you?"

"I've eaten worse," Margaret grunted.

Clara turned her attention back to Erin.

"Can you walk unaided? Head a bit light?"

"No, my head is clear, thank you. I should be all
right."

Clara led the way and Erin followed. When they
got to the door, the nurse produced a plastic card and
slid it through a scanner. There was a click and the
lock shot open. Now, they were out in a bigger ward
with more beds and a nurse's work station in the
centre of the room. The bathrooms were beside the
work station. As she passed, Clara picked up a towel

and a bar of soap and led Erin inside. There was a row of open cubicles and another row of handbasins. In the corner, two showers stood.

"Do you want to wash?" the nurse asked.

"Yes."

"I've got to stay with you."

"Why?"

"It's the regulations. But you'll get used to it. Just go right ahead and I'll wait for you."

There was a chair beside the door and the nurse sat down. Erin went into the first shower and drew the curtain. At least in here there was some privacy. She was beginning to realise that Avondale was unlike any hospital she had ever seen. Would she ever get used to the locked doors and constant supervision? She thought bitterly of the roses from Harry and the card: *With all my love.* What a hypocrite! He had signed her in here. She felt like weeping all over again and then she remembered Margaret's advice. She drove the thoughts from her mind and turned on the shower.

When she had finished washing, Clara returned her to the ward and waited while she got back into bed.

"There are a few more regulations you need to know," she announced in her chirpy voice as if she was explaining the rules of the local tennis club. "You can't send or receive telephone calls. You can't have visits. You can't leave the ward without permission and supervision. If you need anything, ring the bell and one of the nurses will come. We can get you newspapers or books from the library. You have a television above your bed. It's operated by remote control. We require you to keep the sound down in deference to other patients. Okay?"

Erin nodded.

"After lunch, Dr McAllister will come and have a little talk with you. When he thinks you are ready, you'll be moved to a general ward and most of these restrictions will be relaxed so you'll be able to have visitors." She smiled. "And one final thing, there's no smoking here."

"I don't smoke," Erin said.

"Well, that's good. Now you just make yourself comfortable and soon we'll start serving lunch."

By the time the food arrived, Erin was starving. She tried to recall the last time she had eaten anything and couldn't remember. But the lunch was surprisingly good, tender slices of roast beef and creamed potatoes with carrots and cauliflower. She ate everything on her plate and polished off the apple pie that followed.

By now, her mind was clearing again. Her first thought was how she was going to get out of here. Once more, she recalled her earlier conversation with Margaret. *What you have to do is be clever.* She mustn't argue with them. Arguing hadn't helped her in the past. She must tell them what they wanted to hear. She must give them no reason to doubt she was a normal, sane person who by some ghastly mistake had found herself incarcerated here. When Clara came to take away the tray, Erin asked if she could get her some newspapers and a book to read.

About an hour later, she was engrossed in *The Clarion,* when she heard the door open and a tall man with blond hair came in. He looked about forty and had a warm, pleasant face. He waved to Margaret and came and sat down at Erin's bed.

"Hello, Erin," he said. "Anything interesting in the paper today?"

"Quite a lot," she said.

"Do you read the paper often?"

"I have to. I'm a journalist."

"Really? That's a very interesting job."

"It has its moments," she replied.

He held out his hand. "I'm Dr McAllister. I thought I'd pay you a little visit."

"I was expecting you," Erin said.

"Oh? Did Clara tell you I was coming?"

"Yes."

Dr McAllister was smiling now and Erin noticed how white and even his teeth were, as if he'd had them specially straightened.

"How do you feel?"

"I feel good, thank you."

"Has your head cleared by now?"

"Yes."

"Do you mind if I carry out a few routine checks?"

He stood up and pulled the screens round the bed, then took a stethoscope from the pocket of his coat and listened to her heart. He made a note on his clipboard and then checked her blood pressure. Finally he took her temperature.

All the while, he continued to smile. Smiling seemed to be mandatory in Avondale. Everybody did it.

"Now the first thing I want to say is that you are absolutely safe here. This is a place of safety. You are in a private sanatorium and we have very tight security. No one can get in here so you are in no danger."

"That's good to know," Erin said.

He looked at some notes on his clipboard. "Do you feel agitated or nervous?"

"No."

"Concerned about anything? Worried?"

Erin shook her head.

"Excellent. Your blood pressure and heartbeat are both normal and so is your temperature. You're in very good physical condition, Erin. Do you get much exercise?"

"I walk quite a bit and recently I've been horse-riding."

"That's fine. Exercise is very important. Now, I understand you were concerned that someone was trying to murder you? Would you like to tell me about that?"

He spoke in a matter-of-fact voice as if they were having a conversation about the weather. But his manner invited confidence. Maybe, at last, she had found someone who would believe her.

"It's a long story," she began. "Bad things began to happen to me. A baby's cot was left in the nursery while I was asleep. And then the buggy was left on the lawn. And no one would listen."

As she spoke, she knew these were the wrong things to say. They made no sense. To Dr McAllister they must sound like the ravings of a lunatic.

"That would frighten anybody," he said. "It would frighten me. And as a result of these events, you decided that your life was in danger?"

"My baby died."

"Tell me about that."

She related the history of little Emily's death.

"That must have been a terrible shock for you."

"It was devastating. We all loved her. You've no idea . . ." She broke off as she felt all the grief and sadness return.

Dr McAlister reached out and gently patted her hand. "I do have an idea, Erin. I've spoken to lots of women who have had similar experiences. It is one of the most traumatic events that can happen to anyone. You've given birth to this child, your own flesh and blood, and you've watched it grow and develop. Then to find the child is dead is absolutely shattering."

"Thank you, doctor."

"If you're finding this difficult, we can leave it till another time."

"No," she said, "I'd like to continue. I'd like you to understand exactly what happened."

For the next half hour she went back over her experiences with the Kavanaghs from the very first time they had been introduced to the final confrontation in her bedroom. Dr McAllister listened patiently and took notes. When she was finished, he began asking questions.

"You felt they didn't like you, is that right?"

"Some of them liked me and some of them didn't."

"But you were made to feel like an outsider?"

"Exactly."

"Did that make you angry?"

"Sometimes."

"Angry enough to want to harm them?"

An alarm bell went off in Erin's head. This was a dangerous question. It was a booby trap carefully concealed among the other more innocent inquiries. She had to be careful how she replied.

"No," she said. "I never wished them any harm."

Dr McAllister seemed satisfied. He put his pen away and stood up.

"We'll continue this conversation tomorrow, if that's all right. I'm going to ask the nurse to give you a sleeping tablet tonight, just to help you relax."

"No," she said quickly. "I won't need it."

He looked at her for a moment. "Okay. But if you have difficulty sleeping, ring for the nurse and she'll give you something."

He shook hands again, pulled back the screens and was gone.

"Well," Margaret asked when the door had closed, "did you do what I said?"

"I tried."

"Did you give him the right answers?"

"I hope so," Erin said.

Chapter 34

The following morning at eight Clara arrived with one of the catering staff to serve breakfast.

"Wakey, wakey!" she announced in her cheerful voice.

She pulled back the screens around Margaret's bed then took four tablets from her pocket and poured some syrupy liquid into a little plastic cup.

"Let me see you take your medication," she said.

Margaret sat up and rubbed the sleep from her eyes, then swallowed the tablets and the liquid.

Next the nurse turned to Erin. "Nothing for you today. How did you sleep?"

Erin hadn't slept at all. She had lain awake for most of the night brooding about her situation and what she could do about it. But she was learning to heed Margaret's advice.

"Very well," she said.

"That's good," Clara said pulling back the curtains

and flooding the room with light. "Look at that lovely morning. Now who is having boiled eggs and who is having poached?

"Boiled eggs, please," Margaret said in a slurred voice and Erin followed her lead.

"Two for boiled eggs," Clara announced and the catering lady proceeded to serve them with a tray containing tea, toast, orange juice, boiled eggs and a slice of ham.

"*Bon appétit*," Clara said and was gone.

"Where does that young one get all the energy?" Margaret asked, pouring out the tea. "I wonder is she taking something herself?"

After breakfast they were taken separately to the bathroom to shower and then they were led out to the garden for exercise and fresh air. The garden had seats and flower-beds and high walls topped by barbed wire. As soon as they were out in the open, Margaret took a packet of cigarettes from her pocket. She opened it and offered one to Erin.

"I don't smoke," she replied.

"Well, I do," Margaret replied, striking a match and sucking deeply on the cigarette. "It's one of the few pleasures I've got left."

They began to walk around the perimeter of the garden.

"Why are we locked in?" Erin asked.

"Because we're category A."

"What does that mean?"

"It means they think we're dangerous."

"Dangerous?" Erin asked in disbelief.

"Yeah, or they think we might try to escape or maybe harm ourselves."

"But you're not dangerous," Erin said.

"Want to bet? I told you I set fire to the house. I also stabbed my partner and tried to throttle one of the doctors. They had to restrain me."

"But you look so calm."

"That's because I'm doped up to the eyeballs. You saw the medication she gave me this morning. It would knock out a racehorse."

"I'm not dangerous," Erin said.

"Then maybe they'll let you out. If you keep on the right side of Dr McAllister he might release you into the general ward. But be careful with him. He's a sly one."

"A sly one?" Erin asked.

"He's nice as pie, isn't he, always smiling with his nice white teeth? But that's so he'll get you to talk. He's like a detective with his questions. Just be careful what you tell him. He's the one who'll decide your future."

"And will there only be the two of us in the locked ward?"

"Who knows? There could be two more when we get back. It all depends who comes in today."

Margaret finished her cigarette and lit up another one and smoked it down to the butt. On the way back to the ward, Clara searched them both and removed Margaret's matches and cigarettes.

"They'll be waiting for you tomorrow," she said with her permanent smile.

Erin spent the morning lying in bed and thinking about what Margaret had said. Dr McAllister would decide whether she got out of here. But he was sly so she had to be careful what she told him. She had already told him too much. After lunch, he came to see her again. He began with general inquiries about how she was feeling and how well she had slept. Then he began questioning her.

"Tell me about your family life?" he said. "How did you get on with your parents?"

"Very well. They were loving parents. We are a very close, happy family."

"When you were a child was there any animosity?"

"How do you mean?"

"Were there any fights or arguments?"

"None that I can remember."

"What about your sister? How did you get on with her?"

"We got on very well. We still do."

"Was there any sibling rivalry? Did you ever think your sister was treated better than you?"

"I don't think so."

"Did either of your parents drink?"

"They drink socially. But they aren't regular drinkers."

"Was there any violence in the family?"

Erin shook her head.

"Tell me about your father. Was he a dominant figure in your life?"

The questions went back and forth. Some of them seemed meaningless but others were quite personal. If it wasn't a doctor who was asking, Erin would have refused to answer.

As she gave her replies, he took notes on his clipboard. When the session was ended, he stood up and shook hands and said he would see her again the following afternoon.

On the third day, Dr McAllister came in with a frown on his face. It was the first time she had not seen him smile. She immediately felt apprehensive.

He sat down beside the bed and took out his pen and looked at her for a long time with his pale blue eyes.

"I don't believe you've been honest with me," he said.

She felt her chest tighten. She knew the power this man had over her. She desperately wanted to please him.

"How do you mean?"

"You're holding something back. I want to return to the death of little Emily. It seems to me that's when all the trouble began."

She felt frightened. There was no telling what went on in Dr McAllister's head or what he was going to decide.

"What do you want to know?"

"Tell me how you felt when you found your baby dead."

"I was distraught with grief. I couldn't believe it had happened. I was in a state of shock. I don't remember much about the immediate aftermath because Dr Bellows sedated me."

"Afterwards, did you wonder why it had happened?"

"Yes."

"Would you say you were depressed?"

"I suppose so."

"Did you think that God was punishing you for something you might have done?"

"No, I never thought like that."

"Are you sure?"

"I'm certain. The God I believe in doesn't punish people. People punish themselves through their own actions."

Dr McAllister paused. As he asked the questions, his eyes bored into her. Only now, they were no longer soft and kind but hard and challenging.

"Did you ever think your life wasn't worth living?"

"No, I never thought that."

"Did you ever consider taking your own life?"

Erin was shocked. "No. That thought never entered my head."

"You told Dr Bellows you didn't believe it was a SIDS death. You said you believed your baby had been murdered."

"Yes."

"Why did you form that opinion?"

"Because it happened so quickly and she had never

shown signs of illness before. She was a perfectly healthy child and then she was dead."

"Was there any other reason?"

"I told you about the threatening notes. I assumed there was some connection. I thought the person who had sent the notes had also killed Emily."

"But your husband said the notes had come from a crank."

"I think he was wrong."

"So you still believe she was murdered?"

Erin sensed she was on dangerous ground. The answer she gave could condemn her. She swallowed hard.

"Yes – I think that is possible."

"Do you have a suspect in mind?"

An image of Susan flashed into her head, the scowl on her face when she received the necklace at the Christmas lunch from Mrs Kavanagh. And it was quickly followed by another picture of the groom Cornish, carrying away the baby's buggy from the front lawn.

She shook her head.

"No," she said.

Dr McAllister brought his face close and stared at her.

"Did you talk of murder because you had considered killing the child yourself?"

Erin gasped. She reeled from the brutality of the question. This was the most outrageous thing she had ever heard. Thinking of killing her own child! How could he even suggest such a thing? She felt like reaching out and clawing his face.

"No!" she shouted. "How can you sit there and say that?"

"Why not? It happens. The child gets on the mother's nerves, particularly a mother who is highly strung or depressed. It's always crying, looking for attention. She kills it in a moment of anger."

"No!" Erin screamed. "I loved my child! I loved her more than myself. I would never have harmed a hair on her head. I'm devastated by her death. You should be ashamed of yourself to even suggest such a thing!"

There was silence when she finished. Dr McAllister continued to stare at her. Then he folded away his pen and stood up.

"That's enough for today," he said. "Thank you for giving me your time."

She didn't watch him go. She heard his footsteps echo across the floor and then the sound of the door banging firmly shut and the lock snapping into place. She lay on the bed and listened to the sound of her heart pounding in her breast. She was furious with Dr McAllister but just as much, she was furious with herself. Despite her resolve, she had allowed him to provoke her and she had reacted in the worst way possible – by screaming at him. Now he would certainly regard her as deranged and possibly even violent. She would never get out of here.

But what a provocation! Her mind still reeled from

the horror of his questioning. How could he possibly believe she would have hurt little Emily? How could he suggest such a thing? He was a psychiatrist. Yet he seemed to have learnt nothing about her in the days he had been interviewing her. He couldn't see that she would rather have died herself than see her child harmed.

She felt pity and frustration and outrage well up in her breast. She was incarcerated in this place and at their mercy. A criminal in prison was in a better situation because he had a sentence and knew when he would be released. But she could be kept here indefinitely until Dr McAllister deemed her well enough to go out into the world again. And her husband had signed the authorisation which allowed this to happen.

Deep feelings of resentment welled up inside her. Harry had been responsible. Without his authorisation, Dr Bellows could not have committed her. Harry was the one who had sent her here. He had sided with his family against her and not for the first time.

She thought what would have happened if the positions had been reversed. Would she have done the same thing to him? Not in a million years. And he had signed the authorisation solely on the word of Dr Bellows without speaking to her. He hadn't even given her a chance to defend herself. His behaviour had been outrageous. He had sent her roses but that was probably the action of a guilty conscience. How could she ever forgive him?

And then another thought came to her. What if Dr McAllister had been testing her? What if he had been voicing a suspicion that was already forming in their minds? What if they had decided that little Emily had indeed been murdered *but that she, Erin, had been the murderer?*

The horror of such a scenario overwhelmed her. Suddenly she realised just how helpless she was. If they accused her of killing her baby, how would she prove her innocence? It would be impossible. And now she could see exactly how they would go about it. They would say she was depressed, her mind was upset. The child had been getting on her nerves. She had tipped over and murdered the baby in a fit of rage. It would be her word against theirs and already they had her locked up here in a mental hospital.

She sank her head in her hands. This was worse than she had thought. It was turning into a nightmare. To be accused of murdering her own child when she knew exactly who had done it. And possibly to be convicted! How could she live with it? Now she wished she had some of those tranquillisers that made poor Margaret so calm and placid. She needed something, anything to numb her feeling and give her a few hours of blessed oblivion.

She heard the screen rustle. It was Margaret come to sympathise with her.

"Dr McAllister certainly left in a hurry," she said. "Did you give him the wrong answer?"

Erin forced herself to look at her. "It was worse

than that, Margaret. I screamed at him. You heard me."

"That wasn't a very clever thing, now was it?"

"I didn't mean to do it. He just pushed me too far."

"I told you he was a sly one," Margaret said. "Now what are you going to do?"

Erin shook her head. She had no idea what was going to happen next. But she knew one thing – whatever it was would be bad.

The day crawled by. She lay in bed staring at the ceiling, alternatively feeling sorry for herself and trying to figure out what she was going to do. To be accused of murdering her own baby would be the ultimate horror story. It was so awful that she tried to blank it from her mind.

She thought of escape but she knew it would be impossible. The ward was locked, the walls were high and topped with barbed wire and she was in her nightclothes. How far would she get? She had no option but to stay here till they decided otherwise.

When it came time for tea, she couldn't eat.

"What's wrong with you?" Clara asked. "No appetite?"

"I'm not feeling well. Dr McAllister said you would give me something to make me sleep."

Clara looked at her. "Is that what you want?"

Erin nodded. Sleep would be escape for her. It would release her from the raging torment in her mind.

The nurse came back with a tablet and a glass of water.

"Here we go," she said. "Sweet dreams."

Chapter 35

It was morning when Erin woke again and the ward was filled with light. She opened her eyes to find Clara bending over her again.

"How did you sleep?"

"Well."

"Good. You're to get your stuff together and come with me."

"Where are we going?"

"To the general ward."

Erin rubbed her eyes. Was this some cruel joke they were playing on her? By now, she was so confused she didn't know what to think.

"You mean, I'm getting out of here?"

"That's right."

"Why?"

"Don't ask so many questions," the nurse replied. "Just do as you're told."

The general ward had eight beds and most of them were occupied. The patients ranged from teenage girls to elderly women. But for Erin this was freedom. Patients could move around or sit and chat at a table at the top of the room. And the doors were open. They could use the bathrooms unescorted. They could wear their own clothes, although Erin had no clothes to wear since she had been brought here in her nightdress. But most important, she had achieved a small victory. However she had managed it, she had got herself transferred out of the locked ward.

It was this feeling that buoyed her up. For the first time since she had come into Avondale, she saw a small ray of hope. She was convinced she had damned herself with yesterday's outburst. Yet for some reason, Dr McAllister had felt confident enough to let her come here to the comparative freedom of the general ward. It was surely a positive sign.

And then something else struck her and cheered her further. Now she could make phone calls and receive visitors. She made inquiries and learnt there was a pay phone in the hall. But she had no money. The ever-helpful Clara came to the rescue.

"How much do you need?" she asked.

"Enough to make a few calls."

Clara went to the nurses' station and returned with a handful of change.

"Don't spend all day on it," she warned. "Others will want to use it too."

Erin had no intention of hogging the phone. She

knew exactly what she had to do. She was going to ring the one person she could trust – her sister, who must surely be back from Cork and would come and help her. She went quickly to the pay-phone and fed in the coins. By now she was desperate to hear her sister's voice. She rang the number. But there was no answer!

Disappointment and frustration came at her like a wave. What should she do? She left a brief message telling Anne where she was and begging her to make contact at once. She had enough money for one more call. Who should it be? She immediately thought of Ger Armstrong. He answered on the second ring.

"Thank God," she said, hardly daring to believe that she was speaking to him. "I'm in trouble, Ger. I need you to help me."

"Trouble? What sort of trouble?"

"I can't go into it right now but I need you to contact my sister. Write down her number."

She gave him Anne's mobile number.

"Will you keep ringing till you get her? This is vitally important. Tell her I'm in Avondale Sanatorium and must talk to her urgently."

"Avondale . . .?"

"It's a long story, Ger. I'll explain it when I see you. Promise you'll do that for me."

"Of course, I will."

She heard the pips begin to sound as the money ran out. She was about to be cut off.

"Thanks, Ger. You're a star."

She put the phone down and returned to bed. She

was bitterly disappointed that she hadn't got Anne but
at least she had made *some* progress. She had finally
made contact with the outside world. She trusted Ger
to locate Anne and she knew that Anne would do
everything in her power to help her. Now it was just a
matter of waiting.

But waiting wasn't easy. When lunch came round,
she greedily attacked her plate. She tried to watch
television but now her mind was racing. There was so
much to do. Finding Anne was only the first step.
There were still a lot of obstacles to overcome. The
biggest challenge was going to be convincing them to
release her from Avondale altogether.

She paced the ward, constantly checking her
watch. It was now four hours since she had talked to
Ger Armstrong and nothing had happened. Where
was Anne? What was keeping her? Why hadn't
someone turned up?

Doubts began to creep into her mind. Maybe Anne
was still detained at Cork. Maybe her phone was out
of order. She was sorry that she hadn't given Ger
Armstrong her sister's address but there had been so
little time to talk. She thought of borrowing some
more change and ringing again. She looked for Clara
but she was nowhere to be seen. She decided to ask
another nurse.

She started for the work station. Just then, the
doors swung open. Erin turned to look and her mouth
fell open. Anne was coming into the ward carrying a
huge bouquet of flowers.

Erin never thought she would be so pleased to see another human being. She ran to her sister and flung her arms around her neck.

"Oh Anne, thank heaven you're here!"

"Careful!" Anne said. "Don't crush the flowers. I paid good money for these."

"Never mind the flowers. You're here. You don't know what this means to me."

She looked at her sister and tears began to well in her eyes.

"Let's sit down," Anne said, gently, "and you can tell me everything."

A nurse appeared from somewhere and offered to put the flowers in a vase.

Anne pulled out a chair and Erin sat on the bed.

"Did you get my message?" Erin asked.

"Yes and a phone call from your news editor. He was very concerned about you. I've just returned from Cork. I'd no idea you were here."

"I've been here for four days. It's been awful."

"Start at the beginning," Anne said. "Tell me what happened."

Erin told her about the intruder and the cot and doll and finding the broken piece of plastic the following morning. She told her about waking to find the buggy on the lawn and seeing Cornish take it away to the stables. She ended with Dr Bellows and the Kavanaghs waiting for her and the letter of authorisation that Harry had faxed to enable her to be committed to Avondale Sanatorium.

When she had finished, Anne sat with an astonished look on her face.

"This is incredible. I don't know what to say. Someone must have made a terrible mistake."

"No, Anne, there was no mistake. Whoever is responsible for Emily's death planned this. I'm sure of it. It all fits into a pattern. Someone wanted me in here. They wanted me certified insane. They want me to take the blame for the baby's death."

Anne looked uncertain. "Are you sure, Erin?"

"I'm positive. Have you ever had a gut instinct, a knowledge about something that you can't prove but you know is true?"

"Yes."

"Well, that's how I feel about this. I don't believe any of it was an accident. It was all planned, the cot, the buggy, everything. Emily was murdered and I have been set up to take the blame. Dr McAllister hinted as much yesterday when he interviewed me. He asked me if I had ever thought of killing her."

Anne bit her lip. "Do you suspect anyone?"

Erin lowered her voice. "My sister-in-law."

"Susan?"

"Yes. I've thought hard about this. I saw her groom, Cornish, take the buggy from the lawn. It wasn't imagination. I witnessed it with my own eyes. And I found the doll in the stables where he works. It was with the rest of Emily's baby stuff. And here's the interesting thing. *Emily never had a doll.* Someone went out and bought that doll and put it in the cot to frighten me."

"But why would she do this? It doesn't make sense."

"Jealousy. She has always wanted a child of her own to please her mother. And she never had one."

Anne sat for a moment, turning things over in her head. "It seems to me the doll is central to this. Did you tell anyone where you had hidden the broken piece you found?"

Erin paused. This was something that hadn't occurred to her before.

"I only told one person."

"Who?"

"Harry."

Eventually Anne left, promising to return again the following day. She had a friend who was a solicitor and she said she would talk to him about the possibility of securing Erin's release. She said she would also get in touch with Harry and see if he could be persuaded to rescind his authorisation.

"Keep your chin up," she said, hugging Erin close. "We'll have you out of here by hook or by crook."

She spoke so confidently that Erin believed her. Anne kissed her and left.

Erin got back into bed and pulled the sheets around her. Just talking to her sister had been like a tonic. She felt enormous relief in sharing her doubts and fears with her. And Anne had been so positive that some of it had rubbed off on her too. There *was* a way

411

out of this nightmare and now she was confident they would find it.

That night, she slept soundly, a natural, drug-free sleep that had her feeling energised when she woke at eight o'clock. She had just returned from the bathroom when Clara came to her bed to take her breakfast order.

"Sleep well?" she asked.

"Like a log."

"Well, that's good to hear. Do I take it your appetite is in order?"

"You certainly can. This morning I want the Full Monty – bacon, eggs, sausages, toast and tea."

"That will do wonders for your cholesterol," Clara said.

"I'm not in here for my cholesterol."

Clara smiled and went to move away when Erin called her back.

"How is Margaret?" she asked.

"I think she misses you. She's all alone in there now. She has no one to talk to."

"Tell her I was asking for her."

After breakfast, several of the patients wandered up to Erin's bed to admire the flowers that Anne had brought.

"Did your husband get you those?" one woman asked.

"No, my sister."

"They're beautiful. They smell so nice."

The conversation set Erin thinking. She had been in

Avondale for five days now and Harry hadn't visited her once. He hadn't even phoned or left a message. This thought sparked her resentment back into life. Harry had put her in here and he hadn't even bothered to visit. What sort of loving husband was that? But she quickly reined in her resentful thoughts. She needed all her energy focussed on positive things. She'd had enough of feeling sorry for herself.

At ten o'clock, a nurse came to tell her there was a phone call for her at the work station. It was Anne.

"Did you speak to Harry?"

"Afraid not. He was tied up at a business meeting. I'll try him again this afternoon. But I *have* got some good news. I spoke to my solicitor friend and he says there may be a legal route to get you out. He thinks, as your sister, I might be able to take an injunction to have you released."

Erin felt her spirits rise. "That's great news."

"There's more. I went out to Belvedere last night and got some of your clothes and, very important, I got the doll. It was in your bedroom."

"Did they make a fuss about giving it to you?"

"No. Mrs Kavanagh just took me to your room and let me pack your stuff."

"Did she say anything?"

"She asked how you were and I told her."

"How did she react?"

"I think she was sad, Erin. She looked kind of guilty." Anne paused. "I also told my friend of your suspicions about Emily's death. He suggested we hire

413

a private detective to do some digging for us."

"Why not go to the police?"

"He thinks the police will be slow to believe you without any evidence and he could be right. This way we can conduct our own inquiries. I've got a man who will take it on. His name is Jim Burke. He's a retired police detective. He doesn't charge very much."

"Go ahead and hire him," Erin said.

"Okay, I'll be in to see you around lunch-time."

"I'm grateful, Anne. You don't know how grateful I am."

"I can guess," her sister said and switched off.

Erin put down the phone with an enormous feeling of relief. Anne was a terrier and she would move heaven and earth to get her out of here. With her sister in charge, she was confident they would succeed.

The morning drifted by. But now there was hope. Erin had the comforting feeling that wheels were moving and things were getting done. Shortly after midday, Clara arrived to say that Dr McAllister wanted to see her in his office. This took Erin by surprise. After her last session with the doctor she had thought he was finished with her. But apparently, he had more questions to ask. It was with some trepidation that she followed Clara out of the ward and along a corridor till they came to his office.

When she opened the door, she found him sitting with a younger man with dark hair and a serious look on his face. Dr McAllister stood up and introduced him.

"Take a seat Erin. I want you to meet my colleague, Dr Baker."

The man smiled and extended his hand. Erin took it gingerly. She tried to conceal her growing unease. There were two of them now. What were they up to?

"I've asked Dr Baker to sit in with us today. I want his opinion. He's going to ask you some questions. Just answer them as best you can."

Dr Baker produced a notepad and began.

"Erin, I'd like you to go back again to the death of your child. Tell us exactly how you felt when you found her."

At the mention of the death, she felt her chest tighten. So Dr McAllister hadn't let go after all. He still believed she had killed little Emily. And now he had brought this new doctor along to confirm it.

She forced herself to keep her nerve. Whatever happened she mustn't react like the last time. If she did that she would be completely doomed.

"I felt distraught," she replied. "It was the worst thing that had ever happened to me in my life."

For the next half hour, she answered Dr Baker's questions as calmly as she could. When they had finished, Dr McAllister asked her to take a seat outside in the corridor.

She waited anxiously. Inside the office she could hear the low hum of voices. By now her fears were growing. She knew Dr McAllister was devious. She had witnessed his methods. Was this another trick he was playing on her? Was he planning to send her back again to the locked ward?

After what seemed like an eternity, the door opened and Dr McAllister called her back into his office. This time, he smiled as he held out a chair for her. He sat across the desk and fiddled with his pen.

"Erin, I have come to the conclusion that you are suffering from depression as a result of your child's death. Dr Baker agrees with me. In our opinion, that is to be expected after what you have been through."

She felt her heart sink. "What does that mean?"

"It means you are not insane."

She stared across the table. "You've changed your mind?"

"No. My mind was always open."

"But I lost my temper. I screamed at you."

Dr McAllister shrugged. "You reacted the way any innocent person would respond to the question I asked. I would have done the same."

"So what happens now?"

"I'm releasing you. This is not a prison, Erin. It's a hospital for sick people. Your depression isn't severe. I'm prescribing you some medication. You are free to go."

He scribbled his signature on some papers and Dr Baker did the same. Dr McAllister handed them to her.

"Your prescription and your discharge documents," he said, flashing his perfect white teeth at her. "Make sure you don't lose them."

Chapter 36

She couldn't believe her good fortune. At long last something positive was happening. She rang her sister and told her the good news and Anne turned up half an hour later with some clothes for her to wear. Erin drew the screens round her bed and quickly exchanged the hospital nightdress for a pair of jeans, blouse and a warm fleece jacket. Since her interview with Dr McAllister she had been unable to contain her excitement at the sudden turn of events.

"You look good," Anne said.

"Do you think so? I certainly haven't been feeling very good."

"No, you look just fine."

"I'll look even better when I've been to the hairdresser."

"So, are you ready to go?"

But there was still one thing she had to do. She found Clara at the nurses' station.

"I'm leaving," she said.

"I know. I heard. I wish you well, Erin. If everyone was easy as you, my job would be a walk in the park."

"Will you do me a favour?"

"Depends."

"Will you take me to say goodbye to Margaret?"

She found her sitting alone in the locked ward, staring aimlessly out the window at the sparrows quarrelling in the grass.

"I've come to thank you," she said.

"What for?"

"Helping me when I arrived, giving me advice, looking after me. I appreciate it."

Margaret looked her up and down. "Going somewhere?"

"I'm leaving," Erin said. "I've been released." She took Margaret in her arms and kissed her. "I won't forget you."

A crooked smile crossed Margaret's face. "You're one smart cookie. So you did give them the right answers, after all."

Outside, it was another beautiful day. The sky stretched like a brilliant blue canopy with barely a cloud. The roses in the flowerbeds were in bloom and from a nearby tree Erin could hear a thrush singing. She felt her breast fill up with emotion. She had seen these things a thousand times but never again would she take them for granted.

Her sister's apartment was in Smithfield in the

heart of the city and close to *The Clarion* office. It was in a new gated development of three eight-storey blocks.

"You can stay with me as long as you want. It won't be as grand as Belvedere…"

"It will be safer," Erin said.

"Yes," her sister replied. "I think you can say that."

The apartment was on the fifth floor, a nice spacious unit with a large living-room, kitchen and bathroom, plus two bedrooms. It had good views over the river. Erin's first action was to walk out onto the little terrace and gaze across the rooftops and spires glinting in the bright afternoon sun.

She turned back into the room.

"You don't know what it feels like," she said.

"No," Anne said. "That's certainly true. But it's behind you, Erin. Now you've got to look forward."

She showed Erin to her room and left her to take a shower.

When she emerged again, Anne had set out the tea things and a tea brack already cut into slices.

"I'm sorry it's not a bottle of champagne but I didn't expect you'd be out of there so soon."

"Right now, this is better than champagne," Erin said, pouring out the rich brown tea.

Anne took her hand. "Was it very hard?"

"Not in a cruel way. They were all pretty decent. But you have no freedom, Anne. That's the part I found most difficult."

"Well, now you're out and we have work to do. I spoke to that detective. He needs to sit down with you as soon as possible and get all the facts together."

"So, what are we waiting for?"

Anne punched a number into her mobile and spoke for a few minutes. She switched it off and turned back to Erin.

"He's on his way. He'll be here in twenty minutes."

Jim Burke turned out to be a fit-looking man in his early fifties with close-cropped hair, dark brown eyes and a quiet, unassuming manner. He shook hands with Erin and took a small voice recorder from the pocket of his leather jacket.

"Do you mind if we tape this?" he asked. "It saves time writing it all down."

"Not at all, go right ahead."

Burke switched on the recorder and placed it between them in the middle of the coffee table.

"Now, start at the very beginning," he said. "And don't rush. Tell me everything that you think is relevant."

By now, Erin had told her story so often that she knew it by heart. Nevertheless, she took her time, occasionally breaking off to answer questions from the detective. When she had finished, he switched off the machine and put it back in his pocket.

"I'm going to need recent photographs of the Kavanagh family and this man Cornish. Any idea where I could get them?"

She thought for a moment. There was a group wedding photograph back at Belvedere which contained all the family members. But getting a picture of Cornish was going to be more difficult. And then she remembered a photo of Susan receiving a prize at the Malahide gymkhana about six months earlier. It had been published in one of the local papers. Cornish had appeared beside her, holding the horse.

"I can get those for you," she said.

"And one final thing, do you still have this doll you found?"

"Yes."

She went to the cupboard and returned with the doll. Burke put it into a plastic bag and stood up.

"I'll be in touch," he said.

"Any idea how long it might take?"

He shrugged. "Depends on how lucky we get."

When he had left, Anne came to join her.

"Well? How did it go?"

Erin had felt reassured talking to Burke. He hadn't given her any sales talk nor made rash promises. He had an air of quiet confidence like a man who knew exactly what he was doing.

"I think it went pretty well," she said.

Next, she rang the *Malahide Gazette* and spoke to the editor, a man called Eddie Shaw. She introduced herself and asked if it would be possible to purchase a print of a photograph that had been taken at the local gymkhana six months earlier. Once he realised who she was, the editor was anxious to help her.

"That shouldn't be a problem, Erin. I'll ask someone to dig it out. When do you want it?"

"When will it be ready?"

"I could have it for you by four o'clock this afternoon."

"That will be perfect," she said.

She had to brace herself to make the next call but there was no escaping it. She had Harry's personal mobile number. He answered on the second ring. He seemed taken aback to hear her voice.

"Where are you calling from?"

"Anne's apartment."

She heard him catch his breath.

"Why aren't you in Avondale?"

"They released me."

"Are you okay? I mean . . ."

"I'm not mad, Harry. They said I was perfectly sane."

"But why are you with Anne? You should be here in Belvedere. This is your home."

She shook her head in disbelief..

"You know, I could find that hilarious, Harry. Somebody in Belvedere murdered our child. Somebody in Belvedere tried to drive me crazy. Various people in Belvedere, including *you*, had me committed to a locked ward in Avondale!"

"Let's not get into that."

"Why not? It's the truth. I've spent the past year trying to get out of Belvedere. And you want me to come back?"

He seemed taken aback by the vehemence of her response.

"How long are you planning to stay with Anne?" he said after a pause.

"I'm not sure yet. But it could be a while."

"For God's sake, Erin, is there any need for this?" She could hear the exasperation in his voice.

"I think there is," she replied.

"You're sore at me for signing that authorisation, is that what this is about?"

"Yes. But it's not the only thing. I don't think you have supported me very well throughout this whole business, Harry. At least, not the way a husband should."

"I find that very hurtful, Erin."

"That's how I feel. You never visited me once in that sanatorium. You never called."

"I was told you weren't allowed calls or visitors."

"You never checked. They would have told you I had been released into the general ward."

"For God's sake, I've always tried my best to stand by you. It hasn't always been easy but I have. And I was in London when this latest crisis blew up and Bellows told me he thought you were becoming delusional. He said he was afraid you might try to kill yourself. I thought it was the best thing for you, Erin."

"And you believed him?"

"Yes, because I love you."

"You never thought of talking to me?"

"We had already talked, if you remember. And it

had turned into an argument."

"But with something so important, don't you think I should have been allowed to say something in my own defence? Even a common criminal is allowed that. And I was innocent. I had done nothing wrong."

"I'm sorry, Erin. But I was told there was no time to waste."

"I'm sorry too, Harry. But now you can see why I must have time and space to work these things out."

He started to reply but Erin cut him short. The conversation had gone on long enough and she could see where it was headed.

"I need to come over to Belvedere this afternoon to pick up the rest of my clothes and my computer," she said.

"You really mean to go ahead with this?"

"Yes."

"Then come whenever you like. I'll tell the staff to expect you."

She asked Anne to drive her. There would be safety in numbers. But when they arrived at Belvedere at half past three there was no sign of her husband. Tommy Murphy was at the front door to meet them and took them up to Erin's bedroom where she spent twenty minutes gathering her remaining belongings. She made sure to include the picture of the wedding group. When she had finished, there was nothing left to remind anyone of her stay at the house. They got back into the car and drove off down the drive.

"I hope I never set foot in this place again," Erin said bitterly as they arrived at the high wrought-iron gates and made their way out onto the road.

"Was it really so terrible?" Anne asked.

"Yes. I'm afraid that house will always have bad memories for me."

On their way through Malahide village, they stopped while Erin went into the office of the *Gazette*. True to his word, Eddie Shaw had the print ready in a brown hard-backed envelope. Erin took it out and examined at it. It showed a perfect profile of Cornish. It was exactly what Jim Burke would need.

"How much do I owe you?" she asked, reaching for her purse.

But the editor waved her away. "No charge," he said. "It only took us a few minutes to find it. And I've always admired your work, Erin. Say hello for me to Ger Armstrong. We started off as cub reporters together on the *Dundalk Democrat*."

"Thank you very much," she said. "I'll make sure to do that."

Out on the street again, she went into a nearby chemist and presented Dr McAllister's prescription. She picked up the medication and got back into Anne's car. When they returned to the flat, she called Jim Burke to tell him she had the photos and he arranged to pick them up the following day. He sounded busy so she didn't detain him with small talk. Besides, she had already formed the opinion that Burke was a man of few words. When he had something to say to her he would let her know.

By the time evening arrived, she was exhausted. She had spent the past five days lying in a hospital bed with nothing to do and now she had all this excitement back in her life. Anne prepared a meal of chilli con carne and salad and they shared a bottle of wine and ate in front of the television. By eleven o'clock she was ready for bed.

Her medication sat on the bedside table in the spare room. She picked up the box of little white tablets and a thought crossed her mind. She seemed to have been medicating for weeks. And right now she felt fine. She would see if she could get along without it.

She cuddled under the duvet and closed her eyes. She was free at last from Avondale and Belvedere and free of Harry too. But she felt safe in her sister's apartment. No harm could come to her here.

Chapter 37

When she woke the next morning, Anne had already left for work. She pulled on an old tracksuit and running shoes and went jogging through the busy city streets. When she returned, she had a hot shower, percolated a pot of coffee and made a plate of pancakes. She took them onto the little terrace and ate breakfast in the glorious morning sunshine.

Afterwards she sat down at her laptop and started work on a list of feature articles she was planning for Ger Armstrong on the theme of *The Villages of Dublin*. The city was rapidly being turned into a busy metropolis. Old districts were being demolished and new housing developments were springing up to replace them. The idea was to visit places like the Liberties and Ringsend and talk to people about the way their area had changed in the last twenty years.

She waited till after the morning news conference before ringing her boss.

"Erin! Where the hell are you?"

"In my sister's apartment."

"So they've let you out of Avondale?"

"Yes. There was nothing wrong with me."

"Well, I'm sure glad to hear that. How did you end up there in the first place?"

"It was all a mistake, Ger. I'll tell you about it some time but, right now, I'm reporting for work and I've got some ideas for you."

"Shoot," he said.

She spent the next five minutes telling him about her proposed series.

"We could illustrate it with old photographs. And it will be a good circulation booster. People love to read about their own local areas."

"I like it," he said. "How long would it take?"

"Shouldn't take very long, couple of weeks, I'd say. I've got an outline prepared which I'm going to email to you."

"Tell you what," he said. "Write the first one and if I like it, I'll commission the whole series."

She felt the old adrenalin rush return.

"By the way, Eddie Shaw sends his regards."

"Eddie? Where did you run into him?"

"I had to call into his office. Some business I was taking care of."

"He's a character," Ger Armstrong said wistfully. "We had some times together when we worked in Dundalk. Did he tell you about the time he got thrown out of the town hall for disrupting a council meeting?"

She eventually put down the phone with a smile on her face. She would put her heart and soul into this article. She would write a piece that would bowl Ger Armstrong over and compel him to commission more.

She decided to begin with Howth, a fishing village on the northern outskirts of the city. It was one of the oldest parts of Dublin with a Viking settlement going back to the 9th century. And it was also an area of immense natural beauty. It was one of the places she used to visit when she first came to Dublin when she wanted to escape from the pressures of the city and breathe some clean fresh air. She knew she would have no problem illustrating the article with wonderful scenic shots.

But the town had also seen rapid development in the last twenty years. A new marina had been built, with expanded facilities for the fishing community. Howth had become a very desirable place to live and property prices had soared as fancy new restaurants and fashionable shops opened up. However, not everyone was happy with this new prosperity and many of the local people were complaining that their children couldn't afford to buy houses in the town any more. Erin knew it would be the perfect place to start.

She got on the phone and spent a couple of hours setting up interviews with the local chamber of commerce, community groups and people involved with environmental protection. They would all have strong points of view. But she also wanted to include the voices of ordinary residents. And the best way to do this was to go out there and talk to them.

She got the DART out to Howth and began with people in pubs and shops and restaurants. They were keen to talk and gave her the names of old residents whose families had been living in the town for generations. She met fishermen and anglers, hill walkers and yachtsmen. They all had views about how Howth was developing. She spent a busy couple of days in the town and when she had finished, she had a notebook crammed with material.

The following morning she took her laptop out to the terrace and began to write. She found the article very easy to compose. She had so much material that her hardest task was cutting and revising. But she finally managed to trim the piece back to 1500 words. She sent it into Ger Armstrong and waited for his reaction. It was immediate. He rang the following day in a rhapsody about the article.

"It's perfect. You know, you really have a talent for this sort of thing, Erin. I've shown it to the editor and he loves it too. We're going to give it a full page. I'm thinking nice layout, plenty of white space, fabulous pictures. Now when can you have the second one?"

"Do I take it you're commissioning the series?"

"I think that's a reasonable assumption," said Ger.

Over the next couple of weeks, she repeated the same exercise with the other villages she had identified: Clontarf, Sandymount, Blackrock, the Liberties and Dalkey. It was a labour of love. Erin buried herself in the work. It was the kind of reporting she liked best: talking to people, listening to their views and recording them. And it gave her scope to indulge her creative skills. In a very short time, Ger Armstrong had six articles on his desk and the series was ready to run. He rang two days later to congratulate her.

"This stuff is fantastic, Erin. I think it's the best work you've done for us."

She felt a thrill of satisfaction. It was nice to be complimented by her boss.

"So everyone is happy?"

"Everyone is delirious. All except the editor, that is."

"Oh?"

"He wants more. After these articles are finished, he wants another series. So you'd better get your thinking cap on and come up with some more places to write about."

She put down the phone with an enormous feeling of satisfaction. It had been hard work but it had been good for her and she felt rewarded. And now they wanted more. She immediately began thinking of places she could visit: Inchicore, Rathfarnham, Smithfield where she was now living – it had changed out of all recognition in the last few years. She would have no difficulty putting another series together. She was lost in thought when she heard her phone ring.

"Hello," she said, thinking it was Ger Armstrong back with further instructions.

But it was someone else.

"Jim Burke," the voice announced. "We need to talk."

Over the past few weeks she had been so engrossed

in her feature articles that Burke had slipped to the back of her mind. But she had not forgotten him and now he was centre stage again.

"Okay, where do you suggest?"

"Can you come into my office?"

"Where is it?"

"Gardiner Street."

It was quite close. She could grab a cab and be there in twenty minutes.

"I'm on my way," she said.

Burke's office was on the top floor of a cramped tenement building above a Nigerian grocery store. It comprised a small waiting area and a larger room where she found him sitting behind a battered desk. It was like something out of a Sam Spade movie.

"Would you like some coffee?" he asked after she had seated herself on a hard plastic chair.

"Yes, please."

He boiled a kettle and poured hot water into a plastic cup and added instant coffee and powdered milk. It tasted awful.

"Before we begin, I've asked someone else to join us." He glanced at his watch. "Should be here any minute now."

They sat in the small interview room and waited till at last they heard the sound of footsteps climbing the stairs.

The footsteps came closer and finally the door opened. Erin turned to look.

Susan came into the room.

Erin stared at her in amazement. So she had been right! She had suspected that Susan was the culprit and now Jim Burke had come to the same conclusion. But what was she doing here?

She opened her mouth to speak but immediately closed it again. She was too dumbstruck for words.

"I've identified the person who purchased the doll," Burke said.

Erin's gaze shifted between Susan and the detective.

"Cornish?"

"No, this man."

He reached for an envelope and selected a blown-up photograph. He slid it across the desk.

Erin was looking at a picture of Tim.

Chapter 38

She gasped in astonishment. Surely there was some mistake? Tim of all people couldn't possibly be mixed up in this.

"Are you sure?"

"I'm certain. I've got witnesses."

She shook her head in disbelief. Once again, words failed her.

Burke continued speaking.

"For the past few weeks I've been trawling the shops and toy stores in the Malahide area trying to find the person who purchased that doll. Three days ago, I located two shop assistants who recognised it. It was part of a special consignment made in Taiwan. What's more, they were able to produce till receipts.

"The doll was purchased on the 20th March at the Pavilions shopping centre in Swords. When I showed them the photographs you provided, they had no hesitation in identifying the purchaser. What is more, they are prepared to make sworn statements."

Erin stared from Burke to Susan.

"I'm sorry," the detective continued. "This will come as a shock to you but your brother-in-law has been spinning you a tissue of lies since the very beginning. These degrees he said he had? They don't exist. This novel he claims to be writing, the one that has the publishers raving with delight? It doesn't exist either."

Erin stared at him. "No?"

"I've checked with every London publisher in the *Writers, and Artists, Yearbook*. Many of them know him all right because he's been sending them manuscripts for years. But they all deny offering to publish his work.

"This woman he says he had a relationship with, Sarah Ferris? Nobody has ever heard of her. But there *was* a lengthy relationship all right. It was with a man. A young guy called Justin Rochford. It broke up a couple of months ago. Rochford ditched him."

He turned to Susan who was nodding her head in agreement. "I've asked Susan along to verify what I'm saying."

"It's true," she said.

Erin was still dazed at what she had heard but suddenly she recalled the time she had come upon Tim in the woods, broody and depressed. It would have been about five months earlier. He had said he was having trouble with his publisher. So the break-up with Justin Rochford was the real reason.

She felt the gentle pressure of Susan's hand on hers.

"Tim's problem was he was always different, even when he was a little boy," said Susan. "He was a sensitive child and quite artistic. I could see from an early age that he wasn't cut out for the rough and tumble of business which was where my parents wanted him to go. He liked reading and painting. He preferred my company to Harry's or the company of other little boys. I remember one time he persuaded me to let him dress up in some of my clothes and there was an unmerciful row when my father found out.

"Tim was punished and sent to a harsh boys' boarding school in an effort to toughen him up. He hated that school and refused to study. He was bullied and was forever getting into trouble. Eventually, his results got so bad that my parents took him out and sent him to a private grind school where he seemed to settle down. He got sufficient grades to gain admission to Trinity College and study English Literature."

Despite her shock, Erin found herself getting drawn into Susan's story.

"Tim loved it there. He fell in with a crowd of like-minded individuals who congregated around the literary society. He was in his element. But he seemed in no hurry to take his degree and enter the company. This infuriated my father. He had already had several warnings about his health and told to slow down and take things easy. He was anxious for Tim to shoulder some of the burden along with Harry but Tim refused point blank and announced that he was going to write a novel that would be a bestseller and take the world by storm.

"My father was enraged. He regarded Tim as a wastrel and several times threatened to cut his allowance. But Tim simply ignored him. And then about six months ago, two things happened to change matters. I had always suspected that my brother was gay but one evening, he confided in me that he was in love with a young man he had met at college called Justin Montfort. He said they were planning to go off and live together on one of Greek islands.

"When my father got wind of this, he moved quickly to cut off Tim's allowance. As a result there was a falling-out with Justin and the pair broke up. Then my father had his heart attack and, when he recovered, he decided to alter his will. These two events had a profound effect on Tim. He became increasingly depressed and broody. At the same time, he was growing bitter. He began to make wild accusations about people."

She paused and turned again to Erin.

"Don't take this personally but he said you were a gold-digger who had trapped Harry into marrying you for the family money." She smiled and shook her head. "I knew it wasn't true. Neither is the story he told you about my mother having a cot death and asking you to call your baby Emily because that was the child's name. My mother *never* had a cot death. The truth is, she has always wanted a grandchild. Toby and I have been trying for years without success.

And Tim was obviously never going to provide one. When she heard you were pregnant she was delirious with joy. Here, at last was the grandchild she wanted so much. She asked you to call the baby Emily because that was her own mother's name. And *her* name is Caroline Emily. She wanted the child named after herself. It was as simple as that."

Susan sighed and continued.

"I began to get worried about Tim. His behaviour was becoming increasingly erratic and his lies more outrageous. I thought he might be suffering some sort of nervous breakdown. And then little Emily died.

"At first, I accepted it was a SIDS death but then I began to get suspicious. Tim was going around telling people you were becoming suicidal. He said you told him you were planning to burn the house down when everyone was asleep. My parents began to get extremely concerned.

"Then came the episodes with the doll and the buggy. My groom, Cornish, was coming into work that morning when he saw the buggy on the lawn in front of the house. As you know, Harry had put the buggy and the rest of the baby's stuff in a storeroom at the stables. Cornish went to retrieve it and when he returned to the stables, he saw a man running away. He chased after him but the man escaped. But he left his cap behind.

"By now, you had gone back to the house. My mother and father had become so worried that you were going to do something crazy that they had summoned Dr Bellows. He had already persuaded Harry to sign the committal authorisation for your own protection. Later, I examined the cap that Cornish had found and I discovered it was Tim's. When I realised Tim's part in all this, I did something I shouldn't have done. I persuaded my husband to let me see my father's will. It was Toby who had taken it down. He was reluctant but he finally agreed. I discovered something that shocked me."

She raised her eyes and looked directly into Erin's face.

"My father had cut Tim entirely out of his will. His portion of the inheritance had been transferred to Baby Emily. And in the event of her death, it was to go to you."

For a moment no one spoke. There was utter silence. You could almost hear a pin drop. Then Jim Burke spoke again.

"There's your motive," he said.

Erin's face had gone pale. She had wronged Susan. She had wronged a lot of people. She had been so arrogant and blinkered. But she had just listened to so many bizarre revelations that her mind was reeling.

"So Tim murdered Emily?"

"Yes," Susan said. "And he wanted to drive you insane. He might even have murdered you too if he got a chance."

So she had been right all along. But she had suspected the wrong people.

"How did Tim know about the will?"

440

Susan shrugged.

"I don't know. Maybe my father told him."

Erin turned again to Burke. "What do we do now? Call in the police?"

"Slow down," the detective said. "All we have is some very strong circumstantial evidence. And purchasing a doll is a long way from murdering a baby. We've got some road to travel yet."

"So what do you suggest we do?"

"I think you and Tim have got to have a talk."

Chapter 39

Tim was at his charming best when Erin rang him later that evening.

"Erin, what a pleasant surprise! I heard they had let you out of that dreadful Avondale place. It must have been awful for you. How are you bearing up?"

She gritted her teeth. It wasn't easy talking calmly to him after what she had learnt.

"I'm not too bad, Tim. You know I'm staying with my sister now? I couldn't face returning to Belvedere again."

"And who can blame you after everything you have been through? I think it was appalling the way the family treated you. They never accepted you from the first day you appeared at the house. And then to have you committed to a lunatic asylum! Doesn't that just show you what they are capable of?"

"I need to talk to you Tim, I need your advice."

"Sure, Erin, how can I help you?"

"It's about Baby Emily."

"Go on."

"Not on the phone, Tim. I don't trust it. I need to speak to you privately."

"Where do you suggest?"

"Could you come here, to Smithfield?"

There was a slight pause.

"When?"

"Could you come tomorrow morning? The flat will be free. My sister will be at work. We'll be able to talk."

"Okay," he said. "I could get there about eleven."

She gave him the address and the gate code.

"That's excellent, Tim. I'm really grateful."

"Don't even mention it, Erin. You're my friend. I would do anything for my friends."

The following morning after Anne had left, she tidied the flat, laid out a cake she had bought at a nearby bakery and percolated a pot of coffee. At ten past eleven she heard the buzzer sound to announce Tim's arrival.

He came into the living-room, wearing a smart blazer and slacks and with a large smile on his face. Immediately, he took Erin in his arms and kissed her.

It took all she could do to bear contact with him.

"Sorry I'm late. The traffic was dreadful."

"Tell me about it."

He stopped to look around the room. "This is a very cosy place you have here, much more comfortable that dreary old Belvedere."

"It suits me fine. It's close to work for one thing."

He sat down on the settee and stretched his legs.

"You look good, Erin. You seem to have survived your ordeal."

"Thank you, Tim. Can I get you some coffee?"

"That would be nice."

She poured two cups and placed a slice of cake on a plate for him.

"Thank you for coming," she said.

He waved his hand. "I told you to forget it. It's nothing."

"I need your opinion. You see, when I was in Avondale, I had a lot of time on my hands and I began to think. I'm convinced that Emily was murdered, Tim. But I've no way of proving it."

"You mentioned this before. Have you any evidence?"

"I have circumstantial evidence."

He put down his coffee cup and leaned forward. "How do you mean?"

Erin paused. "We're talking in confidence, Tim?"

"Of course."

"I've discovered that your father changed his will after his heart attack. A family member was excluded and their share of the inheritance was given to Emily."

Tim looked startled. "Really?"

"Yes. Don't you think that might provide a motive for that person to kill the child?"

For a moment, he appeared flustered but he quickly regained his composure. "But Emily died from

445

SIDS, Erin. Isn't that what the autopsy found?"

"Tim, I thought you agreed with me that her death was suspicious? She died from smothering. Someone held her head into the pillow till she suffocated."

"But who could do such a thing?"

"You might be surprised what people can do if they're driven to it."

He lowered his voice almost to a whisper. "Are you at liberty to tell me who was excluded from my father's will?"

"Yes, I can do that. It was you, Tim."

"Me?"

Erin nodded.

He stared at her and their eyes locked till his face went red.

"This is ridiculous."

"Is it? There's more. That doll that was placed in the nursery, I've had a private detective searching for the person who bought it. A few days ago he struck gold. He found two shop assistants in Swords who identified the purchaser. And guess what, Tim? It was you again."

At this revelation, his face flushed with anger.

"What are you accusing me of?"

She felt her heart thunder in her breast.

"I'm accusing you of murder, Tim."

He jumped up from his chair.

"This is preposterous. I won't sit here another minute and listen to this rubbish!"

Erin continued in a calm voice.

"The door is locked, Tim. You've no option but to hear me out. Let me tell you what I think happened. You were the one who didn't like me from the very beginning. You were the one who sent me those anonymous notes because you saw me as a potential threat to your inheritance long before I had even married Harry. You pretended to be nice to me while all along you fed me a web of lies about your mother and Susan to make me feel uneasy. You said your mother had suffered a cot death when it was patently untrue. You even hinted that Susan's marriage was in trouble. You did all this to confuse me and instil a sense of fear in me.

"You were the one who placed the doll and the cot in the nursery when I was asleep. Somehow you'd managed to get your hands on a key to my apartment. And you got an unexpected bonus when I fainted and you were able to remove the doll and cot again. You weren't expecting that – your plan was that the family should think I'd set up the cot and doll myself in my madness – but making them disappear played even more neatly into your attempts to paint me as deranged. You placed the buggy on the lawn. I know it was you because you left your cap behind. And after I told you I had discovered a piece of the doll, you came to my bedroom and searched till you found it, then took it away.

"Somehow, you learnt about your father's will so you set out to remove poor little Emily and then me. You were the first person to turn up after I found her dead. That should have alerted me but I was too distraught to think straight. You killed Emily and you instigated a campaign of terror to drive me insane in the hope that I would kill myself or be blamed for Emily's murder and locked away forever in that sanatorium. Isn't that true? You murdered my baby, you bastard!"

As she spoke, Tim's face had slowly been changing. Now his eyes stared at her with burning hatred and a line of spittle dribbled from his lips.

"Yes!" he screamed. "I killed her and now I'm going to finish the job!"

There was a flash and Erin realised he had a knife in his hand. She jumped up but he quickly followed her, a crazed look in his eyes.

"You should have left the Kavanaghs alone, Erin. I warned you but you wouldn't listen. You thought you could just bewitch that stupid brother of mine and waltz away with my inheritance! And you're not even a member of the family."

He swung at her with the knife and the blade went whistling past her face.

"And now you have left me with no option but to kill you too."

"Don't do it!" she screamed. "Other people know about it."

He swung again with the knife and it narrowly missed her arm.

"But you'll be dead, Erin. After I've set fire to the flat, there will be nothing left of you. They'll say you went crazy and burnt the place down. They'll never be able to prove anything."

Erin felt herself gripped with terror. The knife swung once more. She managed to kick out and caught him on the shin but it didn't stop him. He kept coming towards her, his eyes burning like the eyes of a panther closing in for the kill, the knife jabbing mercilessly at her throat.

And then a figure appeared from the kitchen. A hand went out, followed by a swift jab to the neck. Tim let out a gasp. His knees buckled and he collapsed in a heap on the floor.

Jim Burke stepped over his prone body and removed the knife. He turned to Erin.

"You okay?"

She took a deep breath and wiped her brow. Her legs were trembling. She slumped down on the settee.

"Just about. Another minute and he would have had me."

"Have you got the voice recorder?"

She reached into her pocket and took out the small machine. She pressed a button and Tim's voice boomed out around the room.

"Condemned from his own mouth," Burke said. "The police will certainly be interested in this." He looked at Erin and smiled. "You did well. We have him now, game, set and match."

Chapter 40

In the days that followed, Erin threw herself back into her work. She welcomed the distraction and the relief it gave her from the dreadful events that had turned her life upside down. She still had the second series of articles to write for Ger Armstrong. She decided she would kick it off with a profile of Ringsend.

It was an old working-class district close to the centre of Dublin, with a long seafaring tradition. But it had been gentrified in recent years with new office blocks and smart apartment complexes. It would capture in miniature the way the whole city was changing. She drew up a list of people she would need to talk to and began ringing to set up interviews.

She spent the next few days visiting the area and talking to people and then she sat down to write. The moment she began, she found her creativity return. Her imagination was fired as she remembered the smoky old pubs where, a hundred years before, pigtailed sailors on shore leave caroused with the local judies as the ale and porter flowed. Her fingers flew over the keyboard and she became engrossed in the article. When she had finished and checked the time, she saw it was five o'clock.

She read it over and made a few corrections. She emailed it to Ger Armstrong with a note saying: **Will this do?** By now she felt the need for exercise and fresh air. She pulled on her old track suit and set off to jog along the Liffey quays to the Phoenix Park. When she returned, there was a short reply on her computer from her news editor: **Pulitzer Prize-winning material. More to follow, please**.

She smiled, had a shower and sat down on the sunlit terrace with a book and a glass of wine.

As the time passed, she heard nothing from Harry or the Kavanagh family. She could only assume that Belvedere was not a happy place right now. She didn't envy Susan's task of breaking the news that Tim was about to be charged with the murder of little Emily. In particular, she thought of her father-in-law and his heart condition. How would he take it? Would he blame himself? And Mrs Kavanagh – the news would be certain to distress her enormously.

She could see now how badly she had misjudged the situation. Her instincts had been right and they had saved her life. But she had accused people, particularly Susan and Mrs Kavanagh and attributed blame that didn't exist. And all the time, the murderer was the one person she didn't suspect – the smiling, suave, sympathetic Tim who she had considered her friend. If the sorry episode had taught her one lesson, it was how naïve she had been. In future she must learn to be less critical, to keep an open mind and not to rush to judgement.

Over the next couple of weeks, she completed the remainder of the articles and already she was thinking of other features she could write. There had been a strange missing-person case in Galway where a man had left his clothes on a beach and gone for swim but and had never been found again despite numerous sightings as far as away as Paris and New York. It had received huge media attention at the time but now the interest was beginning to fade. It would be interesting to go down there and write a thorough investigative piece.

One morning, she received an invitation from Ger Armstrong to go to lunch. This was a rare honour from the harassed news editor who usually ate his meals at his desk from a paper bag. He took her to a little Italian restaurant on Baggot Street. He opened proceedings by ordering a bottle of Chianti Classico.

"How are you coping, Erin?" he asked, sympathetically.

"I'm trying to put it behind me."

"It can't be easy."

"It's not. But I've got to move on, Ger. I can't live in the past."

He gently patted her hand. "I think you've been

453

very brave. Well, I've got news for you that should cheer you up. The editor has instructed me to offer you a new job."

"Oh," Erin said.

"He loves this stuff you've been writing. He thinks it's exactly the kind of material the paper should be printing. And we've put on circulation. You were right about that. Every area you wrote about saw an increase in sales."

"He's not sending me to the circulation department, is he?"

A wry smile crossed Armstrong's face. "That would be such a waste of talent. He wants to make you a full-time features writer."

She couldn't believe it. This was the job she had long dreamt of. It would suit her perfectly. She put down her glass.

"I don't know what to say. That's brilliant."

"There are a few things you should know," Armstrong continued. "You'll be working for me."

This was even better. She liked her boss and got on well with him.

"It's going to cause some tension. The features editor won't like it. She'll see it as an encroachment on her territory. It's going to cause a turf war. But you can leave the infighting to me. Now, are you interested?"

"Does the Pope have a balcony? Of course, I'm interested."

The news editor smiled again. "That's what I hoped you would say. Now let me explain the terms.

We'd expect you to produce eight articles every month. You would work your own hours under my direction. I won't dictate to you but I will expect you to consult with me."

"Go on."

"There will be an immediate increase in salary plus a weekly expense allowance. You can work from home. Any money you spend on meals, hotel accommodation, travel, drinks or entertainment, just give me the receipts and we'll reimburse you. So what do you say?"

A wide grin spread across her face. "I say we've got a deal."

Armstrong held up his hand and she gave him a high five.

At that moment the waiter arrived.

"Are you ready to order?" he asked.

She arrived back at the apartment in mid-afternoon to receive a phone call from Jim Burke. She hadn't heard from him for some time.

"Can I drop by?" he asked. "We need to talk."

"Sure."

He arrived twenty minutes later, looking slightly harassed.

"I thought I'd bring you up to speed with developments," he said. "The case is proceeding smoothly. I've been talking to the legal people and they expect it to go to court in the next few weeks."

Privately, Erin had been dreading the case. She had

covered trials as a reporter and knew what was involved. She feared the thought of taking the witness stand day after day with Tim's cold eyes watching and the jury hanging on her every word. His defence team would do everything in their power to discredit her.

They would go into every little aspect of her background. All the details of her marriage would be uncovered, her erratic behaviour, the arguments she had with Harry and Mrs Kavanagh. They would try to destroy her. And worst of all, she would be asked about finding the dead baby. She would be forced to relive those terrible events yet again. It would be a searing experience. Would she be able to withstand it?

"I know you haven't been looking forward to it," Burke continued, "but I have good news for you. He's signed a confession. It's an open-and-shut case. The prosecution won't be calling any witnesses."

She sat still for a moment. This meant she wouldn't be called to give evidence.

"That's an enormous relief," she said at last.

"I realise that. Just thought I'd let you know."

He shifted uneasily from one foot to the other.

"There's something else I have to mention – the matter of my fee. I've got an invoice all made out."

He produced a paper from the pocket of his leather jacket and gave it to her. Everything was noted, phone calls, stationery, photocopying, petrol.

"Fifteen hundred euros, Jim? That wouldn't cover your time."

"It's enough," he said, "It was interesting work."

"But you're robbing yourself."

"I'll make it up from my next wealthy client. Don't worry about it, Erin. I'm not going to starve."

The case was scheduled for November 27th. It would be straightforward. The prosecution team would demand a guilty verdict based on Tim's statement confessing to the murder. His defence team would admit the charge and attempt to plead for clemency. There would be thin pickings for the lawyers.

Erin debated whether she should go. She didn't want to face Tim and the rest of the Kavanagh family. But she did want to see justice done. She wanted to witness his conviction and hear the judge pass sentence. And she was also anxious to hear what his lawyers would say in his defence. In the end, she decided to take the risk.

It was a cold, miserable winter's day. Her mother and father had travelled up from Mountclare and Anne had taken leave from work so that they could all support her. The hall of the Four Courts was crammed with people. There were a dozen cases going on the building and wigged barristers seemed to be everywhere, conferring with clients in corners and corridors.

They entered the court and took the places that had been allocated to them. Because the case featured a prominent business family, there was intense media interest and Erin recognised many of the reporters crammed into the press bench. The presiding judge

entered and everyone rose till he had taken his seat.
Erin studied him. He was a well-fed man in his sixties,
his plump, red jowls giving him the look of a strutting
turkey-cock. After a few moments, Tim was brought
in.

She barely recognised him. He came in between
two police officers, his head bent and his eyes fixed on
the floor. He looked a thin shadow of the man she had
known. His face was pale and he had lost weight in
the months since she had last seen him. He didn't look
up and only raised his head to give his name and
acknowledge the charge against him. Then he sat
down and the case began.

The prosecuting barrister demanded the maximum
sentence for what he described as 'the cold-blooded
murder of a defenceless infant'. He talked about the
shock and grief that had been inflicted on the child's
parents and immediate family by this 'wanton
destruction of an innocent human life'. After five
minutes, he sat down and the defence put their case.
They were very brief. They simply asked the court to
take into consideration their client's guilty plea, his
previous good record and his obvious remorse for his
actions.

Tim was found guilty of murder. The judge then
addressed him. A hush descended on the courtroom.
Erin felt her mother grip her hand tight.

The judge said that in his long years on the bench
he had not come across a crime of such brutal
callousness. He described little Emily as 'a lovable

child whose life had been snuffed out when she had hardly begun to live'. Under the circumstances and as a warning to others, the court had no option but to impose the mandatory sentence that the law stipulated. He sentenced Tim to life imprisonment with no right of appeal.

There was a gasp from Mrs Kavanagh. Erin saw her father-in-law put an arm around her for support. Her gaze shifted to Susan who looked at her without emotion. Then she moved on to Harry. He sat beside his father. Briefly, their eyes met and for a moment, she thought he was trying to express something before he shifted his gaze and looked away.

The court was breaking up. Tim was led away, his eyes still fixed on the ground. By now, the press bench was emptying as reporters rushed outside to phone the verdict to their news desks. Erin made her way across the room to the prosecution lawyers and thanked them individually for their work.

Then they were outside once more in the damp, misty November rain and Anne was leading them through the crowds of photographers to her waiting car and a chapter in her life was closing.

Chapter 41

At Christmas, Harry sent her a card. She'd had no contact with him since the trial. Indeed she hadn't heard from him at all since her release from Avondale apart from that single brief telephone conversation when she asked permission to pick up her belongings from Belvedere.

The card was a simple painting of a nativity scene with a plain message: *Best wishes from Harry.* But the card had broken the ice. There was something unexpressed between the lines. She detected an appeal for a response from her and in the spirit of the season she went out to the nearest bookshop and bought a card with a picture of the Madonna and Child. Borrowing a fountain pen from Anne, she wrote in her best handwriting: *Hope you have a good Christmas, Erin.*

The season passed. She went down to Mountclare and spent the holiday with her family. But all the time she was wondering how Harry was faring. It would be a sad, lonely Christmas at Belvedere. She couldn't help thinking of that other Christmas and the tree and the crackling fire and the good cheer around the table where they ate lunch unaware that a potential killer was sitting in their midst.

She returned to Dublin and went back to work. The frenzy of publicity that the trial had unleashed had now died down. Ger Armstrong rang to ask her for a feature article about the New Year sales. It was a routine task that each paper did every year in the dog days after Christmas when nothing much was happening. Erin wrapped up well against the cold January winds and set off for town, prepared to brave the heaving crowds of shoppers who would be cramming the big stores around Henry Street and Grafton Street.

This article was a routine piece. She would begin with colour impressions and later she would ring the store managers and get some sales figures and reaction. Was volume up or down? What were people buying? Writing these features had become a formula and there was little excitement or creativity involved.

By four o'clock, she had completed her initial research. She sought out a quiet little bar she knew in Chatham Street but even here it was packed with noisy drinkers laden with bags of shopping and she was lucky to find a seat. She had just ordered a gin and tonic from a harassed waiter when she became aware of someone standing at her table.

"Hello, Erin."

She looked up and saw Harry. He was clutching a glass in his hand. There was an awkward smile on his face.

"Happy Christmas," he said and raised the glass.

"Happy Christmas," she replied.

"Mind if I join you?"

What could she say? She could hardly refuse. So she shifted her seat and Harry brought his stool from an adjoining table and sat down beside her.

"You didn't buy anything?" he said.

"No, I'm not shopping. I'm working."

"Ah," he replied. "I came in to buy some late presents but I gave up. You know how I hate shopping. It reminds me of the terraces at Lansdowne Road for a rugby international."

There was a brief silence.

"How are you getting on?" she asked.

"Okay. And you?"

"I'm back at work now. I'm writing features mainly."

"I know. I've been reading them. They're very good."

"Thank you," Erin said. "It suits me. I can work at my own pace and choose my own subjects and I do most of the work from the apartment. How are things at Belvedere?"

"Not good," he said. "Mum is devastated by what has happened. We all are to various degrees. Dad blames himself for being too tough on Tim. He feels if he hadn't cut him out of the will, none of this would have occurred."

"Has anyone been to see Tim?"

"Mum and Toby have been in. I'm afraid he's not well. He's taking his sentence very badly. "

Erin nodded. "I have mixed feelings about Tim. You know I liked him. I had an empathy with him. I can't get my head around the fact that he murdered our baby and tried to destroy me too."

She lowered her head and Harry gently placed his hand over hers.

"Are you getting your life together?" he asked.

"Slowly," she said. "My work is going well and I'm happy living with Anne. But I'm thinking of renting a place of my own."

"Larchfield is empty. You could live there if you wanted. I'm staying at home now."

"No," she said.

They finished their drinks and left.

Erin went back to Smithfield and made her phone calls to the store managers. By eight o'clock she had the article completed and emailed it to Ger Armstrong. Anne had recycled the remainder of the turkey their mother had given them and produced a spicy Thai dish which she served with rice and salad. They drank a chilled white wine.

"I met Harry in town today," Erin said.

"Oh! How was he?"

"Down in the dumps. The family are taking Tim's conviction very badly."

"I'm not surprised. How would you react if it was your brother or son?"

"He offered me the new house if I wanted to move in. I turned him down."

Anne regarded her over the edge of her wine glass.

"Was that a good idea? The house is lying idle, isn't it?

"Yes, but I'm not ready," Erin said.

"That might change," her sister replied. "They say time is a great healer."

But the meeting had an unexpected effect on her. She couldn't help thinking of Harry. He had looked so lost and forlorn. She wondered if the time had come to forgive him. From what she had learnt from Susan, Harry wasn't the prime mover in having her committed to Avondale. And he had acted from fear that she might kill herself. Perhaps she been too hard on him?

In the days that followed she found herself thinking about him a lot. She tried to put herself in his position. He had been in London when the incident occurred and the situation was put to him second-hand. To any objective observer, her behaviour must have seemed bizarre and frightening. She was agitated and argumentative and Tim was whispering that she was suicidal and threatening to set the house on fire.

He had consented to her committal for her own safety. She remembered what Dr McAllister had said the first time he came to interview her in Avondale: *"You are safe here. This is a place of safety."* Harry had told her he had done it because he loved her. Perhaps he was right?

January gave way to February and the cold, dreary weather continued. She grew sick of waking to see the rain falling like a grey mist across the city. But March brought sun and the buds appeared on the trees and the birds began to build nests in the rooftops outside her window. Spring was on the way. She remembered that she still had the keys to Larchfield somewhere among her possessions and decided to go down at the weekend and see it again.

She borrowed Anne's car and drove out to Kinsealy. It was a bright, sunny day and the sea from the coast road looked blue and peaceful. Larchfield sparkled in the sun but already it was showing signs of neglect. The grass was overgrown and there were weeds sprouting through the gravel on the drive.

Along the verges, she could see the daffodils pushing up through the damp earth. Harry must have planted them. And suddenly, her mind travelled back to the first time she had visited Belvedere. There had been daffodils there that day too. She remembered Harry pointing them out to her and thinking how observant he was.

Inside the house, the smell of fresh paint had long vanished. Now the rooms smelt of trapped air and a musty odour hung over the place. She went around opening windows to let in the fresh breeze. But Larchfield still looked spectacular. She let her eyes take in the beautiful new furniture and the drapes, the ornaments she had chosen with Anne.

She climbed the stairs and entered the room she

had selected as her office and study. The desk was waiting for her computer beside the window where it would catch the light and she could look out over the garden. She remembered the thrill of anticipation she had felt at the prospect of moving in here. She closed her eyes. If only they had done that, if only they had moved here straight away without waiting at Belvedere, how different their lives would have been.

She went back downstairs to the kitchen with its gleaming appliances, its mammoth fridge and worktops. She had chosen these too with Anne's help. She was lost in thought, when she heard footsteps and turned in alarm. She had forgotten to close the front door. She hurried back out to the hall and to her amazement, she found Harry standing there. He looked every bit as surprised as she did.

"What are you doing here?" she asked.

"I came out to look at the house. I was going to talk to you about putting it on the market." He glanced around the hall and his eyes eventually returned to Erin.

"It looks fabulous," he said. "This was to have been our dream home."

"I know."

"It still could be, Erin, if you could find it in your heart to forgive me."

She didn't know what to say. He had caught her entirely by surprise.

And then he moved closer. She didn't move. She didn't resist as his strong arms went around her and next moment he was holding her in a deep kiss.

She felt the thrill of his warm body close to hers. She hadn't felt like this for a long time and now she realised how hungry she was for his touch. She clung to him and kissed him back.

Eventually they drew apart. But her body was still burning with pleasure.

"Come back to me," he said.

"Give me a few days to think," she said.

Later that evening she talked to Anne about what had happened.

"He wants me to go back. What do you think I should do?"

Anne studied her face. "Why are you asking me? I think you've already made up your mind."

On Friday afternoon, Harry called to invite her out to dinner the following evening. Erin flew into a tizzy. She rang around the hairdressers till she eventually found a cancellation. She spent Saturday morning having her hair cut and styled, her nails polished and trimmed, her face cleansed and massaged. She spent the afternoon choosing what to wear – a red evening dress, black jacket, black tights and red shoes. For the *coup de grace*, she put on the gold necklace and pendant that Mrs Kavanagh had given her as a Christmas present before all the bad stuff had happened. When she finally checked herself in the mirror, she knew she looked fantastic.

At five to seven, the buzzer sounded. Erin let him

in and a few minutes later, Harry stepped out of the lift. He looked magnificent in his well-tailored suit, white shirt, blue tie and matching pocket handkerchief. In his hand, he carried a single red rose.

His eyes travelled over her and he smiled.

"You look beautiful," he said.

Chapter 42

The housewarming party for Larchfield was held on a warm August evening. Harry had trimmed the grass and erected a barbecue. The trees were in bloom and the scent of the night stock that Erin had planted near the patio mingled with the smell of cooking steaks and the charcoal smoke that drifted across the lawn.

They had invited their families and friends, business contacts of Harry's, colleagues of Erin's and their close neighbours. Mrs Kavanagh hadn't come, pleading illness. Instead, she had promised to visit them some evening for a quiet dinner. But Susan and Toby were there and Charlie had sent a gift of a crate of champagne. Jim Burke was standing under a tree wearing his trademark black leather jacket, his face inscrutable as ever as he chatted with a reporter from *The Clarion*. Altogether about seventy people had turned up to sample their hospitality and welcome them into their new home.

In the intervening months, Erin and Anne had tidied up the house, thoroughly aired all the rooms and Harry had seconded a couple of gardeners from Belvedere to knock the gardens into shape. Borders had been dug, trees planted and flower beds laid with bright yellow and crimson roses.

The patio had been paved with flagstones and turned into a suntrap with terracotta tubs of pink and red geraniums and little pots of basil and mint and chives. All through the summer, she had sat out here with a little table and chair and worked on the features that Ger Armstrong was demanding with increasing frequency because, as he said, 'the readers are clamouring for more'.

And Erin had slowly let go of the past and found a measure of peace and contentment again.

She stood now and gazed out over the lawn. Harry had strung lanterns from the trees and they cast bright shadows on the grass. People were chatting in small groups, nursing glasses of wine or cans of beer. The sun had almost set and the stars were beginning to come out. The night felt warm and balmy. All that was required was a gentle breeze to cool the air.

She saw Harry framed in the light from the kitchen as he came out of the house carrying two glasses of wine.

"Shouldn't you be sitting down?" he asked, handing her a glass.

She allowed a smile to play around her mouth. A week ago, she had been told she was two months pregnant and already Harry was beginning to fuss.

"Harry, I remember having this conversation with you once before. I am not an invalid!"

"Nevertheless, I think you should rest. You've been on the go all day."

"You want me to sit like the President and receive people in a line?"

"That's a good idea," he said, with a grin. "Why didn't I think of that?"

It was nice to be fussed over. It was nice to know he cared. To please him, she sat in one of the wicker chairs. Harry sat beside her and held her hand.

"This is my idea of bliss," he said, stretching his long legs. "A balmy summer evening, our friends, a glass of wine and the woman I love seated beside me. Thank you for making my life complete."

She felt something stir inside her. It was such a beautiful thing to say. She leaned over and gently kissed his cheek.

"Thank you for asking me," she said.

THE END